THE WOLF OF THE NORTH

ALSO BY DUNCAN M. HAMILTON

THE WOLF OF THE NORTH

DUNCAN M. HAMILTON

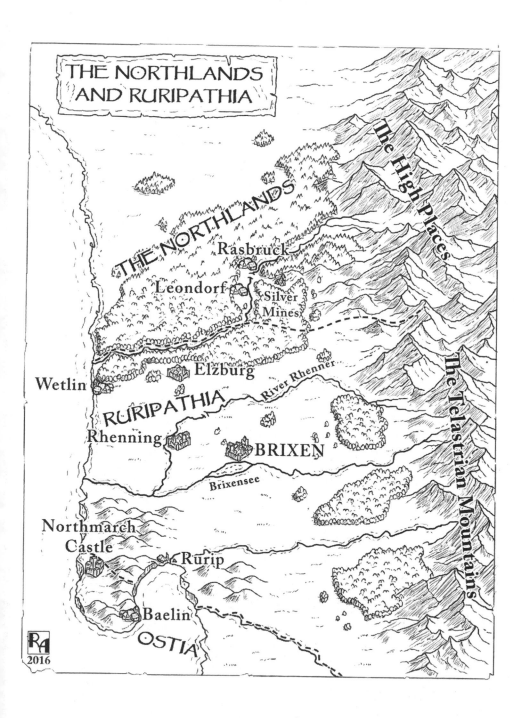

THE NORTHLANDS
AND RURIPATHIA

The High Places

THE NORTHLANDS

Rasbruck

Leondorf

Silver Mines

The Telastrian Mountains

Wetlin

Elzburg

River Rhenner

RURIPATHIA

Rhenning

BRIXEN

Brixensee

Northmarch Castle

Rurip

Baelin

OSTIA

RA
2016

PROLOGUE

THICK-CUT STONE WALLS and a roaring fire kept the winter cold and the vicious bite of the Niepar wind at bay. The Maisterspaeker paused when he entered the inn's taproom and breathed deeply the sour smell of ale interlaced with the tang of pine smoke. The room had a rough, earthy charm and a welcoming cosiness, two things the Maisterspaeker always looked for. He had no idea how long he would be there, so he had chosen it carefully. His friend would certainly make the meeting, but Northlanders were never the most careful keepers of time.

He took a stool by the bar and scratched his beard, all grey but for a few stubborn hairs that refused to acknowledge that he was no longer young. He waved to the barkeeper, busy with other patrons, and savoured the prospect of his first mouthful of cool, bitter ale. It couldn't push away the flutter of excitement that beat within his chest, however. It was a sensation that he had not felt in a long, long time: the anticipation of an impending fight.

It had been many years since he had given up the sword for the story, and he had not once regretted the fact. It was only now that a chance encounter had dragged things from the distant past into the present that he noticed its absence. He would take up the sword once more and do battle with his best friend fighting at his side, before the gods called him to his rest. The thought made him feel like a man of twenty summers once again, grey beard or not. Vengeance had been a long time coming for his friend, but with the Maisterspaeker's recent discovery, that wait was now almost at an end.

He allowed his mind to drift on the sound of the crackling fire, the bustle of the taproom, and the voices of tired men enjoying a well-earned drink. Places like the inn were what made the Maisterspaeker love the Borderlands. Life was simple here, away from the machinations of court and the constant struggle to find favour with the powerful. There was no need to take care with his words, or force small talk. Men spoke their minds and would punch you in the face rather than stab you in the back, a refreshing change from the drama of noble courts. It was why he chose to stay in the village inn rather than the Graf's great hall on the overlooking hill where he had told a tale the night before. No one knew him at the inn. No one would ask him for a story. It would be a welcome rest for his tired voice. That the ale was good only helped his affection for the place.

'I know you,' a voice said.

The Maisterspaeker closed his eyes and prayed to the old gods that the voice was directed at someone else. So much for anonymity, he thought.

'You're the Maisterspaeker. I saw you in the Graf's hall last night.'

'You have the advantage of me,' the Maisterspaeker said.

'My name's Conradin. Liegeman and sergeant-at-arms to Graf Sifrid.'

'I hope you enjoyed my story,' the Maisterspaeker said.

'I had to leave just as you started,' Conradin said, his face a picture of disappointment. 'Had my duties to attend.'

'A pity.'

'It was, my Lord. I'd been looking forward to it ever since I heard you were coming to Graf Sifrid's court. You told "Dal Rhenning's Last Stand", didn't you? About Ulfyr the Bloody—Jorundyr's chosen warrior—and his comrades fighting those southern devils in Darvaros.'

'You've heard it before then?' the Maisterspaeker said.

'Of course,' Conradin said. 'I've heard all your stories, but never you telling them.'

Conradin's use of the old god's name struck a chord with the Maisterspaeker. Jorundyr and the old gods had been all but forgotten in Ruripathia before the Maisterspaeker started telling his tales. Now everyone spoke the name with familiarity once more, for the first time in nigh on a millennium. It occurred to the Maisterspaeker that perhaps his friend Wulfric—Ulfyr as he was known to all but those closest to him—was indeed chosen by the old god, and for a very simple reason. Jorundyr's fame was spread hand in hand with Wulfric's, and what was once relegated to the shadows was now again in the light.

'You're right,' the Maisterspaeker said. 'I told "Dal Rhenning's Last Stand". It seems to be everyone's favourite.' He said it with reticence, knowing what was coming next, his hopes for a quiet repast fading.

'I was wondering if you might be of a mind to tell a bit of it here?' Conradin said. 'I've always wanted to hear it told from the mouth of the man what wrote it.'

The Maisterspaeker grimaced and started to shake his head. 'Graf Sifrid paid me one hundred crowns to tell that story…'

Conradin blushed with a mixture of embarrassment and disappointment. He shrugged. 'I'm only a sergeant-at-arms…'

It was the Maisterspaeker's greatest weakness, the desire to entertain and delight, but it was also his strength, and why he could command five hundred crowns for a single night's recital, even after three decades of telling the same stories. He had nothing to do while waiting there, other than sit by the fire and drink and doze, and he didn't feel old enough to relish such things just yet. His only reluctance was that there might not be time, and there was nothing so disappointing as a story half told.

There was something he was working on, though, a tale that put all the others and more together into one great epic. It would be his defining work, and he thought it fitting that he tell it now, unfinished though it was, for it was about the man he awaited. Wulfric—Ulfyr the Bloody, Wolf of the North. When he arrived, the two of them would create its ending in blood and steel and flame.

'I've been working on something new; it's a long story, though,' the Maisterspaeker said quickly, his decision made.

'It's winter; the night's long too,' Conradin said, his voice hopeful.

'Fair point. So long as my throat stays wet, I doubt we'll have a problem.' He couldn't give his tale away without some consideration, after all, and storytelling was thirsty work.

Conradin smiled, turned and beckoned to the people in the taproom. Where there had been only a sergeant-at-arms, there was now half a village. The Maisterspaeker smiled, flattered by the draw the prospect of his story had.

'If you're all ready and of full mugs, I'll begin. My new story is called "The Wolf of the North"; the full tale of the legendary warrior you all know as Ulfyr the Bloody, Scourge of Belek, Draugar, and Dragons, Jorundyr's

Chosen, from boyhood to his last great deed. You will hear of his famous band of warriors; Enderlain Greatblade, Varada of Darvaros, and Jagovere the Skald, as well as others just as brave, whose names have been scattered by the winds of time. Some parts you will have heard before, but not a living soul has heard it all, nor told like this.'

No one stirred. All eyes were locked on him. The Maisterspaeker had to suppress a smile, not wanting to detract from the solemnity of his tale. His skin tingled. It was the moment that made it all worthwhile; the intoxicating anticipation, the impending joy of a great story well told.

'This story, like so many others, exists because of a woman, and the love one man had for her…'

PART ONE

CHAPTER ONE

WULFRIC LET OUT a strained grunt as he pulled the sword from the water. The metal was cold from having been in the icy river. Despite spring being well underway, the river came down from the High Places, where the snow and ice never melted. His fingers went numb at the touch of the cold steel, and he did his best not to drop it. The blade was covered with a thin coat of rough brown rust that felt gritty to the touch, but he knew the metal was still good underneath. The leather of the handle was intact—it had not been in the water long. He was barely able to lift it with both hands, so he scrambled backward up the riverbank hauling it with him. When clear of the slippery mud at the water's edge, he stopped and allowed the tip to sink into the earth. Supporting the sword with one hand, he tentatively touched the edge with his finger. It was still sharp.

He stared at the sword for a few moments longer, confirming in his mind that it really was what he thought it was; it was the first time he had ever held a real one. He was never allowed near his father's. Swords were expensive and he wondered if this one could be returned to pristine condition and sold. His mother would find the coin useful, although his father scorned money. He was not interested in anything that could not be won with skill and force of arms. Money was for tradesmen and the sly merchants who passed through the village, coming from the cities in the South to sell their wares. It was beneath a warrior's contempt, even if it was sometimes necessary. Even rusty, the sword held a captivating appeal for Wulfric. A warrior was rarely seen without one. The best ones had names, and tales of great deeds behind them. Wulfric wondered if it might be one of those. Perhaps his mother would let him keep it?

He looked away from the sword and along the riverbank to see if there was anything else of value. The river was not wide; when he tried his hardest, he could throw a stone all the way over to the other side. The water was still too cold to wade through, but there was a shaky wooden footbridge downstream where he could cross if he spotted something worth a closer look.

There must have been a battle farther up-river, Wulfric thought. He couldn't believe anyone would be careless enough to lose such a fine weapon. His theory was confirmed when he saw a bloated corpse caught in a bush on the other side. It bobbed gently on the water that flowed past it. Wulfric felt his stomach churn as his mind filled in the details that his eyes could not make out. The sword was probably that man's, whoever he was. A pang of panic struck Wulfric. What if the slain warrior turned into a draugr, and wanted his sword back? He stared at the body, but saw no sign of foxfire. Aethelman the Priest said draugar and foxfire always went together. Nonetheless, his desire to keep the sword was greatly diminished. Merely holding it gave him a sick feeling in his stomach.

'What have you got there, fatty?'

Wulfric jumped in fright. His first thought was that the voice had come from the body, but it came from behind him. The fact did not make him any less afraid, however, for he recognised it well, and knew what it meant. Rodulf and his three cronies, Rorik, Helfric, and Walmer stood a few paces away. They were all apprentice warriors—they thought they could do anything they liked. For the most part, they were right.

'Well? What is it, fatty?' Rodulf said, squaring up to him.

'It's a sword,' Wulfric said, his eyes barely level with Rodulf's chin.

'What's a fat little turd like you doing with a sword?' Rodulf stared Wulfric down, his eyes like dark coals against his pale, angular face and sandy hair.

'Found it,' Wulfric said.

'Hand it over.' Rodulf held out his hand, standing there with the confidence of knowing they were four, and Wulfric was one.

Wulfric thought about defying them. His father might scorn money, but his mother did not, and his father was perfectly happy to enjoy the nice things she bought with it when she could. She would have been able to sell the sword for a good price, which would buy fine cloth and spices from the south. If he handed it over, Rodulf's mother would be doing that, and his family would enjoy Wulfric's good fortune. He knew he would be going home without the sword, one way or the other, but something stirred within him. It would not let him give it to Rodulf.

'Hand over the sword. Now!' Rodulf said.

Wulfric knew what his defiance would bring, but he could not help himself. He flung the sword back into the river with as much strength as his flabby arms could muster. It was far heavier than a stone, but he put more into that throw than he ever had before; every ounce of anger, frustration, and impotence that he felt at that moment. It plopped into the water—the icy-cold water—almost exactly in the middle of the river.

'What sword?' Wulfric said, with a feeling of satisfaction so great, the experience of it almost made the beating he was about to get worth it.

❈

'Wulfric! Wulfric! Look what I found,' Adalhaid rushed up to where Wulfric was sitting by a tree in the glade next to the village, and she flopped down beside him. His face hurt, as did many parts of his body. He realised that his dark blond hair was matted with blood after the earlier encounter with Rodulf at the river, and he tried to free it up before she noticed. The effort only drew her attention. She frowned and touched his face gently with her fingertips. It was puffy and hot. His skin felt tight from the swelling, and he knew he must have looked a hideous sight, but her touch seemed to make it feel a little better.

'Are you all right?'

Wulfric nodded. 'It looks worse than it is.' In truth he had no idea how it looked, and it was agony.

'You're sure?' She gave him a pained smile.

He nodded again.

She held up a blue flower, which contrasted starkly with her copper hair. It meant nothing to Wulfric, but Adalhaid seemed to think it was something special, and he was glad of something to distract him from his wounds.

'It's the first of the year,' she said. She studied it intently, her green eyes narrowing as she did. 'It means spring is truly here.'

He wasn't really paying any attention to what she said—the pain was too great an imposition on his concentration—but he enjoyed listening to the sound of her voice when she was excited about something. He watched the way the sun glistened on her burnished copper hair, and her nose scrunched up as she studied the flower, and let his worries drift away. Being in her company made him forget about everything else; how his face hurt when he forgot not to smile, how the bruises that covered his body sent jolts of pain through him every time he bumped against one of them. She was his sanctuary, his happiness, and had been for as long as he could remember.

There was no snow left now in the glades and pastures around the village. The brown grass was beginning to take on a green hue once again, after being covered in snow all winter, and the sun had dried the ground where they sat. Sitting there on that dry patch of grass with Adalhaid in the warm sunlight, he really could believe that none of his problems existed. He could almost forget the shame of returning home without the sword, of hoping that maybe his mother would not notice the cuts or bruises, that she would not tell his father that he had been beaten up by the other boys. Again.

The only consolation he could take was that they did not get the sword either. They may have been brave when facing him down, four of them while he was alone, but none was brave enough to enter the freezing water to retrieve the sword. As Wulfric had lain on the riverbank nursing his newly acquired injuries, he watched as they squabbled amongst themselves over who would fetch it. Rodulf tried to get the others to do it, although they knew that he would take it, telling everyone that he had found it; that he'd pulled it from the icy water.

Rodulf accused them of cowardice, weakness, and a host of other names that would shame any warrior or anyone who wished to be one when they refused to do as he ordered. There was never any question of him being the one to venture in, however.

Wulfric pushed the memory and shame of it from his thoughts. The happiness in that moment with Adalhaid was marred by the knowledge that eventually they would have to go back to the village where the other boys were, but he could choose not to let them spoil it, so that was what he did.

❀

'Who's Wulfric?' someone in the gathering asked.

'Is he a famous warrior?' another said.

'Shut up!' Conradin said. 'Don't interrupt.'

'It's all right.' The Maisterspaeker held up a hand to still Conradin. 'Wulfric is the boy who grew into the man you all know as Ulfyr. It's the first time most of you will have heard him called that, however.'

'That can't be true, then,' someone said. 'No one could beat Ulfyr in a fight.'

The Maisterspaeker smiled. 'And he was born full grown with a sword in his hand and pissing fire,' he said, his rich, sonorous voice rising to a boom.

Everyone laughed. The group had grown larger in the short time since the Maisterspaeker had started telling his story. From the look of it, he reckoned almost the entire village was now there, all but those tucked up in their beds.

'Don't forget, he wasn't Ulfyr then; he was merely Wulfric, a young boy trying to find his way in the world. This story starts at the very start, and ends at the very end. Just because a story's beginning is not audacious does not mean it will remain that way…'

CHAPTER TWO

THE HOUR FINALLY came when Wulfric and Adalhaid could stay in their little patch of sunlight no longer. The sun was low in the sky and the warmth it had provided earlier was gone. They were both shivering as they made their way back to their homes. Their village, Leondorf, was a cluster of wood and stone thatched buildings surrounded by an earthen bank and wooden palisade. The warriors guarding the gate all recognised Wulfric, and all noticed his bruises and cuts. It was humiliating to pass under their stares.

Wulfric dreaded going home, knowing that his mother would make a fuss over him, both out of concern for his injuries and from a wish to make him feel better. He appreciated it, but he disliked the attention.

His mother's attention was one thing. The disappointment from his father was another entirely. Wolfram the Strong Arm. He was the bane of anything that ordinary men feared. He cast a shadow that eclipsed all around him. The expectation it placed on Wulfric was more than he could ever hope to live up to. It was crushing.

Wulfric walked up the wooden steps to his home and hesitated before pushing open the door. He cast a final glance over his shoulder and saw Adalhaid watching him from the doorway of her home, several houses up the muddy lane. He could see her smile at him and wave. He smiled back; he wished that he could have stayed with her by the tree forever. He stepped inside.

There was a cut on his arm from where Rodulf had hit him with a stick. It had grown itchy over the course of the day, and now it was hot to the touch and far more painful than when it had happened. There were a multitude of other bruises and sore spots, and he knew how swollen his face was. He rubbed at it as he walked through the house, hoping to get to his small room before his mother took a proper look at him.

'Supper's nearly ready. Where have you been?' his mother said, without looking away from what she was doing.

'I was down in the glade. Adalhaid told me to give you this.' He held out the blue flower that Adalhaid had picked.

His mother looked over at him and took it, her eyes widening when she saw his face and the tear in his sleeve.

'What happened?' she said.

'I fell.'

She grabbed him by the chin and turned his face into the light, looking it over with a mix of anger and concern. 'How many times did you fall?' she said. 'It was those boys again, wasn't it?'

He hated lying to his mother. He hated disappointing her even more. Once she knew, his father would find out and his shame would be complete. That hurt worse than any of the blows the boys landed. He nodded.

Done inspecting his face, she pushed up his sleeve and grimaced as she looked at the gash on his forearm. As she did, the door opened and his father came into the house.

'Wolfram, go and fetch the priest,' she said.

His father drew his sword from its scabbard and hung it by the crossguard from a pair of wooden hooks on the wall. Satisfied it was secure, he began to remove his sword belt. 'Why?' he said.

'Wulfric's got a cut. I think it's going bad.'

Wolfram sighed. 'What happened this time?'

His mother shook her head.

'I'll bring Wulfric over to see him in the morning, Frena.' Wolfram made his way over to his chair by the fireplace, not bothering to inspect Wulfric's injuries.

'You'll fetch the priest now. Wulfie could have a fever by the morning if it's going bad. You're the First Warrior of the village. The priest comes to us. We don't go to him.'

Wulfric cringed. He hated it when his mother called him 'Wulfie'.

'You're not going to give me peace until I fetch him, are you?' Wolfram said.

'No supper either,' Frena said.

Wolfram groaned and got to his feet. He was a mountain of a man with long hair so blond it was almost white. Despite not having a beard, he was never clean shaven, the dark stubble a strong contrast to his hair. He towered over Wulfric and there was not a pinch of fat on his body, while there was not a pinch of muscle on Wulfric's. He could not have been more different from his father, and he knew it was a continued source of disappointment. There were even some who whispered that Wulfric was not his son; that someone else had sneaked into his mother's bed without his father's knowledge.

Wulfric knew about these whispers because he had seen his father beating a man senseless outside the Great Hall in the centre of the village one day. When he had asked someone why, they had told him what the man had said and that nobody spoke ill of Wolfram without discovering for themselves why he was called 'The Strong Arm'. It was why he was the village's First Warrior; the bravest, the most skilled, the most feared. To insult him was the act of a man who no longer cared for life.

❖

Ritschl's old bones ached as he sat in the crook of a branch on a great tree overlooking the village of Leondorf, wrapped in a damp, threadbare cloak for what little warmth it gave him. Everything he had was damp. It was impossible to keep anything dry in the forest. Even his grey hair was plastered to his skin. He didn't need to worry much about his appearance, however, as he was invisible to the warriors who maintained watch—a trick he had discovered he knew when confronted with a pack of hungry wolves many years previously, at a time when he had no idea where or who he was.

His memory was a blur of disconnected images. It took great concentration or a sight, sound, or smell to bring him moments of clarity. As with the wolves, when he first saw the priest he had experienced one such moment. When he saw him for the first time in many years, that was.

He watched the priest as he walked across the square outside his kirk. He tried to match the old face to the picture of the young man called Aethelman that he had in his memory. Instinct told him they were one and the same, but a voice in his head urged caution. The prize was too great to make a mistake.

Ever since the memories had returned, his dreams had been haunted by one in particular. An image of a stone. The Stone. No bigger than his fist, covered in strange markings, it promised all things to the man who possessed it. Could that shabby, nondescript priest making his way through the village have it? How could he live in so humble a fashion if he did? It seemed almost too much to hope for, so Ritschl continued to watch, instinct telling him he was in the right place, reason demanding caution.

❉

Aethelman the Priest was an odd-looking man. He had a narrow, jowly face with ears that seemed too big for his bald head. The only hairs on it were the two dark, bushy eyebrows that moved animatedly each time he changed his expression.

'Fell again?' he said, as he rolled up Wulfric's sleeve while Frena watched.

Wulfric nodded his head, all the while trying to think up some interesting questions for the priest. Aethelman knew everything and Wulfric loved to get the chance to pick his brains. There was one above all that he wanted to know the answer to, but no matter how many times he asked, Aethelman smiled and shook his head.

'That boy, Rodulf,' Aethelman said. 'I presume tripping over him was the cause of your fall?'

Wulfric said nothing, ashamed that yet another person knew how easily Rodulf could beat him.

'You're right,' Aethelman said to Frena. 'It's going bad. The boy would be in a fever by the morning. You have a good eye for these things.'

His mother's face flushed with pride. The priest always had a way of making people feel at ease.

He held his hand over the cut on Wulfric's arm and paused. 'No questions for me today?' he said.

'Just one,' Wulfric said.

'Let me guess…'

Wulfric could feel his arm grow cold. The priest's hand hovered over the wound, not touching him, but Wulfric could feel his skin tingle on the area beneath.

'How do you do that?' Wulfric said.

At first Aethelman did not answer. He stared at Wulfric's arm, holding his hand still above the wound. It was as though his mind was entirely elsewhere. After a moment he drew a deep breath, and for an instant a look of extreme weariness appeared on his face, but it passed quickly.

'That, my young friend, is for the gods to know and you to be thankful for.'

It was more of an answer than he usually gave. Wulfric looked down at the wound. Where it had been red and angry, it now appeared as though it was several days old; the redness had faded to a benign pink and the cut had closed completely.

'It's clean now,' Aethelman said, turning to Wulfric's mother once again. 'And well on its way to healing.' He turned back to Wulfric. 'You need to be more careful.'

Wolfram grunted in disdain from his seat by the fire. 'It's not care that he needs.'

The words cut Wulfric more painfully than the stick had.

❋

'What can I do about it, Frena?' Wolfram said.

The walls in their house were thin, and although muffled, Wulfric could make out most of what his parents were saying from his bed. They thought he was asleep, but the remaining injuries hurt each time he moved and he knew from experience that he was unlikely to sleep much that night. Instead he would have to be tormented by his parents' conversation as well as the injuries Rodulf and his friends had inflicted.

'You can speak to the boy's father,' Frena said.

'The boy's father is a merchant. I'm not going to speak with him. He's a peddler of useless trinkets, and his son can beat mine. Over and over. The shame would be too great. In any event, he's a warrior apprentice and Wulfric is not. There's little that can be done.'

'His son is two years older,' Frena said.

'It shouldn't matter. Their blood is weak. Ours is strong. Wulfric will have to learn to take care of himself. It's bad enough that he still hasn't started his training. He's fourteen, for Jorundyr's sake. He should have been in training for two years already. I'd have forced him to put himself forward for selection last year if I thought I could have coped with the shame of him being rejected. I'd rather he get beaten every day than suffer the indignity of having to beg that man to make his son stop beating mine. It shames you, me, and my entire line back to its very beginning when the gods still walked this land. And the boy too; better to be defeated in battle than beg your enemy to leave you be.'

'They are saying that Rodulf will be First Warrior some day.'

'My arse! The only person who says that is his father, and maybe one or two of his lickspittles. He can pay for Rodulf to train as a warrior, but he can't pay for him to become one. The lad will have to pass the trials like everyone else. If he can, then he deserves it. I doubt it though; no one from that family has ever been a warrior. Even if he does, he will never lead this village; mark my words. A First Warrior leads by inspiration, not by bullying and intimidation.'

'But he doesn't stand up for his son? Some day, Wulfie will get beaten so badly he'll be maimed for life. What will you do then?'

'Enough. I'm going to sleep.'

Wulfric felt a pain in his chest that had nothing to do with the beating, as he tried to do likewise.

CHAPTER THREE

THE MAISTERSPAEKER PAUSED for a drink. He used the short break to take a close look at his audience. Their reaction was exactly what he was looking for. Wide eyes, open mouths. They were transfixed.

He took a deep breath and was about to continue when the silence was broken by a voice from the crowd.

'How do you know what they said?' asked a boy far too young to be out of his bed at that hour. 'You weren't there.'

The Maisterspaeker could see Conradin's face screw up with irritation. It didn't bother the Maisterspaeker. Sometimes it was good to let a story breathe, to take a pause to allow the listeners digest what they had heard, and consider what was to come.

'You're right,' he said. 'I wasn't there, but I've made it my life's work to find out every detail and fact about the stories I tell. What I can't find out for sure can usually be inferred. Don't forget that a story is just a story after all…'

❉

'Why don't you take Wulfric with you?' Frena said.

Wolfram shifted uncomfortably. 'I prefer to hunt alone.'

'All the other boys go hunting with their fathers. Maybe it's what he needs.'

Wolfram grunted. 'I don't like anyone slowing me down. There're few enough warriors in the village I'd consider bringing along.'

'But none of them are your son.'

Wolfram looked at Frena, and realised that he had no choice in the matter. 'Fine, but if he gets gored by a boar it's on your head. There's a reason I haven't brought him before; it can be dangerous.'

'So is getting beaten every other day.'

Wolfram knew that he wouldn't peace until he agreed. 'Put his things together. I'll bring him.'

❊

Wolfram led them away from the thatched roofs and gently smoking chimneys of the village and toward the High Places. Their craggy, snow-covered peaks dominated the eastern skyline and loomed ever larger as they rode. Wulfric shifted uncomfortably in his seat with increasing regularity. He didn't spend nearly as much time in the saddle as the other boys, and the insides of his thighs began to chafe after only a couple of hours. Men of the Northlands, particularly those with warrior blood, were born to the saddle and were expected to be as comfortable in it as out of it, but Wulfric did what was expected of him and no more.

That was not to say Wulfric was a poor rider, it was just that his body was not as hardened to long periods on horseback as it should be. Still, he could not complain. He had overheard his father's discussion with his mother and knew how reluctant he was to take Wulfric along. It was only to be expected, but at least he would have the opportunity to prove his father wrong. How he would do that was an entirely different matter.

'You see that peak there,' Wolfram said, pointing to one that stood out from the others surrounding it.

Wulfric nodded.

'To the right is the valley where Jorundyr's Rock stands. That's where you will go to become a warrior.'

Wulfric stared at the peak his father pointed out as they rode. It seemed so very far away. 'You went there?'

'Yes. Me and the other young men who were to become warriors. The snow never melts up there. I'll never forget the cold.' He chuckled at the reminiscence.

'Is the journey difficult?'

'Very,' his father said. 'Twelve of us went up. Only eight came back.

Jorundyr does not allow those too weak of mind or body to join the warriors' ranks. Those not strong enough to complete the pilgrimage would fail their comrades on the battlefield. The Rock is where Jorundyr sits, with his wolf, Ulfyr, as they pass judgment on fallen warriors, and decide if they are worthy to join his host to hunt belek and battle draugar.'

'He's there?' Wulfric said.

Wolfram smiled. 'Yes, but not for the eyes of the living. Don't be fooled though. He's watching. He's always watching. Making sure he knows who the brave and worthy are.'

They continued on in silence, Wulfric left to mull over what his father had said. He stared at the peak and felt a shiver run across his skin. It stood there, dominating the horizon; majestic but foreboding.

It was nearly noon when Wolfram told him to dismount. They had been making their way through forest game trails for some time, having left the cleared glades and pasturelands well behind them, and it seemed his father had spotted something of note.

Wolfram knelt by a disturbed patch of leaf litter and gently ran his hand over it. 'See here,' he said. 'These are boar tracks. There was a sounder here. Five or six of them, I'd say. One big one. Not long ago.'

Wulfric looked over his father's shoulder, but could not see what he was talking about. Yes, the ground was disturbed, but how anyone could distil any more information from it than that was beyond him. As if reading his thoughts, Wolfram continued.

'You see this mark here?'

Wulfric nodded.

'What is it?' Wolfram said.

'A hoof print,' Wulfric said. It was a guess. It looked like a smudge in the dirt to him.

'Good. It's large, and deep, so the animal that made it is big and heavy. See how the soil in the print is dark, and the edges are clear?'

Wulfric nodded.

'And how the disturbed leaves are damp?'

Wulfric nodded again.

'That means the tracks are fresh. The soil in the print hasn't had time to dry. Nor have the undersides of the leaves that were overturned. Understand?'

'I think so,' Wulfric said, as the scene before him did indeed begin to make sense.

'Now, get back on your horse and let's see if we can find them.'

Wulfric's legs had grown stiff and they protested as he hauled his body back into the saddle. Once again, his father led the way, urging his horse on at a slower pace than they had been keeping up previously.

There were weapons strapped to Wulfric's saddle. His father had put them there, and Wulfric was not sure if they were brought along as spares or if his father intended him to use them. He had never handled either of them before: a long spear with two arms branching out from just behind the head, and a weapon that looked like an oddly shaped and unusually long sword.

'Follow me closely,' Wolfram said in a whisper. 'But stay back when I charge the beasts. You must do exactly as I say, when I say. Understand?'

Wulfric nodded, feeling a building nervousness take hold of him.

They moved on slowly, their horses carefully placing each hoof as though they realised that the hunt was on. Even their breathing was quieter. They never ceased to amaze Wulfric. Traders with dark skin from the very far south came all the way to his village to buy them, so famed were they for their prowess. Each warrior in the village was given one of the finest from their communal stock when he returned from his warrior's pilgrimage. Men like his father had many, some of which were prizes taken in battle.

The foreign traders called them Northlander destriers. To Wulfric they were simply war horses. Big, aggressive, and spirited. He had always been terrified of them when he was younger; he still was. The one he sat on had treated him well enough so far, but he knew that he needed to impose his will on the beast or it would come to ignore him. It was a daunting prospect; the horse was so huge and he was so small.

Wolfram glanced back over his shoulder with an expression that said more than any words could. His eyes were wide with excitement and Wulfric knew that he had found their prey. His father reached for his spear and spurred his horse to a gallop. Wulfric's horse needed no such encouragement. By the time he had lifted his foot to spur it on, it had already started its pursuit. They plunged through undergrowth and dodged trees as they galloped on. He was thankful his horse needed no guidance, as he could barely react quickly enough to each approaching obstacle.

Gone now was any semblance of stealth, as the horses crashed through the brush with a thundering of hooves, rustling of leaves, and snapping of branches. Wulfric's thighs burned as he gripped onto the saddle with all his strength. With or without him, his horse would complete the chase.

His father struck down with his spear. It looked as though he was stabbing a bush, but there was a loud squeal. Wulfric managed to stop his horse, and waited for his father to bid him forward. Wolfram urged his horse on as he stood in his stirrups, pressing forward on his spear with all his weight as well as the strength of the horse.

'The long sword! Draw it!' Wolfram shouted above the squeals and thrashing in the bush in front of him.

Wulfric's ears were flooded by the raging noise, and he could feel his heart pounding as he tried to do his father's bidding. He drew the odd-looking weapon from its sheath, his hands shaking so much he feared he would drop it. It had the handle and cross-guarded hilt of a sabre, but the blade—if it could be called that—was long and straight. It was square in cross section, and unsharpened for most of its length. Only the final part, about the length of Wulfric's forearm, splayed out into a double-edged blade with spear-point tip. It was an unwieldy thing, and Wulfric had to concentrate to keep it under control.

'Come forward! Quickly!' Wolfram shouted.

Wulfric's horse moved forward, eager to be part of the action. His father's spear was embedded in the shoulder of the largest boar Wulfric had ever seen. He was struggling to keep it pinned to the spot with his spear. Despite this, it was far from beaten. Its eyes were red with rage and its mouth foamed. It squealed and snarled and Wulfric found it hard to tear his eyes away from the large jagged tusks that curved up out of its mouth.

'Finish it! Quickly!' his father said. 'Stab it through the throat, and on as far as you can reach.'

Wulfric took a deep breath. He had never killed anything before and knew that this was the moment that would make or break him in his father's eyes. He struggled to hold the long sword steady and felt his heart race. He looked at the raging boar as it fought to remain standing under the weight of Wolfram's spear. Wulfric lunged forward with the sword, while he clung onto the saddle with his legs so hard they burned.

As he did, he heard a violent rustle in the bushes behind him, and a ferocious snarling screech. Wulfric's horse turned in reaction to the new danger, throwing Wulfric off balance. A boar, almost as large as the one his father was struggling with, emerged from a bush. Wulfric's horse kicked at it. Wulfric dropped the sword and grabbed onto the first thing he could for support; the hunting spear secured to his saddle. The horse kicked again, and Wulfric went flying through the air.

He could see his father struggling to keep his horse under control, while also continuing to pin the first boar in place with his spear. The scene felt as though it was playing out in slow motion, all but for the ground, which rushed toward Wulfric far more quickly than he would have liked.

His fall was not as heavy as it might have been; he landed in a bush that bore the brunt of his weight, but he was dazed and battered. As he shook the stars from his head, he realised that he was still clinging onto the spear, which had been ejected from the horse along with him. His father was twisting in his saddle, trying to get into position to kill the huge boar he had trapped. Until he did, he would not be able to help Wulfric. To let the first boar go now could mean a violent and painful death for them both. He supposed that his father could always have more sons. Wulfric knew that if he was to survive the next few moments, it would be up to him.

His horse was stamping at the second boar, but not having any success. While it was huge for a boar, it was smaller than his mount and more agile. It ducked and dived out of the way, squealing and snorting in rage. It spotted Wulfric, and paused for a moment. Wulfric made a more attractive opponent than a raging warhorse.

'Run, boy! Climb a tree!'

There was panic in his father's voice. Wulfric did not think he had ever heard him sound like that before. The boar stamped its hoof on the ground and with a loud snort, charged. Wulfric pushed himself backward into the bush with his feet and lowered the spear, his eyes fixed on the boar's long tusks. They looked as though they could cut right through him.

Still on his backside, he wedged the spear butt against his shoulder and leaned forward as the boar came within reach. The shock of the impact knocked the butt free with a tremendous, painful jolt, and the shaft struck him hard against the jaw as it was twisted from his hands. There was a blood-curdling squeal, and with his wits knocked from his head for the second time in as many minutes, Wulfric feared it might have come from him.

He fought through the confusion in his head, and the maelstrom of noise and movement around him. He caught hold of the spear and threw his full body weight on top of it. Wulfric's heart beat against his chest so hard he thought it would break through. He gasped for breath as he tried to hold the spear down. The boar thrashed about in fury. The tugs on the spear grew less forceful until they were no more than twitches. There was another loud squeal to Wulfric's right. He looked up to see his father finishing off the first boar.

A moment later his father was standing over him.

'Are you all right, boy?'

'I think so. My shoulder hurts.'

'It's never a good idea to brace a spear against yourself; always use the ground and press on it with your foot if you can. Anything else solid will do if you can't. I doubt you'll forget that lesson though.' He chuckled and reached down to the boar impaled on Wulfric's spear. He dabbed his fingers into the blood before he turned to Wulfric and smeared the blood across his face. Wulfric was taken by surprise and flinched.

Wolfram smiled. 'You're a blooded hunter now. It's a fine kill. Well done. Your mother will be pleased.'

CHAPTER FOUR

WULFRIC COULD FEEL the bulk of the boar he had killed slung over his saddle behind him, matching the one on his father's horse. It was the most satisfying thing he had ever experienced.

He was still amazed that he had managed to kill it. It was only a boar, and he realised that as a warrior he would be expected to kill a man without hesitation, but how much more difficult could it be? Could he perhaps have what it took to be a warrior after all? The thought kindled the faintest flicker of hope inside him, but it still seemed too much to believe.

With a fine kill to each of their names, they could return home that evening rather than spending the night in the forest as originally planned. At a good pace, they would be back not long after nightfall, with him a newly blooded hunter. He couldn't wait to tell Adalhaid.

They were moving through a clearing when his father held out his hand and halted. He was staring at the tree line to their right so Wulfric followed his gaze. The light was failing and it was difficult to make anything out. He moved up beside his father.

'What is it?' he whispered.

'There's no sound.'

That was exactly what Wulfric thought, not seeing his father's cause for concern.

'The insects have gone quiet over there. That means something big moving about.'

'Men?'

'Perhaps. The scent of a freshly killed carcass can attract far worse than men, though. Stay as quiet as you can. Let's get moving. Keep your eyes and ears open.'

Wulfric could sense his father relax when they reached the tree line and returned to the cover of the woods. As soon as they were concealed within, he turned to the right and they made their way along the edge of the clearing, still hidden by the trees, heading toward the source of Wolfram's concern. It occurred to Wulfric that they would be better off heading away from it, but that was not how warriors behaved.

His father halted and again held out his hand for Wulfric to stop. It was almost completely dark, and Wulfric could make out the faint flickering of light against the trunks of some of the trees. Wolfram slipped down from his horse and gestured for Wulfric to do the same.

They crept toward the source of the light, moving between bushes and trees in the hope of staying out of sight. Wulfric spotted the source a short distance away and crouched down behind a bush beside his father. There were four men gathered around a campfire, chatting quietly, their voices barely audible over the crackling of the fire.

'Who are they?' Wulfric whispered.

'Not from Leondorf anyway.'

'Rasbruckers?'

Wolfram nodded. 'Quiet now. Don't let them hear us.'

Wulfric was more interested in watching his father than the men sitting by the campfire. He had taken a step in the right direction that day by killing the boar, even if he had been terrified on the inside. Either he had done a good job of concealing it, or his father had chosen not to see it. He had no desire to undo all he had done by making a mistake or doing something foolish.

Watch, listen, and be careful, he thought. He could learn a lot from this experience, and he did not intend to waste the opportunity. His father crouched on one knee and was completely still, watching the campfire between a gap in the leaves of the bush they were hiding behind. He barely blinked and Wulfric could see the firelight reflected in his eyes.

Wulfric had never been so close to Rasbruckers before, and had certainly never seen one. The name of the neighbouring village was a byword for anything bad; any individual of questionable moral character was assumed to have Rasbruck ancestry, irrespective of where he came from, and to be called a Rasbrucker, or have your behaviour likened to that of a Rasbrucker, was one of the most potent insults available to someone from Leondorf.

They did not look any different to people from Leondorf. He realised that it was silly to think that they would, but nonetheless it came as something of a surprise when they looked so ordinary. He half expected deformities, crazed, manic behaviour; something, anything, that would mark them out as being his natural enemy. He was disappointed. It was more difficult to hate someone who looked just like the man who lived in the next house.

'I've seen enough, let's go,' Wolfram whispered.

As Wulfric moved back, he brushed against a bush. Not so much as to cause noise, but enough to disturb what was sleeping within. A partridge burst from it in a racket of rustling, squawking, and flapping as Wulfric looked on in horror. There was an immediate reaction from around the campfire. Wulfric's was to freeze on the spot. Would they dismiss the noise as nothing more than a bird spooked by a nocturnal animal?

It didn't seem that his father was willing to take the chance. 'Run,' he whispered, placing a guiding hand on Wulfric's back as he started to do so himself.

'Hey!'

The call came from behind. They were spotted. No hope for getting away unseen now. Wulfric knew he was holding his father back, as the pressure of his hand urging Wulfric on was constant. He went as fast as he could, but as with all other things, in running he had always lagged behind the other boys of his age.

He could hear the men from the campfire crashing through the undergrowth behind them as he and his father ran for their horses. The thought occurred to Wulfric that one of their pursuers might have a bow, and that at any second an arrow could skewer him in the back. The notion sent a shiver down his spine—but they reached the horses unperforated, where Wolfram grabbed Wulfric under the armpits and threw him onto his horse.

'Ride for home. Don't look back, and don't stop for anything,' Wolfram said, as he expertly swung up into his own saddle.

Wulfric nodded as he wheeled his horse around. Then they were off, and the sounds of the Rasbruckers, still on foot, faded into the forest night.

❈

They rode hard all the way home. By the time the forest gave way to the outer-lying pastures of Leondorf, his backside and thighs hurt like he did not think possible. It was only then that his father slowed to a trot, and allowed the near-exhausted horses to catch their breath.

He looked over at Wulfric with a smile on his face. 'Nothing like a little excitement to give you an appetite, eh?'

His face was animated. Wulfric's barely concealed the terror he was feeling. He tried to mirror his father's levity, but even feigning it required more energy than he had left.

❈

Wulfric sat in the classroom and shifted on his hard wooden seat, his backside still sore from the hours he spent in the saddle the day before. It had been too late to call on Adalhaid when he got home, and he was impatient for the class to end so that he could tell her all about his adventure.

He realised that Aethelman the Priest was staring at him, distracted by his squirming. Aethelman ran the small school in the village's kirk, teaching the basics of reading and numbers to the town's girls and the children of tradesmen and merchants. No warrior's child attended, aside from Wulfric. The skills learned there were not considered necessary for hunting, ranging, or defending the village. At first he had attended because Adalhaid spent every morning there, and then, as his peers all began their warrior training, because he had nothing else to do. He was not the most attentive of students, and usually spent the classes dreaming up great adventures. That day, he had a real one to pore over.

'Wulfric. Wulfric!'

The second call shook him from his imagination and dreams of being a warrior, and he looked up to see Aethelman standing by his small desk.

'Be so good as to go into the back room and fetch out a fresh bottle of ink.'

Wulfric nodded and got up from his seat while Aethelman continued with the lesson. He always asked Wulfric to do the small errands, an acknowledgement of his lack of participation in the class. Wulfric was glad to be a help, however, so did it without hesitation.

The back room was Aethelman's private space. It was where he slept, kept his personal things, prepared his potions and poultices. Aethelman made the ink for their classes himself from powders and liquids that he stored in small glass bottles that fascinated Wulfric. He quickly spotted the freshly prepared bottle, took it up and turned to leave. As he did, his eyes lingered on a strange object that he had not seen before. It sat on a small table beside Aethelman's modest cot-bed. He stepped closer for a better look; it was too fascinating to ignore. The room was dim, but the object— which looked not unlike a large potato—glistened as though made of metal. The surface was rough, and it was only as he neared it that he realised it was covered in finely etched symbols.

It was an ugly thing, and Wulfric could not understand why it intrigued him so. He stared at it a moment longer before giving in to temptation. He reached out. His fingertips tingled in an uncomfortable way as they touched the cold metal. His heart quickened and he quickly withdrew his hand. For a moment the object seemed to emanate a pale blue glow, causing Wulfric to panic that he had started whatever it was it did. The glow faded as quickly as it had appeared. He took a deep breath of relief, but felt dizzy, and his stomach turned in the way it often did before he vomited. He took another deep breath to steady himself and walked out of the backroom, hoping he had not delayed too long to draw questions.

He handed Aethelman the bottle of ink without a word and sat at his desk, trying to swallow the feeling of nausea and ignore the headache that had joined it.

※

Aethelman placed the stack of rough paper pages on his desk, writing exercises that he would have to correct before morning. Wulfric's sat on top, easy to spot for it was little more than a series of smudges and blots. He looked at it with a mixture of sadness and disappointment. Wulfric was a bright boy with a good heart, but he had no interest in learning and that seemed unlikely to change. He spent most of his time daydreaming of being a warrior, of heroic deeds that he was central to, but the reality of that seemed equally unlikely. Aethelman hoped more than anything that Wulfric could find some of his father's mettle, and begin his journey to being a warrior. There seemed to be little else for him. He would certainly never be a scholar, and a life could not be made sitting under a tree watching the clouds and dreaming.

Aethelman muttered a short prayer under his breath that Wulfric would find his way and apply himself to it, as he sat on his cot and pulled off his boots. He stopped mid-pull and spotted the Stone sitting on his bedside table. Aethelman frowned. He had forgotten taking it out of its box. He was old, and had noticed for some time that faculties he had so long taken for granted were starting to let him down. It was careless to leave the Stone out like that; foolish to have even taken it from its box to begin with. His ageing mind was weakening; the temptation it presented would grow harder to resist. It was long past time to get rid of it.

He covered the Stone with a cloth to avoid touching it, then returned it to the box which he shut and locked. The box sat under the table, a chastising reminder that Aethelman had ignored it for far too long.

❈

'What was it?' a woman's voice said.

'Shut up!' Conradin said with such vigour the people around him shied back.

The Maisterspaeker gestured for Conradin to relax. 'Would you like me to go directly to the end of the story?' he said to the young woman.

She shook her head vigorously.

He was pleased the bluff worked. His story did not yet have an end. 'You'll learn everything I know about the Stone in due course, but you'll have to be patient.'

The young woman smiled.

The Maisterspaeker took another mouthful of ale, and continued.

CHAPTER FIVE

WULFRIC WAS LOST in his thoughts, walking toward the schoolhouse to meet Adalhaid when someone shoved him, knocking him to the muddy ground. He had enough time to roll onto his back before Rodulf pounced on him and punched him in the stomach.

'Gonna fight back today, fatty?' Rodulf said, as he delivered another blow.

Wulfric didn't have time to answer before Rodulf hit him again.

'Didn't think so, you fat fucker. My dad says you must really be the privy cleaner's son. No way you're the Strong Arm's boy.'

His cronies laughed, as they always did. The taunt hurt Wulfric as much as any of the blows, but he didn't fight back. He reckoned if he just lay there, it would be over sooner and he could get on with his day. He was determined he wouldn't cry this time, though.

Adalhaid's voice cried out and the barrage of blows ceased. Wulfric turned his head and squinted through swelling eyes to the direction of the voice. Rodulf's knees still pinned his arms to the ground. She stood there, her face twisted with pain and anguish. Wulfric realised immediately that it was his beating that caused it. It shamed him, more than his inability to fight back ever could. It also made him feel something else, something he had never felt before. Anger.

He heard Adalhaid's voice calling out again.

'Why don't you piss off, you interfering bitch!' Rodulf said. 'Perhaps when I'm done with your little pal, I'll come over and show you what a real man is like.'

The others all laughed. They were now at the age where the older boys began to notice girls as something more. They all noticed Adalhaid, her long hair the colour of burnished copper and tall, slender figure. Her green eyes were clever and mischievous. Wulfric cared about her more than anything in the world. She was his friend, his only friend, but he realised that even he had started to look at her differently. When he dreamed of heroic deeds now, they were all done for her. He felt his heart quicken at what Rodulf said. When Rodulf looked back at him to finish the job he had started, Wulfric was staring directly at him, intently.

'What are you looking at, fatty?' Rodulf said.

'You shouldn't say that to her,' Wulfric said. His voice was still weak.

'What was that, fatty? What the fuck did you say?' He punched Wulfric in the stomach.

Wulfric gasped and was unable to reply.

'What? Cat got your tongue?' Rodulf said.

The other boys standing behind him laughed again.

'Not going to stop me from making a woman out of your little tart then?'

The others laughed even harder and Wulfric could see a predatory, lustful sneer on Rodulf's face.

Wulfric punched him. He punched Rodulf squarely in the face and paused for a moment. He was almost as shocked as Rodulf at what he had done. He couldn't remember deciding to do it. It had just happened. Everyone fell silent and Rodulf's eyes widened with surprise. Wulfric wasn't afraid anymore. He realised in that moment that he hadn't been afraid at any time that day, merely accepting of what was to come. Too lazy to fight back, rather than too afraid. Now, all he could think about was what Rodulf had said. All he could feel was rage.

He hit Rodulf again. Rodulf's expression changed to one of anger. Still Wulfric could only think of that one thing; of what Rodulf said he would do to Adalhaid.

He punched again, and again. Rodulf's expression changed to one of shock, before finally to something else. Fear. Then Wulfric was kneeling over Rodulf who was on the ground, on his back, trying desperately to cover his face. It felt as though Wulfric was watching it all from a distance, as though his body was doing things all by itself. He kept punching and punching, until his anger abated and his arms burned and his lungs screamed for air. He looked down and was horrified by what he saw. Rodulf's face no longer bore any expression; it was a pulped mess. The other boys were silent and had not moved from where they stood. Wulfric looked down at his hands which were coated in blood, confused by what he had done. He turned to Adalhaid, who stared wide-eyed and in silence just like the boys. She stared at him for a moment longer before turning and running away.

Wulfric looked back at Rodulf, who groaned and moved. Adults arrived, and on seeing Rodulf's moaning, bloodied body they demanded to know what had happened. Aethelman was sent for, while Wulfric was subjected to a barrage of questions. He felt so tired, and let their voices wash over his head. No one seemed to believe that he was the one who did it. They asked the same question over and over, and also of the other boys, but the answer was always the same. It was Wulfric. Wulfric did it.

Aethelman arrived, followed shortly after by Donato, Rodulf's father. He was a lean man with sandy hair like his son, and sharp, cunning eyes, like a rat. The priest declared that it was likely Rodulf would lose an eye. Donato was in a rage and made for Wulfric. One of the villagers had the presence of mind to stop him.

Wolfram was one of the last to arrive. The arrival of the Strong Arm silenced the crowd. The villagers were terrified of him, as was Wulfric. The fear returned now. He was fearful of what would happen, of what his father would do when he found out the trouble he had caused. In the back of his mind though, he was more afraid of what Adalhaid thought. The look she had given him made his fear stronger than ever. He wanted to go after her, but knew he had to stay and discover the consequences of what he had done.

'What happened here?' Wolfram said.

Wulfric said nothing, timidly waiting for his father's famed rage.

'There was a fight,' someone said. 'One of the lads is badly hurt.'

Wolfram looked at Wulfric, a confused expression on his face. 'He looks fine to me.'

'Not Wulfric. The other one. Rodulf.'

Aethelman turned from where he was kneeling next to Rodulf's supine form and nodded. Wolfram looked down at Rodulf's bloodied face. Wulfric waited for his reaction, for the anger, and the punishment that would surely follow. His father's face was impossible to read.

Donato broke free from the man who had been holding him back. 'Look what he did! Look what he did to my boy! What are you going to do about this?'

'He's a warrior apprentice, isn't he?'

'Yes,' Donato said, hesitantly.

'If he can't defend himself from a boy two years his junior, I don't hold out much hope for him completing his training.' Wolfram turned to Aethelman. 'Will he live?'

'Yes, but I expect he'll lose an eye.'

Wolfram nodded. 'No chance of him becoming a warrior then. He's learned an important lesson in not provoking his betters. It will serve him well in the future if he remembers it. As for him picking a fight with my son? Boys will be boys. I won't hold a grudge against you for it.'

'That's not what I meant. You know that's not what I meant. You, you—'

Wolfram back-handed Donato across the face with a loud crack that drew a gasp from the gathered villagers, and sent him sprawling to the ground beside his son.

'Perhaps you need to learn the same lesson your boy just has, but I promise you won't enjoy it.' Wolfram's voice had dropped to a growl and Wulfric could see the fury in his eyes.

The crowd fell silent and the air was thick with tension as the crowd strained to hear what Donato would say in response. Already his disrespect had brought him perilously close to the point where Wolfram could kill him and not have to answer to the council in the Great Hall for it. Donato knew this, knew he had overstepped the mark, but was too enraged to back down as quickly as he should have. Everyone in the crowd could see this, and all waited with the expectation of being about to witness a killing.

Donato gritted his teeth. 'I'm sorry. I'll see that the boy watches his manners in future.'

'See that you do,' Wolfram said. 'Have a thought for your own while you're at it.'

He turned and smiled at Wulfric, before putting his hand on Wulfric's shoulder and leading him home.

❄

Adalhaid sat by the tree on her own, thinking over what she had just seen. It had seemed as though there was no trace of the caring, considerate boy who was her friend, only a savage animal. She had thought Wulfric would kill Rodulf, and had never believed him capable of such a thing. It was what separated him from all the others. Now she didn't know. It was as though in that moment, the person she thought she knew the best had been taken from her, and replaced by someone entirely different.

She stood and started walking home, with a pervading sense hanging over her like a dark cloud that the inevitable had finally happened.

❄

He was sitting by the tree where he and Adalhaid had so often sat, one evening a few days after the incident with Rodulf. She had not spoken to him since his fight with Rodulf, and the fact constantly played on his mind. He had barely seen her, and her absence left him with a constant hollow feeling inside that he could not explain. Usually he enjoyed the warmth of the sunshine, but that day it did nothing for him.

She was beside him without making a sound, in the spot she had occupied so many times in the past. She broke a piece from a bread roll that she was eating and handed it to him. They ate in silence for several minutes before he spoke.

'I'm sorry,' he said.

'For what?' There was an edge to her voice but the expression on her face made it clear that she had not intended it. 'Sorry for what?' she repeated, her voice softer now.

'For what I did and for upsetting you,' Wulfric said.

She smiled. 'That's all right. I was just surprised. I didn't expect to see you doing that. I shouldn't have been. All boys are like that, I suppose. I just didn't think that you were.'

Wulfric felt disappointment drop in his stomach like a lead weight. 'I'm not, it's just, what he said, I mean…'

She reached over and put her hand on his. 'It's all right, there's nothing to be sorry about,' she said. 'I should be sorry for the way I behaved. Part of me is glad you did it. The others will leave you alone now. Things will be so much better for you. Even my parents were talking about it. We're all growing up. Life changes.' She looked down at her feet and seemed sad.

Wulfric didn't like it when she got sad. It filled him with the overwhelming desire to make her happy again. He had no idea of how to do it, though.

She held out her hand with something in it. 'I made this for you, to say sorry.'

He took it carefully and wished he had something to give to her. It was a small silver coin that had been worn away to a smooth finish. She had engraved her initials onto one side, and his onto the other, in ornate lettering that must have taken hours of careful work. She had also punched a small hole close to the edge and threaded a leather lanyard through it. Putting aside his embarrassment at not having anything for her, he immediately tied it around his neck.

'I love it,' he said. 'I'm sorry that I have nothing for you though.'

'That's all right,' she said, smiling. 'Seeing you wear it is enough.'

CHAPTER SIX

WULFRIC STOOD QUIETLY among the other boys, who joked and laughed nervously as they waited in the glade, basking in the autumn morning sun. Although they had all been preparing for, and anticipating this day for as long as they could remember, none of them knew exactly what to expect. For Wulfric it had long seemed like an impossible dream to stand there, to finally start his training. His presence was two years overdue and for him there would not be another chance, so he remained silent, not joining in the skittish banter.

In the months since he beat Rodulf, Wulfric had thought about little other than putting himself forward for training. The few days surrounding that incident had sowed the seed in his mind that being selected was a possibility. His life had changed substantially. There were no more attacks, no more snide comments. Between the boar and Rodulf, he stopped thinking of himself as feeble, inept, incapable. Something had changed in his mind. The doubt had departed and was replaced with belief. Being left alone gave him the time to focus and train, and that was what he had filled his summer with. Running, lifting heavy weights, everything he had seen warriors and apprentices doing. He tried his best to keep it a secret. Part of him still feared failure, and if that happened he did not want anyone to know how hard he had worked.

Jorundyr's festival day was the day that marked this event for all young men. It was the day on which training to be a warrior began for some—and for others, the day on which their training ended and they were faced with their final test.

Those who considered themselves ready to start their apprenticeship mustered in a glade near the village. At its centre there was a single standing stone, said to have been placed there by Jorundyr when he still walked the realm of men. He had waged a war against the draugar, and had needed brave men to join his ranks. He placed the stones near villages throughout the land, where warriors could gather and make their desire to fight by his side known.

Draugar were little more than a legend now and Jorundyr had long since gone to his hall in the High Places, but the stones remained, as did those who sought to become Jorundyr's disciples. The village's warriors would deliberate, and decide which of the boys would be allowed to remain in the glade to start their training. What made up the selection process was a secret known only to those already chosen. It was this, as well as the fear of being rejected, that twisted the guts of every young man there. Failing to be accepted for training would be a shame that would follow him for the rest of his life.

Another group were gathered there that morning; those who had finished their training and were about to depart on their pilgrimage to Jorundyr's Rock, an isolated spot deep in the High Places. They were even more nervous than Wulfric and the other hopefuls. They looked lonely and lacked the cocky confidence that they had developed over their years of training. They all knew that for some of them, the reticent, backward glances they took as they walked away from the village would be the last look of home they ever had. The pilgrimage was a rite of passage that every warrior had to undertake. They all went willingly, even in the knowledge that some of them would die.

Those who were still in the middle of their training, not yet ready for the journey, were also in the glade—returned after the short break for harvest— watching in a smirking, chuckling group while Wulfric and his fellow hopefuls waited to discover if they would be considered worthy to join them.

Wulfric stared at the stone at the centre of the glade. The writing on it was so old not even Aethelman could decipher it with any certainty. Only warriors were supposed to go near the stone, and simply being that close to it brought home the reality of the step he was about to take. The glade was screened off from the village by trees and undergrowth, which gave it the feeling of being a secret place. A sacred one, even.

One of the warriors, Eldric, a friend of Wulfric's father and a man that had always been friendly on the many occasions he had eaten at their home, walked up to the assembled group. His neat black beard was punctuated by the scars that most of the village's warriors bore. He held a great sword, different from the usual type of sabre favoured by warriors. Northlanders fought from horseback whenever the situation allowed, and they preferred a one-handed sabre with a single curved edge. This sword looked old—ancient—with long straight edges meeting at a rounded tip. The guard was short and thick, and engraved with what seemed to Wulfric to be the same type of symbols as were on the standing stone.

Eldric placed the sword down on the ground in front of the gathered boys with reverence. He stood and looked at it for a moment before returning his gaze to the boys.

'Who thinks he can lift the sword? The sword touched by the hand of Jorundyr himself?'

Aethelman stood behind Eldric, just to the side of the standing stone. His face had been solemn all morning, but when Eldric asked his question Wulfric thought he saw Aethelman's mouth curl ever so slightly in a knowing smile.

Hane stepped forward. He was tall and broad, with short brown curly hair that was in keeping with him being of farming stock, rather than of a warrior family. Wulfric wondered if he would let it grow longer should he be chosen to start his apprenticeship, an odd thought that made him realise he was searching for anything that would distract him from the anxiety he was feeling.

Although the same age as Wulfric, Hane had not been chosen to start his training until now. He was larger than the others, and stronger, but his father had needed the help of his eldest son to work the farm. He had bought a slave that summer, which had given Hane the chance to be a warrior. Wulfric liked him. Even when the bullying had been at its worst, Hane was never involved. Wulfric wondered if his greater age made him feel as though he had something to prove. Wulfric knew that in his case, it certainly did. Should he have put himself forward to try?

'Hane. A bold statement. Please,' Eldric said, gesturing to the sword, 'pick it up.'

All the boys watched Hane intently, but none were brave enough to offer words of encouragement. After seeing Aethelman's smile, Wulfric was more interested in watching him. As Hane approached the blade, Aethelman stared at it and Wulfric could see his jaw clench and his face tighten. Hane leaned over and put his hand on the hilt. He hesitated for a moment before pulling back. His body jerked, but the sword did not budge. He tried again, and again, the final time with so much effort he lost grip and fell backward.

One of the other boys laughed, and Eldric snapped his gaze on him.

'Would you like to try?' he said.

The boy looked about himself nervously, and at Hane who was still sitting on the frosty grass kneading his shoulder. The boy shook his head.

'When you can lift the sword, you will be ready to make your journey to the High Places. Not before. Jorundyr invites those he wishes to test in the High Places by allowing them to lift his sword. Eight young warriors lifted the sword this morning and started their pilgrimages. Not all of them will come back.' He paused, allowing his words to sink in.

'The life you choose for yourself is one of danger,' Eldric said. 'To fail is to die. Being a warrior is not a privilege. It is a responsibility. You bring life to those you defend and death to those who would harm them. You must be willing to lay down your lives to satisfy that responsibility. The pilgrimage proves you have that commitment, but it is our responsibility to you to ensure that you are ready for that journey when your time comes.'

He walked forward to where the boys had lined up. He continued along the line slowly, looking each of them up and down as he went. He stopped at one, the smith's son. One or two boys who, like Hane, were not from warrior families put themselves forward every year; few were chosen.

'Try again next year,' Eldric said. 'You'll have a better chance when you're taller and heavier. No shame in having to wait another year.'

The smith's boy had gone pale with disappointment, but he nodded and did as he was told, likely taking solace in the hope that the next year it might be different. Wulfric felt a flutter of nerves as he wondered what Eldric would do when he reached him. His heart started to race as Eldric got closer. Wulfric knew him well, thought of him as almost an uncle, but now he seemed like a complete stranger. He stopped at Wulfric and looked at him as though he had never before laid eyes on him. Wulfric held his breath, but did his best to hold Eldric's stare. Eldric moved on without uttering a word or revealing anything with his expression.

Wulfric took a deep breath and had to take care not to let it out with a loud sigh of relief. The release of tension was dizzying, and knowing he was past the first obstacle his curiosity turned to how the others would fare. In all of the anxiety and uncertainty, Wulfric had not paid much attention to who else was there to put themselves forward. When he spotted Rodulf standing farther down the line, it came as a surprise. He had already been in training for two years, although this was his first day back since he and Wulfric had fought. Surely they could not be making him put himself forward again?

Rodulf's injuries appeared to have healed well, all but for the eye which he had lost. He wore a finely crafted leather patch over whatever was left beneath it. Wulfric felt no remorse for the injuries he'd caused; quite the contrary. He felt anger kindle within him every time he saw Rodulf, which was rare enough since their fight. For whatever reason, Rodulf was rarely seen out of doors since losing his eye. No amount of injury would ever settle things between them as far as Wulfric was concerned.

Wulfric watched Eldric reach Rodulf's place in the line and stop. He didn't bother with an appraising look; he merely shook his head as soon as he stopped.

'You have no place here,' Eldric said. 'Not anymore. You have already been told that. You should not have come today. Losing an eye to another warrior is a badge of honour. For an apprentice to be beaten by an ordinary boy who has not yet even put himself forward for training? Go, and don't come back.'

Rodulf's mouth dropped open as though he was surprised, but he must have expected to hear what he just had. Everyone had said that he would never become a warrior with only one eye. He shut his mouth without uttering a word, and it twisted with anger. He turned and looked directly at Wulfric before storming back to the village.

Three more were sent home, two with hope of returning the next year, one with his dreams of becoming a warrior shattered. When each had been scrutinised, and all of those found lacking sent home, Aethelman spoke.

'You are all now apprentices of Jorundyr. He expects you to bring your best every single day. Anyone who does not will be sent home. Congratulations.'

For Wulfric, the relief of having been selected was short lived. The true test would begin the next day, when their training began.

CHAPTER SEVEN

AETHELMAN STRETCHED OUT on the cot in his small private quarters at the back of the village kirk. The boy, Wulfric, had done well, and Aethelman had no reservations in saying he was ready to begin on the path to becoming a warrior; a Disciple of Jorundyr, as they were referred to by those of his order, the Grey Priests.

Aethelman had arrived in Leondorf on the eve of Wolfram's birth, watched him grow to manhood, and was now doing the same for Wulfric. To bring two generations of a family into the world made Aethelman feel privileged. He had convinced himself it was acceptable to remain to see Wulfric take his pilgrimage and become a man. Then, he had promised himself, he would move on and attend to the Stone, whatever that might involve.

It was the longest he had ever spent in one place; longer than his childhood home, the Hermitage—the monastery where he trained—or any of the places his calling had led him over the years. It also meant it was far past time to consider leaving. Usually another priest would pass through the area, and if the incumbent at that time felt he had remained for long enough, they would exchange places. Priests were supposed to be loyal to the gods and all of the people they presided over; never to any one tribe or village. It made for a lonely life—but few ties, and there was appeal in that also.

His eye fell on the old wooden box beneath the bedside table, and the sense of contentment that had filled him a moment before fled, replaced with unease, fear, guilt. He had always known what lay within that box would have to be dealt with eventually. It was called the Gods' Stone by some, the Fount Stone by others. He had no clear idea of what to do with it, that oddly shaped lump inscribed with symbols that even he could not read.

The rector at the Hermitage, the place where all Grey Priests trained, had sent them out to search for Stones many years before as part of their ordination. He had said they were a source of great power, and could only be safe when in the custody of responsible guardians—the priesthood to which Aethelman belonged.

There was only one problem with the task the rector had set them. No one had seen a Fount Stone in generations, and no one knew what to do if one was found. Aethelman always thought it a good example of the folly of suspicion. Knowledge that was so important—and guarded in such secrecy—that it was now forgotten altogether. It did little to ease his conscience, however. Not knowing was not an excuse for having left it sitting in a box under his bedside table for decades.

The only saving grace was that neither he, nor anyone else, knew how to use the Stone. At times he still had trouble believing he had found it. The Grey Priests' rite of passage was called 'the Search'. To complete their ordination, each young priest spent a year and a day scouring the land for the Stones. Once, it was said, there were many of the Stones, relics of an ancient time, artefacts of the gods. No one really knew. None had been found for centuries, and there was not a young priest who did not grumble at the futility of their task. Aethelman had thought it nothing more than a tradition. A show of devotion to their creed and a way to prepare them for the itinerant lives they would lead. Then he had found one, he and another young priest.

If they found a Stone the gods would give them guidance, the rector had said. Aethelman had prayed every night for years, but the gods never saw fit to tell him what to do. It was little consolation that he had never tried to learn its secrets, or bend its power to his will. He knew he should have done *something*, but the fact was he had no idea where to begin. He had waited patiently in the hope that the gods would tell him. And waited. Sometimes they tested a man to see his true worth. Perhaps the Stone was his test?

Aethelman knew he was being harsh on himself. There could only be so much expected of any one man. That he had kept the Stone safe and secret for so long was something in itself. He knew what he had to do when he left Leondorf. He would discover how to destroy it and do so, for there was one thing of which he was certain: it had no place in the world of men. It would be his final quest, the thing that defined him. He found the idea strangely appealing.

He continued to stare at it, its mere presence like a great weight on his chest. It seemed to occupy his mind ever more frequently. Were the gods finally telling him it was time to act?

❋

Wulfric didn't get home until well past dark that Jorundyr's Day. It had gone by in a blur of celebration, food, drink, and backslapping. To have warriors that had terrified him ever since he knew what it meant to be afraid walk up and shake him by the hand, all smiles, was disorienting—but Wulfric had never felt quite so elated. He had achieved something that not everyone did, and he had accomplished it all by himself. He knew that there would be plenty of opportunities to make a mess of things, but he had surmounted the first great obstacle and the view from the top was intoxicating.

He was tired and his legs ached from standing all day as he clambered up the two wooden steps to his home's porch. A sound in the darkness startled him.

'Not yet, boy,' his father's voice said. 'Come this way. I've something to show you.'

Wulfric wanted his bed more than anything, but there was no refusing his father. Certainly not on Jorundyr's Day. What if there was one more test that he did not know about? Wulfric followed him back toward the village. The feast-day celebrations were still going strong, with the usually quiet village evening filled with the sounds of revelry that only large amounts of alcohol could bring.

They walked in silence, skirting around the festivities, until they arrived at the corral behind the village stables. Wolfram let out a shrill whistle through his teeth. There was a snort and then the sound of a large beast walking toward them. A great, black horse loomed out of the darkness. It made straight for Wolfram and nuzzled at his hand.

'His name is Greyfell,' Wolfram said.

Wulfric frowned. 'He's not grey.' He realised he sounded ungrateful, and regretted saying it as soon as the words left his mouth.

Wolfram laughed. 'No, he's not. That's not why he's called Greyfell. One of Jorundyr's horses, his best, was named Greyfell. This fellow here would be a worthy mount for a god if they ever chose to come back to the realm of men. I've bred many horses in my life, but he is the best.'

Wulfric put up his hand to stroke Greyfell's muzzle, but he snapped at Wulfric as soon as his hand was within reach. Wolfram laughed again.

'He's proud, arrogant, and vicious, and he won't suffer you for an instant unless you can prove to him that you're worthy.'

Wulfric nodded.

'I gave him his freedom when he was young; let him roam the pastures, but he always came back,' Wolfram said. 'Our lines are intertwined, and he knows it as well as I do. My grandfather rode his great-grand sire into battle, and the connection goes back farther still. Greyfell's sire died beneath me, but only after carrying me from harm. Greyfell barely needed any breaking when the time came. It was as though he knew what he was meant for. I knew there was something special about him from the moment he was born, that his line's blood runs true and is still strong. Just like you showed ours does today.

'Look after him, earn his trust and respect, and he'll see you right up to his last breath. He's the finest horse I have ever laid eyes on. It has been my joy to rear and train him. Now he is yours.'

❊

Adalhaid sat on the porch to Wulfric's house long after the air became chilly enough to be uncomfortable. She clutched the small, cloth-wrapped parcel to her chest, but knew remaining any longer was pointless. It was a gift to congratulate Wulfric on becoming an apprentice. She realised that he might well not be home until after dawn, and felt foolish for sitting there as long as she had. There was no way she would wait that long for him.

As she stood and started for home, she realised that there would be many callings on his time now that he was starting his training. She wondered how much would be left over for her.

❊

Watching the revelry of others was hard on Ritschl. For the most part, his self-imposed isolation in the forest was not difficult for him to bear, but watching them enjoying themselves and one another's company ate away at his very being. It flooded his mind with images of the life that had been taken from him. Two little girls and a wife who had held him tenderly when he woke in the middle of the night with terrors that he could not explain. Taken off by the bloody flux, only a day between each of them. But that was not all. There was more to it than that. A time before his wife, that even now he could only remember fragments of.

Before their deaths that time had been a complete blank, as though his life had begun when he had awoken on a riverbank full grown, one cold afternoon. He had stumbled through the forest for what seemed like weeks, before finding a village that took him in and gave him shelter. In time, a wife and daughters too.

The trauma of their deaths had brought the terrors that haunted his sleep to him in greater detail. Memories of falling; of cold, furious water; of panic. Memories of a stone, a powerful and ancient thing. Memories of a man. The priest he now watched.

It had taken years of travelling from village to village until he had found a face that matched that image in his mind's eye, and now he was certain that he had. As he watched the priest in his grey robes, something seemed oddly familiar. Then it dawned on him. He had been a priest himself. Ritschl the Priest. The thought made him laugh. It was a strange thing, the way the mind worked and things long forgotten could return to the memory as fresh as the day they were made.

Aethelman the Priest had taken the Stone from Ritschl, he was certain of that. Now it was time to take it back. It would give him everything he wanted and more. It would be his, and he would let nothing stand in his way.

CHAPTER EIGHT

WULFRIC'S FATHER HAD shown him his way around a sword since he put his mind to becoming a warrior; how to hold it properly, how to swing it through basic cuts and parries. He had a great deal of work to do if he was to catch up with his peers, however.

There were already several others in the glade by the time Wulfric arrived for his first day of training, well before the appointed hour. Among them were Eldric and Angest, two of the village's better-known warriors. Angest terrified Wulfric and had done ever since he first laid eyes on him as a young child. His presence only added to Wulfric's nerves; it made him question if he really wanted to be there. His bed seemed a far better option.

Angest was also called the Beleks' Bane, for having killed at least a half dozen of the ferocious beasts over the years. The joke in the village was that he had killed so many of the large, fanged, catlike creatures that no one bothered to count them anymore. He had paid a heavy price for his heroic cognomen however, which was the source of Wulfric's fear. He was hideously scarred, each belek scratching a keepsake of itself onto his face. Wulfric wasn't alone in his fear; the younger children in the village would scatter and flee when they saw him coming. Now it seemed that the most terrifying man in Leondorf was to be his instructor.

All of the apprentices were present by the appointed hour. It was early, and everyone looked tired. Wulfric certainly felt that way, not having gotten much sleep the previous night. It didn't feel like the ideal way to be starting, but there was nothing to be done about it.

Angest approached the beginners, his gaze settling on Wulfric and Hane.

'Do either of you know how to use a sword?' Angest said.

His voice was harsh and raspy, no doubt a consequence of the scar across his neck. Wulfric tried not to stare, but it was difficult not to wonder how he had managed to survive the wound that had caused that scar.

Both Wulfric and Hane nodded eagerly. Wulfric did not feel nearly as confident in his assertion as Hane appeared. Swords still felt like clumsy dead weights, not the nimble, graceful things they seemed in the hands of an experienced warrior.

Angest looked to Eldric and smiled, an expression that made his face even more hideous than it was previously. 'Well, that won't be much use to you today. We start with quarterstaffs.'

Wulfric groaned, but made sure to do so too quietly to be heard. He had never even held a quarterstaff before. The rest of them all rushed to pick up a weapon from the pile. At the back of the pack, Wulfric took whatever was left. When he looked around, Helfric was the only other apprentice that remained unpaired.

Helfric wasn't all that much bigger than Wulfric despite being two years his senior, but he was strong. His brown beard was starting to grow in, which made him seem even older to Wulfric, and he bore the confident demeanour of someone in no way threatened by his opponent. The years of torment he and Rodulf's other cronies had inflicted on Wulfric caused his gut to twist. He was vicious, but had always been a follower. Perhaps without someone to tell him what to do, he would not be such a challenge.

Helfric pushed his curly brown hair back from his face and smiled at Wulfric as they squared up to one another.

'Well, fatty,' Helfric said. 'Looks like you've missed a few meals over the last couple of months.'

Wulfric said nothing. If he kept talking when the order to begin was given, Wulfric might be able to get the jump on him.

'I don't know how you managed to get taken into training, but after I've beaten you about the place a few times, I'm sure you'll be sent home to your mother.'

'You looked bigger when you were standing behind Rodulf,' Wulfric said.

Helfric glanced over his shoulder to where Eldric and Angest stood. Wulfric followed his gaze. There was a bright flash behind his eyes and he stumbled backwards. The dull sound of Helfric's quarterstaff striking him on the temple lingered in his ears. It was joined by the word 'begin' a moment later.

He was barely in control of his wits when Helfric came at him again. He wondered if either Eldric or Angest had seen what Helfric had done, but he knew Helfric wouldn't have been so foolish as to be spotted. There was no time to dwell on it, however. It was clear that Helfric intended for Wulfric's humiliation to be swift.

Wulfric did his best to keep up with the blows coming at him from both ends of the quarterstaff. Even had his head not still been spinning, he would have struggled; Helfric had far more practice with the quarterstaff than Wulfric. He caught Wulfric on the thigh with a low strike, then on the shoulder with a high one. It knocked Wulfric off balance, and left Helfric free to sweep his legs out from under him. He was sitting on his backside before he knew what had happened.

He looked up to see Helfric standing over him. With care verging on the delicate, he tapped the butt of his quarterstaff into Wulfric's face, squarely onto his nose with a painful crunch. Wulfric did his best to stifle a cry of pain, and when he had blinked the tears from his eyes, he could see a second figure standing over him; Angest.

'It's broken all right,' the scarred warrior said. 'You weren't the prettiest to begin with, so it won't matter much. Best go see the Grey Priest and get it set.'

Wulfric could hear Helfric sniggering as he got to his feet. He felt his shame grow worse, his impotence overwhelming. Other than Rodulf's absence, it was just like the old days. Things couldn't continue like that. Not if he hoped to keep his apprenticeship.

❋

Rodulf watched the apprentices at their training, but took only mild satisfaction from the hiding Helfric had given Wulfric. He only wished he'd been able to do it himself. He felt sick watching them, knowing he should be there, proving as he had each day in two years of training that he deserved his place there. He was as good as any of them, even with one eye.

The humiliation of being turned away on Jorundyr's Day burned within him, but did not cloud his realisation that his dream of being a warrior was over. His father had been furious at first. It had been his great plan, to gain access to the Great Hall through his son, the warrior. Rodulf cared little for his disappointment, however, only what it meant for him.

He wondered what Wulfric would look like with one eye. Hate simmered within him, but his father had expressly forbidden any retribution. Now that he was no longer an apprentice, their position was tenuous. Once again they were a mere merchant family, and any warrior would be within his rights to kill one of them for a perceived insult. If Rodulf got caught taking revenge it would mean death for him, and likely his father.

His father had said they had too much to lose, but he hadn't lost an eye and a lifelong dream. At times Rodulf's hate for Wulfric made him feel dizzy, but that did not mean he was a fool. There was something to what his father said. There was no point in throwing his life away to ruin Wulfric's. One day, the opportunity for revenge would present itself. When it did, he would be wealthy and powerful. Untouchable, and his revenge would be absolute. Until then, he had to be patient.

The first days of training had been so taxing, Wulfric had all but forgotten about Greyfell. He got up before first light, forced himself to eat, trained, ate some more, then collapsed into bed. It would only be a matter of time before their training moved to horseback and he needed to have as strong a relationship with Greyfell as he could by then. The last thing he needed was to battle against his mount, as well as his fellow apprentices. Tired though he was, he forced himself to head out the door rather than straight to bed and walked toward the stables.

His father had left Greyfell in the paddock to make things easier for him. If the stallion was allowed out to the pastures, it might be weeks before he returned. Greyfell stood proudly, but alone. All of the other horses in the paddock were gathered at the opposite side.

Greyfell watched Wulfric's approach with interest. Ordinarily the other horses would come over when someone arrived at the fence, hopeful for an apple or a handful of oats. That day they all stayed away, as though they were too afraid of Greyfell to make the prospect of treats worth the bother. It made Wulfric second-guess his own carefree approach. He had been asking around how best to deal with an animal like Greyfell, from the stable hands to some of the best riders in the village. The advice was all the same: when dealing with a spirited beast, show no fear.

Wulfric had already faltered in his step. Had Greyfell seen it? He put his doubts to one side and strode forward purposefully. His plan was to spend some time walking Greyfell around the paddock so they could get used to one another. To do that, Wulfric needed to get a bridle on him. In principle, this was a simple thing that he had done many times before. In reality, it felt far more daunting. Greyfell was an enormous horse, the largest Wulfric had ever had any dealing with. His coat was jet black, but when the sun fell on it, it had a rippling grey sheen. He was a magnificent, terrifying beast.

Wulfric decided to try putting the bridle on from the other side of the fence, it providing enough protection to boost his confidence. He arranged the various strands of leather and pieces of metal so that all he would have to do was slip the assembly over Greyfell's muzzle and then fasten it.

'Greyfell, I'm Wulfric, and we are now brothers.' It felt ridiculous to say, but he couldn't think of anything else. Considering the future they would likely share, it didn't seem so far-fetched.

Greyfell showed no sign of reaction. Wulfric reached forward with the bridle, and Greyfell snapped at him viciously. Wulfric withdrew his hands in the nick of time, narrowly avoiding a nasty bite. So much for the horse's sense of tradition and duty, Wulfric thought.

'Show him the whip,' a stable hand shouted. 'He's tried to kill me twice already today. Needs some manners put on him.'

Wulfric knew no self-respecting warrior ever showed his horse the whip. The stable hand walked around the paddock with a long whip. He proffered it to Wulfric.

'Does that usually work?' Wulfric said, already having dismissed any possibility of using it.

'Lets them know who's boss.'

The whip was an ugly, wicked looking thing; a long, slender strip of ox hide. The thought of using it on a living creature made Wulfric sick to his stomach. Wulfric reached forward again with the bridle, knowing the stable hand's eyes were on him. He stared at Greyfell with all the authority he could muster. The horse's lips twitched, as though he was readying a bite, but Wulfric kept his stare fixed and his hands moving forward. His heart was racing as he felt the bridle's leather touch Greyfell's muzzle. The great horse shifted slightly, but did not move away. Wulfric stretched to slip the bridle over Greyfell's ears. He held his breath as he fastened the buckle, but Greyfell allowed him. It seemed almost as though he had understood Wulfric's conversation, and was behaving to spite the stable hand.

With the bridle fastened, and the bit in Greyfell's mouth, Wulfric stroked his muzzle. Wulfric's heart still raced, and he expected Greyfell to snap at him at any moment, but the feared-for bite never came. They had taken the first step on their journey together, but there were many more to come. Wulfric doubted Greyfell would submit to any of them without opposition.

❊

Waiting and watching was driving Ritschl near to insanity. As sure as he was that Aethelman the Priest was the man in his memory, he could not be sure that he still had the Stone. The fact that he lived such a modest life gave Ritschl the worry that he had lost it, or that someone more worthy had already taken it from him. One way or the other, he had to know for sure.

His ability to dissolve into the background was of limited use. As best he could tell it only worked front on. Anyone behind him or to the side would still be able to see him. In a crowded village, it would be almost impossible to go unseen. Even at night, there were warriors on watch, not to mention dogs, chicken, geese, and pigs, any of which could raise enough of a racket to alert the villagers to his presence. The risk was great, but he knew he had to take it. He had to know for sure.

He waited until night and watched the palisade for an opportunity to present itself. When it did, he clambered up at a low point and swung himself over. He fell to the other side and knocked the wind from his old chest. He struggled to catch his breath as quietly as he could, hoping upon hope that he had not alerted the guards.

Satisfied that he was undetected, he made his way farther into the village, moving from shadow to shadow. The kirk was almost at its dead centre, surrounded by open space. He could not imagine a worse location for it—for his purposes at least.

He heard voices, and saw the glow of a lantern. He threw himself into a dark shadow and pressed himself as deeply into it as he could until the sound and light had passed. Then, on all fours, he crept forward.

He had not gone far before he realised that his body was far too old for such a carry on. His joints screamed in protest, and if the need to run arose, he would be found wanting. Everything would fall apart, and the Stone would never be his. Still, he had to know. He had to have it. He continued, crouching as he followed the cover of a low wall until he reached the point where there was nothing but open space. There he stopped, not needing to go any farther.

The presence of the Stone made itself known to him. The feeling was as solid as a warm, loving embrace. He could feel the way the energy of the gods swirled around it, surrounding the kirk like an invisible whirlpool. He closed his eyes and smiled at the joy it brought him. It wanted him as much as he wanted it. The Stone was there, only paces away. The priest still had it. The fool must not have been able to work out how to use it.

Aethelman's face popped into his mind, as clear as though he was standing right in front of him. Standing on a bridge, watching. Watching as Ritschl fell and fell and fell, then plunged into freezing water. It all made sense. Aethelman had wanted it for himself, and had tried to kill him. He must have pushed Ritschl from the bridge. Ritschl thought of returning the favour, but realised the joy in allowing Aethelman to live—knowing that the Stone had been taken from him, that he had not been worthy enough to tap its power—was far more satisfying.

The fact that the Stone was so close made his skin tingle. He wanted to rush forward and take it, but even in the dead of night there was no way he could get to the kirk unseen. The risk of his old body betraying him was too great, and he could not fail, not now that he was so close. He saw movement to his right and looked over. A grey robe hung from a line, drying in the gentle breeze. He reached out and took hold of it, a new plan forming in his mind.

CHAPTER NINE

RODULF SAW HELFRIC walking across the square with a spring in his step. It must feel good to still be on the road to becoming a warrior, he thought. He hadn't spoken to Helfric since the day he was dismissed from selection. Or any of his friends, now that he thought about it. He had been so caught up in what he was going to do with his life now that he wasn't going to be a warrior, that he hadn't noticed their absence. He jogged across the square toward Helfric.

'Helfric!' Rodulf smiled broadly as he caught up to his friend. 'How's training going?'

'Good,' Helfric said. 'Not much time for anything else, even sleep.'

'I wish I was there with you,' Rodulf said. 'Maybe next year they'll change their minds. Let me back in.'

Helfric nodded. 'Maybe next year,' he said, but there was no enthusiasm in his voice. 'I knocked that little prick Wulfric on his arse the other day,' Helfric said, laughing now. 'I put his nose in with my quarterstaff for good measure, sent him squealing off to the kirk to get it put back together.'

Rodulf smiled. 'I can't see him lasting long. Everyone knows he's not up to it.' Rodulf saw Helfric's pale eyes flick to his eye patch. Did he really think that was anything more than luck? Could he think Wulfric would manage it a second time?

'You're probably right,' Helfric said. 'A few more beatings like the one I gave him, and Eldric'll send him packing.'

'We should take bets on how long he'll last,' Rodulf said, laughing. 'I thought we could get Rorik and Walmer and go hunting one day next week.'

Helfric winced. 'I don't think that's a good idea. You understand, don't you? No hard feelings?'

'No hard feelings,' Rodulf said, as Helfric continued on his way. He understood perfectly. With no chance of ever being a warrior, they wouldn't be seen with him now. His thoughts turned to Wulfric again, filling with rage.

❋

Identifying the joy that could be had in the simplest of things was something Aethelman prided himself on. The touch of the sun on a summer's day, the beauty of a cloud as it passed across the sky, gently shaped by the wind that bore it. Even as winter showed its first signs of arrival, there was beauty to be seen. He often stood at the top of the steps to the kirk and searched out such things as he watched the village and its people.

He saw Adalhaid stop by a small dog lying at the side of the square. He had seen it limping about the village for a day or two, stray or turned out by its owner because of its injury, Aethelman did not know. One way or the other, life would be short for it. The Northlands was a harsh place, particularly in winter, and cruel to anything that could not fend for itself.

The girl had a kind heart, one that he worried was too kind for the North. She certainly had a mind that would be wasted there, and it saddened him to think that her life might come to nothing more than domesticity. He considered suggesting the priesthood to her. She had a passion for learning, and the Hermitage was the only place he knew of in the Northlands with a library. It was not the ideal life, however, and he feared not one she would enjoy. Would being the wife of a tanner or a smith be any better? He would have to give it further thought.

She stood, and walked away from the dog. Aethelman stepped back into the kirk's doorway, not wanting her to know that he had been watching her. The dog got up and ran after her with no hint of a limp, its tail wagging furiously. Aethelman raised his great, bushy eyebrows and his mouth opened wide, then curved into an equally wide smile.

❋

'What are you doing?' Adalhaid said.

Wulfric looked up from the pile of sawdust and woodchips. 'I'm making myself some training weapons.'

'Do they not give them to you?'

'They do. It's just I need to put in some extra time.'

'I'd be surprised if you can find it,' she said. 'You seem to spend every spare minute training. I've not even seen you the past few days.'

There was a hurt tone in her voice, and Wulfric realised that she was right. He'd been so busy it hadn't even occurred to him. He looked up from the piece of wood that was beginning to resemble a sword to apologise, and noticed a small furry grey face peer out from her skirts.

'You know you've got a dog hiding in your skirt,' he said.

'Of course,' Adalhaid said, as though it was the most normal thing in the world.

'Is there a reason for that?'

'No. He's been following me around all day. I'm going to ask Father if I can keep him.'

'You know it's going to get a lot bigger, don't you. That's a scent hound pup.'

'I don't mind,' Adalhaid said. 'I can't get him to stop following me anyway.'

'What's his name?'

'I hadn't thought of that,' she said. She scrunched up her nose for a moment as she thought. 'Spot.'

'He's plain coated…' Wulfric said.

'And you've got a black horse called Greyfell.'

Wulfric shrugged.

'It's cute, and it suits him.' She reached down and scratched Spot behind his ears, which he seemed to love. 'I'm going to take him for a walk. I was wondering if you'd like to come?'

Wulfric looked down at his half-finished weapons, and thought of the secluded spot behind a stand of trees where he could practice in secret. He knew what he should be doing, and he knew what he would far rather do.

'Hold on a moment,' he said. 'I'll get my cloak.' His new regime could wait one more day.

CHAPTER 10

FOR SOME TIME, demand for Northern goods in the south had outstripped Leondorf's—and more importantly Donato's—ability to supply. Few Northlander villages traded south, particularly not those to the north of Leondorf like Rasbruck. They would have little clue of what their wares were worth in the South. Donato knew all too well. All that remained was for him to get his hands on as much as he could.

Rasbruck was the only village for miles around to rival Leondorf in size, and thus production. He could spend months travelling around the small villages, doing deals to get what he needed, or do it all in one fell swoop. The risk was high—Rasbruck and Leondorf were traditional enemies, although a state of peace had existed between the two villages for some time. Nevertheless, the profit was always the largest where the risk was the greatest, and Donato did not want his southern contacts looking elsewhere for their supply.

With Rodulf's dream of becoming a warrior at an end he needed to learn the family business, and a trip to Rasbruck would be a perfect opportunity. Financial gain was the main motivator, however. There was no future for them in the Northlands now. Rodulf would not get Donato his access to the Great Hall, and Donato would not stay in Leondorf while he and his family had to bow and scrape to the warriors.

He already had plenty of coin, but it was not enough to be a man of substance in the south. Being comfortable was not what he had worked so hard for so long to achieve. He wanted more. He wanted influence and power. Both could be had in the south if he was wealthy enough. Coin was the only thing that mattered, and the Northlands was the ideal place to earn it. When he had enough, he would uproot his family and move south, where they would be merchant princes, and the Northland warriors could roll around in the muck in their furs and rough-spun cloth until the gods returned, for all he cared.

There was never any time to waste with new opportunities. If one rested on his cogitations, he would be beaten to the goal. He made his arrangements quickly, and planned to leave before dawn the following morning—before any of his rivals were taken by the same idea.

Rodulf was sullen and quiet the next morning. All Donato got from him was a few grunts of acquiescence as they saddled their horses and rode out of the village. The Northlands were now firmly in the grasp of winter, and Donato expected it would only be a matter of days before snow drifts made the roads all but impassable. They were wrapped up warmly, and their breaths filled the air around them with a lingering mist. It mattered little to him. His only concern was how much gold it could put in his pocket. There was a seemingly endless appetite in the south for furs, amber, precious metals and gems. There was only so much one village could produce. If Donato could get his hands on Rasbruck's, he would be a very happy man indeed.

As they rode from the village, the only sounds were hooves on the muddy road and the occasional snorts from the horses. Donato let his mind drift to thoughts of what this new opportunity might mean.

Everything would be better in the south. The weather, the food, the culture. Everything. If only they had the same respect for money north of the border, how different things would be. Land and wealth were the things the rulers of the south coveted most, and the Northlands had plenty of both. Dense forests and ferocious warriors bred for fighting in it had always kept the southerners on their side of the border, however, letting so much opportunity go to waste. Donato would exploit them for everything they were worth. By the time anyone realised the true value, he would have made a fortune several times over and would be counted among the most powerful men of the south.

'My knees and hips are getting too old for all this walking,' Belgar said. 'You'll be taking these walks on your own before too much longer.'

'Your belek wrestling days are certainly long behind you,' Aethelman said.

'Ha! Belek wrestling. Have you even seen one of the beasts?'

'I have,' Aethelman said. 'As well you know.'

Belgar became reticent. 'Of course. I'd forgotten.' They walked in silence for a moment. 'How could I have forgotten something like that?'

'It happens to the best of us,' Aethelman said, hoping to sound as dismissive of the mistake as he could.

Aethelman and Belgar walked together in the morning from time to time. Aethelman always looked forward to it. They were the two oldest people in the village, him by quite a substantial margin. Considering Belgar had been a renowned warrior in his day, and the village's First Warrior for two decades, his age was far more impressive than Aethelman's, even if it was the lesser by decades. Despite his white hair and heavily lined face, Belgar's blue eyes were still intense with the vigour of a man a fraction of his age. That he still lived was testimony to his great skill in arms.

Aethelman knew his own longevity was largely down to his connection with the energy that came from the gods, the same power which allowed him to mend bones and keep the old sword pressed to the ground every Jorundyr's Day, among other things. The energy had been called the Fount beyond the southern border in the old days, when the Empire reigned and its mages travelled the world trying to learn its secrets. With the Empire long gone and magic outlawed, it had been all but forgotten there, in the great cities like Brixen or Ostenheim. Where the old gods held sway, magic still lived. The energy had other, older names, but most were long forgotten, or written in that unusual, ancient script that none could read. That was the time the Stone locked up in his room came from, a time when magisters walked beside the gods and were limited only by their imaginations.

Aethelman liked to think that his own skill as a priest and healer was in some small way responsible for Belgar's continued vitality, but he knew it could not last for much longer and the thought of losing his friend of so many years pained him. It was the curse of priesthood, and one of the many reasons they were encouraged to move on before they ever grew too attached to one place or one people.

Aethelman enjoyed the conversations on their walks, content to listen as Belgar recounted the tales of his youth; the battles, the women, the mischief. Aethelman had been present for some of those tales, but he was content to hear them again all the same, enjoying how an old man's weakening memory coloured events that were still as clear as crystal to Aethelman. It almost made the priest wish he had been born to the sword rather than the grey.

Belgar's voice was the only sound to break the still of the morning air until they neared the end of the pastureland, and the edge of the forest. Aethelman held out his hand to stop Belgar, pointing in the direction of a new sound. They rounded a stand of trees and were presented with the sight of Wulfric beating the hell out of a tree trunk.

'He seems quite intent on killing that tree,' Aethelman said.

'Anything that can hit back seems to be too much for him to manage,' Belgar said.

'Oh? The broken nose wasn't just a one off?'

Belgar shook his head. 'He's coming to it too late. The others his age are far ahead of him. If he's still in training by next summer, I'd be amazed. It'll be disappointing for Wolfram, but that's the way of things sometimes. Not everyone's made for this life.'

'He seems eager enough,' Aethelman said. 'I don't see any of the others out here putting in extra hours.'

'Hacking lumps out of a tree will teach him how to cut lumber, not how to be a warrior. He's wasting his effort.'

'Perhaps a little guidance would help.' Aethelman let the comment hang in the air.

It took Belgar a moment to pick up on the not-so-subtle hint. He tugged on the braids in his long white hair as he thought.

'You mean I should help him?' His grizzled old face contorted in disbelief.

'Don't you think all the extra effort he's putting in deserves some acknowledgement? Reward, even?'

'Come now. We're training warriors, not milksops. Rewards aren't deserved, they're won. They're taken. It's his father's responsibility anyhow.'

'His father is First Warrior,' Aethelman said. 'I don't recall you having much time for anything when that was your responsibility.'

'He's not the only one who doesn't have time,' Belgar said. 'I have little enough of it left to be wasting it on him.'

'I see potential in the lad. It's late in coming, I admit, but it's there. It would be a shame to let it go to waste.'

'You're giving me a headache to join my knee and hip aches, Priest,' Belgar said. 'You're supposed to take them away, not add to them. I'm going back. See you later.'

Aethelman remained where he was and watched Belgar walk back toward the village. Belgar's surliness amused him. Aethelman knew the seed had been sown, although it might take a day or two for the idea to gnaw away at Belgar to the point where he acted on it. With a wry smile he turned back to look at Wulfric, still hacking at the tree oblivious to his audience. Aethelman was confident that if the boy kept coming back each morning, in a few days at the most he would be getting some unexpected private instruction.

CHAPTER ELEVEN

WULFRIC TRUDGED TOWARD his secret training spot while it was still dark. He had struggled to drag himself from bed, his tired body aching with every movement. He forced himself on in the knowledge that he desperately needed the extra practice. He reached the tree that served as his sparring partner. He had worn away all the grass near its base, and his constant attacks had cleared off a patch of bark revealing the pale wood beneath. He winced as he let go of his training sword, intending to start the day with the quarterstaff. The blisters on his hands were open and weeping. In the time since picking up his things before leaving the house, the wood had become stuck to his hand. Another day or two and he would not even be able to hold a weapon, let alone use it. He would have to call at the kirk on his way to training to get a salve from Aethelman.

He tried to convince himself that it was all character building; that one of the tests of a warrior was enduring hardship and demanding the best from yourself all the while. He made a tentative jab at the tree with his quarterstaff. His hands seared with pain, while his muscles felt slow and heavy. It was a half-hearted attempt at best, a feeble one if he was being hard on himself.

'Train smarter, not harder, boy!'

Wulfric jumped at the sound of the voice, and it took him a moment to recognise it. Belgar stepped out from the trees. Just seeing Belgar made Wulfric feel inadequate. He had killed a belek at only fifteen, fought and won over a hundred personal combats, and earned his byname 'Belgar the Bold' many times over. He had been First Warrior for most of his life, before he handed that mantle over to Wulfric's father. Now, at an age that few lesser warriors could hope to reach, he spent most of his time guiding the village council. Wulfric had heard him referred to as Belgar the Old once or twice, but never when he was within earshot. He was a man everyone wanted to impress.

'Let me see those hands, boy,' Belgar said.

Wulfric set the quarterstaff down and gently separated his palms from the now sticky wood. Belgar was not a man to refuse, so Wulfric held out his hands.

'You bloody little idiot,' Belgar said. 'They look like chopped meat. What do you expect to achieve with hands like those?'

'I don't know,' Wulfric said.

'I thought you were supposed to be a smart one, boy. I'd wondered if any of that learning would stand to you, but it looks like the time would have been better spent banging your head against that tree.'

'I have to at least try,' Wulfric said. 'If I'm thrown out of training, it won't be because I didn't try hard enough.' There was anger in his voice.

Belgar studied him for a moment, scratching his short, white beard. 'Go see the priest to sort those out. Then go home.'

Wulfric's heart dropped.

'Eat, sleep, get those hands better. Come back to training in three days. Meet me here that morning. I'll show you that training smarter doesn't mean training harder.'

'I didn't want anyone to know I was doing the extra work,' Wulfric said.

'No. I didn't imagine you would. I won't tell if you don't. I'll have every apprentice in the village knocking on my door if I do. Now go and do as you're told. Back here in three days. And tell Aethelman if he doesn't have your hands fixed by then, I'll want to know the reason.'

❖

Wulfric headed straight toward the kirk as Belgar had instructed him. He didn't like missing training, but when Belgar told you to do something, you did it. Wulfric only hoped that he would let Eldric know, as excuses and explanations were never well received on the training glade.

By the time Wulfric got to the kirk, the first pupil was arriving—the most diligent pupil, Adalhaid, with Spot only a few paces behind.

'You're up early,' she said cheerfully. 'Excited at the prospect of another day of bashing lumps out of each other?'

'Something like that,' Wulfric said. Spot circled them, then made for Wulfric's hands, which he tried to sniff and lick. Wulfric pulled them back protectively.

'What's wrong?' she said, reaching out and taking one of his hands. 'What have you been doing to them?' she added when she saw the damage.

Wulfric shrugged. 'Training's been hard.'

'It'll be a lot harder without any hands. Which is how you'll be if you continue like this. You best see Aethelman right away.'

'That's why I'm here,' Wulfric said.

Adalhaid frowned. 'You mean it wasn't to see me?' She let him stew for a moment before smiling and punching him playfully on the arm. 'Come on. There's time for him to look at them before classes start.'

He went inside with her, where Aethelman was setting up for the day's class.

'Wulfric,' he said. 'Planning a return to scholarly ways?'

'He's hurt his hands,' Adalhaid said, before Wulfric had a chance to answer.

She was looking after him, as she always did, but he didn't need looking after anymore. He wondered how he could make her realise it, then wondered why it felt so important that he did.

'Let's take a look,' Aethelman said. He winced when he saw Wulfric's hands. 'That's quite a mess, but nothing we can't fix.'

Aethelman held out one of Wulfric's palms and lifted his other hand to it, then paused.

'No,' Aethelman said. 'Let's try something a little different. Adalhaid, give me your hand.'

She did so, but with a puzzled expression on her face which mirrored the one on Wulfric's. Aethelman lifted it and held it over Wulfric's wounded palm.

'Now, why did you bring Wulfric in to see me?'

'Because I wanted you to heal his hands.'

'Heal his hands. Exactly. Think about that desire. Concentrate on it.'

Wulfric could see her brow furrow, as it always did when she was applying her mind completely to something. He stared at his hand, but nothing appeared to be happening. The furrow on Adalhaid's brow increased to a full frown, and then she let out an exasperated sigh.

'I can't do it,' she said with a sigh. 'I don't know how.' She turned and walked away in frustration.

Wulfric said nothing. He was dumbstruck by the fact that he had felt a chill on his hand in the moment when she had frowned, just like he did when Aethelman healed him. It was not as strong, but he had not imagined it. Aethelman looked at him with the knowing expression he often had, the one that said he understood far more about the world around them than anyone else. Before Wulfric could say anything the chill returned, but with far more strength as Aethelman applied his own powers of healing.

❊

Rodulf was surprised when they arrived at Rasbruck the day after setting off. It didn't look all that different to Leondorf. Like Leondorf, most of the buildings were built of wood and thatch, and several of the larger were constructed of cut stone and tiled with slate. The village was clustered around a cobbled square that was reached by a number of dirt roads and it was all surrounded by an earth mound and a wooden palisade. Just like Leondorf. People worked, children played, dogs barked. It was far removed from the vicious den of savages he was expecting. He could be forgiven for thinking he was back home. Perhaps his father's plan to trade with them wasn't such an insane idea after all.

They were approached by armed men within moments of drawing into view of the village. Rodulf and his father carried no weapons, and wore none of the accoutrements that could cause them to be mistaken as warriors.

'Who are you, and what do you want?' one of the men said.

'We're friends of Rasbruck,' Donato said. 'We're here to discuss trade with your village.'

'From Leondorf?'

'Yes,' Donato said.

The man gave both Rodulf and Donato a close look. 'There's an inn by the market square. Wait there and I'll have someone meet with you.'

Donato nodded his head. 'I'm obliged to you.'

They continued into the village and then headed toward a building that was unmistakably the inn. They tied their horses to a post outside, and went in.

Everything about Rasbruck was a disappointment to Rodulf. For so many years he had believed it to be a stain on the face of the world, yet nothing he had seen so far stood out in any way from what he would expect at home. Rasbruckers, it seemed, were little different to Leondorfers.

It was early in the day and the inn was quiet. Rodulf was glad to be out of the cold, having barely slept at their campsite the previous night because of it. They sat at a table, and Donato looked around. Rodulf tried to let the warmth penetrate his cold limbs.

'What do you make of the place?' Donato said, in a hushed tone.

'Seems little different to Leondorf. I hope it's worth having made the trip in that cold.'

'It'll be far colder in a few weeks,' Donato said. 'We'll have the thought of all the extra trade to keep us warm then.'

'Assuming the Rasbruckers let us leave here alive.'

'Oh, they'll let us leave,' Donato said. 'Trade is good for everyone. The trick is to make sure it's best for you though. Watch, listen, learn. That's why I brought you with me.'

There was an innkeeper eyeing them curiously from behind his bar, but he said nothing and gave no indication that he would come over to see if they wanted anything. A bowl of hot broth would have been very welcome, but Rodulf suspected not forthcoming. They might even try to poison them. As similar as everything in Rasbruck was, he could not forget that they had been enemies for generations and despite the current peace, they were in danger for as long as they remained. The sooner their business was concluded and they were on their way home, the better.

They had not been waiting long when two men came into the inn and looked around. Their gaze stopped on Rodulf and his father.

'You the Leondorfers?'

Donato nodded to Rodulf and smiled. 'We are. Who are we speaking with?'

'I am Emmeram, this is Thietmar. We're the First Warrior's men. I'm told you're here to discuss trade.' Both men sat at the table Rodulf and his father occupied.

'We are,' Donato said. 'I am Donato, and this is my son Rodulf.'

The men nodded to Rodulf before returning their attention to his father.

'We have authority to negotiate on behalf of the village,' Emmeram said. 'We're interested to know what you have in mind.'

'I'd like to trade with you. Furs, amber, metals and gems,' Donato said. 'I'm also interested in woollen cloth, if the quality is high.'

'And in return, what do you offer?' Emmeram said.

'Gold,' Donato said. 'I'll pay a fair price for anything that meets my standards.'

Both of the Rasbruckers laughed, leaving Rodulf to wonder what was so funny.

When their mirth had subsided, Emmeram spoke. 'Gold? The First Warrior would take out my tongue for wasting his time bringing an offer like that. Cattle or horses.'

Donato nodded. 'It'll take a lot of amber and cloth to pay for a cow.'

'We have plenty of both; furs, metal, and gems too. Everything you could want. Better quality than what you have in Leondorf too,' Emmeram said.

Donato leaned back in his chair and smiled. 'If the quality is as you say, and you've enough of it, I can pay you in cattle.'

Emmeram looked at Thietmar, who nodded.

'Thietmar will take you to our storehouses. I need to speak with the First Warrior, and will join you after to discuss a price.' He stood, and offered his hand to Donato, who shook it.

❄

Thietmar led them across the village square and along a muddy road that took them to the outskirts of the settlement. Donato dropped back to walk alongside Rodulf, out of earshot of Thietmar.

'Two important lessons there,' Donato said. 'Never let them know who you're selling to, and never let them think they can go direct and cut you out. You need to make it seem easier to do business with you than anyone else.'

Rodulf nodded. 'How do you plan on getting the cattle? Do you really think any of the warriors will sell you some?'

'We can worry about that later,' Donato said. 'First, we need to see what the good people of Rasbruck have to offer us.'

Thietmar stopped by a number of storehouses constructed from rough wooden planks. He opened the door to one and gestured for Rodulf and his father to go in. Rodulf felt his stomach clench. What if the Rasbruckers meant to lure them inside to murder them? There had been plenty of time for them to plan it. Donato gave Rodulf a reassuring smile and walked in without hesitation. Rodulf did hesitate, but felt he had no option but to follow his father.

It was dark inside the storeroom. Rodulf scanned it for any sign of danger, but could see nothing. That did little to allay his concern; between the gloom and the hulking mass of the things stored there, it would be easy for a few warriors to hide unseen until their chosen moment. Thietmar followed them in, but left the door open. He took a lamp from a hook by the door and worked to light it. Only then did Rodulf relax.

'Furs, bales of cloth and casks of rough amber,' Thietmar said. 'There's another storeroom filled like this. We keep the ore down by the forge. There's some Godsteel ore too. Emmeram will bring a sample of gems. They're all rough cut.' The lamp's wick took a spark, and the storehouse was filled with a dim orange light.

Donato whistled through his teeth. 'Another storehouse like this, you say?'

'Just as full,' Thietmar said.

Rodulf looked around. The hulking shapes in the darkness turned out to be stacks of fur pelts, bales of spun cloth and several casks. Even Rodulf knew enough about trade to realise how much they could get for it all in the south.

Donato walked farther in, and up to one of the cloth piles. He inspected the material, rubbing it between his thumb and forefinger.

'Rough spun?' he said.

'No. That's top quality,' Thietmar said.

Donato sniffed and moved to a stack of pelts. 'Your trappers look a bit heavy handed with their knives.'

'Our trappers know what they're about. There's nothing wrong with those pelts.'

'I didn't say there was,' Donato said. 'They're just not quite of the quality I was hoping for. I can certainly sell it. Perhaps not for as much as I would like though.'

'You can say what you like about them,' Thietmar said, 'but we know what we have and your words won't change the price.'

Emmeram arrived at the doorway with a small wooden chest under his arm. 'I've brought a sample of the gems,' he said.

They all went back outside. Emmeram opened the chest and proffered it for Donato's inspection.

He picked a rough stone from the chest at random, and held it up to the light. He squinted at it for a moment before taking a second, then a third, and subjecting them to the same scrutiny.

'Excellent,' he said. 'Now these are very fine. I'll be able to get an excellent price for these.'

Rodulf was as surprised by his father's reaction as it seemed the two Rasbruckers were. Once their surprise subsided, Rodulf could see the all too obvious signs of greed. What was his father thinking? He couldn't be that big a fool, could he?

'If you can get me a full inventory of what you are willing to sell,' Donato said, 'we can start to discuss a price.'

'That shouldn't take long,' Emmeram said, still visibly pleased by Donato's reaction to the gems.

'Excellent. My son and I will wait in the inn, if that's agreeable.'

'We'll call on you when we have the full list,' Emmeram said. 'It won't take more than an hour or so.'

Donato smiled and nodded, before gesturing for Rodulf to accompany him back to the inn.

'Why did you show them how much you liked the gems?' Rodulf said as soon as he was sure no one would hear him.

'Your second lesson of the day,' Donato said. 'They now think that I am either honest or a fool. In either case, they expect to get a better deal and to have an easier time negotiating it. I have no problem paying a fair price for the gems, or over-paying for them, because I only plan to buy a handful or two. A fraction of the value of the entire deal. I'll use that to distract them on the cloth and fur, which is what I really want. I'll take everything they have and at a price of my choosing. Now, I'm in want of a hot bowl of broth.'

Rodulf nodded in agreement, reckoning that the danger of poisoning was now well past.

❄

Ritschl stood atop the steps leading into the small kirk in Rasbruck and watched the newcomers with interest. He recognised them both from Leondorf, and thought it odd that they would come to Rasbruck, their traditional enemy. Rasbruck had been his home for only a short time. Once he remembered that he had been a priest, some of the knowledge that went with it returned. In his attempt at sneaking into Leondorf, he realised there was no chance of getting the Stone and escaping with it. The cold, damp forest shack in which he had made his home was another incentive to find an alternative approach, so he had walked to Rasbruck and announced himself at the kirk. The previous priest had been only too happy to leave, with Ritschl equally pleased to replace him.

He was enjoying life in Rasbruck, enjoying being around other people and the comforts that brought. Decent food, his clothes washed for him by the local women, a warm, dry bed. His appearance had changed since arriving. The women had insisted on trimming his grey, receding hair, and he had grown a short beard to fill in his hollow cheeks and help him better fit the image of a benevolent priest. The good living conditions had even lessened the ache in his bones, and he stood straighter. It didn't make his desire for the Stone any less, however. His being there was all part of his strategy to secure it. In his observation of Leondorf, he had learned that they had warred many times with Rasbruck over the years. He hoped it wouldn't take much to inspire them to do so again. It could provide the distraction he needed to get into Leondorf's kirk, take the Stone and disappear. That death and destruction would be the consequence of his plan mattered little. The Stone was all that counted. Everything would be well when he had it. The arrival of these two Leondorfers might be something he could exploit to precipitate war, and the perfect opportunity to take the Stone from Aethelman.

CHAPTER TWELVE

WHATEVER AETHELMAN HAD done to Wulfric's hands left them feeling like two pieces of old leather. He was confident he could have carried around a glowing-hot coal all day and not noticed. Quite why it had not occurred to him to see Aethelman before turning his hands into chunks of bloodied meat was beyond Wulfric, but at least it had turned out all right in the end.

It was the morning of his scheduled appointment with Belgar, and Wulfric felt a rumble of nerves in his gut. He had no idea what to expect from Belgar, knowing little about him other than his reputation. It was hard to believe that Belgar had done all those things. Even more so that he lived to tell the tales.

The few days of rest had also left his body feeling fresh and ready to go. He did not like the fact that he had missed training, but going against Belgar's instructions was not an option, and, he realised, probably for the best.

The old man was already there when Wulfric arrived, leaning on a quarterstaff. His posture showed the ease of one so familiar with an object that it has almost become part of him, which looked odd with one so old.

'Ready to start?' Belgar said.

Wulfric nodded, dropping his training sword in favour of the quarterstaff.

'The hands?' Belgar said.

Wulfric held up one of his palms.

Belgar scratched his white beard and smiled. 'That priest can work miracles. Now, attack me.'

Wulfric did as he was commanded, although hesitantly. He did not want to be the one responsible for putting the old man on his funeral pyre. He was still considering that thought when he landed on his backside, quickly followed by wondering how he ended up there. Belgar stood over him, his quarterstaff held in a relaxed, comfortable grip.

'I'm nearly five times your age. If I can move faster than you, you've got a very serious problem.'

'I'll try harder,' Wulfric said.

'You'd better, or you'll be taking a beating from an old man every morning.'

Belgar moved with the easy fluidity of a man so well-practised in his field that his age did not seem to be of any hindrance. Wulfric knew it must have been, however, and realised that Belgar must have been all but invincible in his prime.

'Watch what I do, boy,' Belgar said. 'Copy my movements. Smarter, not harder. That's how we achieve the things we desire.'

Wulfric nodded, determined not to get left behind by a man old enough to be his grandfather.

※

'Wulfric.'

Adalhaid's voice startled him from his train of thought as he plodded toward home. He stopped and turned to the sound of her voice.

'How are you? How are your hands?' she said.

'I'm fine,' Wulfric said. 'Tired. Always tired. My hands are healed. Better than they were before.' He held one up and forced a smile exhaustedly. 'How are you?'

'The same,' she said. 'I haven't seen you… How's training?'

Wulfric felt awkward that he hadn't spent any time with Adalhaid since the day Aethelman healed his hands. It felt odd, and came as a surprise that it had been a few days since he had last spoken to her. Before then, a day or two was a rarity, and felt like losing a limb, but now he was always so busy.

'It's hard,' Wulfric said. 'All I seem to do is train, eat, and sleep. Then train again.'

'It doesn't look like you've been doing enough of the eating part,'

Adalhaid said. She prodded his midsection playfully. 'You're wasting away. Your mother is going to have to alter all your clothes.'

'How are classes going?' he asked.

'Well,' she said. 'You're missed. Aethelman hasn't found anyone to fill your seat yet. Or his ink bottles.' She smiled.

Wulfric felt his face flush. Ink bottles… He wished she could see him train with Belgar. There were moments when the old man actually praised him.

'What are you working on?' he said.

'Numbers mainly. He got some books from the south, and he has us read them aloud.' She wrinkled her nose. 'They aren't very interesting.'

Wulfric felt very left out. Only a few months before, he had known every detail of her life. He was usually present for all of it, and now it was going on without him, he was overcome with the oddest sensation of loss.

'I…' Wulfric wanted to say something, but he had no idea what it was. He was so tired he could barely order his thoughts. 'I need to get home. I need to eat and have to be back at the glade soon.'

The smile faded from her face, and he felt rotten as he walked away. He struggled to work out why he found it so hard to talk to her. Perhaps it was because he was so tired. He felt guilty and stupid all at once.

He thought nothing could add to his confusion, but he had only gone a few more paces when he was proved wrong. A tall, blonde girl with features that looked as though they were carved from alabaster was walking toward him. On the rare occasions that she had even looked at him before, it was with the same expression as she would her shoe after having trod in horse manure. Her name was Svana, the daughter of the Second Warrior, and the girl to whom he had been promised since birth.

He watched her out of the corner of his eye as he walked. It was difficult not to be swallowed up by her beauty. He saw her look in his direction and quickened his pace. He continued to watch her as surreptitiously as he could manage. Her gaze lingered on him longer than it usually would, and she smiled at him. He almost collapsed in surprise.

❀

For his first meetings with Greyfell, all Wulfric had done was put the bridle on the horse's head. After that, he would sit on the paddock fence beside his horse for as long as he could. Sometimes he would talk to Greyfell, and occasionally pat his muzzle. He brought an apple each visit, and ate it all himself the first dozen or so times. Today, he had something more in mind. He cut a piece and held it out for Greyfell. He was aware of the biting danger that he was inviting, but knew it was the next necessary step. He'd sat well within range of Greyfell's teeth on each occasion up to that point, and acted with nonchalance; the horse had plenty of opportunity to bite Wulfric had he chosen to do so. Wulfric's confidence that their relationship had reached a point of equilibrium did little to ease his tension as he held up the piece of apple.

He pretended not to look, but strained his eyes to see how Greyfell reacted. He stared at the slice, but made no move; a display of his usual haughtiness. However, Wulfric could tell by the way his nostrils quivered that Greyfell was interested. Eventually, and with a great show of reluctance, Greyfell peeled back his lips and gently took the piece of apple from Wulfric's hand. The treat eaten, he brushed his muzzle against the side of Wulfric's head.

❊

Rodulf sat on a wall watching the construction of his father's new warehouse. It was to be built over the winter and would be ready in time for the first transport of goods from Rasbruck after the snows melted. His father had still not given him any indication of where they were going to get the cattle to pay for it all, and he felt sick every time he thought of it. He fully expected that his father would have every last pelt, bale of cloth and piece of amber sold within a few days of receiving them, but Rodulf was certain that all the money in the world wouldn't convince a warrior to sell a single beast from his precious herd. Rodulf doubted that any amount of smooth talking would calm the Rasbruckers, and no amount of the smaller southern cattle, which could be had for coin, would settle the bill. He wondered if any one man had been responsible for starting a war before. It occurred to him that there were two of them in it now.

❊

All the village girls gathered in the afternoon at a spot that gave them an uninterrupted view of the glade where the apprentices trained, but allowed them to stay largely out of sight. It had always been where the older girls went, but Adalhaid's friends had started going in the previous few months, which meant that she did too.

It struck her as a silly practice, and she could think of far more useful ways to spend her time, but she didn't want to be the odd one out. It wasn't the worst though, sitting out in the sun. There wouldn't be many more days like that before Leondorf was blanketed in thick snow.

They all had their favourites, but for most of the girls, marriage to a warrior was an unlikely thing. Some might be fortunate enough to catch the eye of one who was not already promised in a dynastic marriage, and the thought caused Adalhaid a sudden pang of envy, something that took her by surprise. She had always rued the knowledge that one day she would lose her closest friend to Svana, the haughty blonde who walked around the village with her little group of followers like a queen with her ladies-in-waiting. Arranged marriages seemed like a ridiculous thing to Adalhaid. There was something more to it, however, a feeling she couldn't quite put her finger on.

'Who's that one?' one of the girls said.

'Which one?' another said.

'The new one. I don't think I've seen him before.'

'That one? That's Wulfric,' another said laughing.

'Ohhh,' came the reply.

Adalhaid sprang to her feet and strained to see from behind them. He was sparring with someone, Kolbein she thought from the mop of shaggy red hair. She had noticed how much Wulfric had trimmed down, but now that the girls pointed out the other changes, she noticed them too, and felt her heart beat a little quicker. His jaw was defined now, and bore the smudge of an early effort to grow a beard. His arms were corded with muscle and glistened with sweat in the winter sun. *Ohhh* was her reaction too.

✸

'Better make it look good,' Kolbein said, nodding to the spot where the girls spied on them from.

'What? Why?' Wulfric said, taking the opportunity to grab his breath. He continued to circle Kolbein, wary that it was a ruse to put him off guard.

'See anyone you recognise?' Kolbein said.

Wulfric cast a glance over his shoulder, looking up to the hill. He could see the cluster of girls gathered there, thinking themselves obscured by the undergrowth. In their midst was Adalhaid. Their eyes met, and even from that distance, he could see her face go bright red. Wulfric stood straight and sucked in what was left of his gut as best he could, and she dropped from sight as though she had dived for the ground. He smiled, and was rewarded with the hard crack of Kolbein's training sword across his arm. It didn't take the smile from his face, however.

CHAPTER THIRTEEN

SPRING SLOWLY LOOSENED winter's grasp on the village of Leondorf, and where for months there had been nothing but white, there were once again browns and greens. As soon as the winter snows thawed enough for safe travel, Donato began his search for cattle. The Rasbruckers would not wait long, and Donato needed every moment to secure what he required.

He stood watching a herd of cattle that belonged to the warriors of a village called Belindorf, two days west of Leondorf. He was as interested in the herdsmen as the beast, and was quick to note that there were not enough to control a herd that size if someone was trying to steal them.

'Who are you?'

Donato did his best not to jump at the unexpected voice. 'Fine looking beasts,' he said.

'They are fine beasts,' the previously unnoticed herdsman said. 'Who are you?'

'Urrich dal Sonburg,' Donato said, holding out his hand to shake.

The herdsman did not reciprocate. 'Southerner?' he said.

'Ruripathian,' Donato said, his accent and clothing both tailored for that deception. 'I'm interested in buying some cattle. These beasts are the best I've seen. Are they for sale?'

'My lord's not interested in selling,' the herdsman said. 'No right-minded man would be.'

It was exactly as Donato had expected, not that he had any interest in paying. 'I'm sorry to hear that,' he said.

'Not likely to have much luck,' the herdsman said. 'Best off heading south again. Those fancy clothes don't look warm enough for hereabouts.'

Donato didn't need to be told twice. He had seen all he needed to see.

❉

Progress with Greyfell felt tediously slow, but Wulfric knew he was building a relationship for life. He had spent the winter months working on it, and did his best to be patient. After weeks of walking Greyfell around the paddock and sharing apples with him, Wulfric knew he had reached the point where he could not put off trying to ride him any longer. It was a daunting prospect, and as well as their relationship had progressed, Wulfric knew saddling and mounting him were steps up to a higher level—a level that Greyfell might not be at all happy about.

Wulfric's father had said Greyfell was saddle broken, but Northland stallions had to be broken again by each individual rider. The stallions seemed to have their own concept of social status, and were more discriminating in that than even the most snobbish person. Greyfell might like Wulfric—and might enjoy the apples Wulfric brought him—but that did not mean he would condescend to allowing Wulfric on his back.

Wulfric started as he always did, by putting on Greyfell's bridle and sitting on the paddock's fence, eating and sharing an apple. He had brought out a saddle with him, and left it sitting beside him on the fence, where Greyfell could see it. He undoubtedly knew what it was, and Wulfric reckoned he knew what it meant. He shaved slice after slice from the apple with his knife, far thinner than usual, making it last longer, putting off for as long as possible what Wulfric was sure would involve many hard falls to the muddy ground.

With the apple whittled down to the core—Greyfell's favourite part—there was no more delaying. Wulfric swung his legs over the fence and dropped down into the paddock. Greyfell remained where he was; usually he would move into the centre of the paddock in anticipation of being walked, but today he knew there was something different.

Wulfric did his best not to show any fear, and focussed on all the steps he needed to take to saddle Greyfell. He took the thick woollen blanket and placed it over Greyfell's back. The horse watched him suspiciously, but made no effort to move or bolt away. Wulfric reached back for the saddle, not taking his eyes from Greyfell for a second. To turn his back on the horse would be to invite disaster. He hefted the saddle from the fence slowly. Greyfell twitched his head and stamped one of his feet, but remained still as Wulfric approached him with it.

Wulfric held his breath as he stretched to lift the saddle up to Greyfell's back. He expected Greyfell to bolt, and add in a kick for good measure. Wulfric had seen his response when another horse got too close to him in the paddock, and had no desire to be on the receiving end of that kind of treatment. He eased the saddle down onto Greyfell's back, ensuring that it was square and centred. Still no response. Wulfric let his breath whistle out from between his teeth. So far so good, but the hardest part was yet to come.

He loosened the cinch and set the stirrup before returning to the other side, Greyfell watching him closely all the while. He fastened the cinch and checked it twice before setting the second stirrup.

Wulfric thought about trying to mount there and then, but the sudden shock might be enough to push Greyfell beyond the boundary of his patience. Wulfric went to his head and stroked his muzzle, wishing that he had brought a second apple with him. He tried to read something, anything, from Greyfell's eyes, but whatever was going on in his mind was a mystery to Wulfric.

There was no cause for further delay. Wulfric went to Greyfell's side and took a firm hold on the saddle. He lifted his foot and slipped it into the stirrup, gradually increasing the weight he placed on it. He could feel his rear foot start to rise from the ground when Greyfell shifted. Wulfric's rear foot was thrown from underneath him, and it was only the firm hold he had on the saddle that stopped him from falling backward.

He pulled hard on the saddle's pommel and swung his leg over. He slowly sat upright, and wondered how long he should wait to allow Greyfell to get used to the idea before urging him to walk forward. The decision was made for him.

Greyfell bucked, kicked, and started around the paddock at a canter. It was only Wulfric's caution that saved him. His knuckles had been white on the pommel from the moment he laid his hands on it. Clinging on desperately, he squeezed his thighs for all they were worth in an effort to keep his feet in the stirrups.

The other horses scattered to stay out of Greyfell's way, voicing their protests loudly. The commotion drew the attention of the stable hands, who came out of the stable building to see what was going on. A few shouted words of advice, but Wulfric was too occupied to pay them any heed. It felt as though his brain was being rattled out of his skull as Greyfell bucked and thrashed wildly. Still Wulfric clung on. With an audience, there was also his pride to think of. To be thrown would make him into a joke.

He could feel his palms grow slick with sweat. Each jolt tugged at Wulfric's grip, and with each one his hand slipped a little farther. Greyfell screamed in anger, showing no sign of tiring. The shouts were still coming from the stable hands, and out of the corner of his eye he could see that other passers-by had joined them.

Greyfell twisted and kicked. Wulfric's right foot slipped from the stirrup and he was tossed to the left. Somehow his other foot remained secure, and between it and his grip on the pommel, he was able to stay in contact with the saddle. He could hear the gathered audience's reactions, but fought to keep his head clear of any distraction. His arms were starting to burn and his hands had gone numb. Would the horse ever tire?

The idea of letting go and throwing himself clear was growing ever more appealing. If it looked intentional, it might even allow him to save some face.

As abruptly as he had started, Greyfell stopped dead. There was no sign of him having tired himself out—it felt more like he had simply gotten bored with his behaviour and chosen to end it. Wulfric slipped his loose foot back into the stirrup and adjusted himself so he was secure in his saddle.

He sat counting each breath as he waited for Greyfell to do something, anything, but he remained still, drawing in great lungfuls of air and glowering at the people gathered by the fence. Was he waiting for Wulfric to do something? Wulfric tentatively lifted his feet to spur Greyfell, but reminded himself what any hint of hesitation would bring. He urged the horse on as authoritatively as he could. On command, Greyfell broke into a trot.

Wulfric turned him when they reached the fence, then spurred him on to a canter. Greyfell responded instantly and Wulfric smiled broadly as they accelerated. The onlookers were still there, still watching, and Wulfric suspected they were disappointed he had not been ejected from the saddle. He had to force himself not to laugh aloud when Greyfell snapped at anyone within reach as they passed by.

Chapter Fourteen

ADALHAID SAT AND placed a rectangular wooden box on the table before sitting down. Without saying a word, she opened it to reveal a collection of polished discs of ebony and bone and two dice.

'What is it?' Wulfric asked, as she began to space the discs out along the patterned interior of the box.

'It's a game,' Adalhaid said. 'Aethelman got it from a southern trader and gave it to me. He said it's very popular there. I thought it'd be fun to play.'

'All right,' Wulfric said, eyeing the pieces suspiciously. He could feel Spot flop down on his feet under the table, and wondered why the dog always chose to sit on them. It was of little inconvenience when he was small, but he was growing fast and his weight pinned Wulfric's feet to the floor. He returned his attention to the board and could think of many things that struck him as being more fun than moving polished pieces around a wooden board. 'How do you play?'

'It's probably easiest if I show you as we go along. Basically, you have to move all of your pieces to the end of the board. You roll the dice, and each turn you can move them that many places. If you land on one of your opponent's pieces, that piece goes all the way back to the start. Understand?'

Wulfric nodded.

They got started, and at first, Adalhaid's pieces seemed to move toward their goal at a blistering pace. As the rules became clearer to him, his began to catch up, until it was obvious even to him that they were heading toward a stalemate, one that would be decided by whoever had the luckiest roll of the dice.

He rolled a four, moved his final piece, and realised he was holding his breath as Adalhaid took her roll. A six. He hadn't expected to win, but his competitive instinct had been well honed by all the training, and he couldn't help but feel disappointed.

'Can we play again some time?' he said.

Adalhaid smiled. 'Any time. I didn't think you'd like it.'

He gathered up some of the pieces, and Wulfric handed them to her. His hand brushed hers. He could feel her warmth, and how soft her skin was. He realised she was looking at him oddly, their hands still touching. He wanted to take hold of it properly, but as he tried to build up the courage to say something, do something, Spot let out a thunderous fart.

❉

'You've been spending a lot of time with her lately,' Frena said.

Wulfric looked up from his plate. The comment was entirely unexpected and out of context. However, there could be no doubt it was Adalhaid she was referring to. He suspected his mother had been looking for a way to bring the matter up for some time, but failing to see the opportunity, had decided to force the matter.

'Yes. I see her most days,' Wulfric said. His father was out, so there were only the two of them at the dinner table.

'Do you think that's wise?'

Wulfric frowned. 'Why wouldn't it be?'

'You're not children any more,' Frena said. 'People will start to talk.'

'About what?'

'You know that one day you'll be married to Svana. It's been arranged ever since you were infants. How do you think it makes her feel to see you with Adalhaid all the time?'

'I don't really care. She's haughty, and has never once in her life said a friendly word to me.'

'Be that as it may, she will be your wife and it will make your life far easier if you start off on good terms with her. It won't be long before you're formally betrothed to her.'

Wulfric said nothing. The uncomfortable silence was only disturbed by the crackling of the fire. Wulfric took a moment to swallow his growing anger. 'Are you saying I shouldn't see Adalhaid any more?'

'Of course not. You two have been inseparable since childhood. I just think that you should see less of one another. Spend more time with your new friends.' Frena smiled in the way she always did when she thought she had won an argument with his father.

The smile made it more difficult for Wulfric to quell his anger. That she would think it a good idea he disregard the one person who had been true to him his entire life and prioritise people who would not even have spat on him only a few months before was beyond his comprehension.

'I'll see who I like, whenever I like, for however long I like,' Wulfric said.

'Be careful,' Frena said. Her voice was harder now. 'The mistakes you make now, you may have to live with for the rest of your life.'

❉

At first, Donato would not say why they were taking a sudden trip south to Elzburg. Rodulf assumed it was to watch him negotiate the sale of all the items they had stored in the new warehouse, but once they were well on their way his father revealed that he had found the solution to their cattle problem, and they were on their way to discuss the terms. He would not be any more specific than that, and most of the journey was carried out in silence. It frustrated Rodulf to be fed information piecemeal, but he was glad of the trip to the city. He had never been there, and was eager to see for himself all of the things he had heard about it. Everything a man could want was said to be there, a source for every pleasure and an outlet for every vice.

It was not all idyllic, however. Rodulf realised that one needed money to enjoy life there; the more the better. He had heard tell of people begging on the streets, dressed in filthy rags. Coming from Leondorf, where nobody went without, it amazed him that a person could become so despised and overlooked. No one there ever went hungry, or without shelter. The fact that someone could fall so low terrified him. He wondered what they had done to end up there, whether it was misfortune or the just reward for some misdeed?

The journey was not a comfortable one. Still only being spring, it was cold, but the roads had started to thaw and were a churned up mess in places. He would far rather have spent the time in front of a fireplace than in the saddle, but getting to the city was reward enough to make it worthwhile. His eyes widened with awe as the great redbrick walls with their copper green and slate grey roofed towers came into view. Even at a distance, he could see the steady stream of traffic in and out of the main gate; merchants and their goods going to and coming from all sorts of foreign, exotic places. It made the world seem so huge. Rodulf could still remember the first time he had ventured beyond Leondorf's pasturelands. It had seemed like such a long way from home. He had no idea then just how much farther he could go. He still didn't, but at least he was no longer steeped so deeply in ignorance.

His father knew the city well, having visited it countless times over the years. Its merchants were his main contacts in the south, and the city was where he did most of his business. He led Rodulf up to the city gate, where they stabled their horses and continued on foot. Even outside the gate, there were hawkers, beggars, and boys offering to carry baggage. Donato shooed them all away and headed for the inn he always stayed at when there. When they realised he knew where he was going, and was not a naive bumpkin visiting Elzburg for the first time, they lost interest. Rodulf did his best to match his father's indifference, not to stare at everything wide-eyed.

The inn was a behemoth that made their new warehouse in Leondorf look like a small shack. Like all the other buildings on the street, it was coated with white plaster and capped with orange roof tiles. Inside it was spacious, bright, and busy. Men of all shapes and colours came and went, while others lounged on comfortable chairs in a communal area surrounding a great, crackling fireplace. His father chatted to a receptionist before a boy led them to a room three floors up. It was the highest Rodulf had ever been—higher even than the tallest tree he had climbed. He tried to peer out a window, but from that vantage point he could not make out the street below. It made his heart race to think of what would happen if he were to fall through it.

The boy showed them to their room, and Donato gave him a penny. When the door was shut, and only the two of them remained, Donato spoke.

'I've been put in contact with a band of reavers. They may be able to help us with our problem.'

'We've come all this way to treat with thieving scum?' The greater part of a warrior's life involved chasing off or hunting down reavers. Northland cattle, oxen, and horses were in high demand in the south, and roving bands of thieves did their best to help themselves to the herds. His father's face darkened at his comment, so Rodulf thought better of saying any more.

'I identified several small villages with few warriors. Their herds are ripe for the plucking. They reave the cattle, I provide the maps and information, and we split the take.'

'Think they'll agree to it?'

'It'll make them rich,' Donato said. 'Offer to satisfy a man's greed, and he'll dance like a puppet for you.'

'It sounds like a big risk,' Rodulf said.

'Fortunes aren't built by playing it safe.' Donato paused, then fixed his gaze on Rodulf. 'Whatever it takes. Understand?'

Rodulf nodded, but was not convinced. 'What's to stop them taking the lot and betraying us?'

'Nothing, other than the promise of the names and locations of other villages that are similarly soft targets. I can just as easily set warriors on them, and I'll make sure they know it. All the southerners know how treacherous the Northlands are. They're terrified of the place, even if they won't admit it, and that's to our advantage.'

❧

One of Donato's business associates, a prosperous-looking man dressed in silks and furs called Henning, met them at the inn. He brought them through a warren of streets to a tavern in what Rodulf assumed was a less salubrious part of the city. Down one side alley, he saw a man being beaten by three others. Despite there being a number of people passing by, no one stopped to help the unfortunate. Rodulf certainly did not; another man's misfortune was no concern of his.

Henning spoke when he stopped outside the tavern door. 'I'll make the introductions, then I'm leaving. I don't want to know what you've got planned. The fewer who do, the better for you.'

'Sounds reasonable,' Donato said. 'I appreciate your help on this.'

'Just you remember that when you bring all those furs down to the city.'

The tavern seemed to be a repository for the dregs of society. There were whores—a sad, bedraggled-looking lot caked with rouge and kohl—and men who looked like they had not changed their clothes in a decade, nor taken them off for ablutions. There were those with a predatory look in their eyes, whose gazes instantly locked onto Rodulf, his father, and their business associate. It seemed like the type of place where you went after you had fallen through the cracks, or where you would be given the final push. The people here were vermin; beneath his contempt. Rodulf could not wait to leave.

Henning brought them over to a booth at the back of the room where a motley group of men sat with nearly empty mugs. The word 'reaver' sounded dashing and dangerous to Rodulf—as a child, 'watch out for reavers' was often his mother's last call before he went out with his friends. He always knew they were more interested in cattle rustling than kidnap, though. He had never actually laid eyes on one before, and he found the men in that booth to fall sadly short of the image he had in mind.

'This is the man I was telling you about, Captain Morlyn,' Henning said. 'Burgess Donato, Captain Morlyn.'

Donato and Morlyn nodded to one another. Rodulf had never heard the term 'burgess' before and wondered what it meant. It wasn't the time to ask. Morlyn sat casually at the centre of the group, his black hair pulled back into a pony tail and several days' worth of dark stubble on his jaw. He looked like a man who stole and killed for a living, but there was nothing dashing about his appearance. The others were an equally motley bunch, and one of them, with long hair and beard that were not the fashion Rodulf had seen in the city thus far, he took to be a Northlander.

'I'll leave you to arrange your business, gentlemen,' Henning said. He gave Rodulf a curt nod as he passed, seemingly as eager to get out of the tavern as Rodulf was.

'Gentlemen, sit, please,' Morlyn said. 'I'm given to believe you might have some work to put our way.'

Rodulf and Donato sat. Rodulf cast an uncomfortable glance around the tavern's taproom, but no one was paying them any attention. There was something exciting about the clandestine nature of what they were doing, and of consorting with dangerous men.

'I need help acquiring some cattle,' Donato said.

'We've experience in that line of business,' Morlyn said. 'Bart there used to be a herdsman. Weren't you, Bart?'

The largest of the reavers, the one Rodulf thought to be a Northlander, nodded. Rodulf wondered what misfortune brought him to that miserable place in the company of these miserable people.

'How many cattle do you need?' Morlyn said.

'A dozen at first, but a regular stream of them after,' Donato said.

'Regular work, lads,' Morlyn said. 'Haven't had a regular job since before I took up reaving the Borderlands. What will you pay?'

'My payment is this,' Donato said. 'I know of a number of villages throughout the Northlands where the herds are lightly protected. I also know the best trails for you to drive the cattle south. My information will ensure your safe passage through the Northlands to cattle ripe for the picking. We divide the spoils between us, even split. When you've taken as much as you can from one region, I'll give you the details for the next.'

Morlyn remained silent.

'You know as well as I do how much a purebred Northland cow fetches in southern markets,' Donato said. 'At least, you would if you know this business as well as you claim. Bear in mind, you're not the only sell-swords in the city.'

Rodulf saw Morlyn's eyes flick over to the former herdsman, Bart, who nodded with conviction.

'I'm interested,' Morlyn said. 'But we'll have to take it on a job by job basis. If your information doesn't prove to be as good as you say it is, we'll be keeping whatever we take and heading south as fast as we can drive them. I don't want to end up stuck on some bloody savage's spear, no offence.'

'None taken,' Donato said. 'The information's good. We both stand to do very well out of this.'

'The brands,' Rodulf said.

Everyone turned to look at him.

'How will you deal with the brands on the cattle?' Rodulf said.

'Don't you worry about that, lad,' Morlyn said. 'We've got that covered.'

'I do worry about that,' Rodulf said, 'and don't call me *lad*.'

Morlyn smiled and raised a hand in apology. He nodded at one of the other reavers. 'Arbo there was training to be one of your grey priests. Didn't take to it though. Prefers the life of a wandering reaver to that of a wandering priest. Don't you, Arbo?'

'If I knew I'd have to put up with you, I'd have been more patient with the priests,' Arbo said.

Morlyn laughed. 'Arbo stayed long enough to learn some healing. Enough to heal the branding marks. The cattle'll be clean as a whistle. As far as branding goes, leastways.' He laughed again.

CHAPTER FIFTEEN

THERE WAS A pile of quarterstaffs in the glade when Wulfric arrived to training. It was his least favourite weapon—he far preferred the sword—but there was nothing to be gained in grumbling, so he picked one up, and looked around for a partner. He found himself staring at Helfric. Wulfric had avoided him all winter, but there was no way out of it now.

'First to three hits wins,' Eldric shouted. 'Show me some spirit; I'm in the mood to send people home today. Who wants to be a carpenter or a tanner?'

No one answered. Wulfric wasn't sure if anyone believed the threat, but he certainly wasn't willing to take the chance. Neither was Helfric. Even before the command was given, he attacked. Having seen this tactic before, Wulfric was ready for it. Helfric swiped at him, holding his staff with both hands down near the base like a sword. Wulfric jumped out of the way and blocked the follow up. Helfric seemed to think he had the upper hand, and the confident smile was still firmly fixed on his face.

Wulfric continued to block. Helfric's attacks were incessant, leaving him no time to put together a counter. As much as his confidence had grown, Helfric still represented a spectre in the back of his mind. Finally, Wulfric saw an opening and went for it. The months of hard work had stripped away the excess from Wulfric's body, leaving him faster and more agile. Helfric was caught wrong footed. Wulfric knocked his quarterstaff aside, and followed in with a fast jab to the gut.

There was no pause between the scoring of hits, and Wulfric did not plan on giving Helfric the chance to recover. The jab had left Helfric even more open, allowing Wulfric to slam in a heavier hit that Helfric would feel for days to come. With a sense of righteous indignation, he rounded off his three hits with a jab to Helfric's face, which connected with a crunch and a splatter of blood.

Helfric dropped his quarterstaff and fell onto his backside, both hands lifted to his nose. Wulfric stepped back to survey his handiwork. He was amazed and delighted in equal parts at how quickly and smoothly he had done it.

Eldric appeared, and gave Wulfric a curious look. He leaned forward and took Helfric's chin in his hand, scrutinising Helfric's face. 'Want to go home? Want your mother?'

Helfric shook his head adamantly, but Wulfric could see his lower jaw trembling.

'Go see the priest,' Eldric said. 'Think about the beating you took. Next time it might not end at three hits.'

Helfric did as he was told, got to his feet and started back toward the village in a limping jog.

Eldric stood and looked around. The glade was silent as everyone had stopped to watch. 'Back to it, the rest of you,' he shouted.

❀

The tavern keeper made a huge cauldron of stew which was ready for the apprentices every day after training, and they were welcome to refill their bowls as many times as they liked. Wulfric had yet to see the stew cauldron emptied, no matter how much they stuffed into their hungry bellies. Wulfric spent the first hour after training there every day, eating and joking with the others. He realised the time with them eating was as important as the hours they trained together. As Eldric had said, they would stand together in battle one day and camaraderie was as important as respect. The hour took him to the point of the day when Adalhaid's classes ended, allowing him an excuse to walk home with her, something he looked forward to even more than the bowls of hot stew.

He wiped the residue of stew from the thickening stubble around his mouth of which he was increasingly proud. It was a long way from being a proper beard, but it was a satisfying development from the smooth, soft skin of boyhood.

'Where're you off to?' Hane said, as Wulfric stood.

They were almost a match in height now, Wulfric having had a spurt over the winter, a situation as satisfying as his fledgling beard.

'Things to do,' Wulfric said.

'He's off to see his girlfriend,' Farlof said, a mischievous grin firmly affixed to his face. Wulfric had quickly come to realise that little Farlof said was ever meant to be taken seriously. The short, stocky redhead more than made up for his comparative lack of size with that of his mouth, but Wulfric would have preferred it if his wit were directed elsewhere.

Roal backhanded him on the shoulder. 'Shut up, Farlof.'

'What?' Farlof said, raising his hands and acting the injured party. 'Just saying, he spends a lot of time with her... And she's pretty easy on the eye...' He raised his dark red eyebrows lasciviously.

'He's meant to be marrying Anshel's sister Svana,' Roal whispered, loudly enough for everyone to hear.

'Really? When?' Farlof said, the grin even wider on his face. 'I love a good wedding.'

'Shut up!' The exhortation came from everyone else there, except for Anshel.

Wulfric glanced in his direction, but he did not meet Wulfric's eyes. Anshel was the best of them: faster, stronger, more skilled. He shared his sister's blonde hair, but where her features were fine and delicate, his were strong and angular. If he chose to view Wulfric's friendship as disrespectful to his sister, he was more than capable of dishing out a beating that Wulfric would be unable to stop. Wulfric walked away, angry with Farlof, but knowing that he was only casting light on something that was true. It was an uncomfortable situation that Wulfric was very happy get away from as quickly as he could.

❀

Wulfric was quiet as he and Adalhaid walked along the tree line that divided the village from its pastures, Spot bounding along ahead of them. Adalhaid talked about her day, and the sound of her voice helped ease his worries, but did not dispel them completely. His future marriage to Svana had always lurked in the background, but it had remained there. Now it seemed to be coming up more and more often. He wondered what type of life they would have together. Would they ever go on walks in the evening talking and laughing as he did with Adalhaid, or would it be a life of silence masking frosty contempt?

Svana and her family lived on the other side of the village, so he rarely saw her at anything less than a healthy distance—one he was more than happy to maintain. The thought of why Adalhaid had never featured on his list of potential future partners popped into his head, but the answer was so simple it was barely worth considering. Her father was a lanceman, not a warrior. A lanceman aided a warrior in battle, helping him with his weapons and equipment, and when called upon would also fight. It was better than being a merchant or a craftsman, but it was unthinkable for the son of a First Warrior to marry the daughter of one. It seemed that other people's expectations often made life more complicated than it needed to be.

'You're very quiet tonight,' Adalhaid said, pulling him from his thoughts.

'Tired,' he said, his stock excuse. 'Always so tired.'

'We can go back if you like,' she said, stopping.

He looked at her, and felt his heart quicken at the thought of not seeing her again until the next day. 'No,' he said. 'I can go a little farther.'

❈

Captain Morlyn squeezed the trigger on his small crossbow and smiled at the satisfying thrum of the string. It was the weapon of murderers and assassins, and south of the border they were illegal. In the Northlands, they were the ideal weapon and there was no law to tell him he couldn't use them; one of the few things he liked about the Northlands. Light, convenient to carry about, and still powerful enough to accurately hit—and kill—a target at a hundred paces, the small crossbow was a gift from the gods to men who made their living in the shadows.

The target that evening was a herdsman. He had been standing near a tree, but now lay in a heap at its foot. If the bolt hadn't killed him, the poison on its tip would. Morlyn turned and smiled at Bart, the dark shape lying in the undergrowth beside him. He had hit his last dozen targets, satisfying a long-standing bet between them. Bart's share of that night's proceeds would be going to Morlyn. Bart grunted an unhappy acknowledgement, making Morlyn's smile even wider. Bart's share would pay for a case of the best Ostian wine, a pouch of Darvarosian tobacco infused with dream seed, and at least a dozen of the finest whores; enough to keep that smile on his face for a month or more. Or perhaps just one exceptional night.

Their first job for the Northlander merchant was going perfectly. He was true to his word, which gave Morlyn hope for the future of their joint venture. Other than that one herdsman, there was no one looking over the herd, as best Morlyn could tell. It was an out-of-the-way village, a fair stretch from the border, and it seemed they didn't think they had anything to fear from reavers. Northlanders did that type of thing differently. There was no honour in stealing your neighbour's cattle. Apparently you had to kill him first. Only then was taking his cattle worthy of songs and epic tales. Savages, one and all, Morlyn thought.

Savage or not, if the Northlander could give them the locations of more such places, he was correct in saying they would all get very rich indeed. Morlyn nodded to Bart. He was the one who knew cattle. He would give the orders until they had the herd rounded up and well on their way south. Then it would be Arbo's turn to clear the brands off them, before dividing the spoils with the Northlander at their arranged meeting place. All in all, it was a very satisfactory start to their business relationship.

❈

Ritschl's months in Rasbruck saw him gradually become a part of the community. It was an advantage of the tradition of priests moving from village to village over the course of their lives; it made people accept and trust a new face far more quickly. He was a long way from being able to exert the influence he required, but everything he did each day made him ever more indispensable. A time would come when his word would be acted on without question.

He stood on the steps of his small kirk as he did every morning, watching the village come to life, greeting all those who passed his door. Even so long after forsaking his vocation, he could see the appeal in the life he was masquerading behind. Given different circumstances, he thought he might even have enjoyed it. The feeling of being of value to another person was enticing, but it brought back memories that were painfully clear. Memories that made him feel sick. Family. The life he'd had. It had been a good life, one that had made him not care how much he had forgotten. His wife. His two girls. So much had been taken from him. The thought of their lifeless bodies lying next to one another made him want to collapse and weep.

The illness had taken them so quickly. Within a day of the first person in their village falling ill, his wife and children had been on their death beds. If the Stone had been in his possession, he would have been able to save them. He knew that. He would not let anything be taken from him again, nor would he allow Aethelman to keep something that was rightfully his. With the Stone, nothing could be taken from him ever again.

❀

Adalhaid was sitting on a wall, waiting in their usual meeting spot, but was not alone. Wulfric squinted to see who she was talking to. His name was Sigert, a slight, studious boy with mousy hair who went to Aethelman's classes. His father was a leatherworker, and he had been second only to Adalhaid in their studies, which meant he and Wulfric had never had any contact beyond when Wulfric handed out pens and papers. They were chatting and laughing. Sigert playfully touched her on the shoulder, and Wulfric felt a flash of anger that he could not explain. He felt himself hoping that Spot would jump up and savage him. He quickened his pace, and delighted in interrupting them.

'Sorry I'm late,' Wulfric said. Spot gave him a warm welcome, which Wulfric played up. 'Hello Sigert. Thanks for keeping Adalhaid company while she was waiting. You needn't delay any longer.'

There was an uncomfortable silence for a moment as Sigert worked out what Wulfric meant. He gave Adalhaid a smile before nodding and leaving. Wulfric was an apprentice warrior, and Sigert was a leatherworker's son. He should have known better than to delay.

'What was that all about?' Adalhaid said. 'Did he do something to you?'

'What do you mean? Of course not. It's just, well, I'm an apprentice now, and he should show a little more respect.'

'Really? You were very short with him, for no good reason,' Adalhaid said.

'I didn't mean to be,' Wulfric said, backtracking as quickly as he could.

'I've seen a change in you recently,' she said. She stood from the wall and gathered the few things she had with her. 'I'm not sure I like it. Spot!'

She walked away without another word, with Spot close on her heels.

❋

The end of planting in spring was always marked by a festival, the last one before Jorundyr's Day at harvest time. The apprentices held a display of horsemanship that became the talk of the village in the days leading up to it. It was only supposed to be an entertainment, but it always became competitive as each apprentice tried to prove himself the best. Wulfric was no different. He believed he could win.

The contest gave Wulfric the chance to show everyone in the village what he had made of himself, how he had changed from timid boy to budding warrior in less than a year. It gave him the chance to show Adalhaid that he was a man, and could look out for himself, that he was someone to be admired rather than pitied.

Posts had been driven into the ground throughout one of the pastures, and a ring was attached to each one. Tall haystacks were littered throughout the pasture to prevent the riders from being able to gallop between the posts in straight lines. Speed, acceleration, manoeuvrability, and the horseman's skill in controlling his mount were all tested as the participants raced around the pasture gathering as many rings with their spears as they could. The rider with the most rings at the end was the winner.

There had been little talk of the event amongst the apprentices in the lead up to it—a surprise considering it was all anyone else spoke about—but Wulfric knew that it was dominating all of their thoughts. They all wanted to win it. Part of a warrior's life was about acquiring fame through brave deeds, and this was the first chance any of them had to do that. They all dreamed of the glory victory would bring, none more than Wulfric, but dreaming alone would not bring it about.

CHAPTER SIXTEEN

THE RIDERS LINED up along one side of the pasture, horses snorting, equipment rattling, and breaths creating little clouds in the air, but not one of the apprentices uttered a word. It was early and the morning mist hung over the grass, almost obscuring the spectators lined up along the other side. The tension surrounding the riders was as palpable as the mist—everyone was eager to impress.

Wulfric's father was watching, but that was not the only person on his mind. If anything, his father was secondary. Adalhaid was there too, and her presence was what Wulfric was thinking about most. They had not spoken since she got angry with him. He wanted her to see how much he had achieved. He couldn't explain why the need felt so great, but her opinion was the only one that mattered.

Greyfell was stamping his hoof and casting aggressive glances at the other horses. Wulfric admired him his single-mindedness—the flutter of nerves in his own stomach was difficult to ignore. The previous night he had felt much as Greyfell was now behaving; confident and eager to get going with it. Now all he could do was wonder if he was going to throw up. Every person in the village was there watching, even his mother who usually eschewed such things.

The piles of hay and the ring posts loomed in and out of view amongst the clouds of mist. In order to keep the apprentices on their toes, not all posts had a ring. They had been randomly laid out that morning, so no one could plan their route in advance. It was going to be a mad dash to find them.

The rules were sparse on physical contact. Actual combat was forbidden, the test being designed to show speed, agility, and horsemanship rather than brawling, but barging someone out of the way was perfectly acceptable. In that, Wulfric had an advantage. He had grown big over the past year, but Greyfell was huge and the other horses remained terrified of him.

Waldegrim presided over the event. He was a dour-looking man, who always dressed head to toe in black, but he was acknowledged as the finest horseman in the village and was deferred to in all such matters. He inspected each rider, checking their equipment for anything that went against the spirit of the contest. It was not unheard of for dirty tricks to be employed, as in the heat of the contest it was often hard to work out who the offender was. Such was the desire for victory.

When Waldegrim was satisfied no one had concealed spikes anywhere, he moved to the side and raised his right arm. Wulfric felt his heart race. Despite the cold morning air, he was sweating. He cast a glimpse along the line of assembled horsemen. All of the horses grew agitated as they sensed the moment growing closer. They snorted and stamped, revealing the emotion that each of their riders tried to conceal. Anshel was three down from him, and probably Wulfric's greatest threat. He looked straight ahead, his angular features betraying nothing. It was as though he was carved from a block of ice. Was he just better at hiding his nerves than Wulfric?

He caught Helfric casting him a sideways glance. He was a weaker horseman than Wulfric, and if he tried anything underhand Wulfric was determined to make him regret it. He was so caught up in his thoughts, Wulfric almost missed Waldegrim drop his hand.

If Wulfric's reactions were a fraction late, Greyfell's were not. Both horse and rider bolted from the line. Wulfric, his mind back where it needed to be, focussed on the nearest ring. Quick glances from the corners of his eyes showed that he was pulling away from the others, but speed was not everything, and with a large stack of hay close by the post, stopping quickly was as important.

Wulfric aimed the tip of his lance at the ring's empty centre, and stretched forward. Hearing it rattle up the lance's wooden shaft went a long way to steady the turmoil in his gut. The ring needed a firm pull to free it from its mounting on the post, and for a panic-filled instant, Wulfric felt the spear tug in his grip as he passed it at speed. He held firm, felt the ring give way and breathed a sigh of relief. He urged Greyfell to the left and grazed one of the haystacks, sending a cloud of hay into the air. He cut back to the right hard. Greyfell gasped with the exertion but responded perfectly.

As Wulfric rounded the haystack, he saw some of the others charging in and out of the mist. He spotted his next target and spurred Greyfell toward it. Hane was going for it with everything he had, but Wulfric got there first, scooped it from its post and added a second ring to his lance. He gave Hane, whose face was a picture of disappointment, a nod, but the ring was fairly won. Wulfric wheeled Greyfell around and headed for the next ring, one he had chosen when riding for the previous that took him close to where the spectators were gathered. With his confidence built, he planned to give them a show.

He did his best to stay focussed on the ring, but his eyes drifted across the assembly and he spotted Adalhaid. Standing next to her, his attention most definitely not directed at the contest, was Sigert. The moment's distraction was all it took for Roal to thunder across Wulfric's path, making for the same ring, and well ahead. Wulfric urged Greyfell on, but the gap between them was too great.

Roal was on it—he leaned forward from his saddle and stretched out with his lance. The tip struck the ring's edge, sending it spinning into the air. Roal shook his lance in frustration and reined in his horse to go back for it. Wulfric watched the ring's flight through the air until it landed on the soft turf. He cast another glance in Adalhaid's direction. She was watching him, but Sigert's eyes were still firmly fixed on her.

He twisted the leather reins around his palm and gripped them as tightly as he could. With a final look to Adalhaid, his eyes catching hers, he spurred Greyfell toward the fallen ring. Greyfell was at full gallop along the edge of the crowd when he leaned from the saddle. Gripping firmly with his legs he slid sideways until he was perpendicular to Greyfell's flank. He heard the crowd gasp and could not help but smile. The lapse in concentration almost cost him as he slipped farther than he had intended, his head almost brushing the ground. He clamped down hard with his legs and arrested his descent, his thighs screaming and his joints twisting with the effort.

He had tried this manoeuvre twice before when riding Greyfell, and on both occasions it had ended with him flat on his back. He had done it this time without hesitation, common sense replaced by a desire to ensure Adalhaid did not spare a single thought for Sigert again that day, or any other. Every muscle in his body strained to the point of agony as he fought to remain attached to Greyfell.

The ring lay flat on the ground. He scooped it up into the air with the tip of his lance, then speared it, to a chorus of cheers and applause. He would have smiled were it not for the need to get back into his saddle. Each jolt of the horse threatened to throw him free. Sliding down was the easy part; he had not yet had the opportunity to try getting back up.

He pulled with every fibre of his body, the taut reins wrapped around his hand cutting off the circulation in his fingers. His grip threatened to falter, but if he fell to the ground he would be disqualified from the contest and all his hard work would be for naught. With one last effort, he pulled on the reins and pressed on the stirrup as hard as he could. He launched himself back into the saddle; it was far from graceful, and was certainly not a stylish end to his act of bravado, but it was far better than the alternative.

His showboating had cost him precious time, and Wulfric wondered if it had been worth the effort for that single ring. He looked around in the hope of seeing another one nearby. He reckoned a fourth might be enough to take the win. He spotted one and charged for it without wasting an instant.

As he passed a haystack, Helfric emerged from the other side, making for the same ring as fast as he could. Greyfell needed no encouragement; as soon as he saw Helfric, he redoubled his effort. Wulfric crouched low, standing in the stirrups, trying to move in concert with Greyfell. His hooves thundered on the ground and Wulfric could hear his breath rasping, but he showed no signs of faltering. Slowly but surely, they drew Helfric in, until finally they were alongside one another.

Helfric looked over in dismay. He whipped his horse on, something that was anathema to Wulfric, but despite its increased effort, Greyfell matched it without any such encouragement. Helfric looked over again to see if he was pulling away. When he realised there was no difference, he swerved and shouldered into Wulfric and Greyfell. Caught off guard, Greyfell stumbled, but recovered with the next step, and pushed on to bring them level again. Helfric repeated the tactic, but they were ready for it, and he bounced off them ineffectually.

Not one to let the behaviour go unanswered, Wulfric urged Greyfell to the left, barging into Helfric and his horse. They had already played this game on foot, and Wulfric thought Helfric would have had more sense. Helfric veered away after the impact, but disappointingly remained in his saddle.

The ring was growing close. Wulfric looked over and saw Helfric glaring at him, his face a picture of spite. Wulfric spotted three rings on his lance. He followed the lance's movement and realised that it was heading toward him faster than it ought to be. The realisation came too late. A bright light flashed behind Wulfric's eyes when it struck him on the temple. He managed to remain in the saddle, but his head was rattled by the blow.

'Helfric Bertholdson! Disqualified.' Waldegrim's stentorian voice thundered across the pasture.

It served him right, and Wulfric did not spare him another thought, focussing instead on the ring. Anshel blasted from behind a hay stack and lanced it. With considerable dismay, Wulfric saw that it joined the four that were already on it. He looked around, but saw no more. There was no way to catch him.

Anshel slowed to a canter and wheeled his horse around, holding up his lance as he did. Wulfric reined Greyfell to a halt, both of them breathing heavily. He wondered if Greyfell sensed his disappointment. Everyone else was trotting around, most sporting two or three rings on their lances, but none with more than that, other than Anshel. He was the only one smiling. Everyone else, Wulfric included, did their best to hide their feelings. He looked toward Adalhaid, who was playing with her hair as she chatted with Sigert, without so much as a glance in Wulfric's direction. It was a bitter medicine to swallow. Belgar's words echoed in his ears: 'Smarter, not harder.' That day had been very hard, but it appeared he had not been very smart.

As Wulfric put Greyfell away for the night, he sensed that the horse was as disappointed by the day's result as he was. He trudged home, ambivalent to how the day had played out. The decisions he had made were poor, and he had allowed himself to be drawn into things that had hindered him. That day it meant losing. On the battlefield it could mean dying.

'That was my ring.'

The source of the voice was behind him, but he didn't need to see it to know it came from Helfric. Wulfric stopped, but didn't turn.

'It belonged to whoever could get it. Anshel, as it turns out,' Wulfric said.

'I'd have taken it if you hadn't gotten in my way.'

'Well, I did, and I'm not in the mood to discuss it with you, so get over it.'

Rorik and Walmer stepped out in front of him.

Wulfric nodded. 'So it's like that. You know you're not able to do it on your own, so you recruit help. All we need now is Rodulf. He must feel very left out.'

Wulfric turned and stepped back to try and put all three of them on one side of him. With his back secure, he had a chance, even if it was a slim one.

'I might not win this, but one of you is in for a bad evening,' Wulfric said, with as much bravado as he could muster.

'Reckon more than one of you is in for a bad evening,' Hane said, stepping out from the shadow of a nearby building. He walked over, shouldered Walmer out of his way and stopped beside Wulfric. He turned to face the others, with folded arms.

'Get them,' Helfric said. Nobody moved.

'Taking over Rodulf's job?' Wulfric said. 'You don't seem to be as good at it as he was.'

'Now,' Helfric said. 'Get them!'

Still nobody moved. Eventually, Rorik did.

He stepped back and faced Helfric. 'Get them yourself,' he said. 'I told you this was a bad idea. I'm going home.' He turned and left.

'Two on two,' Hane said. 'Don't fancy your chances. Didn't fancy them before, either.'

'Well?' Wulfric said. 'Are you going to get us?'

Helfric's face was a picture of enraged impotence. Walmer was staring at him uncertainly.

'Did Rodulf put you up to this?' Wulfric said.

Helfric sneered. 'I wouldn't do anything for a merchant's son.'

'So you came up with this plan to beat a brother apprentice all by yourself?' Hane said.

Helfric remained silent.

'I'm going home too,' Walmer said, backing away before he turned and disappeared into the night.

'Probably time you went home too,' Wulfric said. 'We both know how it ended the last time it was just the two of us.'

Helfric glared at him a moment longer before storming off. Wulfric watched him go, then turned to Hane.

'Thanks. That wouldn't have gone well for me on my own.'

'No need for thanks,' Hane said. 'We're brothers now.'

'It would be nice if Helfric realised that too.'

'He will. Just takes some longer than others.'

CHAPTER SEVENTEEN

WULFRIC WAS HEADING toward the glade, eating a bread roll while he walked. He went as quickly as he could manage with a mouthful of food while not suffocating himself in the process, as he was running late. His last session with Belgar had been that morning, and it went on longer than usual as he took the opportunity to ask the old warrior every question he could think of.

Svana was walking through the square with some of her friends. Wulfric spotted her and rushed to brush the crumbs from his woollen tunic.

'Good morning, Wulfric,' Svana said. She smiled as they passed.

Wulfric halted in surprise and inhaled a chunk of bread. The girls laughed as he hacked and spluttered as he tried to bring it back up. She had never spoken to him before. He looked back, and as he did she cast a glance over her shoulder and smiled again as they walked away. Wulfric raised an eyebrow as he drew his first unimpeded breath. What had brought on that change in treatment? It left him with a feeling of nagging concern in his gut.

❊

Wulfric had not been able to stop thinking about his brief encounter with Svana for several days, wondering if it meant their formal courtship would begin soon and feeling sick at the thought, all the while trying to conceal his worries from Adalhaid. The time for dwelling on it was taken from him, however, as preparations began for the apprentices' first expedition.

The instruction given the previous day was to arrive to training with their horses ready and supplies and kit for a two-day ranging, the first that they would be in charge of themselves. Several apprentices were already there when Wulfric arrived, and the glade was filled with the sound of excited chatter and laughter. Eldric, Waldegrim, and Angest were gathered by the standing stone chatting with a more casual air than Wulfric would have expected. It seemed they too were looking forward to what was on the agenda.

'You can all put your kit down and relax,' Eldric said, when everyone was assembled. 'We're going to do things a bit differently this time around. Usually, we spend a couple of days wandering around the forest looking at prints in the dirt and nothing much happens, so Angest and Waldegrim here are going to answer their true callings and play at reavers for the next two days.'

He turned to the two warriors, who looked as though they were relishing the task ahead of them. 'Off you go, lads. Don't make it easy for them.'

They both laughed and mounted. Angest gave them all a smile that sent a chill down Wulfric's spine. Farlof said his father told him that Angest ate the hearts of the men he killed. With Farlof, it was impossible to tell whether he was being serious or not, but looking at Angest, Wulfric could well believe it. He could imagine Angest choosing not to eat anything else.

The pair galloped away to the south. Eldric watched them go for a moment, before turning back to Wulfric and the other apprentices.

'You can relax for a while,' Eldric said. 'Give them two hours. They've been told not to put up a fight if they're caught.' He glanced in the direction they had gone and shrugged. 'But with those two, you can never really tell.'

It was only now that Wulfric noticed Eldric did not have a horse with him, or ranging kit.

'I'll be in the ale house if anyone needs me. I'll be very impressed if anyone catches them. If you're not back in two days, I might come looking for you.' He started to walk back to the village. 'Then again, I might not.'

'Who's in charge?' Anshel said.

'The man who asks the question first is usually a good choice,' Eldric said, 'but you'll have to work that out for yourselves. See you in two days. Try not to die.'

'Will they stick together or split up?' Anshel said.

'Your guess is as good as mine,' Eldric shouted back. 'Enough questions, I've a mug of ale waiting for me.'

'Mug of ale?' Hane said. 'I've only just had breakfast.'

'It's made from grains, stupid,' Farlof said.

Hane grunted and the others laughed.

'We need to get organised,' Anshel said, silencing the banter. 'We need to put the two hours to good use.'

There were murmurs of agreement.

'We should split in two,' Anshel said. 'Even if Angest and Waldegrim stay together, we'll be able to cover twice the distance, and there are more than enough of us. There's no need for all twelve of us to stick together. I'll take one group. Wulfric, you take the other.'

It took Wulfric a moment to realise Anshel had spoken his name.

'Wulfric, you take Hane, Kolbein, Berun, Roal, and Helfric. The rest come with me.'

Wulfric wanted to groan out loud at the mention of the last name, but was still so taken aback at Anshel having appointed him that he kept quiet.

'Wait,' Helfric said. 'Why's he in charge?'

Anshel fixed him with one of his icy stares. 'Because I said so. Problem with that?'

Helfric cast Wulfric a filthy look, but shook his head. Wulfric felt a twist of nerves, not just at the responsibility being placed on him but at the prospect of having to manage Helfric.

'I'll take my lot east of the southern road. You take yours west,' Anshel said.

Wulfric started to nod, but paused. 'Shouldn't we go north?'

Helfric sniggered, and Anshel frowned.

'North?' Anshel said. 'Why would we go north?'

'Because we saw them go south,' Wulfric said.

Anshel smiled, the first time Wulfric had ever seen him do so. 'You're right. It could be a double bluff, though.'

Wulfric shrugged. 'No way to know, but they aren't going to make it easy for us.' He hoped his voice sounded more confident than he felt.

'Go north for six hours. If you don't pick up any trace of them, cross over the river to the east bank and come back south. We'll head south for the same amount and wheel east if there's no trail. With any luck, we'll have caught them before we meet in the middle.'

'Sounds good,' Wulfric said.

'Check your kit and be ready to move off as soon as we get word,' Anshel said. 'We're not giving them a moment longer than we have to.'

✿

Rodulf slipped out of the village while all the attention was on the apprentices preparing for their first ranging. Children looked at them like they were all heroes, and the village's young women gathered to see them off, many offering tokens of good luck to their favoured apprentice. The way they behaved, one would be forgiven for thinking they were going to war. Admittedly it was something of a milestone for them, and their departure looked almost exactly as it did when the warriors went out— always an event for the village—but it was still nothing more than boys playing at being men.

Rodulf felt a pang of jealousy. His first ranging, a training trip or not, was something he had looked forward to for as long as he could remember. He had put those dreams behind him now, and knew that his future could offer far more than he had lost. Visiting Elzburg had showed him how much more of the world there was. He wanted to be a man of it, not some ignorant warrior who lived and died within a few paces of where he was born. He had an important task of his own that day. He carried a leather folder with several folios of maps—maps that would direct the reavers to villages he and his father had scouted and considered ripe for the picking.

The reavers were waiting for him at a rendezvous point some distance to the north. Their relationship had proved fruitful—their profits were enormous already. If the arrangement continued, and there was no reason for it not to, Rodulf and his father would amass such wealth they could move south and set themselves up as merchant princes. Wulfric and the others could charge about the place hacking lumps out of one another until the world froze and the gods returned, for all he cared.

✿

'Time to go,' Anshel shouted.

The horses were all saddled, and everyone was mounted. They had been for several minutes, eagerly counting the moments until the order was given. Wulfric's heart raced as they started off in two long lines, he and Anshel at the head. Their route took them into the village as far as the square where they would part and go in their appointed directions.

As Wulfric expected, a number of people had gathered in the village square. The departure of warriors always brought out a crowd, and even though they were only apprentices, it was little different. Several girls came forward and offered some of the apprentices tokens of affection and luck—ribbons or small charms that they had made.

Wulfric scanned the crowd for Adalhaid. She would likely be in class by then, but he was still hopeful. He spotted her, standing across the square, and his face instantly broke into a smile. He wanted nothing more than to make his way over to her, but he could not leave the formation.

'Wulfric.'

Wulfric looked down to see Svana walking toward his horse. She held up a piece of white ribbon.

'Good luck on the ranging,' she said.

Wulfric reached down to take it, but looked over to where Adalhaid was standing. She was watching. He saw her raise an eyebrow, turn and walk away. It felt as though she tore a part of him as she went.

Svana's hand touched Wulfric's as he took the ribbon.

'Thank you, Svana,' he said. It would have been unforgivable to refuse it, but he so desperately wanted it to have come from Adalhaid.

She smiled. Seeing both her and Anshel smile on the same day was unsettling, like the confluence of two great and rare events. Thinking of Anshel gave Wulfric a pang of concern. He looked over, but Anshel said nothing until they reached the point at which they had to go their separate ways.

'Good hunting,' he said.

'Likewise,' Wulfric said, trying to sound as grown up and serious as he could. He took one final glance across the square for Adalhaid, but she was nowhere to be seen. Despite the years he had dreamed of going on a ranging, he had a heavy heart as he led his little band of apprentice warriors north out of the village and into the wilderness.

CHAPTER EIGHTEEN

THEY RODE IN silence for the first hour, fanned out so they could cover the most ground. Wulfric's mind was racing with all the things he felt he should be doing as leader of the ranging party. He tried to imagine how his father would behave. He thought back to the day they went hunting together and tried to remember anything that might be of use. Try as he might, he drew a complete blank. Pensive silence was less likely to make him look a fool than attempting to say and do more than was needed, so he kept his mouth shut as much as possible. They all knew what they were looking for—Wulfric thought it best to leave them to it.

Like the others, he scanned the forest floor for any indication of passing horsemen. To call Angest and Waldegrim experts in forest craft was an understatement. Few real reavers would present as great a challenge and it occurred to Wulfric that it was perhaps not the fairest of tests.

Wulfric looked to both sides—Hane was to one, and Helfric to the other. So far, Helfric had remained quiet, which was a relief. Wulfric had expected far more trouble from him, but knew that simply because he had been silent for that long did not mean the situation would last.

They continued on for several hours. It was difficult to keep track of time under the forest canopy, and the monotony of their task made each moment seem like ten.

'Time to turn around,' Helfric said.

Everyone stopped in their tracks and looked to Wulfric.

'Still a couple more hours by my reckoning,' Wulfric said. He wasn't sure exactly how long they had been going, but it certainly wasn't the six hours he agreed with Anshel.

'There's nothing out here,' Helfric said. 'We're wasting our time.'

'I'll say when we're wasting our time. We'll continue as agreed, and turn back when I decide.'

'You're making a mistake,' Helfric said.

'Then it's mine to make,' Wulfric said. He stared at Helfric, and held his gaze until he looked away. 'Let's move off. Keep your eyes peeled.'

Everyone responded to his order, although Helfric waited defiantly for a moment before moving on. Wulfric glared at him until he did. If the others were to accept him as a leader, he couldn't allow Helfric to challenge him.

As he turned his mind back to looking for any disturbed leaf, broken twig, or scuff on the ground, he started to wonder if Helfric might be right. It would be embarrassing to have led them in the wrong direction.

'This is a waste of time,' Helfric shouted. 'No one has come this way in weeks. Let's turn south while we still have the chance of finding them before the others.'

'It's not a contest,' Wulfric said. 'That was last week.'

Helfric's face darkened. 'Everything's a contest.'

'We work together. We stick to the plan we agreed with Anshel.'

'The plan *you* agreed with Anshel.'

'I didn't hear anyone complain,' Wulfric said. 'Least of all you.'

'I'm going back,' Helfric said. 'Who's with me?' He looked around and shouted it again, louder the second time.

Wulfric's heart was racing. He wanted to look around to see if anyone was reacting, but he kept his eyes locked on Helfric. There was no sound of movement, and Wulfric could see the frustration build on Helfric's face.

'The plan's the plan,' Hane said. 'We should see it through.'

The others remained conspicuously silent, with some staring off in the opposite direction to avoid engaging in the conversation.

'Fine. I'm going back alone.'

'No you won't,' Wulfric said. 'We continue on as planned.'

'You might be the Strong Arm's son, but no one's made you First Warrior. Or First Apprentice. I'll make my own decisions. You'll look like a bloody fool when we find them in the south.'

'I'll take that chance,' Wulfric said.

Helfric turned his horse and with a shout galloped off at far too fast a pace for the forest. Wulfric wasn't sad to see him go—he was relieved if anything—but it left them a man short and meant they would not be able to search as wide an area.

'Let's keep moving,' Wulfric shouted. 'I want to cover as much ground as possible before it's time to head back.' He looked straight ahead and rode forward, satisfied by the sound of the others following his lead.

❊

Helfric whipped his horse with his reins to urge him on faster. The thrill of a fast ride through the forest started to ease the fury he felt at Wulfric's casual dismissal of his opinion. He jumped a fallen tree trunk and swerved around another as soon as he landed. He let out a loud laugh, and felt the tension ease from his body. If he pushed hard he could join up with Anshel's party before nightfall.

It had been a mistake not to speak up when the groups were created, but he had expected them to side with him when it became clear Wulfric was leading them on a fool's errand. He wasn't sure when Wulfric had become so popular, but there was little he could do about it. Perhaps it was time to accept the way things were and get on with it. Wulfric was the First Warrior's son after all; it was to be expected that he would rise to prominence, worthy or not. If continuing to oppose it would be detrimental to his prospects, Helfric thought it best to stop.

His horse screamed and stumbled, and Helfric found himself flying through the air.

❊

The sound was unmistakably of a horse. Rodulf stopped to listen, but there was nothing more to be heard. Considering he had just met with the men he and his father were paying to steal cattle, remaining unseen was important. The apprentices should have been much farther north by that point, and he didn't expect to encounter someone there.

His curiosity getting the better of him, he slipped down from his horse and tied it to a tree, then started toward where he had heard the sound. He crept forward, intending to stay out of sight. It was possible that there were reavers other than those in his employ operating in the area. Ordinarily he wouldn't give a damn—his family did not have the right to keep herds— but more reavers at large in the region could cause problems for him.

He reached the spot where he reckoned the horse had screamed, but there was no sign of one. There were some broken branches and disturbed ground, however. By the look of it, only one horse. He heard a groan, and froze on the spot.

He moved forward with extra care, until he spotted Helfric sitting against a tree trunk. Helfric didn't look well. His skin was grey and covered in a sheen of sweat, his curly brown hair plastered to his skin with a mixture of sweat and blood. Rodulf could hear his raspy breathing from where he stood. He cleared his throat and stepped forward.

'Rodulf?' Helfric said. 'Thank the gods. I fell off my horse. I'm hurt bad. Get help.'

Rodulf stared at him. If he hurried, he could have the priest back there within an hour.

'I thought you weren't interested in speaking to me ever again,' Rodulf said. 'I'm only a merchant's son after all. Are you sure I'm capable of bringing help?'

'I'm hurt. Get help.' Helfric tried to shout the words, but they came out as little more than gasps.

Rodulf sat on a dead log. 'Falling off your horse is a silly thing to do, especially for a big brave warrior like you.'

'Stop playing about,' Helfric said. 'I'm hurt bad. Bring the priest.'

'How bad?' Rodulf said. He stood and walked over to Helfric. Both his legs were broken. A jagged shard of bone had pierced through his trouser leg. Helfric had tied a strip of cloth around his thigh above the wound, but his pallor suggested he had lost a great deal of blood. Every moment was vital if he was to be saved, yet Rodulf felt no sense of haste. 'You're right. You are hurt bad. Still, I'm sure it's nothing Aethelman couldn't fix.'

Helfric smiled and relaxed. 'Thank you, Rodulf.'

'For what? I didn't say I was going to get him. Why would I help you after the way you've treated me? You haven't so much as said hello to me since...' He gestured to his eyepatch.

'I'll die if you don't help me.'

Rodulf nodded. 'Yes. Yes, you will. Be sure to say hello to Jorundyr for me.'

Helfric tried to say something, but Rodulf ignored him. He turned and started to walk back to where he had left his horse. He had only gone a few paces when a thought occurred to him. 'Does Jorundyr take in idiots who die falling from their horses?'

Helfric's mouth was moving, but there was no sound coming out.

'No, probably not,' Rodulf said. 'Bad luck.' He returned to his horse.

❋

As he was about to give the command to turn south, Wulfric spotted a wisp of smoke rising up where the forest was thinner. He signalled to Hane, who had already seen it. The signal was passed along the line of horsemen, and they all stopped. Wulfric had never been in that part of the forest before so had no idea of what might be out there. He dismounted and tied Greyfell to a tree. Hane did likewise with his horse, and together they advanced toward the smoke.

The forest gave way to a clearing, in the centre of which sat a small hunting lodge. Smoke spiralled from the moss-covered stone chimney— there was somebody inside. Who?

Wulfric looked to Hane who shrugged. It seemed too much to hope that they had found Angest and Waldegrim. There was the very real chance that they had found danger. Wulfric drew his sabre, his action mirrored by Hane. The others gathered behind them and readied their weapons.

Wulfric picked up a rock and threw it against the door. He crouched, prepared for whatever came next. The door squealed as it opened. Angest stepped out, a steaming mug of broth in his hand. He surveyed the gathered apprentices and gave one of his stomach curdling smiles.

'Well, aren't you the clever fellows?' he said. 'Where're the rest of you?'

'The other group went south,' Wulfric said.

'You can put your swords away. We'll come quietly,' Angest said. 'Waldegrim, we're rumbled.'

Waldegrim came outside and surveyed the scene. 'Well, looks like our vacation is over. Best be on our way then.'

❋

Their arrival back in the village that night came as a surprise to everyone, no one more than Eldric, who had been enjoying a rare day off. He came out of his house and glared accusatorially at Angest, who shrugged his shoulders.

Wulfric's cheeks began to ache, and he realised it was because he had spent the past hours with a smile permanently fixed to his face.

As they rode toward the stables, Wulfric noticed the ribbon tucked into his sleeve. He had forgotten all about it, but wondered if it had brought him luck. It also reminded him of Svana, and her dramatic change of attitude toward him. It was flattering that she had given him the ribbon, but as he twisted it between his fingers he got a hollow feeling inside that sapped all the joy from the day's success.

A rider was dispatched to fetch the others back, but for the apprentices in Wulfric's party there was time for a well-deserved rest. He wondered how Helfric would react when he found out that Wulfric had been right all along, and that had he waited for only another hour, he would have been able to share in their success. He left the stables clutching his saddle to his chest, looking forward to the prospect of a day off.

He saw Adalhaid after going only a few paces. His initial reaction was to rush over and tell her about his day, but he stopped himself mid-step. The old ease with which they always talked seemed lost to him. It had been growing for some time, but this was the first time he had felt it looming between them like a great obstacle. He realised that he was afraid to speak to her, as if he did not know what to say any more. He considered continuing on without speaking to her when she turned and spotted him.

'You're back early,' she said. Her smile looked forced.

'We had some luck,' Wulfric said. 'Looks like I'll be getting a day off for a change.'

'It wasn't luck from what I heard. You didn't fall for their trick and go south with the others.'

'It wasn't taking much of a risk. The others went south, so one of us was bound to catch them. I was lucky.'

'Perhaps it was Svana's ribbon that brought it.'

Wulfric shifted uncomfortably and wanted to hide under his saddle. 'You saw that.' He knew that she had.

Adalhaid nodded. 'It's nice to see you getting on better. It must make life easier for you.'

'I haven't really thought about it like that. It's all new. I'm not sure how long it'll last.'

'I hope it works out for the best. I need to get going.' She started to walk away.

'Wait,' Wulfric said. He took a deep breath, but it did little to slow the maelstrom in his head and chest. 'I wish that it had been yours. The ribbon, that is.'

Adalhaid blushed, and opened her mouth to say something, but closed it again. 'I have to go,' she said finally. 'I have chores.'

She was gone before Wulfric could think of something to say to stop her, leaving him to feel that he would happily give up being a warrior to have her there for one moment longer.

CHAPTER NINETEEN

WULFRIC OPENED HIS eyes and looked around with the confusion that always accompanied waking from a deep sleep. It was still early, and they had been given the day off as a reward for their quick success on the ranging. It took him a moment to register a commotion outside and pounding on the door. Anshel and the others were due back that morning, but Wulfric didn't see why that would cause such a disturbance, unless they had an encounter of their own. Wulfric jumped out of bed and pulled on some clothes.

'Strong Arm! Wulfric!' A dozen bangs on the door accompanied the shout.

Wulfric got to the door first. It was Eldric.

'When did you last see Helfric?' Eldric said.

'Yesterday. Midday I think. He turned around about an hour before we found Angest and Waldegrim. He said he was going to join up with the others.'

'They're back. They haven't seen him. We're going to have to go out and look. Get your gear and meet at the stables. Bring your father. Everyone's riding out.'

❉

Eldric was not exaggerating when he said everyone was riding out. By the time Wulfric and his father got to the stables, every warrior and apprentice was there, preparing their mounts. The six recently returned apprentices had joined the throng, no doubt ruing the fact that a good sleep in a proper bed was farther away than they had thought. Helfric would not be popular with them when he turned up. Wulfric wondered what had happened to him, and questioned his own behaviour. Could he have been firmer with Helfric the day before?

Anshel walked over as soon as he saw Wulfric.

'What in hells happened?' he said.

'Helfric thought we made a mistake heading north and decided to head back and join your group.' Wulfric almost added 'he wouldn't listen to me', but chose not to.

'He never got to us,' Anshel said.

'He could be anywhere. There was no sign of him when we came back, but I suppose we weren't looking.'

'I'll take a group to the hunting lodge and work our way back,' Eldric said, breaking up Wulfric's conversation. 'Wulfric, you come with me. If he was moving fast to get back to Anshel's group, he'll have left an obvious trail. The rest will spread out for a wider sweep.'

'I'm coming with you.' It was Berthold, Helfric's father.

Wulfric worried that he would be blamed, but Berthold seemed concerned rather than anything else.

'We leave as soon as you're all ready,' Wolfram said. Now that Wulfric's father was there, everyone deferred to him.

The ease with which leadership came to Wolfram and how everyone followed his commands without question was not lost on Wulfric. Had he an ounce of his father's influence, perhaps the whole mess could have been avoided. Wulfric hoped that Helfric would turn up safely. He could not help but feel that the finger would be pointed at him if something bad had happened.

Wulfric felt an obligation to be the one to find the tracks that led them to Helfric. His eyes burned from the constant scanning of the ground in front of him. He had been eager to impress when doing the same task the day before, but now he felt a sense of panic. A leader was responsible for his men, and Wulfric had allowed Helfric to take that control from him. The woods were a harsh place, filled with unpleasant things. A fall from a horse was one thing, but even in late spring, the presence of belek could not be discounted and that was before considering bears or wolves. In that forest, a sprained ankle could be fatal.

Wolfram was the one to spot deep hoof prints in the forest litter—the sign of a rider moving at speed. There was silence as they followed the tracks until they stopped a few paces from a fallen tree trunk. The tracks continued on the other side, but were not as deep. The horse had shed its burden. They found Helfric a few paces farther on.

Wulfric had seen the dead before, but never anything like Helfric. It seemed that he had crawled from where he had fallen to lean against a tree. There were no signs of a struggle around where his body rested. Wulfric hoped that meant he was already dead when the wolves got there. He involuntarily glanced at Berthold, who had not uttered a sound. His face was pale, but his jaw was firmly set. Warriors did not show pain. Death was part of their life; it was something they accepted when they chose that course.

'What will I tell his mother?' Berthold said, breaking the silence. 'She'll want to see him, but I can't let her, not like this.' He choked out the final few words.

Wulfric looked to his father, but his face gave nothing away. He had seen violent death many times; for Wulfric, it was a new experience. Being so close to it made many confusing things seem blatantly clear. When death could come so easily, there was no point in living his life to someone else's expectations.

✼

Helfric's body was treated with all the dignity afforded to a fallen warrior. Eldric went on ahead to have the others notified that the search was over, while Wulfric and the rest of them returned with the corpse. Berthold rode in front with his son tied to the back of his horse. Wulfric and his father gave him space. Wulfric found it difficult to look anywhere other than the supine form on Berthold's horse.

'It's not your fault, you know,' Wolfram said.

'Isn't it? I couldn't make him follow my orders.'

'Not your fault. Most lads starting their apprenticeship see themselves as First Warrior one day. No warrior is born to follow, and they never truly resign themselves to doing it. They fight for men they respect and trust, and those are two things it takes years to earn, not just a morning. Hane told me Anshel named you to lead the party. That means you're on the road to earning those things, but some'll take longer than others to come around. Helfric made his choices, and they led him to being carried home on the back of a horse. That's the way it works sometimes.'

Seeing Helfric drove home to Wulfric how fleeting life could be. The whole way back from finding the body, he felt an overwhelming sense of impatience. One thing stood out above the others. He had avoided confronting whatever was causing the distance between him and Adalhaid; allowed himself to continue in a cowardly state of confusion rather than addressing it directly. Seeing Helfric like that crystallised the problem for him. Had Helfric been able to muster the support of the others the previous day, it might well have been Wulfric who was left alone in the forest. It might well have been his half-eaten corpse they found slumped against a tree. There would be no more confusion. He knew what was causing it, and he knew what he wanted.

As soon as they reached the stables Wulfric jumped straight from his horse and went to Adalhaid's house. He knocked on the door and took a step back to wait. His heart thumped in his chest. Adalhaid opened the door.

'I don't know what's come between us, but if it's my fault I'm sorry,' he blurted out. 'I miss you. You've always been the most important thing in my life, and I want it to stay that way.'

'I miss you too,' she said with a sad smile. 'But that won't change anything, Wulfric.'

'It doesn't have to. I'll be a warrior in a few years, and no man alive will be able to tell me what I can and can't do. My choice will be my own, and my choice will always be you.'

She opened her mouth to say something, but was interrupted by a shout.

'Wulfric! Get over here and help put away these horses!' Eldric's voice carried halfway across the village, making them both look and laugh.

'Not a warrior yet,' Adalhaid said, smiling.

'No,' Wulfric said, with a sheepish smile. 'Not yet. I better go.'

❋

Adalhaid watched him go, a smile still on her face, but it was an uncertain one. There would always be calls on his time that he could not ignore, and demands that he would not be able to decline. She knew she felt the same way as he; seeing Svana fawn over him made her want to vomit. When he had been nothing more than a kind-hearted boy, Svana would not even have spit on him. But now?

She shut the door and returned to her small room, feeling as though she was about to be ripped asunder, her head pulling her one way, her heart the other. She could not forget the fact that her father was a lanceman and Wulfric's was First Warrior. Everyone in the village would oppose their being together, and she wondered how they could ever hope to overcome that obstacle. She wondered how her own life would be, forever dictated by Wulfric's duties.

No sooner had she sat down than there was another knock on the door. She rushed back and opened it, expecting to see Wulfric standing there, but it was not he. It was Aethelman. She was in equal parts disappointed and relieved.

'Good evening, Aethelman. I'll get my father,' she said.

'It's you I've come to speak with. At first, at least. Might I come in?'

'Of course,' Adalhaid said.

'I want to talk to you about this out of earshot of the others,' Aethelman said. 'In recent weeks I've had to accept that you've exceeded my ability to teach you.'

Adalhaid raised her eyebrows, not certain what he was getting at.

'You're a bright girl. The brightest I've encountered, and I feel it would be a shame for your education to stop because of my shortcomings as a teacher.'

She started to shake her head, but he raised a hand to stop her. 'Healing and ministration are my duties, and I think myself skilled at both. I was never intended to be a teacher. The question I have for you this evening is do you wish to continue with your education?'

Adalhaid took a moment to think, but she knew the answer. She loved learning, and had no desire to stop. 'Yes. I'd like to very much.'

'Good,' Aethelman said. 'Perhaps it's time you bring your parents in.'

Adalhaid fetched her mother and father, all the while feeling her excitement grow. The gods must have been watching her, to have Aethelman bring this to her at the time of her greatest uncertainty. Her parents were nervous to have Aethelman in their home, and Adalhaid could see why he had wanted to speak to her alone first.

They both started fussing as they did their best to ensure they satisfied every requirement of hospitality. After Aethelman put them at ease, he got to his point. Adalhaid found herself growing increasingly nervous at what he might suggest.

'Ordinarily, on encountering a young person of such intelligence,' Aethelman said, 'I would suggest sending them to the Hermitage to train as a priest.'

Adalhaid could feel the blood drain from her face at the mention of it.

Aethelman saw her reaction and smiled. 'However, the life of a priest is one of solitude, and knowing Adalhaid as I do, I know she would curse my name every day of her life if we were to send her there. However, there are few other options for a girl in the Northlands. In the south, on the other hand...' He let his words hang on the air for a moment before continuing. 'I have been in contact with some friends in the south, in Elzburg, to explore the options.'

'I have a brother in Elzburg,' Adalhaid's father said. 'He's a captain of the guard there.'

'So I heard,' Aethelman said. 'There are a number of schools there, one in particular that I believe would be perfect for Adalhaid. If she does well there, other opportunities will present themselves. Higher study in a university for example. She could be a physician or a teacher, or, well, anything she wants really. She has ability to spare and will thrive in whatever she chooses.'

Adalhaid had heard of universities, great centres of learning in the cities of the south, but it had never once occurred to her that she might go to one. The thought of going thrilled and terrified her.

'What will it cost?' Adalhaid's father said.

'If your brother would be willing to take her in, virtually nothing. She is more than capable of earning a scholarship, and I can see to making that happen.'

'How long would I be gone?' Adalhaid said.

'The term runs from the start of autumn to the end of spring. You would be able to come home for the summers.'

She nodded, her thoughts swirling around the new possibilities. Part of her wanted to go desperately. Part of her felt ill at the thought of being away from Wulfric. That was a foolish notion however, one that was destined to cause her nothing but pain and heartbreak no matter how desperately she wanted to ignore the fact. She knew his words and feelings were sincere, his intentions good, but the reality of life rarely followed on the heels of good intentions. His life would dominate hers until there would be no room left in it for her own dreams. What if they were prevented from marrying? Where would she be then? Destined to be a ragged old spinster dabbling in herbs and salves that didn't work, like Behrta, living in a shack full of cats on the edge of the village? She had to have her own life. Her own future. The thought made her head pound with terror. She felt as though her decision would rip her asunder.

'I want to go,' she said. 'When?'

'There are still a dozen or so weeks of this term left,' Aethelman said. 'I see no reason for you to wait.'

❀

The Maisterspaeker paused. The candles at the inn had burned down to little nubs surrounded by waxy pools. The innkeeper had been so focussed on the story that he had not bothered to change them, although it gave the Maisterspaeker a good indication of how long he had been speaking. His voice was so well accustomed to use that it barely showed any sign of strain or fatigue. He cast a wistful glance at the door, disappointed that Wulfric had still not arrived. It seemed unlikely that he would that night.

The Maisterspaeker looked at the crowd, searching out any sign of weariness or boredom, but there was none.

'Perhaps I shall pause there...' the Maisterspaeker said.

There was a collective groan.

'...to allow the innkeeper and his staff to clear up a little. I shall start again in ten minutes.'

The groan ended, and people rushed for the door. The Maisterspaeker doubted more than half of them would find a spot at the privy before he started again, with only the quickest and most ruthless managing to relieve their bladders. They jostled to get out, and as amusing as the Maisterspaeker found it, he hoped it wouldn't lead to injury. He had been the inciting presence for more than one riot over the years, and the novelty had long since worn off.

He took a moment to gather his thoughts, and ready the next part of his story.

PART TWO

CHAPTER TWENTY

THE VILLAGE—VELDORF WAS its name—was a small place. The Maisterspaeker had noted on arrival that it could not be home to more than a hundred people or so. There appeared to be at least that many in the taproom when he made to continue with the story. It seemed not everyone had gone to relieve themselves; many had gone to gather up every person they knew. It was flattering, but he also felt slightly guilty, wondering if they had been dragged from a warm bed to hear his tale. He hoped it was worth the inconvenience.

Once again, Conradin was at the front of the group, an enthusiastic smile on his face. The innkeeper placed a fresh mug of ale in front of the Maisterspaeker. A filled tavern, a crackling fire, and a cold mug of ale. What more could a man of his years want for? A good comrade and a hard fight, perhaps, but both of those would be coming soon enough. He lifted the mug to his lips and took a long draught. His throat wet, he cleared it.

'I've thought long and hard on the next part, and have decided to pick up our story again three years on. There is little of note that we will be bypassing, merely the slow progression of a boy to the fringe of manhood. We return to the Northlands at a small forest clearing, by a campfire on a cold, dark evening, and to a man with whom we have only been briefly acquainted…'

❄

Captain Morlyn looked over the writing on the scrap of paper one final time before pressing the tip of his tobacco twist into it. It took light quickly, bathing his hands and face in a pleasant, albeit brief, warmth. Winter was closing its grasp on the Northlands, and he would be damned if he was going to be caught north of the border when the snows came in. A warm inn with a good kitchen and clean beds was the place to be when that happened, and he had more than enough coin to see out his days in that style. The village the Northlander wanted them to reave was a long trek north—farther than he would like at the best of times and more than he was willing to accept at that time of year.

For three years his arrangement with the Northlander merchant had been more profitable than he would ever have believed. Reaving had once been a subsistence living for him, and a source of constant shame for his mother, who had once delighted in telling everyone her son was a banneret. She spoke only of his brothers now—one a money lender, the other a trader in slaves—but that would change. He was a wealthy man, and the hardships of life on the trail were neither attractive nor necessary. One more reaving, and then it was home to a life of idle luxury.

He had come to know the Northlands well since beginning their enterprise. He knew where the biggest bands of warriors were, and he knew the routes they took on patrol. He also knew of a cherry ripe for the picking. He had been eyeing it up for a year, but had left it alone for fear of spoiling their deal. He had no need for the deal with the Northlander now, and no reason not to go his own way. It might be more of a challenge than the others, but they had gotten very good at what they did and he was confident they could pull it off. One big reaving to top them all and retire. The thought warmed him more than the small campfire.

Rasbruck had one of the largest herds of cattle he had ever seen. So many that they couldn't even begin to keep watch on all of them. It made him wonder why Donato hadn't sent them there already. Perhaps he thought it was too much for them. If he did he was a fool, and it would cost him. He would get the cut he was expecting from the other village and no more. The rest would be all theirs. Morlyn expected he could drive off several hundred beasts at least and be halfway to the rendezvous before anyone noticed they were gone. Would it be greedy to try for more than that, he wondered? It was his last job; he wanted to go out with a bang.

❄

'A fine job as always,' Donato said as he watched the cattle being herded into their secret corral deep in the forest. 'You must have stripped them clean.'

'We got the lot,' Morlyn said. There was no need to tell him the truth of it. He had no idea how many cattle were up at the village they were supposed to go to, so had estimated how many to hand over, only a small proportion of what they had actually taken. He was giddy at the thought of how much he would make when he got the rest of them south of the border.

'It's a pleasant surprise,' Donato said.

'That was our last run of the year.' It was his last run ever, but there was no need to tell Donato that.

'I understand. I'll be in touch in spring. There are more than enough beasts here to tide me over until then.'

Morlyn wondered what he needed them all for. He must have had one of the largest herds in the Northlands. The savages liked their beasts more than coin, so he should have been about ready to set himself up as a king. He was welcome to it. Morlyn had no intention of ever coming north of the border again.

❋

Wolfram the Strong Arm sat atop his horse staring down at the tracks on the ground below, trying to contain the excitement he felt at having found them. For three years, he had heard talk of a band of reavers taking cattle as they pleased and disappearing back into the forest, not to be heard of until they struck again. They seemed to have a better knowledge of the Northlands than the average reaver, and no one had so much as caught a glimpse of them. He had expected them to pay a visit to Leondorf one day, and it was a surprise that they never had. So long as they were at large they were a threat, and Wolfram had stayed on the lookout for them every time he went ranging. They were ghosts, however, and the longer they went unseen, the more Wolfram wanted them.

He studied the tracks to be certain of what they told him, although they were so obvious he could hardly believe they'd been made by his ghost reavers. They had never been so sloppy before. The tracks were fresh; no more than a couple of hours old. They were close. He waved the other warriors on and spurred his horse forward. They would have blood by nightfall, and tales to tell on the morrow.

❊

Wolfram was elated as he rode back into Leondorf with two heads dangling from his saddle. Angest and Eldric had one each hanging from theirs, and the others were driving a herd of cattle as large as he had ever seen back to the village. The heads would be mounted on posts, a message to anyone thinking of stealing Leondorf's herds. Such was the treatment for reavers. None of the cattle bore brands, so there was no question of returning them to their owners and taking only a portion as their bounty for recovering them. It meant his share would double his herd. There could be no question that they had discovered and killed the infamous reavers.

He spotted the merchant, Donato, as he rode through the village proudly displaying the heads so all could learn of their victory. The merchant's eyes were locked on the heads, his face a picture of horror. It made Wolfram smile. Merchants had such weak stomachs.

❊

Ritschl watched Thietmar, the First Warrior's chief herdsman, count the cattle as they passed, as he did every time the Leondorfer's payment arrived. It could not have come at a more welcome time for Rasbruck. Their herds had been rustled to nothing only a few days previously, and spirits were low. Trade had softened their attitude toward Leondorf, something that frustrated Ritschl. It could mean that his time there was wasted, and he would have to come up with a new plan. The deal had made the village wealthy, but that had been wiped out in one reaving and the recent payment would not go far in softening the blow. He wondered how he might exploit the discontent it created.

'Stop them!' Thietmar shouted.

Ritschl had been turning back into his kirk, but stopped, curious. The herdsmen halted the slowly moving herd of cattle, and Thietmar walked forward for a closer look.

Two seasons before, not long after Ritschl arrived at Rasbruck, one of Thietmar's calves was set upon by wolves. The herdsman was close enough to drive them off before they could kill it, but the calf's ear was ripped off and it took a number of other injuries. Ritschl remembered it well as he had helped heal some of the more serious injuries, glad of the chance to practice part-forgotten skills on something that could not complain. That calf— now a full-grown cow—had been taken off by the reavers. It stood before him now, among the other cattle Donato the Leondorfer had delivered.

Ritschl made his way down to the cattle, and watched as Thietmar checked the beast for a brand.

'I could swear I recognise that one,' Ritschl said, hoping upon hope, but not really believing the Leondorfer could be that stupid.

'I too,' Thietmar said. 'But there's no brand. The flesh where it should be is as untouched as the day the cow was born.'

He ran his fingers over the area on its flank and looked closely as Ritschl joined him. The damage to the ear was the same, as were some of the scars on its body. Ritschl waved his hand over the spot where the beasts were branded, and Rasbruck's mark appeared. He did so again, and it disappeared once more.

'A simple trick,' Ritschl said, 'but the truth always outs. I suspect you have found your reavers.' The brand was genuinely there, still deep within the flesh, hidden only by a superficial healing. He could barely believe his luck.

Thietmar frowned. 'Take them to the pens and hold them there until I say otherwise,' he said. 'The First Warrior will need to see this.'

❧

'The Leondorfers have never been our friends,' Thietmar said. 'And now it seems they think us fools as well. Do they think a little magic to erase brands will deceive us?'

Gandack, the First Warrior of Rasbruck, stroked his thick black beard thoughtfully. It was his way to let the others do the talking before making his decision.

Not a single voice among the village council was raised in opposition. Ritschl was tempted to lend his in support, but he knew he needed to take care with his words. He was supposed to be a priest, after all. It wouldn't do for him to be the one to incite Rasbruck to war; he had to let them come to that choice by themselves. It was too tantalising a chance to let pass, however. This was the opportunity he had been waiting for. It felt like a gift from the gods. It amazed him that the Leondorfers could be foolish enough to steal cattle only to try and sell them straight back, but it seemed that was what they had done.

With his guidance, Rasbruck could wipe Leondorf from the face of the world, leaving him free to peruse the ruins at his leisure and take the Stone from the ashes of Aethelman's kirk. He sat back and allowed the villagers' vitriol to boil over. If everything went to plan, all he would have to do was give them a gentle shove in the right direction every so often.

He watched as the warriors discussed the theft, the herdsmen adding their testimony that they recognised many of the cattle. Their outrage at the perfidy dripped from every word spoken. It seemed that Ritschl's task was all but done for him. A divide began to form between those who were thirsty for blood and those who wished a more moderate approach. It was time for one of those gentle shoves.

'It's not my place to influence this council, but since taking up my responsibilities here I have come to care for the people of Rasbruck. I do not want to see you be taken advantage of, or suffer as a result. Reputation counts for a great deal, and when word of this event gets out the other villages and tribes will wonder how Rasbruck reacted. They will watch to see how she protects what is hers.'

'What if it was just this one merchant?' a member of the village council said. 'We all know what merchants are like.' There was a chorus of approval. 'War might be a mistake.'

'Do you really think a single merchant could do something like this?' a warrior said. 'Steal our cattle? Clean them of our brands? It was chance that Thietmar was able to recognise one of his cattle, and good fortune that we are blessed with a priest who could confirm his suspicion. Now everyone else has found that some of their animals are included.'

'What say you, Priest?' Gandack said. 'Yours is always the voice of moderation.'

Ritschl smiled inwardly that his careful counsel over the years had managed to position him so well. His patience had paid off.

'How much more proof do you need, First Warrior?' Ritschl said. 'If we allow them to get away with it this time, they'll do it again. All of your neighbours will look on Rasbruck as an unattended market stall, taking what they choose, when they choose. In months we will be left with nothing.' He was careful to use words like 'we' and 'our' and 'us' at every opportunity. 'I cannot condone violence, but neither can I stand by and allow the people I have come to love be stripped of all that is theirs.'

'He's right,' another warrior said. 'They are scum, and we have allowed them to take liberties with us. It is too long since we last showed them their place.'

'I agree,' another said. 'We cannot allow this to go unanswered. All our neighbours will think us weak and take ever greater liberties. The priest is right. We will be left with nothing. We need to prepare our response. Will the gods bless us, Priest?'

'I cannot imagine them withholding their beneficence in the face of such injury.' Ritschl stopped himself from smiling. It wouldn't do for the priest to smile at such a time.

❁

The hour or two before everyone else woke was Wulfric's favourite time of the day. The precious minutes were his own, with no demands from anyone else. He spent them in a fashion more akin to his childhood, quietly watching, thinking, imagining. The only difference was that Adalhaid was not at his side. He realised that each morning, as he looked out across thatched roofs and through the misty air, that he prayed for her return, but it was yet to happen. Three long years. It felt like a lifetime.

There was an arrival that morning, however. A grey-robed man walked through the village. The few people already outside and starting their day paid him no attention—they were still either half asleep or too engrossed in their tasks. Wulfric paid attention though, as he did many of the things that seemed to pass beyond the notice of others. Even after three years of training, growing, and maturing, old habits died hard. Only one type of man dressed like the new arrival, which meant change. It meant a change that Wulfric knew he did not want. The life of a grey priest was a transient one, and there were precious few like Aethelman who established themselves with any semblance of permanency in one place.

A village's priest played an important role in preparing young men for their pilgrimage to Jorundyr's Rock, and Wulfric had taken comfort in the thought that Aethelman would be the one aiding him in that. Wulfric still had two more years training at least before he would be allowed to go, possibly three. Aethelman's presence was always a comfort; he could mend any broken bone and heal any cut. What would the new priest be like? Change was not always for the worse—Wulfric of all people knew this— but he did not want Aethelman to leave.

CHAPTER TWENTY-ONE

LATER THAT EVENING, there was a knock at the door. It was usually Wulfric's job to answer, but his father gestured for him to stay where he was and answered it himself. Wulfric sat by the fire, trying to absorb some of its heat into his sore, tired muscles. He kneaded a muscle in his shoulder with discomfort and irritation. It was always the same one that hurt after a particularly hard day's training, his sword arm being taxed more than any other part of his body.

He stopped what he was doing and looked up in expectation. Every time there was a knock at the door, part of Wulfric hoped it would be Adalhaid. That part had grown smaller over the years, but it remained. She had gone off to school in the south, promising she would be back in only a few weeks when the term ended. In three years she had not returned. He spoke with her mother from time to time, so knew that she was well and thriving. Her absence felt like a hole in the centre of him. She had not written, and his skill with letters shamed him too much to try to initiate contact. He had thought of asking Aethelman to write something for him, but was too embarrassed to reveal his thoughts and feelings even to one he trusted as much as the priest. He didn't resent her though. How could he blame her for chasing her dream? Had he not done exactly the same? In any event, he would soon be betrothed to Svana, like it or not. They had sat together at a number of feasts over the intervening years, but it had always felt stilted and formal, as though they were both fulfilling a role, rather than trying to get to know the person they were to marry. She was to be his future, however, a choice Adalhaid seemed to have made easy for him.

Wulfric still felt a sense of disappointment when Aethelman stepped across the threshold, though. Wolfram led him in and gestured for him to sit.

'I hear that you might not be with us for much longer,' Wolfram said.

'No, sadly not,' Aethelman said, as he sat. He gave Wulfric a nod. 'It's beyond time I moved on. Other responsibilities have been pressing on my mind ever more heavily for several years. I cannot in good conscience put them off much longer. We priests are not supposed to become too attached to any one place. We serve all of the gods' people, not just some of them.'

'You'll be missed. There's no way you can stay?'

'No,' Aethelman said, shaking his head. 'Perhaps one day I'll be able to pass back this way.'

Wulfric felt his heart sink.

'We'll give you whatever you need for your journey,' Wolfram said. 'It's the least we can do. Say what you need, and it's yours. This village is as much your home as it is mine.'

'That's very kind of you, but it's not the reason I came. There's something I have to tell you. A warning.'

Wolfram moved to the edge of his seat, and Wulfric could see he was tense.

'The new priest passed through Rasbruck on his way here. They were gathering warriors and preparing for a battle.'

'Against whom?' Wolfram said.

Aethelman said nothing.

'They can try,' Wolfram said, sinking back into his chair and sitting more easily. 'We'll send them home with a bloodied nose as we always do. It's probably just posturing, like game birds in mating season.'

'There's more to it than that. Warriors from other villages are joining them. They're talking about cattle rustling that's been going on over the past few years. They're saying Leondorf is behind it all. The other villages have all suffered from it, and are throwing their support behind Rasbruck.'

Wolfram frowned. 'I caught those reavers weeks ago. Their heads are still on posts along the road.'

'The blame is being laid at Leondorf's door.'

'Anyone with an ounce of brains will realise we had nothing to do with the reaving. They should be thanking us for putting an end to it. We didn't have to. Our herds were never touched...' Wolfram's eyes widened. 'What good will attacking do them? They'll take a patch of land that we'll take back next year when their extra warriors are gone.'

Aethelman grimaced. 'Donato sold them some cattle. Sold them back some cattle, I should say. Ones that were stolen from them a few days before.'

The veins in Wolfram's temples pulsed. He took a deep breath before continuing. 'Was he behind the reaving?'

'I've no reason to believe so,' Aethelman said. 'It's as likely he bought some of the cattle from the reavers hoping to make a quick profit. You know what he's like.'

Wolfram nodded. 'Thank you for letting me know.' He stood and showed Aethelman out.

Wulfric's mother appeared at the doorway to the back room when Aethelman left. 'Why not hand him over? No one will shed a tear for him.'

'I doubt it would do any good,' Wolfram said. 'As Aethelman said, there's no proof that he had anything to do with the reaving, only that he bought some of the stolen cattle. They're just using this as an excuse. It's our territory they really want and they must reckon they're strong enough to take it. Even if that wasn't the case, Donato is born and bred in Leondorf and my responsibility as First Warrior is to protect everyone in Leondorf, him included.'

Wolfram walked out right away, leaving Wulfric with his mother. He felt frustrated that he was still considered too young and untrained to be involved in the defence of the village. The warriors had ridden out of Leondorf in full battle array a number of times since Wulfric began his training—Rasbruck was not their only enemy—and each time they did he found it a little harder to remain behind.

Wulfric could hear his father call out the names of the other councilmen as he walked to the Great Hall. It was always his way, and everyone knew it meant that trouble was coming.

❈

Homecomings were always said to be something to be relished, but Rodulf found it difficult to view his that way. Each trip away made it a little bit harder to return home. After the wonders of Ostenheim, Brixen, and Voorn on the far side of the Great Sea, or the Middle Sea as the southerners called it, going home seemed like a punishment. At first, being sent away from Leondorf had felt like a failure, as though he was scurrying away with his tail between his legs. The only thing that eased the pain was the fact that he already had a taste of what the south had to offer, and was curious to experience more.

Home, however, was where all their wealth came from. They had no great vineyards or glass foundries or shipyards to earn their coin, but they had a stranglehold on the things that the Northlands was rich in and that the southerners craved. His father had sent him south to learn how business was done there, to learn their culture, their habits, and as often as not their vices.

He had had little time to think of home while in the south. There was always work of some sort to be done, and the merchants he was apprenticed to worked him hard. In his few free moments, there were too many diversions and pleasures to spare the Northlands and its boorish inhabitants a thought. The south would always hold a special place in his heart, but Leondorf would be the stronghold of his wealth. When the village finally hove into view, he could see that little had changed. It was incredibly disappointing.

❄

Wulfric watched the scouts ride out the next morning. The council's reaction was to increase their watch on the northern roads and trails, and get a better idea of what they were all facing. Wulfric hoped they might send some of the apprentices out as scouts, as occasionally happened, but the threat was deemed to be too great to put the young men at risk.

Wulfric lounged in a chair on the porch of his house with Hane and several of the other apprentices. They sat in tense silence, each of them trying to appear more relaxed than the next, aping the calm, distant stares the warriors had in times of crisis, but none of them managed it quite so convincingly. With all the warriors preparing for battle, they were given the day off. At moments like this, when he was anxious and uncertain, he felt Adalhaid's absence keenly. She was his source of comfort and always had been.

Wulfric jumped to his feet when the first of the scouts returned to the village. The others stood too. They sighed in unison when they saw Wolfram shake his head after a brief discussion with the scout and return to the great hall, and resumed their vigil. The scene was repeated over the course of the day, as the scouts continued to return until well after dark, none with any reports of enemy warriors. After they had all returned, the senior figures of the village made their way to the Great Hall.

Wulfric waited until everyone was in the Hall, then hurried to a spot behind it where the wall was thin. He pressed his ear against the wall when he got there, and was able to recognise his father's voice.

'If we can't find them on any of the roads or trails, it stands to reason that they're still in Rasbruck.'

'The scouts only covered half the distance. Not spotting anyone doesn't mean they're not marching toward us.'

Wulfric did not recognise that voice, it was most likely one of the older warriors on the council.

'True,' Wolfram said. 'Making any decision now is a risk, but we have to do so. They're preparing to attack us. Aethelman trusts the information he got, and I trust Aethelman. We all do. If we attack now and they're still gathering in Rasbruck, we can catch them by surprise and scatter them. If they are on the way here, they'll still be too far off to expect attack. If we move fast, we can surprise them. Either way, I think we should attack. Now.'

There was some murmuring and more subdued discussion for a few moments. Wulfric strained to hear, but couldn't make out anything to indicate what the council's sentiment was.

'A vote then.'

Wulfric recognised the voice as Belgar's.

'All in agreement with the First Warrior?' Belgar said.

There was a resounding chorus of assent. Leondorf would ride to war.

❃

The members of the council filed out of the Great Hall and Belgar made the announcement. Peace with Rasbruck had lasted far longer than anyone could believe. While no one was surprised, it meant that the warriors would be riding out to battle and that some of them would not be returning. To have a loved one die honourably was far better than to have them come home a coward.

Armour needed last-minute repairs, blades required a final sharpening, and arrows had to be re-fletched. Despite the late hour, the craftsmen all hurried back to their workshops to prepare for the impatient warriors who'd be knocking on their doors.

While the craftsmen and their families prepared for the rush, the warrior families tended to become reticent, quietly returning to their homes to help the warriors prepare for their departure. Wulfric's mother was no different. He watched Frena drop her head slightly when the news was announced, before turning and making her way back to their house. It was the same for her every time, and Wulfric knew there was no way to comfort her. She'd pack travelling rations for Wolfram while he was readying his horse and giving his equipment a final check. Wulfric would do his best to stay out of the way as he always did. With the added frustration that he was not going along.

He watched his father prepare everything, curious about how he readied himself for war, until everything was packed and there was nothing to do but wait. During those hours, with everything done, Wolfram always preferred to be left alone, trying to doze in his chair beside the fire.

Wulfric knew he wasn't going to be able to sleep, and part of him feared that if he did he would miss their departure. He took a bearskin cloak to fend off the night-time chill and went back out to wander around the village in search of a distraction.

Even at that late hour, the village's activity continued unabated. The air was filled with the ringing sounds of the smith's hammer. Wulfric had nowhere in particular to go, so he walked around, looking out for anyone that he knew in the hope of a moment or two of idle chatter, but anyone still out of doors was busy.

While the village was always tense before the warriors left, this was the worst Wulfric had known. The fact that the Rasbruckers had many additional warriors from the surrounding villages bothered everyone. Usually, it was not difficult to estimate how many men they would bring to battle. Now it was a complete unknown. No one could even guess how many men they would have, or of what quality they would be. Anyone could put on some armour, strap a sword to their waist and say they were a warrior, but as Wulfric knew only too well, it took years of training to truly earn the title.

Svana was walking with some friends on the other side of the square. When she saw him she smiled, but did not move toward him. Since Adalhaid left, the general assumption seemed to be that there was no doubt as to Wulfric and Svana's future together. Their betrothal would happen at some point before his pilgrimage, their marriage not long after he returned from it. It seemed inevitable.

The assumption carried with it certain requirements of propriety, for which Wulfric was grateful. It required that they not spend any time together without an appropriate chaperone, which suited Wulfric perfectly. There were some advantages to formal courting—he was able to avoid her for most of the time without causing offence. The drawback was that, if anything, it seemed to make her keener. At times he felt as though she looked at him the way a butcher looked at a pig being fattened for the slaughter.

❋

Wolfram paced through the village, his temper as great as his sense of impatience. There was little time for anything other than dealing with the crisis. That didn't mean that Wolfram intended to let Donato off the hook. One way or the other, he had brought about this threat. There was no way to prove he knew the cattle to be stolen, or had a hand in their theft, but he should have known better. Why would he have dealings with Rasbrucker scum?

He stopped outside Donato's house, and paused for a moment, wondering if it was the appropriate time to broach the issue. The prospect that he might not have another opportunity decided it for him. Donato opened the door and was unable to mask his surprise at seeing the First Warrior standing there.

Wolfram grabbed him by the scruff of the neck and dragged him struggling and squawking out onto his porch. He leaned down to Donato's face, snarling.

'Don't think that I do not know what you did,' Wolfram said.

'I… I have no idea what you're talking about,' Donato said.

'Of course you do, worm. When I get back, we'll get to the bottom of it all, and you'll answer for it. Mark my words.'

'I, I—' Donato spluttered, but he was cut off by a savage backhand from Wolfram, who dropped him to the wooden floor.

Wolfram looked back to the doorway. Donato's one-eyed son stood there, watching. Wolfram spat and stormed away.

❊

The warriors of Leondorf assembled in front of the Great Hall when the sky began to brighten, sitting atop their war horses. They always rode out in full battle array, magnificent in three-quarter plate armour that covered them from head to knee, with weapons at the ready, even though it could be two days or more before they actually did any fighting. With the forests so thick, one could never be certain of the enemy's position, so caution was taken from the moment they left the safety of the village's palisade. Wulfric felt his heart race as he watched, the thrill of the prospect of being one of them tinged with the disappointment of not yet being so.

Their armour had always fascinated him. Hundreds of hours went into making each warrior's suit; dozens of finely shaped plates tailored to the wearer's body, that would move smoothly over one another so as not to restrict movement. They ranged from the elaborately decorated to the austere. His father's armour was well worn, well used, and well maintained, but his was one of the plainest suits. His helmet was the only concession he made to embellishment. It was rounded and enclosed his head completely, with two oval slits for his eyes and some smaller holes around his mouth to allow him breath. The faceplate was engraved and shaped into a nose, mouth, and stylised beard. The mouth was snarling and fierce; the helmet had terrified Wulfric when he was a child.

The more established warriors that had won fame in battle had similarly decorated helmets. Angest had a helmet modelled on a ravening belek, said to be a terrifyingly accurate likeness, although Wulfric had never yet seen a live one. Others had chosen creatures both real and legendary, and the village's smiths had created stylised helms for them, intended to identify the wearer and declaim their prowess in battle.

Final farewells were said, as riders reached down to hug their loved ones, and then they were off. The square was the only part of the village that was cobbled, and so many horses made a great clattering noise until they reached the edge and passed onto earthen road. Everyone stood in silence and watched them go, no one leaving until no trace of them could be seen. No one liked seeing members of their family ride away to battle, but knowing that there were brave men ready to fight to protect the village was a great source of pride. There was a great victory waiting to be won, and great tales of heroism soon to be told.

CHAPTER TWENTY-TWO

WULFRIC WOKE TO the sound of a wailing woman. Two days had passed since the warriors rode out, so it was possible they had returned, with casualties by the sound of it. He climbed out of bed, pulled on some clothes and went to the window, squinting into the sunlight after the darkness of his bedroom. A lone rider was trotting slowly through the village square as though he was not sure where he was. He was a terrifying sight. His hair was matted and caked with gore, his armour was filthy, and his skin was liberally streaked with wounds and dried blood. Wulfric couldn't recognise him.

He went outside for a closer look. The wail seemed to have woken the entire village; other people were emerging from their homes to see what was going on. Wulfric rubbed the sleep from his eyes and squinted at the bloodied mess of a person who had come back to the village.

It was Gondomar, one of the young warriors who had set off on his pilgrimage to Jorundyr's Rock on the same day Wulfric began his training. This was his first proper battle. He looked little like he had the day he rode out with the other warriors. From the injuries he had suffered, it wasn't likely he would ever resemble the favourite with the village's young women that he had been. He was hurried into the Great Hall by the few members of the council who were too old to go into battle, against Aethelman's protestations.

Wulfric was so shocked by Gondomar's appearance, he momentarily forgot about his father. Wolfram had led nearly one hundred men out from the village and only Gondomar had returned. What had happened to his father? What had happened to the rest of them?

Wulfric started toward the spot at the back of the Great Hall, but stopped. He did not want to hear what was being said inside. He waited until Belgar exited, delaying what he was afraid to hear for as long as he could.

'There was a battle on the road to Rasbruck,' Belgar said.

There was complete silence, as more and more people arrived in the square to hear the news.

'Our warriors were ambushed by a much larger force. Gondomar tells me that there are other survivors, and they will be returning slowly behind him. He could not say who, or how many. There have been heavy casualties, however, so you should all prepare yourselves. I will tell you anything more that I learn from him. There will be wounded among those that return, some badly. They will require help as soon as they arrive.' The news relayed, Belgar returned inside.

Sound returned to the square—a cacophony of murmurs; concerned, fearful, hopeful. Wulfric stood in a stupor. Belgar had not said defeat, but the tone of his voice had done that for him. How could men, indestructible men, like his father, Angest, Eldric and the others have been beaten?

He saw his mother in the crowd, her face as white as fresh snow. Wulfric took her by the arm and led her back home, where they would have to wait for more news.

❄

The survivors arrived later that afternoon, so worn and beaten looking that Gondomar had looked fresh and rested by comparison. There were only a dozen of them, all wounded, most two to a horse. Wulfric ran down to the square when he heard of their arrival. He saw Angest and Eldric sharing a horse, both slumped on the saddle and looking as though they needed one another's support to remain upright. He scanned the other bloodied and swollen faces for his father's. It was not among them.

He felt dizzy as he tried to make sense of what he was seeing. His father was such a powerful, indomitable man. How could he possibly have fallen in battle? It *wasn't* possible. As he stood there, looking from one face to the next, unable to believe that Wolfram wasn't there, he saw Belgar standing on the Great Hall's steps and looking about in consternation. He spotted Wulfric and walked over.

'I know it's not the easiest time, lad, but we'll need to go out and bring the others home. I'll need your help. Round up some of the other apprentices. We should leave as soon as we can.'

'There're no more coming?' Wulfric said. He already knew the answer, and he felt childish and ashamed for asking the question.

Belgar shook his head. 'No one else is coming. The Rasbruckers got it just as bad. The Beleks' Bane said there were twice as many of them; lots of seasoned warriors that he'd never seen before. Not so many of them now though, not that it makes things any better.'

'Will Angest live?'

Belgar chewed his lip. 'I don't know. He's a stubborn bastard, but that's the only thing that's kept him going this long. He's in a bad way.'

'I'll go and get the others,' Wulfric said.

'I'll be waiting in the square. Tell them to bring their own horses. That's all they'll need.' He gave Wulfric a nod and headed back the way he had come.

※

There were three large ox-wagons waiting in the square when Wulfric got back with the other apprentices. The oxen were heavy, squat animals with shaggy dark fur, more biddable than red-coated cattle. Wulfric felt like vomiting, but knew he had to maintain face in front of the others.

All he could do to settle his stomach was to try not to think about the task ahead. Every time he allowed his mind to drift to it, he felt torn between vomiting and weeping. He stared into the distance as the wagons bounced along the road north but could find no distraction—numbness was the best he could hope for. The fat, frightened boy within him threatened to take control; he wanted to retreat from the harsh reality he faced, to pretend that it had not happened in the hope that it would all go away. The pillars upon which his life was built had been knocked down, and he felt as though he would fall with them.

Night fell, but they did not stop. No one wanted to delay their task by a single moment. They travelled in silence, the solemnity robbing them all of their tongues. It was after daybreak when they finally came upon the scene of the battle. They were all armed, prepared for trouble, but there was no sign of the enemy.

Wulfric had never seen a battlefield before. He felt his stomach twist at the smell. The bodies hadn't lain there long, but already the air was filled with the stench of rot and butchery. He saw Roal go pale and retch. Wulfric determined not to follow suit. He had hoped that they would find someone alive when they got there, perhaps even his father. Disappointment hit him like a kick to the stomach, as it was obvious no one remained alive there. The only sound and movement came from the crows that swarmed around the corpses. They scattered in angry, cawing flocks when Wulfric approached the bodies.

He jumped from his horse and wandered forward into the carnage, bodies heaped on the road and all around it. Horses too. One of the old warriors who had come with them shouted at him to be careful, something about belek being attracted to the scent of death, but Wulfric ignored him. He had to find his father.

The stink of it all was overpowering. It felt like passing by the midden heap after his nose had been bloodied when he was a child; not a recent memory, but one still strongly fixed in his memory. Blood and shit and vomit. No heroes, or glorious last stands, just men that he had seen laughing and joking a few days before who were now frozen in their death poses; maimed, gouged, slashed. Barely recognisable even to those that loved them. He heard someone else behind him throwing up.

It looked as though they had met the force of Rasbruckers on the road, but had then been attacked on both sides from the forest. There were a large number of Rasbrucker bodies strewn about the place, meaning they had not the strength or manpower after the battle to bring them home. There were a great many of them, far more than the Leondorfers. That was strangely satisfying. If whoever came out to collect them arrived while Wulfric and the others were there, things would be interesting. He couldn't think of anything he wanted more than to kill a Rasbrucker. To kill a hundred Rasbruckers.

The first body he recognised was Adalhaid's father. He knew the man well, and it was only the familiarity that allowed him to see past the blood and wounds. His body was twisted, skin waxy, bloodied, muddied. Lancemen usually didn't fight, except as a last resort. That he was surrounded by the bodies of armoured Rasbruckers was a credit to him.

Wulfric wondered who would break the news to Adalhaid. It pained him that he would not be there to comfort her when she found out.

He continued making his way among the bodies, feeling bad for ignoring those he recognised while he searched for his father. Eventually he found the face that he had made the long trip to find. There was a pile of bodies around him, and his sword was caked with dry blood. It was a good death for a warrior, one that his father would have been proud of. In that moment Wulfric could not help but think life as a coward was better than no life at all, and it shamed him. His father would not have wanted that.

He continued to look down at the body, unable to will himself to move. Wulfric's mind raced with all the questions he wanted to ask his father, the things he always thought there would be more time for. His father's eyes were wide open and glassy, staring up at the sky. Wulfric expected him to frown, or smile, or wink. Something, anything, but there was nothing. He had been so strong, so vibrant, so full of life, and now there was only this left of him, more statue than man. Wulfric felt as though his chest was being squeezed, and his eyes filled with water. It wasn't manly or warrior-like, and he felt ashamed, but he could not stop himself. It was all that he could do to keep breathing, one heavy lungful at a time.

Belgar placed a hand on his shoulder. 'Every man's eyes get wet when he sees something like this. There's no shame in it. We'll clean him up and bring him home.'

CHAPTER TWENTY-THREE

'I RECKON HE BROUGHT the bad luck with him,' Farlof said. His sense of humour seemed to have deserted him since the battle.

Hane grunted in agreement, but Wulfric remained silent. He watched Rodulf walk from his house toward their shop on the square. He had only been back a week, but in that time the village had experienced its worst ever disaster. Perhaps there was something to what Farlof said. Rodulf's gaze fell on Wulfric for a moment, and Wulfric could tell that whatever there was between them was far from finished, even though it had been two years since they had seen one another. Wulfric doubted it would ever be finished. Hate burned longer and brighter than anything else.

'Doesn't look like the southerners were able to grow his eye back,' Roal said. 'What was he doing down south anyway? The tradesman's version of Jorundyr's Path?'

'If he did, it must be called "Rodent's Path",' Farlof said, but the attempt at humour was strained, his voice lacking its usual enthusiasm for mischief.

Taking Jorundyr's Path, a warrior's adventure to a distant land, was a tempting thought at that time. Part of Wulfric wanted to run away from it all in the hope that distance would make it untrue, but they were the ridiculous thoughts of a frightened child and he felt shamed by them.

There was a muted chuckle, but no one was in the mood to laugh and the joke wasn't particularly funny. Grief blanketed Leondorf like the first snow that had fallen in the days after the battle. In one fell swoop, the entire warrior class had been all but wiped out. Of those who had managed to make it home, half had succumbed to their wounds. The rest would never be the same and none would wield a sword again. Gondomar had pushed his already injured body so hard to bring back word of what happened, the new priest, Belarman, said that it was unlikely he would ever walk again. Aethelman had stayed on in order to help treat the wounded, but the fact gave Wulfric little comfort.

While everyone else in the village came to terms with the disaster, it occurred to Wulfric that he was as close a thing to a warrior as there was in the village, even though he had not completed his pilgrimage. If there was to be an attack on the village, Wulfric and the other apprentices were all that stood against it.

With no warriors capable of taking up arms to defend the village, they were in a precarious position. Even if Rasbruck had broken themselves in the battle as Leondorf had, there were other villages that would be happy to take advantage and swallow up some of Leondorf's territory. There was much to lose; prime hunting lands, pasture lands, cattle, all of which would hurt them over the winter. They needed men to defend what was theirs, and to Wulfric, that only meant one thing. The council would be sending some of the apprentices on their pilgrimages soon, and he might well be one of those going. The thought excited and terrified him at the same time. He was supposed to have another two years to train and prepare for it, but a village without warriors was a village with nothing.

❈

Aethelman sat down on his cot and stretched his aching back. He had not managed more than a couple of hours of sleep at a time since the wounded had returned to the village. Even with the presence of the new priest, Belarman, who was proving himself to be an excellent healer, the demands on him were greater than anything he had ever experienced. As if the lack of sleep was not enough, the act of healing placed great stresses on his body.

His gaze settled on the box containing the Stone. It called out to him every time he was near to it, accusing him of neglecting his duty, but once again the gods had intervened. He had been all set to go, to seek out a way to destroy it, but now he could not. He couldn't leave the village when they were going through such dire straits. Even with Belarman there. It seemed there was always an excuse, though. Always a good reason to put off what he suspected would be the greatest test of his life. Why did the gods insist on confusing him so?

❊

Training was cancelled, leaving Wulfric to dwell on what had happened. He would rather have had the distraction of being ordered about and shouted at, but there was no one to do it. The remnants of the village council spent hour after hour locked inside the Great Hall, with Belgar taking charge. Wulfric sat behind it, listening to the discussions within, waiting to hear something that would affect him.

Belgar and a few of the older, retired warriors were all that remained of the council. Considering the crisis the village faced, many others had demanded to have their voices heard. Everyone was afraid. Merchants and craftsmen were invited into the Hall, a first for the village. If they were to survive the winter ahead, everyone would have to pull together. Wulfric supposed it was only fair that they had their say, considering the extra work that would be required of them. It was likely that some of their families would be elevated to the warrior aristocracy, their children plucked from their trade apprentices and set on the path to becoming warriors. It was clear that much would have to change if they were to survive.

With all of the hours spent eavesdropping behind the Great Hall over the years, Wulfric had grown to recognise the voices of all the council members. Now, however, there were only one or two that he could identify. Belgar had generated a feeling of unity and solidarity in the village by allowing the others in, the only positive sentiment in Leondorf. He was doing everything he could to make everyone believe they could survive if they worked together, but Wulfric wondered if it was a futile effort. Seeing Donato going into the Great Hall before the meeting was difficult for Wulfric to accept. Would Rodulf be next?

Wulfric was most curious about what Donato had to say. He had long resented warriors, and would no doubt have been overjoyed by them being wiped out were it not for the threat that posed to his livelihood. He was certainly far from grateful for the sacrifice, and was probably unaware that anyone suspected it was his duplicity that gave the Rasbruckers reason to attack. Wulfric wondered if he should say something, but did not know enough to start making accusations.

The discussion was focussed on how to best defend the village, things

Wulfric thought beyond the expertise of most of the men in the Hall. He shuffled forward and pressed his ear harder against the wall.

'We can't make young men warriors just by calling them that. We can't send them into battle without them having made the pilgrimage.' The voice was Belgar's.

'Why not?' Donato's voice? Wulfric wasn't sure.

There was a loud sigh. 'Only those who've made the journey will be able to find Jorundyr's favour on the battlefield. Not having it means death and defeat, which means we might as well have no warriors at all.' Belgar's voice again, laden with frustration.

'Rubbish. A few days' ride south and hardly anyone has even heard of Jorundyr, or any of the other gods. Those who *have* heard of them call them the old gods. No one there has suffered from forgetting them for centuries.'

'The gods might not hold sway for the southerners, but they do for us, one way or another. If a man believes he can win, often enough he will. And anyone facing down an army of boys who haven't done the journey will be convinced that he will win. We might as well kill them ourselves.'

'Fine then. Send them on the bloody journey. Send the whole lot of them.' Definitely Donato.

'None of them are ready. If we send them now, half will come back. Maybe. Probably less.'

'Better half than none, don't you think?'

'Don't you think we've lost enough?' Belgar said.

'We'll lose everything if we don't have men to defend the village.'

'The journey is too difficult. Saying half will come back is optimistic.' A third voice, one of the old council members.

'There's another option,' Donato said. 'I have friends in the South—'

'That's not an option,' Belgar said, cutting off the voice.

'We need armed men to defend this village, its lands, and its herds,' Donato said. 'If sending the apprentices early is the only option we have, then we must take it.'

There was silence for a long while.

'Fine,' Belgar said. 'We'll send them. They're not ready, but we'll send them. It'll have to be soon though, before the weather gets any worse. And we'll have to answer to the gods for each one that doesn't come back.'

✿

Donato was elated as he walked out of the Great Hall. He had never been inside before that day, and now he had spoken there, and been listened to. The experience opened a world of possibility. He stopped and looked back at the Great Hall. Within a moment of stepping inside, the thought of retiring to a life of luxury in the south had lost most of its lustre. He had seen what it meant to have power over other men, and he wanted more of it. He would be a rich outsider in the south, accommodated but never allowed into the halls of power. He realised he would always be viewed with the hint of disdain reserved for northern savages. It was not a bad place to be, and money counted for a great deal, but here in the north, he realised he could be far more. Wealth he could earn, luxury he could bring to himself. Real power he would not find anywhere else.

A new generation of warriors would be looking to take their seats on the village council in a decade or so, and they would push him back out onto the fringes. To ensure long-lasting power, he had to make sure that the source of the village's safety resided with him, not the warriors.

Donato did not like having blood on his hands. Having the apprentices sent on their pilgrimage early was as close as he'd get to it, but he could rest easy in the thought that they would be going anyway and if they were good enough they would survive. Those who didn't were weak, and the failure was theirs. No responsibility lay with him.

When only a handful of them returned, even the most arrogant of the old farts on the council would have to agree that they did not have enough warriors to defend what was theirs. Then he could make himself the saviour by using his wealth and southern contacts. He would bring the southern soldiers to Leondorf. He would make sure he was the one to negotiate the deal, and that he could keep control. Then, he would set himself up as a great lord of the Northlands. He had thought all was lost when the reavers were caught and killed. It still chilled him when he thought of the expression on Captain Morlyn's face as his disembodied head dangled from Wolfram's saddle. He had been convinced that terrible consequences would land on his doorstep, all the more so after Wolfram had called at his door. However, it seemed that matters could not have worked out better for him if he had planned it.

❈

Wulfric rushed to tell the other apprentices. It was exciting and terrifying, but it was the goal they had all worked so hard for. He headed for Hane's house first with a spring in his step. His excitement had blinded him to the reality, but as he reached up to knock on Hane's door it hit him.

Nearly half of those who went on their pilgrimage died. Half of those who were properly prepared. He was supposed to have two more years of training before attempting it. What hope could he have when so many of them had failed? Particularly when it was usually undertaken in autumn when the weather was settled. It was winter, and the weather was likely to get worse as each day passed, making a difficult journey a deadly one.

As he brooded over the idea, he became less and less excited by it. Downright nauseous. He turned and went home without knocking, not uttering a word of what he heard to anyone. He felt the absence of his father more keenly than at any point in the days since his death. He wanted so desperately to talk to him about this. He tried to think of what his father's advice would be, and realised that it would be the same as it always was. Ignore his fear. Do his best.

❈

Ritschl's head throbbed with frustration. The Leondorfers had been outnumbered two to one at least. He had made sure that every surrounding village knew of what had happened, and they had all contributed warriors. Yet the Leondorfers had managed to fight them to a standstill. The warriors who returned said Leondorf got the worst of it, that they had no more than a handful of men left alive by the end, but Rasbruck's position was not much better. Once the others had returned home, Rasbruck had little strength left to wield. The council questioned if it was all worth it, if the loss had been too great, but Ritschl didn't care about that. All he wanted was the Stone, and he feared that his best chance had been taken from him. He had thought he would be free to pick through the ruins of Leondorf at his leisure. Now he was back to where he started.

CHAPTER TWENTY-FOUR

THE EVENING OF the council meeting, Belgar came out onto the steps of the Great Hall to inform the village of the decisions that had been made. He looked uncomfortable, but Wulfric could not help but feel conspiratorial glee in already knowing what was going to be said. It was also a comfort to have had the chance to absorb the upcoming news ahead of time. After the initial excitement, the worry of what lay ahead had hit him like a hammer, and it was not a reaction he wanted others to see.

'We have decided to send those apprentices who feel ready on their pilgrimage,' Belgar said.

His voice sounded strong, but Wulfric could tell by the way his eyes moved about the gathered crowd that he was concerned about the reaction. There was silence at first, then a murmur developed.

'They're boys,' someone shouted. 'You're sending them to their deaths.'

A great number of voices sounded in agreement.

Belgar held up his hands. 'Some of the apprentices are at an advanced stage of their training, and we're not going to force those who are clearly unready. We need anointed warriors. Jorundyr will never favour warriors who haven't completed their pilgrimage. If we don't send them now, we'll only be delaying the inevitable when they have to defend the village and our lands come spring.'

Wulfric thought his words made sense, and it was obvious that Belgar had prepared the answer. He had known that the decision would not be popular.

'As you all know, the harvest has been poor. Well, we won't be the only ones to have a poor harvest. If ours was bad, chances are all the surrounding villages will have had bad ones too. If they're short on food, what do you think they'll do?' He paused for a moment, but no one spoke. 'They'll go straight to the easiest place to get food. A village with no warriors to defend it. Us.

'The truth of it is, we might not even have until spring before the reavers come. They might already be on their way. I know this isn't a popular choice, and I'm not happy about it either, but we can't hold on to what's ours with cripples and old men. If we want to survive and prosper, we'll have to work together, and we'll have to make choices we won't like.'

Wulfric had thought the other apprentices would greet the announcement with excited bravado, initially at least. However, the speech felt like a collective kick in the gut to everyone standing there. They all knew the harsh truth that Belgar had laid before them, but to hear it spoken aloud was devastating. Life was not an adventure anymore. It was a struggle for survival.

※

Donato made regular trips south, often at short notice, so making another drew no attention. His visits to Elzburg usually followed a set formula: meetings with his trade contacts, a stop at one of the city's finest brothels, and several excellent meals. This time was different. Donato had never been in the Markgraf's palace before. It was quickly becoming a week of firsts for him.

He felt a flutter of nerves as he sat in an anteroom waiting for his meeting with one of the Markgraf's officials. What he intended to propose would be called treason by some. Belgar would spit him on a spear if he got the slightest inkling of what Donato was up to. In the fullness of time, he knew that he would be considered a saviour. By then it wouldn't particularly matter, however. His power would be absolute, and opinion would be of little concern.

His meeting might be premature, but he wanted to have the groundwork laid for when the apprentices went on their pilgrimages. There was little time to waste. The first snow had come early, meaning winter was not far off and would be a bad one when it arrived. In a matter of weeks, the roads would be all but impassable, and who knew what the state of affairs would be the following spring.

Southern soldiers would guarantee the village's safety, but allowing the Ruripathians to extend their influence north of the marches was unacceptable to most Northlanders, fools that they were. If they had even a taste of what was on offer south of the border, he knew they would change their minds quickly enough. As it was, the hundreds of years the Northlander villages had resisted southern influence was seen as a source of pride. The Imperials had crossed the great river a number of times, but were always beaten back by the dense forests and Northland warriors. The epics were widely populated with tales of those old battles. Donato reckoned the people would come around to the idea, however, once they realised the alternative was death.

The Ruripathians greedily eyed the resources north of the river, but for the most part seemed content to trade for them. On the few times they had tried to cross the river, they had met the same fate as their Imperial forebears. Donato knew what he offered would tempt them—a foothold north of the river, and access to all of those untapped resources. He needed to be careful, though. The southerners were duplicitous and he needed to put his offer over in a way that ensured he got everything he wanted. Baron of Leondorf had a nice ring to it, or Lord of the Northern Marches. There were many titles, and Donato was not fussy, so long as it made him the master of Leondorf and its lands and would be inherited by his son and all of those who came after. He was happy to abide by the southern laws and bend his knee to whoever he had to. The villagers would have no choice but to do likewise. Not if they wished to survive.

❃

Wulfric looked around him, glad to see faces as nervous as he felt. The kirk was small, and with all of the apprentices gathered there, cramped. He was squeezed between Hane and Anshel and his discomfort added to his nerves. Aethelman preferred to conduct religious services out of doors, under the eyes of the gods when the weather allowed. However, the secrets of the pilgrimage were only for the ears of those who were preparing to embark on it. The dim room was as full of nervous energy as it was with bodies.

When Aethelman began to speak, Wulfric and the others fell silent.

'In an ideal world,' he said, 'we would not be having this conversation for a few years yet. Tonight will be your vigil and tomorrow morning you will attempt to lift the sword. Those who succeed will leave immediately. Ordinarily we would spend more time discussing the vigil and how you should conduct yourselves, but after all that has happened I want you to go home, fill your bellies, and do your best to get some sleep. They are the most important things for you right now. Pure of mind, pure of heart, pure of spirit. Those are the sentiments with which you should conduct yourself until the morrow. I think they are self-explanatory. Jorundyr is watching.

'Before you go home, there is a short blessing ceremony to go through, but it won't take long. Everyone, please close your eyes.'

Aethelman continued to speak, but Wulfric could no longer understand what he was saying. He squeezed his eyes tightly shut, not wanting to do anything that might jeopardise the process. He listened to the words, as Aethelman enunciated each one slowly and deliberately. Wulfric started to feel light headed and nauseous, and he became worried that he might throw up, making himself look frightened of what lay ahead in front of the others. He was instantly reminded of the time he'd touched the odd-looking rock in Aethelman's room at the back of the kirk. He felt as though the room was spinning around him. Aethelman stopped speaking, and it all disappeared as quickly as it had started as soon as he did, leaving Wulfric feeling perfectly normal.

'You may open your eyes,' Aethelman said. 'I shall see you all in the morning.'

Wulfric looked around. It was impossible to tell if anyone else had experienced what he had, and he was too afraid of the potential consequences if he spoke up. He kept his mouth shut and filed out after everyone else, trying to push any worries from his head.

❊

Wulfric looked out of the window and sighed with frustration that it was only starting to get dark. The pilgrimage was usually undertaken in autumn, but it was now well into winter. There would be no more fine days, only steadily worsening weather. He wondered how much more difficult the journey would be at that time of year. There was always snow in the High Places, and it was always cold, so perhaps it would not be all that different.

He was grateful at least that there had been no recurrence of the nausea, and he had too many things to think about to give it much concern.

He wondered what waited for them in the High Places. There were things that he could predict, from the living—belek and wolves—to the inanimate—falls and the cold, but the High Places were remote and mystical, home to gods and spirits. What else might lurk there? Draugar? Dragons?

He reckoned he would go out of his mind with hours more like that. There was no chance of him getting any rest that night. He closed his eyes and tried to think of warrior-like things; bravery, courage, honour. The pilgrimage was intended to be a demonstration of these qualities. They undertook it alone. To ask for help or require it was to fail. Better to die in the High Places than seek succour and shame Jorundyr. It seemed silly to Wulfric. The strength of the group was greater than that of the individual—he suspected that together they could all survive the pilgrimage—but his father had told him that a chain was only as strong as its weakest link. The pilgrimage proved that each link was strong, that a warrior in battle could count on the man to each side of him without a shadow of doubt.

He wished Adalhaid were there with him. She was the only one who could bring him comfort at times like this, and it brought home how terribly he missed her. It was a foolish thought, however. Even had she been in the village, he would not have been allowed to spend his vigil with her. The thought of trying to share his worries, or simply find comfort with Svana sent a shiver down his spine. He lay back on his bed and started to twiddle his thumbs. It seemed as good a way as any to spend a sleepless night.

✳

Wulfric was sitting on the edge of his bed, ready to go, by the time it grew bright outside. He quickly checked through his things one last time before fastening his pack shut. He strapped his sabre to his waist and looked over his clothing. Everything had been checked, double checked, and rechecked at that point. It was time to go. His mother was still sleeping. He thought of waking her, but decided against it—he couldn't face saying goodbye. With no further reason to delay, he headed for the glade.

Aethelman was alone by the stone at the glade's centre when Wulfric arrived. It felt odd that Eldric and Angest were not there. Perhaps they watched from Jorundyr's Hall. One by one, the others arrived, none of them carrying on with their usual banter. There were no warriors in the glade that morning, only frightened boys. Everyone watched Aethelman in silence, their breath misting on the cold air, as they waited for him to call them forward to attempt to lift the sword. Most years, one or two hopeful apprentices returned to the village after the attempt, a forlorn look on their faces and the prospect of another year of apprenticeship weighing on them. Wulfric wondered how many Jorundyr would turn away this year—or if Jorundyr had a hand in it at all. He remembered the smile on Aethelman's face that handful of years previously when he and Hane had started their training, and Hane had stepped forward to try lifting it. The sword had not budged that day. Wulfric wondered what was going through Hane's head; if he worried that the result might be the same?

Aethelman reverently placed the ancient sword down on the snow. Its steel was dark with a blue lustre—almost a glow. It was Godsteel, made from the ore found up in the High Places, its hilt decorated with the clear stones that were found with the ore. When the light hit them the right way, they too had a light blue tinge.

'This sword was forged in the days when Jorundyr still walked this land, with his faithful wolf, Ulfyr, at his side. It has seen countless battles, and sent thousands of warriors to Jorundyr's Hall, but has long since served as the gatekeeper for this right of passage. Only those with the strength of body and soul to lift it from the ground may go forward and measure themselves against Jorundyr's challenge. Deep in the High Places there is a rock, not unlike the one beside me now. You will journey there, and place your hand on it. Once you have done this, and shown your devotion to the ideals Jorundyr set down for all men who bear arms, you will have proven yourselves to him. You will have earned the right to call yourself warrior—Disciple of Jorundyr—and will enjoy all the rights and privileges that brings with it.

'I wish there was more time to prepare you all, but it is a time of great need, and we must count on Jorundyr's beneficence in providing us with what we need. He favours the brave, and by setting forth on this journey you show him that you are that and more.'

'How will we find the rock?' Hane blurted out.

Wulfric had been wondering the same thing, but had been too afraid of speaking out.

'If you can lift the sword, you will know the way. Have faith that you will. Is there anything else?'

'How will we know that we've done it properly?' Hane said.

Aethelman smiled. 'You'll know. And when you return, I will too. It is on your honour to complete this journey with fidelity. To lie about reaching the Rock is a grave sin, and one that I will be able to spot immediately. Now, Anshel, you are first among your peers, and have the honour of trying first.'

Anshel nodded and stepped forward. He looked at each apprentice as he walked to the sword. Everyone was silent; the crunch of his boots on the snow was the only sound. He reached down with his right hand and took a firm grip. Wulfric glanced at Aethelman, whose attention was entirely on Anshel and the sword.

Anshel pulled and stood straight. He wobbled, caught off balance, surprised by how easily it lifted. He hefted it in his hand and looked back at the others, a broad smile on his face.

'It hardly weighs a thing,' he said.

Urrich was next, the quiet, clean-shaven apprentice whose family lived in the woodlands outside the village. His unsurpassed skill with the bow gave him his precedence. Wulfric had seen him shoot a half-dozen game birds from the sky in a row without a miss. Even the warriors had acknowledged him as the finest shot in the village a few years earlier. His skill had only grown with time.

He too lifted the old sword with ease. He nodded before handing it back to Aethelman, who returned it to the snow before beckoning Wulfric forward. Wulfric walked to the sword. His skin crawled with the sensation that every eye was on him. What a fool he would look if he could not lift it. He could not decide what frightened him more, the idea of not being able to lift it or what would come after if he managed it.

He reached down and took it by the handle. It was freezing cold, and felt as though it tingled against his skin. He gripped the roughly shaped handle as best he could and lifted. It came away from the ground as easily as it had for the others. He held the ancient blade for a moment. It no longer felt cold, nor the handle misshapen, far from it. He wondered if he had been mistaken a moment before, simply nervous. Now it felt as though it had been made for him. He looked at Aethelman, who smiled and nodded. Wulfric handed it to him, and was struck with the realisation that in a few minutes he would be leaving on his pilgrimage.

❋

Every apprentice succeeded in lifting the sword. Things moved quickly from that point, and Wulfric felt as if he could barely keep up. His heart raced as he tried to look as though he knew what he was doing, and was fully prepared for what was to come. They took up their packs and filed out of the glade.

The entire population of the village had gathered on the square. Having that much attention focussed on him at a time when he would rather be left alone with his thoughts was difficult, but that day was as much for the other villagers as it was for the apprentices. All Leondorf's hopes were pinned on having another half dozen warriors before spring, and the reavers, came. Wulfric wondered what difference they would really make. Perhaps as a source of common hope it was enough in itself. Wulfric worried that might be all they had to offer.

His mother was in the crowd, a proud but worried look on her face.

'I'll see you in a few days,' Wulfric said, doing his best to smile.

'You take care now,' Frena said.

'I'll do my best.'

'Just make sure you come home safely,' she said.

He nodded. There was nothing left to say.

'Pilgrims of Jorundyr, prepare to depart.' Aethelman's voice broke their moment of silence. Wulfric walked away to join the others, feeling his heart pull him back in the direction from which he had come.

'On your divine journey, you may neither accept nor solicit help from man or beast. You will not interact with your fellow pilgrims, nor assist them in any way. Each man must make this journey alone. If you are made from the stuff Jorundyr requires, you will return safely. You may depart.'

CHAPTER TWENTY-FIVE

WULFRIC HAD BEEN walking for nearly an hour before he realised that he had never made any decision about what direction he was going in. There didn't appear to be much to it. The High Places were hard to miss—they loomed imposingly on the eastern horizon.

He had an overwhelming sense of knowing exactly where he was going but no explanation for the fact, which was strange. It felt as though he was walking from the kirk to his home, a journey he was so familiar with it required no thought at all.

He looked around at times to see if he could spot any of the others, but once he entered the forest he could see nothing but trees. It made little difference, as he could have no interaction with anyone else even if they were walking right next to him. They would be funnelled together again when they got to the passes in the High Places. He was curious to see who reached them first, whether his footsteps would be into fresh snow, or following the trail left by others.

Wulfric's mind drifted as he walked. Once the initial rush of excitement had subsided, there was little to it—one foot in front of the other, don't fall over, don't walk into a tree. Wulfric's mind turned to the potential dangers of the journey, as it invariably did. Out there, alone, a broken ankle could be fatal—and covered in snow, the ground could be treacherous. That was not what concerned him the most, however.

Belek came down from the High Places at all times of the year, but winter was their season of choice. They were not beasts of instinct, but reasoning. They liked the cold. They were said to prowl the land alone, not enjoying the company of their brethren, but one of Angest's most famous tales was a fight against two at the same time—reputedly making him the only man to have ever survived an encounter with two, let alone to have killed them both. He tried to remind himself that encountering one was rare, but the fact that it happened at all was enough to send a shiver down his spine. One could have been stalking him at that very moment.

His father had killed a belek; he had the cloak of luxurious steel-coloured fur to show for it. Wolfram had always said a belek enjoyed the hunt as much as the kill, much like a person. Stalking a belek was not so much a hunt as a competition; both parties were there for the kill, and as often as not the belek won. They were the stuff of nightmares, and even Aethelman, initiated in the magics of the gods, spoke of them with a mixture of fear and respect.

Some who had encountered them said that the belek too were initiated in the magics of the gods, that they had the same skin tingling other-worldliness that the priests exuded when healing, or invoking the gods for ceremonies. Whatever the truth of it was, it mattered little to Wulfric. If he encountered one it would be a fight to the death.

It grew dark, but Wulfric went on until it became too dangerous to continue. He found a sheltered place, and after careful consideration decided to light a fire. It might draw a belek, but it would keep away wolves, and he felt he could use the warmth and comfort it would give—the better condition he kept himself in, the quicker he could move. He wondered if anyone else had lit one, and looked around to see if he could spot any. In the thickness of the forest, there could have been someone only a few hundred paces away and they would have been invisible; likewise, their fire. He gathered some kindling and put a spark to them, trying to forget about all the unpleasant ways to die in the forest.

❊

Wulfric woke early the next morning, after a fitful night's sleep. The fire had long since died to nothing but a warm pile of ash, and he shivered with the cold. He didn't tarry long, eating only a little before setting off for the day. The morning walk was gently uphill for the most part, with two small rivers to cross. The forest was thick and bore no signs of having been touched by the hand of man, and there was no trace of the others.

The going was far slower than he had expected and he hoped, selfishly, that it was as tough for everyone else. The last thing he wanted was to meet the others on their way home while he was still miles from Jorundyr's Rock. Surviving the journey was all that was required of them, but a rivalry had grown up over the years of training, and Wulfric had no desire to be last.

In the open pastures around the village, it was never difficult to see where he needed to go. The High Places were always visible, towering over the forests to the east, a constant landmark to get one's bearings. Now that he was in the forest, beneath the tree canopy, the peaks were often obscured. He stopped and looked back in the direction he had come. Despite not knowing where he was, he felt a strange compulsion to keep going, as though some unknown force pulled him forward. For all he knew, he could be walking around in circles, that the force drawing him on was simply a figment of his imagination. In the absence of anything better, he gave in to it.

It stood to reason that as long as he continued uphill, he was going in the correct direction and that was the way his strange compulsion was urging him. Nonetheless, he was eager to reach the tree line and get out into the open again.

His path got steeper, the snow got deeper and the air got steadily colder. The vegetation changed; broadleaf trees gave way to needle-leafed pines. As it became dark on his second night of travel the cold grew to the point that he shivered uncontrollably, but he knew it was as much from tiredness as the temperature. It was time to stop for the night.

❀

Wulfric was cold and stiff when he woke the next morning. He revived his fire and quickly heated some broth with shaking hands. He gulped it down as soon as it was hot enough to have an impact, and he could feel the warmth spread through his insides. As he sipped, he wondered how far away the tree line was, the next indicator of his progress. As soon as the broth was finished, he gathered his things and got underway.

The incline grew steeper as he went. After a few hours his thighs burned as each step felt like climbing stairs. He stopped to catch his breath and looked around. He could not see anyone, nor hear anything other than the sound of his rapid, rasping gasps. The air felt thinner, as though his lungs couldn't draw in enough to satisfy his need. It seemed like he was working far harder than he was. The tree line could not be far off, surely. From there it was nothing but rock and snow and ice until he reached Jorundyr's Rock, assuming he made it that far.

It was only now that the forest had thinned enough to see any distance that the enormity of what lay before him was revealed. He had known it was a long way, a hard climb, but presented with the High Places closer than he had ever been, he was overwhelmed. The mountain before him dominated the sky. He had to look almost directly up to follow it skyward, although the peak was hidden by cloud. He was thankful that Jorundyr's Rock was in a valley, and not at the very top.

The lonely sound of his breath was joined by a snapping branch behind him. Wulfric turned and looked around. He could see nothing, and wasn't sure if the sound had come from the forest floor or a tree. There didn't seem to be any birds moving around, but likewise there were no signs of movement on the ground. He continued to scan the forest in the direction he had come from, but everything was still. Once again, the sound of his own breath was the only thing he could hear. There were no marks in the snow other than his footprints. He realised that his grip was tight on the handle of his sword, and relaxed it. He needed to remain alert, but paranoia did nothing but distract him. If he was to survive what remained before him, he needed to focus, not jump at every unexpected sound.

He pushed on. As soon as he broke out of the tree line, he was hit by an icy wind that sent a chill through him. It was the first milestone on his journey and reaching it without any problems felt like a blessing. There were few points for reference in the expanse of snow and rock before him, and at times it was difficult to determine the pitch of the climb ahead, causing Wulfric to stumble and fall into the snow. It sapped a little more of his energy each time.

After what seemed like hours trudging through the snow, he saw a black shape farther up the mountain. At first he dismissed it as a rock, but it didn't take long to realise that it was not getting any closer, which meant it had to be moving along at about the same speed as Wulfric. There was no way for him to tell which of the other apprentices it was, but it meant that one at least was farther into the journey than Wulfric.

Wulfric stopped for a moment and watched the figure's seemingly relentless advance. If only his own determination to keep moving were so strong. There was no prize for being first, but he knew that each and every one of them harboured that ambition. He wondered what route the other apprentice had taken that allowed him to eke out this advantage.

One foot in front of the other, he told himself. That was all it took. The only benefit of it being so cold was that his feet weren't getting wet from the snow melting. When he lifted his leg, snow fell from the leather of his trouser leg like fine powder. The thick fur lining kept his legs warm and free from the pains that cold could cause. Aethelman had given them all a talk on the dangers they would encounter from the cold and the things to look out for that would give them early warning of a problem. It was not just belek that killed in the mountains.

Fingers and toes were the most at risk, Aethelman had said, as was the face if he didn't keep it covered with the flap of his hat. Wrapped up in his thick winter furs, he looked more like a bear than a man. He checked his fingers and feet quickly. Satisfied that the feeling of warmth and comfort was not imagined, he pressed on once again.

Breathing was becoming ever more difficult. No matter how hard he gasped, he could not satisfy his demand. He left the flap on his hat undone for as long as he could, until his nose, cheeks, and chin became itchy and sore from the cold. Only then did he refasten it.

Aethelman had said that from where the trees ended, it was a day to the Rock, all things being well. He had reached the tree line not long after daybreak; with luck he could be there by dawn the next day. There would be no more stopping until he got back to the trees.

CHAPTER TWENTY-SIX

WULFRIC'S HEAD THROBBED with each movement. A headache had started at some point, growing in intensity until he struggled to think about anything else. Despite slowing in pace, it seemed that he had started to close in on the person ahead of him—clearly he was suffering too. He pulled the flap away from his face and tried to suck as much air into his lungs as he could. No matter how hard he breathed, he couldn't get enough. His face felt wet. At first he thought it was the cold, but when he put his hand up to put the flap back in place his mitten came away covered in blood.

Wulfric pulled his mitten off and touched his fingers to his nose; there was a steady drip coming from it. He sniffed to try and staunch the flow, but all it did was fill his throat and mouth with the metallic tang of blood. It kept dribbling blood and Wulfric felt a twist of panic in his gut. Was this the start of what Aethelman warned them about? Death from the inside? There didn't seem to be anything that he could do about it, so he put the flap back in place, pulled his mitten on and continued on up the mountainside. If the mountain was going to kill him, it wouldn't do so before he touched the Rock.

His head was pounding and the flap was stuck to his face with dried blood when the figure ahead of him, getting closer all the time, disappeared. Wulfric felt his already over-pressed heart speed up. What had happened to him? The valley floor was made of ice deeper than the tallest tree was high. There were cracks in it, crevasses, which could be hidden by a layer of snow. Anyone, or anything, that fell in would never be seen again. Had he fallen?

He continued on and eventually night came, but it was clear and the moon bathed the snowy landscape in ghostly pale light. Wulfric pushed his way through the drifts of snow, not sure if his mind was playing tricks on him or if his path was becoming less steep. After so long struggling uphill, it almost seemed too much to hope for. It only took another few paces to confirm his suspicion. When his foot met ground at the same level as the previous one, he almost laughed aloud. He had reached the valley. He spotted the other apprentice some way ahead, still little more than a dark blot on the landscape.

The peaks stretched up on either side of the valley like great, ancient sword blades, rust replaced by snow and ice. The flat terrain made the going easier, but the snow became deeper, up to his waist in places, and wading through it drained the strength from his legs. The only sounds he could hear were the crunching of the snow beneath his boots, and the eerie sound of the wind, like a distant scream. He fought to suck down lungfuls of air. There was no stopping to rest in the valley; to tarry there was to invite death.

Thin wisps of cloud swirled around the valley like wraiths hanging in the air. He could almost believe they were the souls of fallen warriors, coming out to see the next generation of their brethren approaching Jorundyr's Hall. He found himself wondering if his father might be watching. In the twilight, the valley had an other-worldly feel about it. Might this truly be the place where the gods dwelt?

Wulfric realised that he was rapidly catching up to the shape before him. As he drew closer he saw it was Hane, slumped to his knees. For some reason Wulfric had thought it more likely to be Anshel, but Hane was the fittest and strongest of them, so it stood to reason that he had made the best time to that point. He had a strained, exhausted look on his face. It was the look of defeat. His eyes met Wulfric's, but he said nothing.

Wulfric wanted to stop, but he knew there was nothing he could do. Carrying his own weight was burden enough. Adding Hane's would see them both dead, and excluded from Jorundyr's Hall for eternity. Neither give help, nor ask for it. It seemed like a cruel rule.

Hane spluttered a mouthful of blood out onto the snow. It looked black in the moonlight. The sight of it frightened Wulfric, reminding him of how his own nose had started to bleed for no apparent reason. He checked it again, but it had stopped. The relief was fleeting, however. If the mountain could strike Hane down, the same could happen to any of them.

Something about the mountain was killing them from the inside. Aethelman had warned them about it, and Wulfric wondered if it had him in its grasp, whatever it was. He gave Hane one last look. Hane did his best to force a smile, his lips and chin splattered with blood. He knew he was spent, but he would be welcomed by Jorundyr. He would not have a place at the main table but he would be there, recognised for the courage needed to trek up into the High Places knowing that there might be nothing awaiting him but death.

He thought of the night Hane had stood next to him when Helfric and the others had planned another beating. There was nothing to be done, but that didn't make what Wulfric had to do any easier. He looked away and pressed on along the valley. As he walked, he tried not to think of Hane's family; his mother, and the younger brother who worshipped him.

❊

Dawn announced itself with a fringing of light outlining the eastern peaks. Wulfric had not seen anyone else during the night. He forged a fresh trail through the snow, and knew he was ahead of the pack. His eyes were dry, and stung. Every part of him cried out for sleep. He kept scanning the sides of the valley for anything that stood out. Finally they found something.

At first he thought he was imagining it, but the more he stared, the more distinct it became. A pale blue glow against the dark rock face. Wulfric felt a tingle run across his skin as he stared at the flickering light. He hurried toward it. As he grew closer, he could see that the glow was surrounding an object; a rock. Jorundyr's Rock.

He felt a manic sense of joy rush through him as he stumbled toward it. In only a few moments he would touch Jorundyr's Rock and his journey to be a warrior would be complete. Even if the bleeding took him to his death the instant after he had touched it, he would die a warrior, and join his father at Jorundyr's table.

The tingling on his skin grew stronger the closer to the Rock he got. There could be no mistaking it, just as he had been told. Whatever ancient magic that had guided him, it had proved true. This was Jorundyr's Rock. The place where Jorundyr communed with man, where he chose those he thought worthy of being called a warrior. It was said that Jorundyr would strike down anyone with the temerity to touch the Rock who was not worthy of the honour. Wulfric wondered if he had done enough. Surely making it that far was enough?

After dreaming for such a long time of what the Rock would look like, feel like, of reaching out and touching it, he found himself fearing it. So close to the completion of his goal, what had once been an impossible dream, he hesitated. Aethelman had said the death for those with avarice in their hearts was the most painful imaginable. Their fate after that horrific death was even worse. Jorundyr's wolf, Ulfyr, would gnaw on their bones until the end of time.

Wulfric felt his stomach twist as he stood before the Rock, and thought he was going to be sick. He fought off the sensation and tried to concentrate on it. Like the stone in the glade by the village, it was covered in strange markings. They were familiar to Wulfric, but unintelligible. The familiarity helped to still his nerves, but his hand shook uncontrollably as he reached out toward the Rock. The blue light coruscated on its surface, rippling over the carvings as though it was alive. As his hand got closer, the glow extended out toward him and enveloped his hand. His breathing quickened as it continued up his arm and covered his entire body. He felt the rough surface of the rock with his fingertips. His vision was tinged with blue and his entire body shook. There was a deafening boom and a bright flash.

❧

When Wulfric recovered his senses he was sitting on the snow, the cold starting to permeate its way through his furs and into his backside. He was several paces away from the Rock. It sat there, the blue glow flickering along its surface benignly. Was that it? He wasn't dead, which was something at least. Aethelman had said that touching the Rock was all that was needed, but Wulfric was confused. Was it supposed to respond that way? If this was where Jorundyr communed with mortal men, should there not have been something else? A conversation of some sort?

Wulfric sat there, staring at the Rock, oblivious to the cold. It was not what he had expected. He had always thought that Jorundyr would say something, confirm that the journey was complete, that he was now a warrior. A great booming voice from the heavens to acknowledge his achievement. He decided to try again. He stood and reached forward until his fingertips touched the glow. It offered resistance. It felt as though it was material rather than just light. It was spongy to the touch and created an impenetrable barrier around the rock. One way or the other, it seemed the Rock was done with him.

CHAPTER TWENTY-SEVEN

WULFRIC'S ROUTE BACK took him past the spot where he had last seen Hane. He was still on his knees in the same place. There was more blood splattered on the snow in front of him. He was dead. His eyes were still open, but glassy and lifeless. There was frozen blood around Hane's mouth and his face was twisted with distress. Wulfric stared into the lifeless eyes and wondered if he should bring Hane's body home. He noticed a cold, wet sensation on his own upper lip, and realised his nose was bleeding again. His return was not as certain as he had begun to think. Wulfric continued on his way, wondering how many other old apprentices were in that valley, long buried beneath the snow.

He saw another apprentice soon after, still on his feet and making his way up the valley. Wulfric altered his course to stay well clear, as did the other apprentice. He remembered what Aethelman had said. Jorundyr was always watching.

Despite his heavy furs, Wulfric recognised him as Anshel. He wondered what Anshel would think when he encountered Hane's body. They had all known that some of them would not return, but to see one of their number dead still came as a shock. *How many more would there be?*

Simply disappearing was the worst thing Wulfric could imagine. At least Hane's family would know what had happened to him. It was always harder on the families of those who walked up into the mountains never to be seen again. Was the journey worth it? Hane was a good fighter; strong and fast, but the mountain had killed him. Now his strength was lost to the village forever, at a time when every arm able to wield a sword was valuable beyond measure. Why had Jorundyr been so cruel? It seemed like a foolish waste.

❋

The sky started to darken long before Wulfric got out of the valley, and the snow took on a ghostly glow once more. He thought of trying to dig himself into the snow to get out of the wind and wait for dawn. As tempting as the prospect of rest was, in the cold, people went to sleep and never woke up. The danger posed by starting his descent in the dark seemed to be the lesser. He was tired, but the thought of curling up in the snow for a sleep without end gave him enough energy to keep going.

He spotted another apprentice slowly working his way up the mountain. Wulfric stifled the urge to wave, and counted himself lucky that he was on his way down. The other apprentice had a long journey ahead of him. Wulfric strained his eyes, but the apprentice was too heavily wrapped in his furs to make out who it was. Wulfric would not have swapped places with him for anything.

Cloud had gathered lower down the slope, blotting out the world beneath like a great woollen blanket. The air grew damp and felt colder still as he passed into it. One by one the stars disappeared from sight until only the moon remained. Then it too was gone, leaving him in a mire of misty darkness.

Walking downhill through a mixture of ice, snow, and rock in the nearly blinding conditions was treacherous. With each little slip, Wulfric questioned his decision to continue. Could stopping be any more dangerous than what he was doing?

Exhaustion weighed on him like a tonne of rock. He pushed himself hard, eager to reach the point where he could halt and sleep in comparative safety. With each hasty, careless, fatigued step, his feet slipped a little as the snow beneath gave way to his weight. All he could think about was getting to the shelter of a tree trunk, curling up in his furs and going to sleep.

His foot shot forward. Before he knew it, the wind was knocked from his lungs and he was accelerating down the slope on his back. He clawed at the snow with his hands and kicked with his feet to try and slow himself, but it just turned his uncontrolled slide into a chaotic tumble.

He bounced, flailing through the air before thumping back into the snow and continuing his downward slide. He managed to roll onto his front, his feet pointing down the hill. He dug his hands into the snow to arrest his descent. He was more gentle this time, not wanting to throw himself into another tumble by being too forceful.

Wulfric increased the pressure gradually, and he seemed to slow. He passed out of the cloud and into the night below where he could make out the shadows of distant trees. They seemed to be getting closer at an alarming rate, but Wulfric had to resist the urge to dig in for all he was worth. He was still moving too quickly, and if he was thrown into another uncontrolled tumble he could end up impaled on a branch or broken against a tree trunk.

He couldn't help but think that at least he was completing this section of the journey far faster than he would have otherwise, in minutes instead of hours. Try as he might, he could not stop. The slope was too steep and the snow too slippery. He spotted some smaller bushes that looked a more attractive target than any of the tree trunks that flanked them. He aimed himself toward the them, feet first, with gentle pressure from his hands and heels. He took a deep breath, closed his eyes, gritted his teeth, and shielded his face with his arms.

The next few seconds were a blur of rustling leaves and snapping branches. He was flipped over his feet and felt the branches and leaves clawing at his hands and the exposed parts of his face as he continued his flight through the undergrowth. His momentum slowed as his body crashed through the vegetation, and eventually he stopped, upside down and suspended from branches. He didn't try to move, taking time to catch his breath. His thoughts were scrambled and it took him a moment to work out which way was up. Then he started to extricate himself from the bush.

Once free, Wulfric started pulling all the branches and leaves from his clothes. He noticed his sabre was missing. He paused his tidying and looked back up the mountain to see if he could spot it since it was an expensive thing to lose. He was torn between the desire to get it back and the unlikeliness of finding it in the snow. It could have been torn from his body anywhere, and thrown some distance from his path. The gouge in the snow left by his passage was longer than he had realised. Even in the gloom, he could see it extended all the way up the mountainside until it was lost in the cloud. It would take hours to get back to the top, and he could spend days looking and still not find anything.

He was almost out of food, and tired to the point of exhaustion, not to mention sore. He had banged his knee hard during the fall, and it was already beginning to stiffen. If he didn't get moving on it soon, it could swell to the point where he wouldn't be able to bend it. There was still the better part of two days of walking before he would be home. Being unable to bend his knee was as good as being dead. He gave the slope one last wistful look, and turned back to the forest.

✳

Wulfric's first few steps were tentative. He tested his knee, gradually increasing the amount of weight he put on it until he was satisfied it would hold him. The injury could be properly treated when he got home. He just had to get there. Dawn had made itself known, so he had the slight comfort of increasing light to guide his way.

He felt oddly naked without his sabre. Ever since starting his apprenticeship, he had rarely been without one. His body was so accustomed to the weight of it that it felt as though he was missing a limb. Only the dagger at his belt remained, and that was too small to be of much use if he encountered trouble.

It was a relief to be amongst the trees again. They provided shelter from the wind and concealment from anything that might seek to do him harm. It also meant the hardest part of his journey was behind him. He scanned the ground as he went, worried that tripping on a hidden root would end his pilgrimage so close to his end—he suspected he had already used up all of his luck—but it was difficult with all the snow on the ground.

He heard a branch snap somewhere behind him. Wulfric stopped and looked around, but saw nothing. He listened carefully for a moment but heard nothing. He recalled his nervous reaction to every noise and shadow when passing through in the other direction. After so many hours beyond the tree line where every sound was dulled by the thick blanket of snow, he had become accustomed to the quiet.

Wulfric had only gone a few paces when he heard another branch snap behind. It wasn't within him to ignore it. He stopped again and turned slowly, scanning the forest as he went. Could it be one of the other pilgrims? It was unlikely that any of them could have caught up with him; certainly not after his slide back down the mountainside. Was it possible that someone had gone slowly enough to still be on their way up to the valley?

No. Wulfric crouched and drew his dagger, wishing again that he had not lost his sabre in the fall.

He saw nothing, but remained where he was until several moments had passed in silence. He only moved when he began to feel foolish for jumping at shadows. After only a few more paces, he heard a crunching sound— snow and branches being crushed underfoot against rocks. It was directly behind him, and whatever had caused it was heavy. He stopped and spun around. This wasn't paranoia.

'I know you're there,' Wulfric said. 'Show yourself.' Communicating with another pilgrim was against the rules, but the sick feeling in his stomach said that it wasn't a pilgrim following him home.

There was no reply, and no further sound. Wulfric gave each tree a close look to see if there was anything breaking the line of their trunks. There was nothing. He looked up. Could there be something in the trees? He couldn't see anything there either. He turned slowly to the direction he was heading in, and where a moment before there had been nothing, the source of the sounds now stood. A chill ran over every inch of Wulfric's skin and down his spine. A low, rumbling growl filled the air and reverberated in his chest.

CHAPTER TWENTY-EIGHT

A BELEK STOOD MOTIONLESS, watching Wulfric. His first reaction was that it was a statue, but its great, dark eyes moved as it studied him. Wulfric swallowed hard, trying to contain the shock of being confronted by the object of nightmares. That it had been able to get around in front of him in complete silence was terrifying. If it could do that, then the noises it had made previously were intentional, all for its own amusement. All to toy with and terrify its prey. The expression on its silvery, feline face was one of interest and curiosity, things that seemed completely out of place on an animal. But then again, as his father had always said, belek weren't ordinary animals.

It was larger than he had expected. As big as a large bear, but sleeker, like a cat. A very large cat. Two long fangs curved down from the top of its mouth like sabre blades. Its steely grey fur shimmered in the pale light, its skin stretched over lean, taut muscles.

Wulfric had no idea of what to do next. With his sword and a fresh, rested body, his chances of surviving the encounter would be slim. With a dagger, a knee that did not feel at all right, and a multitude of cuts, scrapes and bruises, things didn't look good. He wasn't dead yet, though.

As a newly anointed warrior, with no great battles, victories or tales of heroism to his name, even in the face of certain death he would need to make some effort to ensure his place in Jorundyr's Host. The belek appeared to be in no hurry; they liked to toy with their prey, as Wulfric now knew first hand. It wanted to see how he reacted; whether he was afraid or undaunted by mysterious sounds in the forest. Whether he would be an easy kill or make for good sport.

The belek gave off a low throaty rumble that resonated within Wulfric's chest so strongly that at first he thought it was coming from inside him. It lifted its head slightly and gave the air a long sniff. That done, it opened its mouth wide, giving Wulfric a clear view of each of its teeth. A taunt. It was inviting Wulfric to make the first move. Without thinking, he took a step back.

He felt ashamed and a fool all in the same moment. He was afraid, and now he had revealed that to the beast. The belek cocked its head and moved sideways, slowly circling to Wulfric's right. It placed each of its four paws carefully, without making the slightest sound, giving its movement an otherworldly quality. The significance of it moving to Wulfric's right was not lost on him. Did it know his knee was injured? If it had been watching him, it might. He wondered how long the belek had been stalking him. Since that first twig snap when he was making his way up the mountain? Had it patiently waited for his return?

He turned on the spot to stay facing the belek. After his first step back, Wulfric was determined not to give the beast another inch. If he was going to die, he would at least do so bravely, holding his ground. Still it paced slowly to the right. What was it waiting for?

'Come on!' he yelled, beating on his chest to make his challenge clear. The belek's expression changed. It understood what Wulfric meant, but it continued to circle.

The belek seemed to enjoy its little game. He shouted again with an ostentatious gesture, hoping to distract the belek as he took a step forward. It didn't react to his movement. He reckoned he was close enough to cover the distance between them with a lunge. If the belek didn't take the initiative, Wulfric decided that he would.

He pounced forward, leading with his dagger. He knew how futile a gesture it was, but he hoped Jorundyr was watching and would not doubt his bravery. Little else seemed to matter. He would sup with his father and those of his line all the way back to the very beginning, before the day was out. He thought of Adalhaid. He would like to have seen her one more time.

It was a wild swipe, and Wulfric wasn't surprised when it missed completely. The belek jumped back and crouched. Its expression of amused curiosity was replaced with something far fiercer, and it hissed at Wulfric baring its wicked teeth. Now it crouched low, its claws flexing and digging into the snow as it threatened to pounce.

When it did, it was so fast that Wulfric was flying through the air before he knew what had happened. It had struck, but he was still alive. He scrambled to his feet, trying to suck some air into his lungs. The belek was slowly padding toward him, crouched, teeth still on display. It was telling him it had the means to cleave him in two, but had chosen not to. Yet. It might be able to kill him with ease, but Wulfric wouldn't be sport for anyone or anything. If it was going to toy with him, he would cause it pain in the process.

It pounced again, leading with its long, curved fangs. Wulfric threw himself backwards, and felt a sharp pain in his knee as he did. A searing pain across his chest joined it, as though two red-hot pokers had been laid on his flesh.

He landed on his backside, still breathing, still alive. He scrabbled backward, away from the belek. It watched him, but didn't approach, patiently surveying the result of its strike. Wulfric's furs were rent open, as though neatly incised with a sharp knife. There were two deep cuts in his flesh. They were bleeding, but unlikely to kill him. Wulfric struggled to his feet.

He crouched and held his dagger out in front of him. The beast crept ever closer, never giving any indication of when it would pounce. Even aware of how fast it was, when it came at him again Wulfric was barely able to react. He slashed wildly, and felt his blade connect with something before he was knocked through the air again.

Wulfric had never been kicked by a horse, but had seen it happen to people. He reckoned he now knew how it felt. He got to his feet again, struggling to catch his breath. His hand was wet. He looked at it. Both his mitten and the blade were soaked in blood. It took a moment to realise it was not his. The belek was limping, its right front paw bleeding from a deep gash. Wulfric knew the wound was caused more by the momentum of the belek's swipe than his own slash, that it was luck—but he would take it.

The belek snarled at Wulfric, clearly angered by the wound. It started to circle again, watching Wulfric and the dagger in his hand more warily. Wulfric knew the games were over. When it struck again, it would be for the kill. He kept turning, keeping the belek in front of him. He glanced left and right, looking for anything that might help him. Even a tree that he could duck behind as the belek pounced might allow him to inflict another wound, perhaps even a fatal one.

Wulfric was no longer thinking in terms of dying bravely, but trying to work out how he might kill the beast and survive. He wasn't sure when that had happened, but it filled him with pride. Other men had killed belek in dire circumstances, might he not be able to do the same? His hands started to shake and he could hear the beat of his heart as blood pulsed through his ears. He wasn't afraid—anger was the strongest emotion he felt—but for some reason his hands started to shake. It was odd, but something he could afford to pay little attention.

He kicked a branch at the belek, but it fell short and the beast paid it no attention. The shadows cast by the trees grew darker and more defined. Wulfric realised that the sun was up and the clouds must have parted, allowing it through. Rays of light penetrated through the sparse forest canopy. He felt the warmth of it on the back of his head. His shadow stretched out before him, reaching forward until it was beneath the belek's paws. The image of his own lifeless body there flashed into his mind.

The belek moved into one of the beams of sunlight. It flinched and blinked its eyes, dazzled by the changing light. Wulfric acted without thought. In the blink of an eye he was draped across the belek's back, one arm wrapped around its neck. He was almost as surprised by his action as the belek. He felt a wave of energy surge through him, driving away any feeling of fatigue.

Wulfric gripped the belek's neck tightly as it bucked and kicked, trying to throw him off. The belek's thrashing made it difficult to do anything more than hold on, but Wulfric knew that he wouldn't be able to do so forever. He struck down with his knife, but the side of his hand bounced off the belek's neck without effect.

The belek thrashed harder, enraged by Wulfric still being on its back. Wulfric wrapped both arms around its neck and held on for all he was worth. His face was pressed into the fur on the back of its head, prickling his skin. The belek's musty, feral scent filled his nostrils. Time was running out.

He released his right arm, drew back and stabbed down as quickly as he could. He would only have one chance. This time the blade struck true. It felt as though the belek leaped directly up into the air. Wulfric could see blood splatter out from the side of the creature's neck. He twisted the dagger as much as he could. The movement caused him to lose grip with his other arm and he was thrown from the belek's back. He tried to keep hold of the dagger, but it was slick with blood and slipped from his fingers as he flew through the air.

Wulfric gasped as the air was knocked from his lungs for the third time in as many minutes. He looked at the belek. It had retreated to a nearby tree, where it was focussed on getting the dagger out of its neck. It was trying to knock it free with its paw, but couldn't reach it. Eventually it caught the handle, but not firmly enough to pull it out. It roared in rage and agony.

The belek rubbed along against the tree and managed to dislodge the blade before turning back to Wulfric and snarling at him. Wulfric looked around for anything he could use as a weapon. The forest was still of pine trees at that altitude, and there was not a decent-sized branch in sight. He looked for a rock, but the ground was covered in snow splattered with red. The belek started toward him. Wulfric held his ground, confused that fury bubbled through his blood, rather than fear.

The fur on the belek's neck was coated in wet blood, which was now starting to dribble to the ground from matted tendrils. It snarled at Wulfric again as it paced closer. Wulfric dashed to his right. He expected to feel a stab of pain in his knee, but there was none. He looked everywhere for something, anything, that could be used as a weapon. He prayed to Jorundyr for a branch or a rock. Surely the god wouldn't let Wulfric complete his pilgrimage only to cut him down a few hours later?

The creature roared again, a strained sound. Pain. Distress. It wobbled, its emotive face showing a mix of fear, then fury. It launched itself at Wulfric, too fast for him to get out of the way, but it fell short. Wulfric crouched and watched in confusion, ready to face his end. Nothing happened. The belek did not move. He kicked it in the face with the sole of his boot, but it didn't react. He did it again, and again, but there was no reaction. It was dead.

Wulfric laughed aloud. Then he vomited. The pain in his chest grew tenfold and his knee burned. All of the fatigue he had felt before encountering the belek returned with a vengeance. He pulled off his mitten and probed the wounds with his fingertips. The cuts were ugly and would leave a wicked scar. The thought filled him with an enormous sense of pride. He looked over at the beast's corpse. Even in death it was magnificent; the silvery lustre of its coat seemed like the armour of a defeated warrior. He glanced at his knife. Not every young warrior won the right to wear a belek cloak, but now Wulfric had. Perhaps Jorundyr was not so cruel after all.

As tired as he was, he knew what to do. Dagger in hand, he went to claim his trophy.

✲

Wulfric stared at the gory scene before him. He had skinned the belek, removed its fangs, and opened it up to reveal its heart, but he was not finished. He had been told of what needed to be done next, but had always hoped that it was an embellishment told to increase the mystique of killing a belek. With no one to ask, Wulfric didn't want to find that he had not done something he was supposed to. He cut the heart free and lifted it from the corpse. It was heavier than he expected, and slippery with blood. He struggled to keep a firm grip on it and the thought of eating it made him want to throw up, but that was what he had to do. He took a deep breath, screwed his eyes shut and bit into the belek's heart.

His mouth was flooded with the taste of blood, and the flesh did not give way easily to his teeth. He tried to imagine it was an under-cooked piece of venison as he tore away a mouthful and started to chew. It was tough, and his teeth seemed to make little impact. As soon as he had softened it enough, he swallowed. *That wasn't so bad.* There was no one he needed to convince but himself, and he was far from believing it. He had no idea how much of the heart he needed to eat, and didn't want to prolong the experience any more than necessary. He bit in again and again, until there was nothing left but the blood on his fingers.

He wrapped the pelt into a bundle and put the fangs into his pack. He could still taste the heart's metallic tang and had to fight down the urge to throw up. It was done though. The heart joined the belek's spirit to his own for evermore and the rest served as proof that he had killed the beast. Part of him still could not believe he had actually done it. Already the experience seemed like a dream, save for the all-too-real weight of the pelt in his hands.

He wanted to make the best of the daylight, but the fight had taken what little was left in his exhausted limbs. He found it hard to concentrate and had not gone far before he knew he could not continue. He was satisfied he had put enough distance between himself and the body, and wouldn't have to worry about drawing animals close. So he lit a fire and stretched out beside it, trying to get as much of the heat into his injured knee as he could.

There was something comforting about the flame. He felt a tension that he hadn't even realised was gripping him ease as the fire's warmth embraced him. He flexed his knee, which was also benefitting from the heat. The wound on his chest was a different matter though. The bleeding had stopped, but the edges were hot to the touch and angry looking. He knew it was going bad. Wulfric shuddered to think where the belek's claws had been before raking his chest—probably in the guts of an unfortunate deer or boar.

For the time being, all he could do was allow the warmth of the fire to soothe his aching body, and rest. So much had happened, and he struggled to take it all in. So many lazy afternoons in his childhood had been wasted dreaming of the things he had done over the past couple of days. It was difficult to separate the imagined events from how it had actually happened. It felt as though his memory had been overloaded and he was in danger of forgetting. He closed his eyes and did not have to wait long for sleep to come.

CHAPTER TWENTY-NINE

WULFRIC WAS SHIVERING uncontrollably when he woke. His skin was cold, but he was covered in a sheen of sweat. He felt weaker than he ever had before. His head throbbed, worse even than when he'd been in the High Places on his way to Jorundyr's Rock.

He fought against the feelings and stoked up the fire. There were still a few embers beneath the ash, which eagerly took to the kindling and wood Wulfric had set aside the previous day. The heat made him feel better, but he still shivered. He peeled back the rent edges of his furs and looked at the gashes caused by the belek's fangs.

The scabs, which had been dark red and black the day before, had a tinge of yellow and green, a sure sign that the wound was bad, if the fever and headache had not already told him as much. He still had plenty of walking ahead of him. The fever was going to get worse before it got better. He was determined not to die there, not after all he had achieved.

He held his palms out in front of the fire for one last caress of its warmth before standing and kicking it out. He stood stiffly and pulled his pack onto his shoulders with a grimace. The skin across his chest was tight, and the movement pulled on it agonisingly. He could feel fluid run down his belly—blood or pus, he didn't want to know which. He had a sickening feeling in his stomach.

✿

Wulfric clung onto a tether of concentration and retreated into his mind as he forced his legs to keep walking. It was the same mechanism he had used all those years ago when Rodulf and his friends made his life a living hell. He had taught himself to detach his mind from what was happening to his body and send it elsewhere. While he might not be able to control what happened to his body, he could always control what happened to his mind. He could choose what he allowed in and what he kept out.

Now his body was deluging him with all sorts of bad signals; weakness, tiredness, nausea, pain. Even his mind threatened to betray him, the light-headedness and headache making it a struggle to build the mental wall behind which he could seek refuge. All he had to do was tell his legs to keep going. He repeated it to himself over and over. *Keep going. Keep going. Keep going.* No matter how hard he tried, he could not block out the pain. The noise it made was too loud for him to hide from it in that faraway corner of his mind.

He had to try something different. He searched frantically through the recesses of his mind for any memory, any glimmer of happiness that he could grab and cling onto for dear life. He found one.

It was summer again, and he was a boy. He was sitting under the tree at the edge of the village, the spot with the view of the pastures and the High Places beyond. It was warm, and the air was fragrant with the pasture flowers. The leaves of the tree rustled in the gentle breeze, and Adalhaid was beside him. They watched the shadows change on the mountain peaks as the evening sun dropped away behind them, not needing to say a word. Being together was enough.

She could never stay silent for long—there was always something she saw that she wanted to make sure Wulfric did not miss—but this memory, his favourite memory, was a moment frozen in time. That brief moment of silence and happiness lasted for as long as he could hold it in his mind's eye. He saved it for when he was at his lowest, since it always put a smile on his face, and contentment in his heart. Now he prayed it could save his life. He tried to imagine a conversation, what Adalhaid might say in that perfect moment. He tried to imagine her voice, but couldn't remember what it sounded like.

From time to time, he needed to make decisions that pulled him from the flimsy haven he had built. Turn left at the stream, turn right at the rock, check for a glimpse of the sun through the forest canopy to ensure he was going the correct way. At times, it felt as though the simplest of decisions would overwhelm him. But then he could retreat back into his mind, though each time the journey back and forth grew a little harder.

Wulfric barely noticed when it became dark. There was no question of him stopping. If he sat down, he'd never get up again. Somewhere in front of him, in the darkness of the forest, he could hear Adalhaid laugh; happy, musical. He forced himself on toward the sound, knowing that when he reached her, he would be safe. Her voice drifted between the trees, urging him on, calling him to her. He could think of nothing better than her warm embrace, the smell of her hair. He staggered on, wanting to reach her more than anything.

❋

Comfort was Wulfric's first thought when he opened his eyes. He had no idea where he was. The darkness did nothing to help matters. He stared into the gloom until his eyes began to adjust. He started to see shapes—a chair, a familiar chair, a table, also familiar. He was home. How had he got here?

He felt tired, but no longer sick. His body was stiff and sore—he felt as though he had taken a beating, but the fever seemed to be gone. It begged the question of how long he had been there. He looked at his chest, which was covered with a fresh dressing. He pressed on it gently but there was little pain. It was well healed. He swung his legs down from the bed and stood. The soles of his feet hurt when he put pressure on them. He must have been bedridden for days. Longer? His knee was stiff, but not painful. The various scrapes and scratches on his face felt almost healed. Everything suggested at least a week had passed.

Wulfric tried to think of the last thing he could remember, and felt a twist of panic in his gut. What had he actually done? What had he imagined? The memory of sitting by the tree was as fresh and real as any of the other things. Adalhaid's laughter. It had seemed so real, but now he realised it had only been in his mind. It was usual to touch the stone in the glade to demonstrate to everyone that the pilgrimage was completed. Wulfric had no recollection of doing that. He worried that he had not managed it. Would they consider him a failure?

The door to his room opened, a silhouette framed in the doorway.

'He's awake,' the voice said. Adalhaid's voice.

Still dreaming, then. But it was a good dream. Wulfric felt the panic and concern fade from his racing heart. He lay back, and sleep took him once again.

❉

Wulfric sat in his bed, trying to separate dream from reality. His head was clear now, and he felt well rested. His mother called in to check on him. Discovering him awake, she made him breakfast but insisted he stay in bed. He could get used to that, but it wasn't in keeping with being a warrior. The thought brought a smile to his face.

There was a knock at the door, and Wulfric was disappointed to see that it was not Adalhaid. He would have sworn on Jorundyr that he had seen her standing in the doorway the night before.

'I'm glad to see you awake and well,' Aethelman said.

'It's good to be home,' Wulfric said.

'Your colour is better. You were deathly pale the last time I saw you. How do you feel?'

'Much better, thank you,' Wulfric said. 'How long have I been here?'

'Nearly three weeks. That was quite a collection of injuries you came home with. You were by far the worst of those who made it back. The only one to encounter a belek as well. I'm not sure if that should be considered good or bad fortune, but seeing as you still live I'm inclined to the former.'

'How many got home?'

'Eight, including you. Walmer, Eckard, Berun, and Hane didn't make it back.'

'I saw Hane in the valley. He was coughing blood up onto the snow. He was dead by the time I passed him on the way back.'

'The others mentioned seeing him. A sad loss, and not one I expected,' Aethelman said.

Hane and Walmer were the only two Wulfric had much to do with. Considering their history, he found it difficult to muster much sympathy for Walmer.

'Eight out of twelve is a good number, though,' Aethelman said. 'More than I would usually expect, and something of a miracle all things considered. Jorundyr has been kind to us. I would have been content if six had returned.' Aethelman's solemn expression changed to a broad smile.

'I need to know,' Wulfric said. 'How did I get here?'

'You walked through the village in a daze, ignoring everything around you. When you got to the stone in the glade, you touched it and collapsed. We brought you back here.'

'I'm glad I made it that far,' Wulfric said.

'It was quite a thing to do,' Aethelman said. 'I've never dealt with a fever as bad as yours. The village is delighted to have eight new warriors to see it through the winter, though. All the more so when one of them can claim a belek to his name.'

Wulfric smiled. He had given only fleeting thought to the belek. Between the confusion and all of the other things to take in, it had seemed distant, something he might have imagined rather than done.

'Killing one on your own is a very fine achievement. One to be proud of and something few men achieve. You should have seen your mother's reaction when we unpacked your things. I only wish you could have seen your father's. Adalhaid and your mother are working on your cloak as we speak. They wanted to have it ready by the time you woke, but I think it isn't quite finished.'

'Adalhaid?' Wulfric said.

'Yes, she got back to the village shortly after you left on the pilgrimage.'

Wulfric could hardly believe it. 'She's back.' He let the thought sink in for a moment. 'There's something else,' Wulfric said. 'Something else I need to ask you.'

Aethelman raised an eyebrow. 'Go on...'

'I... I'm not sure if I touched the Rock.'

'What do you mean?'

'I'm not sure if I touched it or not. I reached out for it, but...'

'You mean you can't remember?' Aethelman said.

'Sort of. I reached out to it and there was a glow all over it, and then all over me. Then I was sitting on the snow. I think there was a bright flash and a bang, but I'm not sure. I can't remember if I managed to touch the rock.'

Aethelman smiled. 'A blue glow, you say?'

Wulfric nodded, more panicked now than before. No matter how hard he searched his memory, he couldn't recall ever having touched the rough, carved surface of the Rock. 'I tried a second time, but it was like it was covered with something invisible and soft. I could push against it, but I couldn't press through it.'

'You did enough,' Aethelman said. 'More than enough.' He studied Wulfric for a moment before speaking again. 'I've heard of what you describe, but never of it happening. I'm not sure if it has for a very long time. Certainly not in my lifetime.'

Wulfric furrowed his brow. 'What do you mean?'

'You were chosen by Jorundyr. Every warrior who remains true to his code will join the Host when he leaves this world, but some Jorundyr chooses for more than that. That he sent a belek to make sure you're worthy of his choice confirms it to my mind. It makes so much more sense now.'

'What does it mean?'

Aethelman smiled. 'You'll have to find that out for yourself. Perhaps nothing, not in this life at least. His touch brings with it gifts, things he will expect you to master by the time he calls you to join his host.'

'Gifts?'

Aethelman shrugged. 'They are different for everyone. Jorundyr bestows the skills he has the greatest need for at the time. That is what you will have to discover for yourself.'

Wulfric smiled to mask his confusion. It was a great deal to take in, and part of him questioned if he was not really still out in the forest somewhere, huddled up by a tree and gripped by the delirious dreams of fever.

'Don't get too pleased with yourself,' Aethelman said. 'It is said that those blessed by Jorundyr's touch tend to get called to his host earlier than most.'

'Why?'

'It's the greatest accolade a man could have. Every time you set foot on a battlefield, you'll draw warriors like moths to a flame. They all want to make a name, prove themselves. Your head will be a very nice way of doing that.'

The windfall no longer felt quite so pleasing. 'How will anyone know?'

'Word will get out sooner or later. Things like this are hard to keep a secret. You'll do something no ordinary man could do one day, without thinking about it. The rumours will start, and once you've done it a few more times you'll confirm it. It's not something to hide away from, Wulfric. It's a two-edged sword, no doubt, but when a god singles you out you do not ignore him.'

CHAPTER THIRTY

WULFRIC WAS ALLOWED out of bed the next day. His mother was still against the idea, eager that he spend a few more days wrapped up in bed, but Aethelman was firm in his insistence that Wulfric go out for some fresh air and exercise. The command was music to Wulfric's ears; he was eager to share stories with the others who had completed their pilgrimages. It was exciting to think that when he stepped out into the daylight, it was as a warrior, anointed *and* chosen by Jorundyr. He wondered if anyone else might have experienced what he had at the Rock. Above all, he wanted to see Adalhaid.

He washed and dressed, and was about to go out when he heard a commotion in the front room. Leaving his room, he saw his mother and Adalhaid busily folding a heavy dark cloak into a linen wrapping. He took a moment to look at Adalhaid before speaking, to convince himself she was really there. She had grown and was taller than his mother now, her long red hair cascading down her back in waves.

'What's that?' Wulfric said, knowing exactly what it was.

'You're not supposed to see it yet,' Adalhaid said with a laugh.

She acted as though she had never been gone, although considering how long she had been back there'd been plenty of time for her to settle back in. It felt strange to Wulfric.

He shrugged. 'Well, too late now.'

Adalhaid held up the fur cloak. The fangs had been polished and trimmed with silver to provide the fastening. Both she and his mother beamed with pride. Wulfric took the cloak, not knowing what to say. It was a far cry from the bloody pelt he had cut from the dead belek. The creature's strong odour was gone, which was a huge relief. He had no desire to be reminded of the beast's smell every time he put the cloak on, nor did he want to smell like it. Adalhaid and his mother had lined it with a fine, wine-coloured cloth, the stitching so fine that it was barely visible.

'Thank you,' he said, throwing the cloak over his shoulders. It was something he had seen his father do many times, and the significance of the moment was not lost on him. Nor was it lost on his mother, whose eyes had filled with tears.

Wulfric didn't know what to say.

'I'm going out for some fresh air,' Wulfric said. 'I won't stay out long.'

'No more than an hour,' his mother said. 'You're not fully recovered yet.'

Wulfric nodded.

'You're still weak,' Adalhaid said. 'You shouldn't go out alone.'

His mother frowned for a moment. 'She's right.'

Wulfric's heart jumped. What would he say to her? Adalhaid took his arm as they stepped outside. He realised she was making sure that he didn't lose his balance, but it felt as awkward as anything he had ever experienced. They had not spoken in nearly three years, and here she was as though her presence was the most normal thing in the world.

✿

They walked in silence at first, Wulfric not knowing what to say. The memory of his journey through the forest, where he was sure he could hear her laugh and speak made him feel awkward.

'How long have you been home?' Wulfric said, unable to bear the silence any longer and unable to think of anything else to say.

'I came back as soon as I got word about my father. I arrived the day you all left on your pilgrimages. I missed you by only a few hours.'

'I'm sorry about your father. He died bravely.'

'I'd rather he hadn't died at all,' she said.

Her accent was a little different, as was the way she spoke. It was only a subtle change, but it was enough to make her seem like a stranger in a friend's body.

'Jorundyr will welcome him,' Wulfric said, not sure if his words would give her any comfort.

'He was only a lanceman. I thought Jorundyr's Hall was reserved for warriors.'

'He died with a sword in his hand, surrounded by his fallen foes. Jorundyr will recognise that.'

She let out a snort but did not reply, and Wulfric felt foolish for saying it. He wondered how much the city had changed her, wondered if the village now seemed like a backward shanty town, and him an ignorant savage, as was the opinion of any southerners he had met.

They walked on in silence. His cloak drew admiring glances from everyone they passed. The white and silver belek-fang clasp contrasted sharply against the dark, shimmering fur of the cloak. Wulfric found it was impossible not to puff out his chest as he and Adalhaid walked toward the town square. It occurred to him that he was the only able-bodied man in the village entitled to wear one. All the other belek slayers had been killed or maimed on the road to Rasbruck. When his mind dragged the memory from its dark recess, it felt like a kick in the stomach. Life in Leondorf would never be the same again, no matter how many times he allowed himself to push the fact from his thoughts. When danger loomed, people would look to him. He could no longer be the frightened child. He was the one frightened children would run to for safety.

How had so much happened so quickly? People were looking at him with the same respect they had shown to the likes of the Beleks' Bane, and his father. It felt strange. He felt like a fraud. He kept reminding himself of what he had done, and wondered if he would ever be able to accept it.

He cast a sideways glance at Adalhaid as they walked. He couldn't tell what she was thinking, and found himself more afraid of speaking than he had been of going on the pilgrimage. He couldn't bear it if she had come to think of him as nothing more than a boorish Northlander.

They arrived at the square, and although he wouldn't admit it, the walk was as much as Wulfric thought he'd be able for. There was a group of men standing on the steps of the Great Hall. Wulfric recognised them all, but didn't know any of them by name; a sign of the changes that had come to the village. Not one of them was a warrior. Not one of them a face he would have expected to see anywhere near the Great Hall only a few months before.

Wulfric nodded to them respectfully. They weren't of the warrior class, but they were all now members of the village council, a fact worthy of some deference. In consideration of how few able-bodied warriors there were, that he had completed his pilgrimage and now wore a belek cloak, Wulfric expected his invitation to join the council to be not far off. The men on the steps all looked at Wulfric, but none responded. He was a warrior and entitled to their respect, but the expressions on their faces said anything but that. He glared at them, but it was a problem for another day.

'When will you be going back south?' Wulfric said.

'I don't know if I will,' Adalhaid said. 'With Mother here alone, I don't want to leave her. I finished my schooling, so there's no need to go back.'

The prospect of her remaining filled Wulfric with a joy that was tempered with discomfort. Would things be the same again, or would her time in the city have changed her beyond recognition? He desperately wanted to ask her why she had not written, and why she had not come back between terms as she had promised she would, but he did not know how to broach it. He chewed his lip for a moment, trying to find the words, but failing. Svana's face popped into his mind, doubling his discomfort. Why did life have to be so complicated?

'I'm getting tired,' he said. 'We should probably go back.'

❋

'Definitely reaving?' Belgar said.

The herdsman nodded, and Belgar swore. A dozen cattle had been taken during the night. It seemed word had finally gotten out that they were left all but defenceless after the battle with Rasbruck, and even winter was not enough to put thieves off such easy pickings. It hadn't been a good year for the farmers, and the crops had been meagre. They were being supplemented from the herds, but it was always a better option if you could feed your people with someone else's cattle. From what passing merchants had told him, it was the same throughout the whole region. He knew the dozen head of cattle was only the start. It was bad luck. Nobody liked to reave in winter. Had the crops been enough, it was likely Leondorf would have been left alone till spring. As it was, their neighbours would nibble away until there was nothing left, unless they were stopped.

Their own crops wouldn't last the winter without the milk, cheese, and meat the cattle added, and Belgar had seen herds whittled to their bare bones by reavers on more than one occasion. He swore again as he stared out over the pastureland. He'd be damned before he allowed that to happen to Leondorf. It was time to send a clear message that Leondorf would protect what was hers, and kill anyone who tried to steal from them.

❦

Wulfric spent the afternoon mulling over his brief conversation with Adalhaid, and knew it would not stop bothering him until he dealt with it head on. After supper, he slipped out of the house before his mother could stop him and went straight to Adalhaid's home. Their childhood evening walks had been so well rehearsed that he didn't need to say anything when he arrived. As soon as she saw him standing at the door, she took her cloak from the peg on the wall and stepped outside to join him.

They walked in silence for a time, until Wulfric thought of something to say that allowed him to completely avoid the issues he had intended to broach. 'What's the city like?' he said.

Adalhaid took a deep breath. 'Wonderful, beautiful, fascinating—'

Wulfric's heart started to sink.

'—soul destroying, disgusting, superficial. It's everything you could imagine, all rolled into one great mass of buildings and people.'

'I'd like to see it one day,' Wulfric said.

'I don't think you'd like it.' She saw Wulfric's reaction. 'I didn't mean anything. I know how much you love the open spaces, the views, the mountains. The city can be claustrophobic; you're hemmed in on all sides by buildings so tall you have to look straight up to see the sky.

'I love those things too,' she said. 'I'd forgotten how incredible this place is. The way the High Places reach into your soul when you look at them.'

Wulfric smiled. 'There's nothing like them. Even up there, in the middle of them all, they can take your breath away.'

'I'd love to have seen what you saw up there.'

'It was a difficult journey,' he said.

'I know. I heard about Hane. I'm sorry. I know what good friends you had become.'

Wulfric shrugged. It wouldn't do for a warrior to show grief over losing a comrade.

'Oh, I'd forgotten what a big, tough warrior you are now,' she said.

They both laughed, and a little part of the distance that had grown between them bled away.

'I'll miss him,' Wulfric said. 'The whole village will miss him.'

'You don't have to be that way with me, you know. I'm proud of what you've achieved, and I know what hard work and strength it must have taken.' She took his hand. 'It doesn't mean you need to change who you are.'

'How can you come back to this and be happy, after all you've seen and experienced in the south?'

'Getting to go to a proper school was amazing, and I'd love the chance to go to a university. But the south is what it is.' She hesitated. 'And you're not there.'

Wulfric's eyes widened. 'You never wrote to me,' he said, his voice uncertain. 'I thought that...'

'I'm sorry,' she said. 'I didn't know what to do when I left. You're the First Warrior's son, and I'm only the daughter of a lanceman. I couldn't see a happy ending, so I left—and once I did, cutting the connection seemed the easiest way for both of us. That's why I didn't write or come back.'

'That was never what I wanted,' Wulfric said.

'I expect you must be getting betrothed to Svana soon.' She forced a smile. 'Married even, now that you've completed the pilgrimage.' She tried to take back her hand, but Wulfric held it tight.

'Svana doesn't matter to me, and I know I don't matter to her. She'd be just as happy with Roal or Farlof or any other decent warrior, as she would me. It's not the person she wants, only the status. And she's not the person I want.'

Adalhaid smiled. He kissed her.

❈

'That's rubbish!' a man said, his voice slurred.

The Maisterspaeker raised an eyebrow. 'Really? How so?'

'Ulfyr the Bloody used to bed a dozen northern wenches a night. Everyone knows that. He'd have bedded that blondie ice queen in a heartbeat. And a hundred more besides. Man like that can't be pinned down by one woman.' He looked around, but did not find the support he had expected. Only silence.

'Any idiot can bed a dozen wenches a night, assuming he has a face like a statue or a purse the size of a cow,' the Maisterspaeker said, to subdued laughter and silence from the man. 'Only a very special type of man can love one woman to the exclusion of everyone else. To the exclusion of everything else. To carry her memory across half the world and back again because of it, knowing that death is likely all that awaits him.' He paused, purely for effect. 'A very special type of man indeed.'

❈

Wulfric's face still tingled from the kiss when Frena led Belgar into the house. Wulfric was sitting in his father's chair, thinking on Adalhaid—and, worryingly, how his gut had grown softer than it had been in some time. Too much rest and too much food. The coddling he had received while recuperating had its drawbacks. It was easily set to rights, and there was nothing to be gained by putting it off. With the mood he was in, he believed he could achieve anything with ease, for he felt as though he had won the greatest prize there was.

'You're looking well, boy. How are you feeling?' Belgar said, before sitting down opposite Wulfric.

'Much better,' he said.

Belgar nodded. 'I'm glad to hear it. You're not going to get the chance for much more rest. We've lost some cattle.'

'Many?' Wulfric felt a flash of excitement and fear.

'A few. We need to show that we have warriors. Make a display of force, small though it might be. Let everyone know we'll take care of what's ours. That they'll bleed for it if they try again. The council has decided to send you out on a ranging.'

It seemed the day would go from strength to strength. Wulfric regretted there was so little left in it. 'When do we leave?'

'The plan is to head out tomorrow morning, ride as far as the winter pastures and circle back. Leave plenty of obvious tracks, let everyone know there's warriors about. I'm to go with you, as is another member of the council.' Belgar's face twisted as though he smelled something foul. 'Now that they have a say in how things are run, they want to have their own set of eyes on everything that happens, so we have to babysit one of them.'

There could be no mistaking who 'they' were. Wulfric couldn't help but feel that Belgar was partly the engineer of his own displeasure, but he agreed that there had been little alternative. They were still far from secure, and input was needed from every corner.

'Ridiculous idea,' Belgar said. 'We should leave him out there, see if he can find his own way home. Might teach them not to interfere in things that are beyond them.'

'Who's going to be coming with us?'

'They haven't decided yet. Now that people actually listen to the prattling that comes out of their mouths, they can't shut them and argue over bloody everything. I reckon they'll have made their decision by tomorrow morning. One way or the other, be ready to ride out by dawn. We'll be back by nightfall, so you won't need to pack.'

Belgar left Wulfric to consider things. That Belgar regretted inviting the new councilmen into the Great Hall was obvious, but it was equally clear that there was nothing that could be done about it now. To try and expel them would tear the village apart. It was the only thing that had held it together, no matter what the older warriors might say. It occurred to Wulfric that there had been no mention of him, or any of the other new warriors being brought onto the council. He wondered if there ever would be.

CHAPTER THIRTY-ONE

ARANGING MEANT THAT the time for inactivity was over. While they might become routine, this was his first real one and everything about it was a new experience. He had to decide what he needed to bring and, more importantly, get himself a new sword.

He owned a set of training armour; cheap, roughly produced metal that protected against the blows of blunt practice weapons, but against arrows and blades with sharp edges he didn't fancy his chances. After that, there were weapons to consider. A sabre would do at a pinch—cattle raiders didn't tend to wear full battle armour—but he thought a lance was a good idea too. Everyone knew he was inexperienced, and he didn't want to emphasize the fact through avoidable mistakes.

It didn't take long to attract his mother's ire with the racket he was kicking up in his search. She led him through the house to a large closet with the patience she had always maintained when he was being petulant as a child. Inside was a mannequin covered in a heavy, oiled cloth. She drew the cloth away to reveal his father's spare set.

'I had it resized when you were recovering. The smith said it will need some more adjustments, but it should serve until you have time to get it altered. I hope it will fit.'

Its oily sheen glistened in the meagre light, and Wulfric could see the hilt of his father's sabre, recovered from the road to Rasbruck, propped up against it. Wulfric took his mother's hand. There was nothing he could think of to say. Without her forethought, he would be riding into danger in little better than tin plates held together with twine.

❊

The newly anointed warriors gathered on the town square the next morning. The way the others were equipped put a damper on Wulfric's enthusiasm. They looked a motley bunch, wearing armour that was cobbled together from their training suits, and better pieces that had been scavenged from elsewhere—the suits belonging to their recently killed fathers most likely. It would not be the glorious, shining promenade of plate-armoured heavy horsemen Wulfric had dreamed of as a child. His own suit, old, and hastily adjusted though it was, outshone the others. Dressed in their patchwork armour they looked like a bunch of boys playing warrior, rather than young men preparing to take their place as their village's defenders—which Wulfric realised was painfully close to the truth. The sight of them wouldn't do much to intimidate anyone. They would have to ensure their actions did that for them.

The villagers stood in groups around the fringes of the square, but there was none of the excited chatter or shouts of bravado that usually accompanied the departure of a ranging. It was the first time warriors had ridden out since the battle on the road to Rasbruck, and the memory was still fresh.

Wulfric could see how eager the others all were to get going, to be away from the melancholy hanging over the village if for nothing else. Like Wulfric, they had all spent their childhoods watching the warriors ride out, dreaming of doing the same, and now they were finally going to get to realise that ambition. Nothing could take that excitement from them. Wulfric thought of the faces that should have been there, but were not—Hane's most of all. Wulfric hadn't realised how much comfort having Hane at his shoulder had given him. He would be missed if they encountered trouble.

A man rode out onto the square and put all the rest to shame. He was clad head to toe in magnificent battle armour, the plates polished to a high sheen, the edges filigreed in gold. The helmet's mask was shaped and engraved to appear like a snarling wolf; it was unique and Wulfric was certain he had not seen it before. He could identify all of the village's warriors by their helmets.

The rider flipped the mask up, revealing Belgar's lined face beneath. He was far too old to be gallivanting around in armour, but he looked the part with the mask closed, and added weight to the threat their little party posed. Wulfric wondered if it would have been worth recruiting some of the other old warriors to fill out their ranks, straw men in tin suits, but they were few enough and armour was too heavy for old limbs. That Belgar managed it was impressive, and Wulfric realised that to underestimate the old warrior was always a mistake. He only hoped it wasn't all an act that would come crashing to a tragic halt at the wrong moment.

The final member of their ranging was the council appointee. Wulfric was curious to see who they chose. Part of him expected that it would be Rodulf, placed there by his father who seemed to grow in influence every day. Before anyone knew it, Wulfric expected that Donato would ensure his son was enjoying all of the privileges of being a warrior. Perhaps he would even see to making Rodulf one, and pay someone to make his pilgrimage for him.

The council appointee walked out of the Great Hall, not looking at all happy with his assignment. His name was Fridric, and while Wulfric recognised him he couldn't say for sure what he did in the village. He didn't look like the type of man prepared for hardship of any sort and Wulfric wondered how much of a burden he would be. He would need to be coddled, but Wulfric hoped that Belgar, used to dealing with the intricacies of the Great Hall, would take care of that.

Those with family or sweethearts said their farewells. Wulfric did his best to look the emotionless, conquering hero atop his horse, but Anshel had him beaten in that. Greyfell reacted to Adalhaid's presence at his side before Wulfric noticed her.

'I wanted to get to you first this time,' she said, holding up a piece of ribbon.

Wulfric smiled and took it, pushing it under his vambrace. 'Thank you.'

'I hope it will bring you luck,' she said. 'And woe and devastation to your foes, and all that.'

He laughed this time, but saw Svana out of the corner of his eye. Her face was, as always, emotionless, but he could see anger in her eyes. There would need to be a conversation when he got back; an awkward conversation, but he knew once she had adjusted to the idea she would likely be relieved.

There was a cheer as they rode out of the village, and Wulfric could not help but enjoy the experience. With their ill-equipped troop of fresh-faced warriors, part of him hoped that they wouldn't encounter anyone hostile, but the desire made him feel ashamed. A true warrior would want confrontation, would seek it out. They had to make the best of what they had and get on with it. They had to show their neighbours that Leondorf could protect what was theirs, and would kill anyone who tried to take it.

❄

They spotted a herd of ruddy-coated Northland cattle mid-morning and headed for them. Their council-appointed comrade carried a banner with Leondorf's sigil of a gold belek rampant on a field of green, so the herdsmen would be able to identify them as friends. He had been given the task for no other reason than it would make him feel involved, and was hard to make a mess of. Wulfric watched him out of the corner of his eye, however. It was bad luck for the banner to touch the ground, and he did not have faith in Fridric not to drop it.

Since leaving the village, Belgar had eased into the role of ranging leader. None of the young men were confident or arrogant enough to object, and Wulfric was glad to have the opportunity to learn from someone with so much experience.

They stopped when they reached the herdsmen, Fridric looking delighted at what he seemed to think was the completion of his first ranging.

'Morning, Skegg,' Belgar said.

The lead herdsman said nothing, but nodded in the surly way the herdsmen often did. They spent a lot of their time alone with their herds in the pastures—too much, some would say—and they didn't tend to be the most sociable bunch. Wulfric had expected small talk of some sort before getting to the core of things, but different people needed to be handled in different ways, and he knew that was something he needed to learn.

Belgar, however, knew how to deal with the herdsman, and didn't waste any time.

'Seen anyone around?' he said.

'Nope,' Skegg said.

'Seen any sign of strangers around?'

'Nope,' Skegg said.

Wulfric could tell from his demeanour that Skegg wasn't trying to be obstructive, he just wasn't the chatty type.

Belgar looked around, and Wulfric could tell he was getting frustrated with the herdsman's brusque manner. 'Lost any cattle?'

'Yup.'

Wulfric almost sighed with relief at the change in direction.

'Six head,' Skegg said. 'Last night.'

'But you didn't see anything?'

'Nope,' Skegg said.

'We'll have a scout around. See if we can pick up the trail.'

Skegg nodded. 'Appreciate it. Let ye know if I see anything.'

❊

'We'll range to the southwest until late afternoon and then return to the village,' Belgar said. 'We'll make noise, and we'll leave a trail a blind man can follow.' He looked around and saw a number of puzzled expressions. 'We want everyone interested to know we were here and that we can come back. It's the opportunists we want to frighten off. Anything more than that is a job for another day.'

Belgar had always seemed like a frail old man in the village, but putting on his armour and riding out on a ranging seemed to have rejuvenated him. He spoke with authority, such that it didn't occur to anyone to question him. The waver in his voice was gone, and the set of his grizzled old jaw seemed firmer. The body might grow weak, but the warrior spirit never declined.

They moved more slowly, with Belgar signalling for them to halt often. He clambered down from his horse and checked the tracks in the snow, before shaking his head and hauling himself back into his saddle. They continued like this until well after midday; halt, check for tracks, continue. It wasn't long before Wulfric was wondering what all the fuss about ranging was. He was bored beyond belief, but at least the winter air didn't bother him as much as it would have before his pilgrimage. It felt balmy in the pastures by comparison. He found himself counting the minutes until they could turn for home. Fridric was the only member of the group who did not seem bored. Although he had grown increasingly uncomfortable looking as his hours in the saddle increased, his face still had the same wide-eyed excitement that it had started the day with. Wulfric had long since given up watching him for fear of the banner being dropped; Fridric's knuckles were white on the banner pole, and Wulfric expected his seized fingers would have to be prised from it at the end of the day.

They stopped again on Belgar's command, but he didn't dismount. 'That's far enough,' he said. 'If we were going to find the cattle, we'd be on the trail by now. The tracks are too confused. Like as not there's been more than one group of reavers in the area. At least in the old days, all you had to do was head toward Rasbruck.' He sighed. 'We'll head for home.'

Wulfric wondered how the uneventful ranging would colour the councilman's perspective on warriors. Whatever report he made to his colleagues would no doubt reflect badly on them. It had been far from the opportunity to prove themselves that he'd hoped for.

※

There was none of the excited energy on the return journey. Everyone felt the job was done and all that remained was the ride home—there was no adventure left in that day, no great deed to be done. Belgar, however, still appeared tense and alert. There was a little chatter now, which Fridric joined in on from time to time—usually to express his desire to be home by his hearth. Wulfric didn't join in, and couldn't ignore Belgar's tension. He wondered if he was equally concerned about Fridric's report. Wulfric didn't like not knowing what was going on, he never had, but it felt as though recovering the cattle had only been of secondary importance.

Belgar raised his hand again, halting their little group. He held it up for a moment and stared across the pasture to the tree line beyond. He reached forward, hesitantly at first, before extending his arm and pointing with more confidence. For an old man, his eyes were impressively sharp. Wulfric looked to where the old warrior was pointing. There was movement among the trees.

'Forward, everyone,' Belgar said. 'At the trot.' He took his spear from the fastening on his saddle.

Everyone else did likewise, and Wulfric noticed that Fridric had dropped the smug expression from his face and was a shade paler. The banner he carried was no longer held quite so high.

'Stop there!' Belgar shouted.

The movement stopped, and Wulfric could see faces looking in their direction from between the trees. A moment later, three men rode out from the tree line and came forward to meet them.

'What do you want?' one of the men said.

'You're on Leondorf's territory. I'll ask you the same question,' Belgar said.

'Passing through. Hadn't heard Leondorfers were bothering travellers.'

'We're not. We're looking for cattle reavers.'

'You'll have to keep looking then.'

'What've you got there in the trees?'

'Just the rest of my party,' the man said.

'No cattle hidden away back there?' Belgar said, his voice filled with irony.

'Listen here, old man. Why don't you take these lads and play warriors somewhere else? It's getting late anyway; you'd probably best be off home to change their swaddling cloths.' The man whistled. Ten more horsemen emerged from the trees.

Wulfric felt his gut twist. Belgar looked from the man to the new appearances. As though on cue, there was a loud bellow from the trees, the characteristic call of a Northland cow.

Belgar raised an eyebrow.

The man who had been speaking smiled. 'Well? Getting close to bedtime for the lads, ain't it?'

Wulfric felt a flash of anger stir within him. He had completed the pilgrimage; such insults could not be allowed to go unanswered, not if they were to earn any respect.

Belgar stared at the man for a moment before wheeling his horse around. 'Back to the village,' he said.

Wulfric couldn't quite believe what he was hearing, but all of the others turned around without questioning the order, leaving Wulfric with no option but to do likewise. Fridric's horse, sensing its rider's eagerness, broke into a gallop and needed to be reined back in. The men behind them roared with laughter. Wulfric glanced back over his shoulder and cast the man as withering a look as he could muster. They were sending a message to all of their neighbours that they could pillage at will. What was Belgar thinking?

Wulfric felt as ashamed as he ever had. How could Belgar turn his back on those taunts? Did he have so little faith in them that he wouldn't lead them into battle?

Belgar rode up beside Wulfric and looked over. 'Well?' he said.

'Well what?' Wulfric replied, unable to contain his anger.

'Well, what do you think?'

'I think we're not going to have any cattle left by winter,' Wulfric said.

'What are you going to do about it?' Belgar said.

'You're First Warrior,' Wulfric said. 'That's your decision.'

'No I'm not,' Belgar said. 'Haven't been First Warrior for near on twenty years. If you were First Warrior, what would you do?'

'What do you mean?' Wulfric said.

'I mean we're about far enough away now to get a good charge at them.'

Wulfric smiled. 'On my word, turn and charge them,' he said, loud enough for the others to hear. A few of them cast Wulfric a surprised look, the rest nodded without question. Belgar smiled.

Chapter Thirty-Two

'NOW!' WULFRIC SHOUTED. He wheeled his horse back around. The cattle raiders were still watching the Leondorfers ride away with their tails between their legs. He kicked at Greyfell's side and the horse launched into a gallop, his spirits as high as Wulfric's, his anger and desire for battle just as strong. All thoughts of second-rate armour and battered old weapons slipped from Wulfric's mind as he focussed on the man who had insulted them. He would be the first to die.

Surprised by the sudden turn about, the raiders hesitated. By the time their leader had gathered his wits, Wulfric and the others had covered most of the distance between them.

'Forward! Forward!' the man shouted to his companion.

The interlopers outnumbered Wulfric and the Leondorfers nearly two to one, but this was their territory and if they did nothing they might as well not have bothered going to the High Places. The three men who had come forward to speak were separated from their comrades by a good distance. Faced with receiving the charge isolated from his men, the reaver's true nature showed through. He broke for the tree line, closely followed by his two pals.

His reaction wasn't fast enough, though. Wulfric was already at full gallop and Greyfell chewed through the distance between them in a heartbeat.

Wulfric levelled his lance and leaned forward in his saddle, as he had done a thousand times on the quintain in the glade. The impact, when it came, was far less than he expected—less than the quintain. After the initial punch, the resistance gave way quickly. The raider let out a cry and flew from his horse. The lance twisted in Wulfric's hand and was pulled from his grip.

His two companions were speared by the riders closest to Wulfric; Belgar took his first kill on the battlefield in decades while Roal claimed the other. The rest charged past them toward the other raiders, who were now galloping toward them with their spears levelled. The only man not in motion was Fridric. Before going after the others, Wulfric cast Fridric a glance and felt pity. If one of the reavers got to him he would be dead before he had time to wet his britches. From the expression on his face, he knew that.

Outnumbered and inexperienced, the odds were not good for any of them. Wulfric followed behind the others. Without a spear he was useless at the front of the charge. Kolbein was ahead of him. Wulfric raised his sabre, ready to deal with whatever came through. The two lines collided with a thundering crunch. Kolbein was launched from his saddle and his spear flicked harmlessly up into the air. He was instantly replaced by a reaver coming toward Wulfric at full gallop, the broken stump of a spear in his hand.

Wulfric slashed at him. His sabre screeched against metal and slid away. The reaver grabbed for his own sabre having dropped the remains of his spear. Wulfric hacked down again, striking this time at the reaver's arm in the hope of stopping him from drawing his sword. Wulfric's sabre found the join in his armour at the elbow and sliced through flesh and bone. The man screamed as his arm fell away from his elbow. His hand still held the sword. Wulfric watched in morbid fascination as the grip went slack and the arm dropped to the ground. He stabbed the reaver through the throat to put him out of his misery.

Wulfric felt himself begin to shake uncontrollably, as though he was struck by an icy wind. It was so sudden and bizarre that it was a moment before he realised how it must look. The others would think he was afraid. His teeth started to chatter, and no matter what he did he couldn't stop it.

The fight had degenerated into a confused mess. Wulfric waded in, but felt lightheaded and couldn't control his shivering. He needed to do something to show everyone that he was not afraid. He looked around at the press of men and horses; it was difficult to tell friend from foe. A strange feeling came over him; it didn't seem to matter, and that terrified him. All he wanted to do was kill. To destroy. He felt as though he was watching himself from a distance. His mind controlled his actions, but the sensations of pain and tiredness could not make their way back to him. He felt invincible.

A man appeared before Wulfric, a wide smile on his face. He must have seen the shaking. Wulfric roared in the hope of drowning out the shaking, and without thinking he slashed. He felt so strong. Unstoppable. He cleaved the man's head and right arm from his body. Men surrounded him as he surveyed the devastation of his strike. Blows rained in on him from all sides. The clattering on his armour and helmet was constant, but it too seemed distant. He couldn't feel a single one.

He hacked at another man, who raised his sword in time to parry. Wulfric's sabre shattered on the impact. He looked at the jagged remains of his blade—it must have been damaged the last time his father used it. Wulfric dropped the hilt and reached across, grabbing the man by the edge of his breastplate. Wulfric head-butted him, smashing his helmet into the reaver's face. The light leather skullcap was no match for Wulfric's faceplate. He roared in pain as Wulfric followed up with his gauntleted fist. He continued to pull him closer, until he was lying across Greyfell's back. Wulfric pounded his fist into the reaver's face over and over, only pushing the limp body to the ground when someone struck him from behind.

Wulfric's helmet rang like a bell. The world swam around before his eyes. He struggled to remember where he was, who he was. The past few minutes seemed like a dream, but as his wits returned, he realised that he had stopped shivering.

Greyfell kicked out behind, throwing Wulfric forward onto his neck. His survival instinct made him cling on with one arm, while he scrabbled with the other to get a grip on his dagger, his only remaining weapon. He was struck on the back before he could get his balance. His armour spread the impact, but it knocked the wind from his lungs. He slashed around blindly behind him with the dagger, but made contact only with air.

Wulfric spurred Greyfell forward, desperate to give himself a moment to gather his wits. His ears still rang from the blow and things were happening too quickly for him to keep up. There were several bodies on the ground now, and as many riderless horses. Wulfric spotted a reaver to the side of the pack. With only a dagger, Wulfric knew rushing back in was foolhardy, but they were outnumbered, and he could not afford to hang back.

Greyfell accelerated into the melee without hesitation. Wulfric swiped at a reaver, but it was a feeble attempt and only luck that he caught him on the side of the neck. Blood gushed from his throat when Wulfric pulled the dagger free. Another reaver approached, seeing his comrade in trouble. Wulfric pulled the dying man's sword from his grasp and turned to face the new threat.

It seemed he had counted on Wulfric not having a sword and attacked rashly. He was overcommitted by the time he spotted Wulfric pulling it free. With what little energy he had left, Wulfric parried and countered. The sword was good and its edge was keen. It parted the reaver's leather armour with ease and cut through to his vitals.

Wulfric found himself next to Belgar. The old warrior smashed his warhammer into a reaver's face, who slumped in his saddle without a sound. Belgar looked at his bloody work with satisfaction, visibly pleased with his victory over a man at least half his age. He did not notice the next reaver until it was almost too late.

Belgar was able to get his armour-plated forearm up in time to meet the blow, but the force of the impact was enough to send him to the ground with a crunch of metal. Wulfric turned and urged his horse forward. The reaver was pressing on, looking as though he planned to trample Belgar to death. Greyfell shouldered into the reaver's horse, knocking it sideways. Off balance, the reaver was slow in turning his attention to Wulfric. He wore a steel breastplate, so Wulfric stabbed into his armpit and on until the wound was mortal.

Wulfric pulled his blade free. He could hear his blood pulse through his ears like the beat of a war drum, and had never felt so energised. He realised his teeth were chattering again. He looked around, hungry for another opponent, but there were none; those that survived were fleeing for the trees and were too far away for him to give chase.

In the blink of an eye, the energy was gone once more. Fatigue, the like of which Wulfric had not known before, hit him like a hammer. He slumped in his saddle, too tired to even sit up straight. He couldn't understand why he was so exhausted. Might he be ill? Still weakened by the pilgrimage? His mind felt as heavy as his body, and he struggled for any clarity in his thoughts. He remembered the strange shivering and detached feeling when he fought. The memory of cutting a man in half popped into his head, vivid and visceral. The memory of not caring who was friend and foe, only the desire to kill. What had come over him? Was this Jorundyr's gift?

It was the first real taste of battle for all of them but Belgar, and the reality of it was far removed from the image Wulfric had of it. The snow was churned through with mud, and splattered with gore. It was not glorious. He felt nearly as bad as he had after the pilgrimage. His throat hurt, his head throbbed, and he ached from a dozen bumps and scratches that he couldn't remember receiving. He was so tired he thought he would fall from his saddle.

Judging by the riderless horses and the bodies on the ground, only two or three of the reavers would be returning home, hopefully with no desire to come anywhere near Leondorf ever again. Wulfric made a quick count. Including Belgar, there were six still on horseback, with Fridric, a seventh, still struggling to control his horse a safe distance away. That meant three unaccounted for. He had seen Kolbein take a spear in the charge. He looked around and saw Anshel dead on the ground not far from him. The blow to his head had shocked Wulfric less. Anshel's glassy eyes stared into the sky, a length of shattered spear shaft protruding from his chest. Wulfric stared, unable to accept it. First Hane, now Anshel. Jorundyr was taking the best of them first. The others sat on their horses, looking around but not moving, as though none of them had any idea of what to do next.

Wulfric took his helmet off. His neck ached so badly it felt as though his head had increased in weight four-fold. There was a large dent on the back of the helmet, and he hoped there wasn't a similar one on the back of his head.

Belgar limped over.

'You all right, lad?'

Wulfric tried to nod, then thought better of it. 'Fine, I think,' he said, his throat painfully dry.

Belgar nodded and turned in Fridric's direction. He let out a piercing whistle that did Wulfric's headache no favours, and gestured for Fridric to come over. He did so with obvious reluctance.

'Go and see if the cattle are still over there. Don't scatter them if they are,' Belgar said.

'What if there are still some raiders with them?' Fridric said.

'We've put enough of a fright on them even for you to scare them off. Pretend you're a man, for once in your bloody life!' Belgar screamed. The old man's renewed vigour still showed in the withering stare he gave Fridric. The councilman finally moved off toward the treeline.

Belgar turned back to Wulfric. 'Looks like we lost three.'

Wulfric hoped the third missing rider would stand up from the bodies on the ground, but that hadn't happened.

'I saw Kolbein go down,' Wulfric said. 'Anshel is there. I don't know who the third is.'

'Rorik, I think,' Belgar said.

Wulfric tried to give a solemn nod, but his neck was too sore.

Belgar looked at him oddly, and spoke after a moment. 'You fought like a man possessed. It's been quite a while since I've seen a man cut in two.' He smiled and slapped Wulfric on the leg. 'Those men were seasoned warriors. You all did very well today.'

Wulfric forced a smile, but it was difficult to be pleased with victory when three of his friends lay dead. Another few raids like that, and none of them would be left. Wulfric thought back to what he had said before the fight started. They needed leadership. He turned to the others.

'Farlof! Roal!' They turned to look at him. 'If you're not injured, go and see if the councilman needs help gathering the cattle.'

They both nodded and acted on his command. The remaining two looked to Wulfric, waiting for their instructions. Wulfric took a deep breath, his head hurting too much to fully appreciate what was happening. 'Let's see to the bodies,' he said. 'Get them back on their horses for the ride home. The cattle thieves can rot where they lie.' Every decision made his head pound more. He wanted nothing more than sleep.

He looked to Belgar for some indication of what he thought about Wulfric's decisions, but it was impossible to tell. Where a moment before there had been steel in his eyes, and a firm set to his jaw, Belgar once again had the tired, weakened look of the elderly man that he was. The sight crushed Wulfric, but there was something stirring in what had happened that afternoon, something in how, just for a few moments, Belgar the Old had been Belgar the Bold once more.

CHAPTER THIRTY-THREE

THE CATTLE WERE discovered, standing with disinterest between the trees. Fridric rode out of the forest behind them with a smile so broad one would be forgiven for thinking that he had chased off the reavers single handed. They drove the cattle back to the herdsman, whose taciturn demeanour showed the faintest hint of a crack when he saw his beasts being returned. That three men died in their retrieval bothered him not in the least.

Fridric chattered the whole way home, his elation at having been part of a battle and taking back the cattle causing a personality transformation. Wulfric wondered how his report to the newly constituted council would sound now. His thoughts of the day were bittersweet. He had gone on his first ranging, fought his first battle, killed his first man. A few weeks before, he had been a boy. Now he was an anointed and blooded warrior. He had also lost comrades and that soured everything else. The image of Hane looking at him with that sad smile and blood bubbling from the corners of his mouth was joined by one of Anshel's pale face and lifeless eyes, and Kolbein being flicked from his horse like a rag doll. They were images he knew he would never be able to erase. The village could ill afford the loss. If every ranging was the same, Wulfric reckoned he would be dead by spring.

He looked over at Belgar. He had not given an order since they turned to charge the raiders. It was Wulfric's commands that were followed and not once had anything he said been questioned. None of them had even hesitated to act on his word. It was a strange feeling, a heavy one. A burden.

❋

Rorik's mother was one of the first faces that Wulfric saw when they rode back into the village. Her eyes fixed on his briefly, before jumping to each of the other riders and only then to the three horses with bodies draped across their backs. It was not the way of Northlanders to display their emotion in public, and Wulfric could see her face screw up as she fought to contain the wail of anguish inside her. Everyone in Leondorf had suffered in the previous months; Rorik's father died with Wulfric's on the road to Rasbruck. Wulfric feared this was the woe that would break their resolve. The cattle felt worthless to him now. It was too high a price to pay for pride, and Wulfric couldn't imagine six cattle being the difference between comfort and starvation.

The council members, alerted to the commotion outside, appeared from the Great Hall and stood atop the steps leading up to it. Fridric pushed his way forward as though he was the most important man alive, and started talking excitedly once within earshot of them. Wulfric didn't give a damn for what he had to say. All he wanted was to get home, put his head down and pull his blanket over his head. It still throbbed, and there was a whistling noise in his ears that had not waned since he'd been hit. He could not explain why he was so tired, nor the strange sensation that had overcome him. He thought of what Aethelman had said about Jorundyr's Chosen. He would have to discuss it with him as soon as he got a chance.

He watched Fridric get ushered into the Great Hall. He realised Belgar was beside him.

'You should be proud,' Belgar said.

'I don't feel that way. It isn't worth six cows.'

'Is it worth a dozen? Or a hundred? If we hadn't done what we did today, that's what we would have ended up losing. Maybe the lot, and our people would starve. Now they know we can fight to keep what's ours, and if they come looking, we'll send them home draped across their horses' backs.' He paused and looked at the Great Hall, his face darkening.

'Are you going to join them?' Wulfric said, nodding to the Great Hall.

'Aye. Assuming I'm still welcome. Should never have let them in.'

Wulfric spotted his mother, with Adalhaid standing beside her. The two most important people in his life. The sight of them together gave him hope that he might be able to keep both of them in it.

Belgar saw the direction of his glance. 'Go,' he said, forcing a smile. Wulfric nodded, slipped from his saddle, and walked to their embrace.

❉

The warmth and comfort of home did little to settle Wulfric. He sat at the table as his mother cooked, his thoughts miles away. He could not forget the way the councilmen gathered at the door to the Great Hall, the possessive, almost hostile way they had regarded the warriors when they had come back to the square. No thanks, no congratulations; nothing but a jealous glare.

Belgar had given Wulfric the responsibility of First Warrior that morning. He wondered if it would be made permanent, but still dared not tell his mother. She put a plate of stew down on the table, and sat. Wulfric started immediately; he had not realised how hungry he was until he smelled the cooking food.

'I've been thinking,' Frena said.

Wulfric stopped mid-chew. That phrase usually preceded something that he would not like.

'Adalhaid was here the whole time you were gone. The pilgrimage, when you were ill…'

Wulfric lowered his spoon to the plate. He was too tired to have this argument. His mind was long made up, and there would be no changing it. As much as he loved his mother and respected her opinion, there was no one who could tell him what to do now.

'She's a fine young woman,' Frena said. 'None finer. I realise that now, and with everything that's happened, everything that's changed…' She paused for breath. 'Well, with your father gone, I've been thinking of the things that are important. The things that are *really* important. I was so afraid that I'd lose you when you went on the pilgrimage. Again when you went on the ranging. Life is short and hard, and you should spend it with the people you care the most about.'

Wulfric opened his mouth to speak, but his mother continued before he had the chance.

'I'll speak with Svana's mother in the morning. If you're not to be betrothed to her, she should know as soon as possible.'

❉

'Hello, Wulfric,' Aethelman said. 'I'm glad to see you looking so much better. What can I do for you?'

He was tired, and had been hoping to go to bed when the young warrior turned up at the kirk. Politeness always seemed so artificial when forced.

'There's something I need to talk to you about,' Wulfric said.

Aethelman raised an eyebrow. 'You best come in then.'

Aethelman's small magical light—called a mage lamp in the South— was all that illuminated the kirk. He sat on a bench, and waited for Wulfric to start.

'We spoke before,' Wulfric said. He chewed on his lip before continuing. 'About being chosen by Jorundyr.'

Aethelman raised both eyebrows this time. 'Yes. I remember.'

'When we were fighting the reavers. I felt... odd. I was wondering if that might be it?'

'Odd?'

'Shaking. My teeth chattering. Feeling like I'm watching myself from a distance, like I'm so strong I could do anything. A thirst; a desire to kill everything in front of me.'

'How long did the feeling last?'

'Until the danger had passed. Then I felt exhausted. Worse than exhausted.'

'Some of those chosen by Jorundyr become devastating warriors. It's a curse as well as a blessing, however, as they can be a danger to everyone around them, not only their enemies. The "berserk" it's been called in the past, but I don't think that a fair name, and was given by those who did not understand it.'

'What use is that?' Wulfric said, his voice laden with frustration.

'Quite a lot, when your foe are draugar and you are surrounded by hundreds of them. In this world, surrounded by friends as well as foes, it can be... a problem.'

'What will I do? What if I hurt one of my friends?'

'That you didn't on this occasion is a good sign. It means you maintained some control, and not all of the berserkir were capable of that.'

'I don't like it,' Wulfric said. 'And I don't want it.'

'But you're stuck with it,' Aethelman said.

'What if I'm not able to make that choice again? What if the thirst takes hold of me and I can't? How can I be First Warrior if I'm as much a danger to my friends as my enemies?' His voice rose in panic as he spoke.

Aethelman shrugged. 'I'm sorry to say I have no answer for you. Only you can explore the gift, and perhaps learn to control it. Some did. Others adapted the way they fought to ensure they could never be a danger to their comrades. Perhaps you can learn to stave the experience off. Then again, one day it might save your life, and those of your friends. Great power can never be given unfettered; it destroys a man's soul if granted without limitation. If Jorundyr thought you strong enough to be given this gift, then he believes you to be strong enough to control it. As do I, once you've learned to understand it. That will take time.'

Wulfric nodded, ambivalent.

'It will likely get stronger as you grow fully to manhood,' Aethelman said. 'It would be wise to begin exploring it now while it will be easier to master.'

'There's one other thing,' Wulfric said, one of his competing concerns laid to rest for the time being. 'It's about Adalhaid. And me. Adalhaid and me.'

Aethelman smiled.

CHAPTER THIRTY-FOUR

'I WANT A SEAT on the council,' Rodulf said.

Donato pushed aside the papers he had been reviewing and gave Rodulf an inquiring look. He had not even bothered to knock before entering Donato's office at the back of their warehouse on the village's outskirts.

'Two voices are stronger than one. You'd know you have one supporter there always.'

'Would I?' Donato said. There were many things about his son that gave him pride, but his avariciousness was such that even Donato was shocked at times.

'You would,' Rodulf said, clearly missing the implication. 'But you need to include me in your plans. For instance, what advantage is there in bringing the southerners here? Surely you realise that once they've got a foothold over the border they won't give it up.'

Donato knew Rodulf was beginning to tire of being kept in the dark about his schemes.

'They're more than welcome to stay,' Donato said, curious to see where Rodulf's line of reasoning would take him.

'They'll take every little bit of power you've brought us. We'll be back where we started, only with masters of another name. The only difference is their contempt of all Northlanders, not just the merchant classes.'

Donato leaned back and smiled. His son's ambition still outweighed his skill in thinking ahead, but he was improving.

'The southerners hate the Northlands, Rodulf. It's wild, dangerous, uncivilised. They do like what they can get here, though. Plenty of wealth to be had, fortunes to be made. That's all they're interested in. They won't want to live up here. To ensure they get what they want without dirtying their expensive leather boots, they'll need someone to take care of things, ensure that the coin keeps flowing south. Someone effective. Someone who understands both the North and the South, and can keep both happy. Why do you think I sent you off on all of those apprenticeships? It certainly wasn't to keep southern whores in business.'

Rodulf blushed at the comment, but Donato paid a visit to one of Elzburg's better brothels every time he was there so he didn't push the issue.

'Keep everyone happy, keep the money flowing south, and the southerners will let us do what we want here. Then, if we run into trouble, we can send south for thousands of warriors to deal with it, and ship them back when we're done.'

'And what if that person isn't you?' Rodulf said.

'I'll make damn sure it is.' The audacity of the question infuriated him. Who else could fill that role? There were one or two other merchants in the village whose wealth approached his own, but they were still a distant second and he had pushed them into the background on the council. His voice was the most frequent, the most prominent, and the one sided with most often. He was the only man for the job, and he glared at Rodulf for suggesting otherwise.

Rodulf scratched at his eye patch. Donato was tired of him trying to find fault with everything he did. Rodulf might be clever—but so was he, and he had years of experience behind him. The warriors' arrogance had brought about their own destruction, whatever that bastard Wolfram might have implied, and Donato had manoeuvred everything perfectly since then. He was already de facto leader of the village—First Warrior, in a sense, even though he could never be called that. The idea made him smile to himself. He made a mental note that he would have to come up with an appropriate title for himself. He gave Rodulf a good look. Since ceasing his constant training, he had grown slender, shedding the unnecessary muscle. Donato knew he still practised with a sword in secret, but used a southern blade now, a rapier that he had bought on his travels. He kept his sandy blond hair shorter, another affectation of the South. Combined with his usual choice in clothes, it made him look far more the southern gentleman than Northlander. He would need to learn to maintain the balance between

North and South if he was to fulfil the legacy he would be left. Everything Donato achieved would one day fall to his son, and Rodulf should be more appreciative of the fact.

'What if the warriors are able to protect the village?' Rodulf said. 'They managed it with the reavers. What if the people don't think we need help from the south?'

'One small skirmish, and three of them were killed,' Donato said. 'How long do you think they'll be able to keep that up? This village has large herds, and the few warriors that are left can't be everywhere at once. I'll see to it that they are out ranging every minute. Captain Morlyn wasn't the only man willing to drive off some cattle for a few coins. By midsummer, every warrior will sup with Jorundyr and the southerners will be our only hope for survival.'

Rodulf nodded. 'About the council?'

Tenacious. It was difficult not to be proud of him at times, even if friction now seemed ever present. 'We'll see. And next time you come in here, knock.'

❄

Wulfric would have been the first to admit that things seemed to be happening quickly, but on the other hand it felt as though he had been moving toward this moment with Adalhaid all of his life. Now that his mother had given him her support, he did not want to give her time to change her mind. He had hoped to keep the matter quiet—a formal betrothal was only a private formality on the road to marriage—but in a small village, it was difficult.

His brother warriors Stenn, Farlof, Roal, and Urrich, as well as Belgar, were waiting for him in the kirk when he walked in with his mother. They gave him a knowing smile, but no one said anything as they waited for Adalhaid and her mother to arrive. Despite it only being a promise ceremony, conducted under the eyes of the gods, Wulfric felt his heart race in anticipation. Might she have a change of heart? Decide that his being with Svana was for the best and leave for the South again without telling anyone? If he were that nervous at the betrothal, what would the actual wedding be like?

He breathed a sigh of relief when she arrived, and then a second to steady himself at the sight of how beautiful she looked. She was wearing her best clothes, a bodice-jacket and long skirt cut from emerald-green southern cloth that contrasted against her dark red hair and fair skin like emeralds and rubies on the snow. Wulfric felt shabby by comparison in his bland rough-spun wool trews, jacket and belek cloak.

He took her hand and they joined Aethelman at the altar in silence. Wulfric had no idea what to say to her, and didn't want to spoil the moment with foolish words. The opportunity was taken away from him as Aethelman began.

'I won't keep you long,' he said. 'More people are here than I'd usually expect for something like this. Adalhaid and Wulfric, do you both wish to enter into a promise of marriage?'

'Yes,' Wulfric said, relieved to hear the word mirrored by Adalhaid.

'Under the eyes of Agnarr, Father of the Gods, you are now betrothed. You shall remain chaste and in this state of half-marriage until at least two new moons have passed. If the gods disapprove of your intentions, they will make themselves known in this time. If not, you will have their blessing to marry at any time after the second moon has waned, and you have come of age.'

For Wulfric, it was a moment where it was difficult to tell reality from the imagined. It was almost like the sensation he'd had when fighting the reavers. It took a shout to bring him back to reality.

'Kiss her, you clown!'

Farlof.

Wulfric blushed slightly and they kissed again. A slap on the back ended the moment.

'Enough time for that later,' Belgar said. 'Now that you're First Warrior, the village will be expecting a betrothal feast fitting to the occasion.'

'First Warrior?' Wulfric said.

'I got the council to confirm it yesterday,' he said. 'It didn't all go my way, but we can talk about that later. You and the others have some hunting to do if you want enough meat to go around.'

'Now?' Wulfric said.

'Is there a better time?' Belgar said. 'The village could use a celebration, and the First Warrior's betrothal is as good a reason as any.'

Wulfric looked back at Adalhaid. 'We've barely said a word to each other,' he said.

She shrugged and smiled. 'What do we need to say?'

'You look so beautiful,' he said.

She laughed. 'Well, I'll let you say that much. Now go with your friends. Belgar's right, the village could do with a celebration.'

CHAPTER THIRTY-FIVE

'THE MERCHANT TOLD me they had plenty of food,' Ritschl said. Gandack stroked his beard, as he always did when trying to appear thoughtful, but Ritschl was confident that his course was already set. Rasbruck was on the verge of starvation. The merchant that Ritschl had spoken with had made no mention of food supplies in Leondorf, only that they had but a handful of warriors, none much more than boys. There would never be a better opportunity.

Gandack looked to Emmeram.

'Even if we rationed heavily, we won't have enough to see us through the winter,' Emmeram said.

'And these paid men will agree to fight for a share of the spoils?' Gandack said.

'They will,' Thietmar said. 'It seems it's common knowledge how weakened Leondorf is. If we don't strike at them soon there'll be nothing left to take. The scouts have seen signs that the smaller villages have already been raiding their cattle.'

'Sending warriors to battle in winter… I don't know,' Gandack said.

'It hasn't snowed in over a week,' Emmeram said. 'The roads are as passable as we could hope for.'

'Still, taking all of their food in winter…' Gandack said. 'It seems the type of thing Jorundyr would frown upon.'

'Jorundyr favours those who look after their own,' Ritschl said. 'Better that they go hungry than those you are sworn to protect.'

It was irritating that Gandack could no longer do so much as visit the privy ditch without reassurance that the gods favoured the act. The battle with Leondorf had gone hard on him; he had lost both of his sons, not to mention the majority of the town's warriors. The prize would make it all worthwhile, though. For Ritschl, at least.

'Fine,' Gandack said, his voice carrying a rare tone of certainty. 'We'll attack them. It seems there is little time to waste.'

❄

Reluctant at first, Wulfric had come to love the hunt. From the skills of tracking the beasts to the mortal struggle against them, he revelled in the thrill of it all. He wanted his betrothal feast to be well provided for. It was another opportunity to show everyone what he and the others were capable of. They rode out of the village in high spirits, with the hunting hounds leading the way, padding through the snow with their long loping run. It was the first time in recent memory that it felt as though the cloud of misfortune above them all had parted.

The dogs chased down a small sounder of boar late in the afternoon, as they were trained to do. Spot led them. When Adalhaid had left, Wulfric took him into his kennels. He had continued to grow and had quickly risen to lead the pack. He was now the size of a small pony and as fine a hunting dog as could be wanted. Spot and the other two ran the boars back to the hunters in a small glade deep in the forest with expert precision. It made Wulfric rue the poor dog's unfortunate naming. He had always thought 'Ulfyr' would be more fitting for such a fine dog, rather than 'Spot'.

They each killed a boar, with the exception of Urrich, and Wulfric was satisfied that there would be enough meat to ensure everyone went home from the celebration with a full belly, and perhaps a little more confidence in their few young warriors.

They left their horses tied up at the treeline and set about bundling up their kills. They were spread across the glade as they went to work, with Urrich standing idly in their midst.

'I wouldn't worry too much about it, Urrich,' Farlof said. 'Not everyone can get a kill. Remind me next time, and I'll show you how!'

'Shut up, Farlof,' Urrich said, clearly annoyed that he was the only one going home without a boar tied to his horse.

A branch snapped somewhere out to Wulfric's left, the crack echoing between the trees. He glanced to the hounds, who had heard it also, and, with ears pricked up, were scanning the forest. He stared out between the trees in the direction of the sound, but could see nothing. It came from the far side of the glade, so could not have been the horses. He strained left and right to get a better look between the trees. The others paid the sound no attention, but he felt concern grow in the pit of his stomach.

Roal, Farlof, and Stenn were spread out around the glade, Roal and Farlof tying the legs of their kills up, while Stenn, already finished, played with one of the hounds with boyish enthusiasm. Urrich walked around kicking at the snow, sulking at not having gotten a kill. It reminded Wulfric of how young they all really were. There was silence in the forest once more. It was always easy to let paranoia get the better of you in the wilderness, Wulfric thought. So many shadows, so many sounds, so many stories to play on the imagination. He turned his attention back to his boar when a grey blur flashed through the glade.

Wulfric was on his feet with his sword drawn before he had the chance to consider what he had seen. Where Urrich had been standing, there was now only air. The dogs whimpered and the others all stopped, looking at the spot.

'What happened? Where'd Urrich go?' Stenn said.

'Belek,' Wulfric said. It was the only possibility. The word was out of his mouth before he had time to consider it, but the tracks on the snow confirmed it. He found it difficult to make his voice come out as anything more than a cloying whisper.

All the others went pale the moment he said it. They jumped to their feet and scrabbled to draw their swords. The dogs paced around in circles, nervous, confused. The horses were straining against their tethers. Greyfell looked as though he might kick the tree down.

Wulfric scanned the forest where he thought the grey shape had gone. He had thought never to encounter a belek again. One was as many as most men ever saw, unless they went looking for them. To have a chance encounter with two seemed dreadful luck. Wulfric thought back to Aethelman's words at the betrothal. Was this the gods trying to put a stop to the marriage?

He looked at the dogs, who circled around him like mewling puppies. The Northland scent-hound was a fearsome beast, and Wulfric had never seen them show even a hint of fear before. With shaggy grey coats and long snouts they were strong yet graceful, but above all brave. One could chase down and kill a man with ease. Packs of them were used in war. To see them behave so was terrifying.

The others looked to Wulfric for reassurance and direction, when it was all he could do to hold his nerve. It felt so much worse this time. On the last occasion he had been so tired it had all felt like a dream. This time was all too real, and it had taken Urrich.

Only a fool did not fear a belek—Angest had always openly admitted each and every one he killed had terrified him. It didn't stop him from hunting them, however. Wulfric tried to calm himself with the thought that he had faced one before, alone, and survived. He wore the cloak to prove it. He had company this time, and a good sword.

There had not been so much as a scream from Urrich. He was not a small man, and the speed and ease with which he'd been carried off was shocking. Wulfric continued to scan the trees, but saw nothing.

'Maybe it won't come back,' Roal said.

It was too much to hope for. When belek encountered men, they killed as much for the sport as for food. It was still out there, somewhere among the trees, watching them. It would not leave until it had killed them all.

'It killed one of our own,' Wulfric said. He could feel his hands start to shake, which added to his concern. Were the others far enough away from him? 'Either it dies, or we do.' There was steel in his voice, but it felt as though someone else was speaking.

There was a low throaty growl and the belek stepped out from the treeline, unconcerned at losing the element of surprise. It walked along the edge of the glade, looking appraisingly at the four men, the three hounds, and the horses. Its eyes gleamed with predatory intelligence. It was bigger than any of the dogs by far, and seemed larger than the one Wulfric killed.

The hounds retreated behind Wulfric. None of the other hunters moved, but they tracked the beast with the tips of their swords, doing their best to prepare for its strike. As afraid as he was, Wulfric felt a tingle of excitement running over his skin. It sent a shiver through him that he worried the others would see as a sign of fear. His teeth started to chatter.

A foolish thought popped into his head—the fame that killing a second belek would bring him. Few enough managed to kill one. Those who killed two became legends. He could hear the name 'Wulfric Beleks' Bane' in his head. He might never see another one for as long as he lived. He had no idea what madness was causing him to think like that, but he realised the fear was gone.

Before he knew what he was doing, Wulfric was walking away from the hounds, sabre held out in front. He felt flooded with energy as his hands shook and teeth chattered uncontrollably. He felt as though he could run for hours, climb without rest, fight until he had laid waste to all before him, but would burst if he did not release all that building energy. Aethelman had said Jorundyr's gift might one day save his life. Would it be that day? He roared a challenge.

The belek snapped its head in his direction. The two large fangs that curved down out of its mouth glistened with blood. The fur all around its mouth was matted with it. Urrich's blood. Wulfric felt a great rage well up inside of him. He wanted to pull it limb from limb. The belek took no further notice of the dogs or the other hunters. It wanted Wulfric first. It wanted Wulfric most of all. It turned to face him, its movements lithe and its muscles rippling beneath its pristine steely coat. It growled, the sound deep and rumbling as it echoed in its great chest. It seemed like distant thunder. Everything seemed distant.

The belek charged at him, its hulking, muscular body moving with mesmerizing grace and speed. Its silver fur shimmered in the evening sun as it pounced. Wulfric watched it come at him as though he had all the time in the world. It felt as though he did, even as he threw himself backward onto the snow and rolled to the side. There was a loud growl as the belek passed by him. Wulfric looked to see one of the hounds hurl itself against the belek, snarling with all the fury it could muster. The belek was momentarily distracted, giving Wulfric time to roll over onto his belly and jump to his feet. There was a yelp, and Wulfric saw the broken body of one of his hounds lying by the belek. The belek took no more notice of the mortally injured dog and turned to face Wulfric.

The belek prowled forward, its gaze fixed on Wulfric. He willed it on toward him. Out of the corner of his eye, Wulfric could see Stenn and Farlof frozen on their spots, watching with morbid fascination. Roal, who had been out on his own, was slowly moving toward them, seeking safety in numbers. Were they waiting for his command to attack?

A distant voice in his head said he should give it, but madness flowed through his veins. He wanted the belek all for himself, and he was tiring of its little game. He let out a roar and charged.

The belek's eyes widened, but it was not to be frightened by a mere man. It roared in reply, bloody spittle spraying from its teeth. Wulfric moved fast, faster than the belek had expected—faster than Wulfric had expected himself. He brought his sword down at the belek's head, but it leapt out of the way and hissed at him. Wulfric closed the distance and attacked again, driving the belek back. The sound of his heart beat out like a great war drum in his ears. Wulfric felt invincible. The belek seemed slow, like nothing more than an overgrown cat. The terror it had inspired in him seemed like a foolish little thing.

The belek swiped at him with one of its enormous clawed paws. Wulfric jumped to dodge, but could not get clear in time. He felt it brush across him, but there was no pain. He leaped forward, bringing his sword down in a great arc. Joy exploded within him as he felt the blade connect with flesh and sinew and bone. He heard the belek screech, was aware of its fangs, its claws, but he ignored them and drove forward with all his strength, seeking out the monster's heart.

It let out a loud hiss. Wulfric had driven his sword into it as far as the hilt. His shoulder pressed against the beast's, and his face was next to its eye. He looked into it and saw the hate that dwelled within. His knuckles were white on the handle of his sabre, and he pressed against the belek with all of his weight and strength. It thrashed its head against him once and then again, trying to bring its great fangs into play, but the second effort was feebler than the first. Wulfric summoned up more strength and pressed with his legs as hard as he could. The belek gave ground. He twisted the sword and it collapsed.

Wulfric pulled his sword free and stepped back. He looked over to the others. They stood in silence, aghast. His eyes were wild and he had a manic expression on his face. He had never felt so alive. He looked at his hands, his chest, and realised he was covered in blood. The belek's, he thought with satisfaction. Then he collapsed.

CHAPTER THIRTY-SIX

ETHELMAN KNEW LEONDORF'S troubles could only justify him remaining for so long, and that time had passed. Wulfric's betrothal celebration would mark, he hoped, a return to happier times for the village. Belarman was settled now, and Aethelman was confident in the young priest's ability. He would serve the people of Leondorf well. Slipping away quietly seemed like the best plan. It was well past time that he did so.

Everything was packed, but for the box containing the Stone. He sat on his cot and stared at it. It would be the focus of the next few months of his life. The next few years, perhaps. He had protected it for many years, and was proud of the fact that he had never once tried to use it. He had been tempted on many occasions, but had not succumbed. He had remained true to his mission for all of those years, keeping it safe and out of sight. Now it was time to see it out of the world of men. His god, Birgyssa—the patron of priests and healers—would guide him. He would seek out a holy place and there she would instruct him on how to ensure the Stone remained safe after he passed from the world. He had done his duty to her, now it was her turn. He hoped he had the strength to see out this final task. He prayed that she would help him in it.

He winced as he stood, his old knees creaking in protest. This was a journey he should have made many years before, but Leondorf had been a good home to him. The only true home he had ever known. It was difficult to leave, even now. He had only made things harder for himself by staying.

There was a shout from outside, and Aethelman's curiosity got the better of him. He walked through the dark nave and out into the bright daylight outside. He shielded his eyes and squinted to make out what was going on. There were a number of people around. They had all heard the shout, but looked puzzled. Aethelman walked down the steps and into the square.

'I heard a shout,' he said to the first person he came to. 'What was it?'

The woman shrugged. There was another shout. Then a scream. Aethelman could hear the sound of galloping horses. For a moment he hoped it was the hunters returning, but he knew it could not be. There was a group of children standing not far from where he was.

'Run away home,' Aethelman said. 'Away now. Don't dally.'

The adults also heeded his words as they all hurried away in different directions. He spotted several horsemen coming toward the village square. Before he knew what he was doing, he turned and started to run.

Aethelman had survived attacks like this before in other places. When they came, survival was the only aim. It wasn't brave and it would never form the basis for an epic tale, but there was no way women and children, tanners, smiths, and tradesmen had a chance against mounted warriors. All they could do was die needlessly. As priest, it was Aethelman's responsibility to ensure as many survived as possible.

He saw a group of villagers standing huddled in a frightened, bewildered group.

'Go to that tree and wait for me there,' Aethelman said.

One of the villagers nodded and ushered the others, too afraid to react on their own, toward the tree. Aethelman looked around frantically, but most people had already scattered to the pastures or gone home to hide. Out of the corner of his eye he spotted Adalhaid and Wulfric's mother, Frena. They were too far from home to have any chance of making it back there.

'This way,' Aethelman called. The air was filled with the sound of screams and chaos. Adalhaid saw him. He beckoned furiously and headed for the tree, keeping a careful watch. He cast a glance toward the kirk, and thought about the Stone. Raiders would not know what it was. In all likelihood the kirk would be burned, and he would recover it from the ashes. If he was very lucky it would be destroyed, but he didn't hold much hope for that.

'I want everyone to sit down by the tree as close to each other as you can,' he said when he arrived. Adalhaid and Frena were only a few paces behind him. He gestured for them to join the others.

'Are we to sit here and wait to be killed?' someone said.

'None of that,' Aethelman said. 'You have to trust me. Sit still all of you, and stay quiet like your life depends on it, because it does.'

He turned his back to the cluster of people and sat before them, cross-legged. Wisps of black smoke were rising from several places in the village. He looked toward the kirk, but could not tell if it was yet alight. He felt a pang of unease, and wished he'd had the presence of mind to bring the Stone with him, but it was too late. No one knew where it was. Or what it was. It looked worthless. There was no reason for it to be touched.

He took a deep breath and felt his skin tingle. It was years since he had attempted this. He cleared his mind as best he could, and reached deep into the place between the worlds where the hands of gods touched the lives of men. His body became energised and the air around him shimmered as it did on a hot summer's day.

Two horsemen came near, and Aethelman heard someone behind him let out a panicky gasp. One of the horsemen looked over, his brow furrowed. His gaze fell on Aethelman, but it was as though he looked straight through him. Aethelman prayed to Birgyssa and Jorundyr, and any other god who would listen, to keep the people behind him silent. A moment more was all he needed. The tension threatened to invade his mind and he fought to hold his concentration. The horseman stared at the tree intently, then scanned the ground. Aethelman could feel blood pulsing in his temples.

✳

Wulfric woke to one of the hounds licking his face. He pushed the dog away and looked around. Stenn and Farlof were standing over him. He collected his thoughts quickly and sat up. Pain made itself known to him across his left arm and shoulder, from a series of claw marks raked deep into his flesh. The wounds would leave scars to match those on his chest, but they were not enough to explain why he had blacked out.

'Are you all right?' Farlof said.

Wulfric stood, feeling more embarrassment than anything. 'Yes. I'm fine. They're only cuts. I'm not sure what happened. We should get back.'

They both nodded, but regarded him with curious looks.

They collected what they could find of Urrich's body—not much, but enough to allow his mother a funeral. Urrich was always a quiet one. Wulfric was more familiar with the sound of his bowstring than his voice. Now he would never hear either again. One less warrior to protect Leondorf, one more argument in favour of Donato's proposal to bring the southerners to the village.

The dog that had given Wulfric the vital few seconds to get back to his feet was Spot. He stood over the hound's broken body and wanted to weep. Spot was the only one of the dogs who had not fled and this was what his bravery had earned him. What would he tell Adalhaid? What would he tell Urrich's mother? What had Leondorf done to so incur the gods' wrath?

❄

Ritschl walked into Leondorf's kirk, his heart racing with anticipation. As he had instructed, it was the only building still standing in the village. Fires raged through the others, filling the air with acrid black smoke and the sickly stench of burning flesh. He took a look around the nave. It was more pleasant than the kirk in Rasbruck, larger too. He wondered where Aethelman might have hidden the Stone. He knew it was close. He could feel it. It called to him. The nave was a public place. Too many people passing in and out; it wouldn't be there. A door led into the back. There was a bed with a full leather satchel sitting on it. Ritschl gave it a cursory look. It seemed to be nothing more than clothes and travelling provisions.

The rest of the room was sparse in furniture. A small table sat beside the bed with a wooden box underneath it. He sat on the bed and pulled the box out from its nook. His breath quickened as he placed his hands on either side of it in preparation to lift the lid. He could already sense what was within. It creaked as he raised it. The poor light in the room glistened on the etched metallic surface. Ritschl laughed aloud when he saw it, and could feel tears form in his eyes. He took a felt bag from his cloak and opened it. He reached for the Stone, but hesitated. He could remember now that he had never touched it. Aethelman had kept it in his possession from the moment they had discovered it, since he was the senior.

What would it feel like? Would it start working as soon as he touched it? The Stone gave the bearer a direct link to the power of the gods. The things he could do with that power were limited only by his imagination. Every piece of magic he had ever worked was feeble in comparison to what he could achieve with the Stone. He grabbed it and dropped it into the bag.

His heart fluttered. He looked at his palm and wondered if the skin felt any different. It looked the same. He took a deep breath. He had to be patient. He had waited so long, he couldn't allow himself to lapse into haste now.

He walked outside, clutching the felt bag. Two of Rasbruck's warriors were in the village square on horseback.

'We've got everything worth taking,' one of them said.

'Good. Time to go home,' Ritschl said.

The horseman nodded to the kirk.

'Burn it,' Ritschl said.

The horseman raised his eyebrows.

'Jorundyr requires a warrior to crush his enemies. We leave nothing standing.'

The horseman nodded.

CHAPTER THIRTY-SEVEN

THE SNOW BECAME grey as they drew closer to Leondorf. At first Wulfric had not understood why, but he realised that it was covered in a coating of ash. It was only when the village hove into view that they could see a few tendrils of smoke rising to the heavens.

Little remained of Leondorf. Wulfric wavered as dizziness swept over him, his brain unable to take in what his eyes were seeing. A few charred timbers still stood upright like grave markers, but that was all. The homes of people he knew were not much more than black smudges on the ground. Only those few built from stone remained. To the side of the village there was a pile of bodies that were partially burned. Roal vomited when he realised what they were. Wulfric wondered if it was the only one, or if there were more piles like it. It was too small for an entire village. He tried not to look at it, not wanting to know who was there, but one face caught his attention, the fine angular features and crystal blue eyes not so far removed in death from what they had been like in life. Wulfric prayed that Svana hadn't suffered. He felt numb.

They dismounted and stumbled slowly into the village, looking around them in shock at the devastation. It was several minutes before they saw a living person, who made to run at first, but stopped when he recognised them.

'What happened?' Wulfric said.

'Warriors came. Late in the morning. They took our food. They started burning down buildings and killing people. They took everything.' The man wandered away into the smoke and ash before Wulfric could ask him anything else.

Wulfric felt his stomach twist in the most horrible way. He was in no hurry as he wandered through the village in the direction of his home, and Adalhaid's. Each step took him closer to the confirmation of something he didn't want to know. However, until he saw it with his own eyes, he knew he would not be able to accept it.

Like all the houses in the village, Wulfric's had been made from timber. Now it was ash and charred wood. Adalhaid's was much the same. He fought to repel the wave of despair that was surrounding and pressing down on him. He felt dizzy as he looked around. The stone parts of the Great Hall and the kirk still stood. The smithy likewise. They were all that remained of Leondorf.

Wulfric walked back to the square in a daze. He wondered what the village must have been like in the moments before the attack arrived. Everyone had been talking about the betrothal celebration when they left. He stared at the well, now only a circle of stone. They had even burned the winding mechanism for the bucket, and the small roof that covered it. The thoroughness with which they destroyed the town spoke volumes for their hate, and how they had likely treated the villagers. It could only have been Rasbruck. Might others have gotten away?

He walked toward the pile. As he drew closer, he could pick out other familiar faces. Not friends or family, but people known to him, their faces frozen in the horror of their last moment of life. They were just ordinary people, not warriors. It was hard to see what reason there could be for killing them.

'Wulfric! Look! There!' Stenn said.

Wulfric felt his heart leap into his throat. He found himself praying to Jorundyr. There were people approaching the village. He squinted, but they were too far away to recognise. He collected Greyfell, mounted and galloped toward them. He had not gone far before he realised how they might react to the sight of a warrior charging toward them, so he slowed. They kept coming, however.

Aethelman's was the first face he saw that he recognised. There were a dozen or so people with him.

'Adalhaid? My mother?' Wulfric said.

Aethelman looked back into the group. 'Frena. Adalhaid.'

Wulfric felt light headed with relief when he saw them both step from the group.

He jumped from Greyfell and rushed over, gathering them up in his arms.

'Wulfric? You're covered in blood,' his mother said. 'Did you get back in time?'

Wulfric shook his head. 'No. They were gone. This was from… before.' He felt a wave of guilt. Might they have been able to stop the attack if they hadn't been away hunting?

He turned to Aethelman. 'Rasbruck?'

Aethelman nodded. 'They came this morning. Took whatever they could carry, killed anyone they saw and burned everything left to the ground.'

'How did you get away?'

'I gathered up as many as I could. I hid them.'

'How?' Wulfric said.

Aethelman smiled in the way he always had when Wulfric was young and questioned him on the workings of his magic, but it was strained. Forced.

'And them?' Wulfric gestured to the pile of bodies.

An expression of shame appeared on Aethelman's face, and Wulfric felt bad for saying it.

'As many as I could,' he said, his voice catching on a lump in his throat.

'You did me a great service today, Aethelman,' he said, holding Adalhaid tightly. 'Thank you.' He knew it was small consolation, as tears streaked Aethelman's soot-covered face.

※

The survivors set to erecting a temporary shelter that very evening. It was cold, and enough had died already without losing more to the chills. There were elderly, young, and injured who would start to suffer sooner than the rest. They had to work quickly.

Enough wood was scavenged from the remains of the village to construct a flat-roofed shack. It was dark and draughty, but it would at least get them all through the first few nights. The proper rebuild would have to wait until the following morning.

There was no privacy there, but at least there was the meat they had brought in from the hunt. They set to cooking one of the carcasses right away. A few more people straggled in over the course of the evening, Belgar and his family, Donato and Rodulf among others, but one boar had been enough to feed them all. All who remained of Leondorf.

In the darkness, Wulfric could hear sobs amidst the snores and whispers. He thought of the belek corpse outside, his glorious second, and how insignificant that achievement now felt. He thought of Urrich, of how the tragedy of his death had been all but forgotten. There was no family to mourn him now, only his brother warriors.

Farlof sat down beside him, disturbing Wulfric from his thoughts.

'Think any more will come back?' Farlof said.

'I don't know,' Wulfric said. 'I hope so.'

Farlof remained silent for a while. 'When that belek attacked us. What were you thinking?' His voice was quiet, serious, something unusual for Farlof. Usually he sounded as though everything he was saying was intended to tease or provoke a reaction. There was none of that now.

'I don't know,' Wulfric said. 'I can't really remember.'

'I'm no coward,' Farlof said. 'But I was terrified when that thing walked into the clearing. Stenn and Roal too. We would have fought it, but we were afraid. You weren't. How?'

'I've fought one before,' Wulfric said.

'That wasn't all, though. You called it to yourself. You weren't just unafraid. You wanted it to come to you.'

'I said I don't remember.' He wasn't lying, but there was a memory swirling in the murk at the back of his mind that he knew would become clearer if he had time to focus on it.

'I tried to lift up its body when you passed out,' Farlof said. 'I couldn't budge it. You pushed it back a few steps when it was still alive. I know you're strong, but *that* strong?'

Wulfric shrugged.

'I've never seen anyone fight like that before. We would have joined in. Helped. But it didn't look like you needed it.'

Wulfric had no idea what to say. His own thoughts were so muddled all he was able to do was shrug again. 'Has everyone got enough to eat?'

Farlof's lips tightened for a moment before he nodded. 'Yes. That much at least is taken care of. This shack won't do for long though.'

'We start rebuilding tomorrow,' Wulfric said. 'No one else is going to die this winter.'

❄

When Aethelman finally awoke, midway through the day after the attack, his first thought was of the Stone. He went to the kirk and walked through the ash, charred wood, and debris. He went straight to the place where his bedside table once sat, and where the box was kept. Nothing remained but a pile of ash. He sifted through it with his fingers, but other than a few fragments of wood there was nothing solid. He stood and looked around, weighing the possibilities in his mind.

Whale oil for his lamps, anointed oils for his ceremonies. There had been plenty of both in the kirk. More than enough to ensure the fire burned long and hot. Hot enough to destroy the Stone? He returned to the ash pile and cleared it away until he reached the hard-packed dirt floor. There was no trace of melted metal, but that meant nothing. The Stone was a holy object, and its destruction might mean it had returned to the gods. Was he being naive in thinking it might have completely disappeared from the realm of man? He didn't know enough to say one way or the other.

Who would have known to take it? The box was plain, the Stone nothing more than a misshapen piece of metal ore covered in runes. It looked no more valuable than many of the other religious artefacts in the kirk. There was nothing to single it out for attention. Aethelman moved to sit down on the edge of his bed before remembering it was no longer there. He looked up to the heavens, but had no idea what he was looking for. Any answers seemed to be escaping him completely. Of certainties, there was only one. He would remain and help rebuild. He had found Belarman's body with the others in the pile. It was a shameful thing to kill a priest—as it was to burn a kirk. All those people killed for no reason. What madness had driven them to it? He had never felt hate before, but in that moment it was all he had within him.

CHAPTER THIRTY-EIGHT

WULFRIC HAD HOPED that more people would return during the night, but there were no new faces the next morning and no one else arrived over the course of the day. Among the missing was Adalhaid's mother. They hadn't talked about it the previous night. After all the beatings and humiliations he had taken over the years, Wulfric knew better than most how healing a good night's sleep could be. He had made sure she had everything she needed and encouraged her to go to sleep as quickly as possible.

Work was already underway when he woke, but progress was slow. All the carpenters and their apprentices were dead, as were the smiths, the tanners, and the masons. Two of the woodsmen had survived, and had spent the morning felling trees which the remainder of the survivors were working to turn into planks. There was so much work to be done, and Wulfric had to wonder if there was any point starting over. There were so few of them now. Would they be better off going to one of the other smaller villages to see if they would take them in? It would make them vagrants and beggars. They would never be able to walk with their heads held high. They would end up in thrall to whoever took them in, if anyone did. As terrible as it was, he would prefer death. Their only saving grace was that what remained could be taken at will; there was no need to kill anyone for it.

Donato and several other men, Rodulf included, surveyed the devastation, riding around slowly in a superior and detached fashion. Wulfric wondered how they had time to find horses with so much to do and when everyone else was so busy. They paid little heed to the people toiling in the ash to rebuild their homes. After completing a tour, they returned to the stone shell of the Great Hall, dismounted and went in. Rodulf walked in behind his father as though it was the most normal thing in the world.

Belgar strode purposefully toward the Great Hall and joined them. Wulfric walked up to him.

'Shall I come in now?' Wulfric said.

Belgar grimaced and shook his head. 'That's the thing I mentioned, lad. You're First Warrior, but that's it. The others felt the title was best limited to the battlefield.'

Wulfric's eyes widened in disbelief.

'Now, don't look at me like that,' Belgar said. 'I did my best. They were going to do away with the title altogether. It was all I could do to save it, and make sure you got it. I'd best get in there.'

He left Wulfric wondering how to deal with the news. He had assumed that he was now part of the council, but his exclusion hammered home how much had changed, if the smouldering ruin of the village was not enough. He did not intend to be left in the dark however, so he made his way to the spot at the back of the hall, and sat against the scorched stones where he could not be seen.

'I think it safe to say, we have no other option now,' Donato said. 'If we're to have any hope of surviving, we need outside help.'

Hearing it said out loud was like a kick in the stomach for Wulfric. He could not shake off the feeling that had he and the others been there, they might have been able to stop the attack, but he knew that was a fantasy. There would merely have been five more bodies in the pile. Donato was right, and the fact that he could not disagree made the reality sting even more. There was a murmuring sound from the others, but it was difficult to tell if it was in agreement with what Donato had said or not.

'We have to plan for what's to come. As things are, Rasbruck can treat us as they like. It will be years before we have enough warriors to defend the village properly. We have no shelter and hardly any food.'

'I know what's coming next,' Belgar said, his voice flat.

'You know what's coming next because as much as age has addled your brains, you still have an ounce of sense left in that grey head of yours,' Donato said, his voice pregnant with conceit.

'There was a time when a mouth like that would have had you dead,'

Belgar said. 'Mayhap that'll be the case again one day. Sooner than you might like. Think on that.'

It was an impotent retort, and Wulfric felt bad for Belgar. It was sad to have lived so long that a man not his equal could talk down to him and not fear the consequences.

'I'll be sure to,' Donato said. 'My proposal is as it was. We send a delegate to Ruripathia and ask for their protection.'

'And why would they want to protect a burned husk of a village and a few hundred people who can't even feed themselves?' Belgar said.

He was fighting every inch of the way, and Wulfric felt proud of the fact, but there was no denying it was a losing battle.

'Leondorf was wealthy and powerful once. We still have a great deal of territory and untapped resources. We can offer them access to both, and give their people safe haven on this side of the river. If we move quickly we might even be able to keep some of our herds. We all know how much the southerners like our horses.'

'I'm sure there're plenty of Ruripathian lords who'd like to add our lands to their own holdings,' Belgar said, his voice defiant rather than combative. The argument was already over, and all that was left was for him to state the obvious.

'It's not my intention to hand our lands over to a Ruripathian lord. Raiding south of the river has always been an irritation for the Ruripathians. Our land abuts theirs, and I am sure they will be glad of having our territory as a buffer. We can offer their merchants and prospectors a safe place to extend their trade networks into the Northlands. They might want more, and we will have little option but to give it.'

There was not a single voice, other than Belgar's, which opposed Donato. By keeping Wulfric out of the Great Hall, away from the High Table, he had ensured that when Belgar died the warrior class would be excluded from government forever.

'I have made connections in the course of my trade with men of influence in the cities,' Donato said. 'I can send word to some of them to see what options there are to provide us with the support we need. As I have said, there will be a price. In order to appear as attractive to them as possible, we will need to know what we still have, and what we can get. Furs are popular in the South, easy to gather and transport. We should consider them a priority. Our horses too.'

There was a murmur of agreement from those assembled. Wulfric wondered at the frustration that Belgar must have been feeling. As much as life had changed for Wulfric, for Belgar, Leondorf must have seemed like an alien place.

Finally, Belgar added his voice to the sound. 'Very well,' he said, defeated. 'Make contact with whoever it is you deal with. See what can be done.'

❉

Having heard enough, Wulfric went to look for Adalhaid. As he walked he considered what he had just learned. As suspicious as the Northlanders were of their southern neighbours, perhaps it would be for the best. There was trade and communication between Leondorf and southern cities. Wulfric was given to understand they were not that far removed from the peoples of the Northlands. His father had told him that once, long ago, they were much the same but that they had become part of a great empire which set them on a different path. That was all so far in the past, the stories had almost the same qualities as those told of when Jorundyr and his wolf, Ulfyr, still walked the land.

As well as traders, warriors went south to fight, to gain fame in faraway lands. It was called following Jorundyr's Path. It was a pilgrimage of sorts, one of experience and braving the unknown. It was something Wulfric had often dreamed of, to see exotic places, meet strange peoples, and fight in great battles. So much would change with the arrival of the southerners, Wulfric could not help but question his role there. His exclusion from the council made one thing clear: the time for warriors in Leondorf was past. Ruripathian soldiers would defend the village in the future, merchants and noblemen would govern it. What would there be for him? He had no trade, no learning. He had more to think of than just himself, however. What of Adalhaid? He couldn't drag her with him.

❉

Wulfric found Adalhaid standing by the remains of her house with his mother, sobbing. Within the burnt-out remains of her home, she had gathered a small pile of charred bones. First her father, now her mother. Wulfric had no idea what to say to her.

It was the tradition in the Northlands to burn the bodies of the dead, and only then to bury what remained. For Adalhaid's mother, that was the only part of the ritual that remained. Wulfric felt a lump in his throat when he saw how distressed Adalhaid was. He thought of Rasbruck. Of flames. Of blood. Donato may have had a hand in causing the first battle, but the attack on the village was unprovoked and without justification. He would see them burn for it, if it was the last thing he did.

Without saying anything, he went to the patch of scorched ground that had once been the small shed at the back of his house. He kicked around in the ash until he found a shovel with enough of the handle remaining to be of use.

He returned to Adalhaid, his meaning obvious. His mother excused herself and went back to help the others. Adalhaid looked at the shovel and nodded. She placed the bones on a piece of cloth and then bundled them up.

'Is there anywhere you want to put them?' he asked. While there was a burial ground just outside the village, many people preferred to inter their loved ones in places that held significance for them.

She nodded again. 'Yes. With my father.'

Adalhaid's parents had a favourite spot by a tree, much like Wulfric and Adalhaid did, albeit on the other side of the village, looking out toward the distant sea to the west. They went there and Wulfric worked in silence as he dug into the bare patch of soil that had so recently been disturbed to bury her father's remains. He was careful not to dig too forcefully, for fear of damaging the bones already there, before removing the loose soil.

Eventually he glimpsed a piece of cloth and stopped. He stepped back, giving Adalhaid some space while she laid her mother to rest with her father. She let out one sob, but quickly regained her composure, the only sign of her distress the stream of tears that ran down her face. When she was done, Wulfric filled the soil back in with as much care as he could muster.

❋

Donato sent the delegation south the next morning. They needed to move swiftly if they were to hold onto what little remained, he said. In that,

Wulfric thought him correct. Now that the decision was made, there was little point in delaying. The cynic in him refused to believe that Donato's motivation was the village's welfare, however. He wondered what Donato expected to get out of it all.

Wulfric watched the delegation go, not a warrior among them. Rodulf rode at their head, as puffed up and full of his own importance as he had been when still an apprentice. Wulfric had expected Belgar to insist on going, but that did not seem to be the case. Wulfric realised he was expecting too much of the old man. He looked more frail every day, and Wulfric feared that the days he could rely on his counsel were numbered.

Until the delegation returned with whatever help they could get, there was little for Wulfric to do other than throw himself into rebuilding as best he could. There was more frustration to be found in that. Despite being young, fit and strong, Wulfric had no skills. Labouring and crafts were all but unknown to him, and he was little more use than a beast of burden. Those with some skill in smithing and carpentry were the most important men in the village, few though they were, and Wulfric felt utterly useless.

He was happy to do whatever was required of him, but the villagers were not accustomed to ordering a warrior around. Wulfric stood with Stenn, Roal, and Farlof to the side of the work gang that was busy chopping down trees and preparing them to be cut into planks. Each time one of the workmen passed by, he would give them a deferential nod, but say nothing. In the end they took it upon themselves to start cutting down trees and hauling them back into the village.

CHAPTER THIRTY-NINE

THE DELEGATES RETURNED to the village a week after the attack with strangers in tow. They were upbeat, but looked tired and wouldn't reveal anything to the villagers. They dismounted before the shell of the Great Hall with the pomp of men who believed they held the fate of all around them in their hands, which Wulfric had to admit was not far from the truth.

A tarpaulin had been erected to keep those within sheltered from the elements but it was difficult to think of it as a building any longer. They went in, and the rest of the village had to wait to find out what news they brought.

People stood idle for a while, but once it became apparent the wait would not be short, they gradually returned to work. Eventually the men emerged from the jury-rigged Great Hall. The new faces had discarded their travelling cloaks, and stood in contrast to the others, their fine, richly coloured clothes marking them out as foreigners. Wulfric felt hopeful. It was unlikely the southerners would have sent men north unless they intended to help. He hated that the prospect of foreign help filled him with hope.

'What do you reckon?' Farlof was standing at Wulfric's shoulder. Wulfric couldn't remember the last time he'd heard the teasing, mischievous tone in Farlof's voice. He missed it, and wondered if it would ever return.

'Your guess is as good as mine,' Wulfric said. 'But it looks like we're getting help of some sort. So long as we can pay for it.'

'I wonder what it will cost?'

'Everything,' Wulfric said.

❈

Donato pushed his way through the others and scanned the gathering crowd, his eyes stopping on Wulfric. 'You!' he shouted, pointing at Wulfric so there was no doubt as to who he was addressing.

Wulfric raised an eyebrow and turned to look behind him, but didn't respond. He had no intention of acknowledging the disrespectful way Donato spoke.

'Wulfric. I need you over here,' Donato said.

There was impatience in his voice, so Wulfric made a point of walking across the square slowly, stopping to exchange a few words with people on the way.

'What do you want, Donato?' Wulfric said, when he eventually reached the bottom of the steps up to the Great Hall. He refused to address him as 'Councilman'.

'I need you to take this man, Sifrud is his name, south to look at the horses. He needs to see how many we have left and what condition they're in.'

Wulfric looked at the man and shrugged. 'Why don't you take him? Arse too good for a saddle now?' The words were out of his mouth before he had time to consider them.

Anger flashed behind Donato's eyes, and Wulfric smiled. He almost wanted Donato to strike at him, as Wulfric had seen him treating his serfs in the past. It would be a mistake Donato wouldn't live to regret.

The merchant swallowed hard. 'It's in the village's best interest that you do as I ask. Take him south to view the horses. Please.'

Wulfric turned and started walking toward the man. 'Fine.' He made a dismissive gesture with his hand, hopeful that all the little marks of contempt would add up and eventually push Donato to doing something rash. As far as Wulfric was concerned, Donato deserved to die far more than those who had done so in Leondorf.

❈

It was late that evening when he returned to the village after inspecting the horses with Sifrud. Those in the southernmost pastures had not been touched and Sifrud seemed satisfied with what he saw. Wulfric had not expected to find anything at all, but clearly the Rasbruckers were complacent about taking what remained whenever they chose. The horses would need to be sold quickly and driven across the border to their new owners before the Rasbruckers decided to collect what they doubtless considered theirs.

The southerner hadn't said much on the ride, but he seemed to know his horses. He would be taking all but a few left for breeding stock. Wulfric was surprised, thinking the southerner would want the lot, but he seemed to be of the opinion that the environment was as much a part of the horses' quality as their bloodlines. Nonetheless, it would take years to bring their herds back up to the size they had once been. Wulfric took grim satisfaction in the fact that although they would be lost to Leondorf, at least they might buy them something useful and the Rasbruckers would never get their hands on a single one.

❋

Frena, unhappy with the lack of privacy and space in the communal shelter, had put up a tent on the remains of their home which was now supplemented by some solid-looking wooden framework that had been added since Wulfric took the southerner to view the horses. As appreciative of the work as he was, Wulfric didn't want special treatment because he was First Warrior. There were those who didn't even have a tent to call their own.

Adalhaid was staying with her, but there wasn't room for Wulfric; he and the other warriors had taken to camping just outside the village. He went to his mother's tent first to check on them, and was surprised to find that Belgar was there, standing outside with one of the southerners.

'What's going on?' Wulfric said. 'Is anything wrong?'

'Nothing to get het up about,' Belgar said. 'This is Aelric. You probably don't remember him. He took Jorundyr's Path when you were a boy.'

'Still not much more than a boy,' Aelric said. 'Good to see you, lad. I was sorry to hear about your father.'

'I don't remember you.'

'Not surprised. I'm Adalhaid's uncle. You were no higher than your father's knee when I left.'

The memory returned to Wulfric. Aelric was a lanceman like Adalhaid's father, who, with no property, had chosen Jorundyr's Path. Adalhaid mentioned him from time to time; she had lived in his household while being educated in the south. He had thrived by all accounts, and was the captain of a nobleman's guard. Now, it seemed, he was returning in their hour of need. Might there be others who would do the same? Enough to tell the Ruripathians to stuff their help in a midden heap?

'You've returned to help then?' Wulfric said.

'Unfortunately no,' Aelric said. 'My responsibilities in the south are many, and I'm just one man. The help that I'm sure Lord Elzmark will send is going to be more than enough to keep the village safe.'

He didn't speak like a Northlander. It was odd to think that he had grown up in the village. His face was lined and his eyes were calm, as though he had seen so much there was nothing left that could take him by surprise. In that moment Wulfric knew a man like him would be a far better choice for First Warrior than he, would be far more able to take back the powers that Donato had usurped, even though he had never gone on a pilgrimage. How could he convince him to stay?

'That's what's happening then? Lord Else…' Wulfric said.

'Elzmark,' Belgar said.

'Elzmark,' Wulfric said. 'He's going to help?'

'Assuming his envoy was happy with the horses. Was he happy with the horses?' Belgar said.

Wulfric shrugged. 'I think so. He seemed to like what he saw.'

'Well then,' Belgar said, 'we can expect soldiers and wagons of food to arrive in the next few days.'

'Are horses all they want?' Wulfric said.

Belgar humphed.

There was a question that remained in Wulfric's head. 'What brings you home, Aelric?'

'When the messengers arrived in Elzburg, I asked for leave to come north with his emissary.'

'I'm sorry for your loss,' Wulfric said. 'Your help now would be a huge boost for the village. If I can convince you to stay.'

Aelric shook his head. 'I really do have to return to Elzburg. I only came to bring Adalhaid back with me.'

Wulfric furrowed his brow. 'What do you mean?'

'I'm taking her back to Elzburg with me.'

'What? She's staying here. With me,' Wulfric said.

Belgar shook his head and took Wulfric by the arm, leading him away from Aelric to where they could speak in private.

'She's an orphan now, Wulfric,' Belgar said. 'She needs to be with people who'll be able to look after her.'

'We're betrothed,' Wulfric said. 'I can look after her. We're as much her family as an uncle who lives half the world away.'

Belgar laughed. 'The world stretches farther than you think, Wulfric. But that doesn't change the fact that we can barely look after ourselves. You're not old enough to marry yet anyway. I checked with Aethelman as soon as I found out about Aelric's plans. Twenty years is what the gods decree.'

'But I'm old enough to go on the pilgrimage? To fight? Die? I'm old enough,' Wulfric said. 'Or I would be if it suited everyone else.'

'Come now, Wulfric. We still don't know what the southerners will offer us. It might be nothing, or not much better than. Donato will take whatever they offer, and I don't have the support to stand against him. We could all be starving in a few weeks' time. Is that what you want for her? The Rasbruckers could come back before any soldiers arrive, to finish what they started. Do you really want her in that danger?'

'Of course not,' Wulfric said. He didn't want her to go. He wanted to marry her and for them to rebuild together. He could provide for her, keep her safe. But now he had a doubt. Was he being selfish?

'She can continue her schooling in the south,' Belgar said. 'She'll be safe and want for nothing. Can you offer her those things?'

Wulfric opened his mouth, but closed it again and shook his head.

'It's been decided,' Belgar said. 'She leaves in the morning.'

'I'll marry her. Then no one can force her to go if she doesn't want to.'

'Don't be daft, boy. You're both far too young. Neither of you are of age yet.'

'I'm a warrior,' Wulfric said, but he felt his resolve weaken. 'You can't pick and choose what I am and am not old enough for.'

'Even if we don't all starve this winter,' Belgar said, 'things will be hard. Very hard. And they won't get easier come spring. This winter is just about surviving. The really difficult part comes in spring when we have to rebuild and stand on our own feet, help from the south or not. Hardship like that sucks the life out of people. Is that what you want for her? I can tell you, if I had anywhere better to be, I'd be gone.'

❄

'Wulfric. What are you doing here?'

It was getting late and Adalhaid was in the process of closing up her section of the shack that had been cobbled together over the remains of his home.

'I need to speak to you,' he said.

'What about?'

'You've spoken to your uncle?'

'Yes of course.'

'So you know then?' Wulfric was amazed that she could react to it all so calmly. Was it that she didn't really care?

'Know what?'

'That he's come to take you south.'

Adalhaid furrowed her brow. 'What do you mean "come to take me south"?'

'That's why he's here. They told me earlier. When he heard that your mother and father are… Well, he plans to bring you back south with him, so you can be with family.'

She moved her mouth as though to speak but stopped. 'He didn't say anything to me. I don't want to go, so I'm not.'

'Belgar said it's been decided.'

'Well it was decided without me, so they can undecide.' She ducked back into the small dwelling and reappeared a moment later wrapped in a cloak. She gave Wulfric a long, penetrating look that made him feel as though he was betraying her. He knew it was for the best, painful though it was.

'I'll deal with this myself,' she said.

Wulfric watched her go a few paces. 'Wait.'

Adalhaid stopped and turned.

'I think they're right.' It felt like stabbing himself in the stomach to say it.

'What?' She stepped closer. 'Do you… want me to go?'

'Yes. I mean no. It's the best thing.'

'I can't believe you're saying this. I thought—'

'I was against it at first too,' Wulfric said. 'Chances are not everyone here is going to live through the winter. Even with the southerners' help. I want to make sure you're one of the ones who does. There's safety in the south. And comfort. I need to know you have both.'

'I'll be needed here,' she said.

'Every person who needs to be sheltered, fed, and protected puts the village under more strain. Most have nowhere else to go, but you do. If things work out with the southerners, we'll be able to start rebuilding properly with the help they send come spring. Until then, it's just about surviving. You can spend the winter at that university you always talk about. Learn things that will help the village, and come back to us. To me.'

She said nothing, but Wulfric could see from the set of her jaw that she wasn't convinced.

'You can come back in spring. It's only a few months.' Wulfric felt empty saying it. He could remember the last time she had gone away for a few months only too well.

❋

Adalhaid left the next morning. Wulfric watched as she and her uncle rode out of Leondorf for the Ruripathian city of Elzburg. One winter. She had said that before, and was gone for three years. This time her leaving was his doing, though. Perhaps it was the previous time also. Considering how much had happened in the past few months, Wulfric felt as though the entire world might be turned on its head in the time she would be away. Would he even still be alive? Change came quickly and in large measure in the Northlands. A voice in the back of his head said he would never see her again. He did his best to ignore it.

He stood staring down the road south. She glanced over her shoulder every so often, and even from that distance, Wulfric could tell that she was crying. He kept watching until she was long out of sight, feeling the hole inside him grow with each passing moment.

❋

The Maisterspaeker stopped talking, and studied the crowd for a reaction. They were silent, staring at him like infants expecting to be fed. There were times to allow a pause, and there were times to grab it by the scruff of the neck.

'Our hero has now been forged in ice, in blood, and in ash—a boy stepped across the threshold of manhood—but has yet to be honed in true battle. Tragedy has followed him like a shadow, and he has been forced to part from the woman he loves with a passion that few of us will ever understand. Our object of mystery, the ancient Fount Stone, has finally found its way into the hands of a man ill-suited to its possession. Men of unbridled and ruthless ambition are in the ascendant.'

The Maisterspaeker considered stopping for the night. He had no idea what the hour was, and his voice was growing gravelly. Conradin placed a fresh mug of ale in front of him, and the Maisterspaeker put the thought from his head. He smiled, and took a deep breath. 'And yet the change to the old order is only at its beginning…'

PART THREE

CHAPTER FORTY

'LEONDORF SURVIVED THROUGH that first winter after the attack. It was difficult, but no one else died,' the Maisterspaeker said. 'The Ruripathians arrived in numbers the following spring, and slowly life in the Northlands grew to resemble life in the south. Buildings were rebuilt by southern architects and workers. The Markgraf sent an ambassador north to oversee his interests, and Donato solidified his position.

'Silver was discovered on Leondorf's borders not long after, which made it a very attractive protectorate for the Markgraf and those who sought to make their fortunes. The population swelled with prospectors, treasure hunters and those who made their livings off them. So life continued in Leondorf.

'The hero of our tale remained. He had an overriding sense of duty to the people of his village, and an undying hope that one day he would wake and discover Adalhaid had returned. Three years have passed when we rejoin our hero, and we find him disillusioned, under-utilised, and questioning his choice to remain in Leondorf now that it is out of peril.'

❊

Wulfric lounged on the porch of his house with Farlof and Stenn, surveying the village. It had changed so much since the southerners arrived. Mixed with the northern buildings of wood, stone, and thatch, there were now many of brick, plaster and slate that towered above their northern counterparts. A group of soldiers rode back into the village, with none of the ox carts they had left with the previous morning. Wulfric would have sniggered at the southerners' misfortune and incompetence were it not for the fact that Roal had been guiding them, and he was nowhere to be seen.

Wulfric sat up and ran his eyes across each of the garrison soldiers' faces. There were two fewer of them also. He didn't care about them, but he was concerned about Roal. He stood and walked over to the sergeant of the bedraggled patrol.

'Roal. Where is he?' Wulfric said.

The sergeant shook his head. 'I lost two men.'

'Don't give a damn about them,' Wulfric said. 'Roal. What happened to him?'

'Rasbruckers. Jumped us just before the bridge on our way back. They killed Roal first.'

Wulfric screwed his face up in anger. In the three years since the battle and the attack, Rasbruck had recovered with miraculous speed. 'Took the oxen? And the silver?'

The sergeant nodded.

'Good luck explaining that to your boss,' Wulfric said, before turning and heading back to the others on the porch. The others looked at him for news. 'Be ready to ride out in ten minutes. Roal didn't come back with them.'

Stenn and Farlof both shook their heads with mournful expressions on their faces. In three years of guiding the garrison soldiers through the forests they had each faced dozens of attacks, but Jorundyr had smiled on them and not one of them had taken so much as a scratch. It seemed only fair after how many of them he had already taken. Now, it seemed his beneficence had run out.

Wulfric watched the soldiers trudge back to their garrison. He didn't like the fact that they were Ruripathians, but as men they weren't a bad bunch. They weren't bad fighters either—Wulfric had trained with them in the three years they had been in Leondorf—but they weren't suited to forest fighting. It was part of why they'd never been able to get a foothold in the Northlands. Before they were invited into Leondorf, that was.

It was the third time in as many months that the ox-train coming back from the silver mine had been attacked, and Wulfric wondered if this one would be enough to finally provoke a response. He didn't know if it was actually Rasbruckers who had carried out the attack, and he didn't care. If it incited the Ruripathians into attacking Rasbruck, Wulfric was all for it. The Ruripathian Ambassador had refused to be drawn into taking any aggressive action since coming to the village. There was plenty of money flowing south and the attacks were usually only a minor irritation. *Why stir up the wasps' nest?* he had said. Wulfric had always stopped short of calling him a coward, but at times it had required considerable effort.

The mine was on the fringes of Leondorf's territory, and the road back passed close to the border with Rasbruck, the only crossing point on the river that the oxen could manage. There was a bridge there now, which made the journey faster, but not safer. The mine's presence ensured the Ruripathians would remain, and that ensured Leondorf would survive, although it little resembled the village it once was.

The other tribes hated the fact that Leondorf had invited the Ruripathians into the Northlands, and expressed their displeasure every chance they got. The silver mine and its ox-trains were a prime target. One of the warriors guided the ox-trains and garrison soldiers each time they went out to collect the silver. There was little else for them to do.

Wulfric spotted Donato watching them ride out from the steps of the rebuilt Great Hall. It was taller and grander than before, but the remnants of the stone walls of the previous iteration had been repaired and reused. The spot near the back where Wulfric had spent so many hours as a boy listening was still there and it had proved useful. With the southern soldiers' arrival, Wulfric had expected that Donato would do away with the warriors once and for all, but that had not happened. Unfamiliar with the region, the southerners needed scouts and guides and the Ambassador had insisted that they be maintained. It kept them relevant, but with each passing day Wulfric lost a little more hope that they would regain their old status. First Warrior meant nothing any more. No one even called him that. The village's children played at being soldiers, not warriors. Half of them were the offspring of the new arrivals anyway.

Wulfric had no doubt that as soon as the garrison soldiers grew comfortable in the forests, they would be done away with, but that had yet to happen. After that? Who knew? Wulfric didn't see himself as a farmer. Adventures in distant lands seemed the most compelling idea. He felt

Jorundyr's Path call to him. Alone, or with the others, it didn't matter. There would be nothing left for him in the Northlands.

The comfort and sophistication of the south also seemed to have finally won Adalhaid over. She had not returned to Leondorf in the spring as they had planned. The memory of the expression on her face when he told her that he thought she should go south was never far from his thoughts. Perhaps he would go looking for her. Sometimes he wondered why he had not already. Fear that she had forgotten him? Fear that she had not forgiven him for telling her to go?

He had remained in Leondorf after the initial crisis had passed in the hope of revenge on Rasbruck. They owed Leondorf a blood debt, and he was determined that they should pay it. As the months and years passed, that hope looked increasingly forlorn, and he grew frustrated that the Ambassador would never order the attack, and had all but given up. But now? With a month's ore lost? If anything spurred the Ambassador to action, it would be this.

They left the village and galloped toward the bridge, the final three apprentices from the pilgrimage that seemed a lifetime ago. Wulfric felt like a warrior for the first time in as long as he could remember. It hammered home his resentment of how they were at the beck and call of the garrison, and left to wallow in idleness the remainder of the time.

It took a few hours to reach the bridge. The road was rutted and muddy from the regular traffic that carved it ever deeper into the forest floor. It made for slow progress, but Wulfric had little hope of finding anyone alive.

Roal was draped on the road's bank, stuck with several arrows. His sword was drawn, and crusted with dry blood. It was as good a death as any warrior could hope for. Wulfric felt an unsettling pang of jealousy. They gathered his body and headed for home.

❖

They rode back through the village slowly, with Roal draped across the back of a horse. They wanted everyone to see that one of Leondorf's sons had died in her service, but hardly anyone took notice. The Ruripathian ambassador had had a house built for himself beside the garrison barracks in the southern style of white plastered brick and red-tiled roofs. It contained all of the famed southern luxuries in great quantities—or so Wulfric had been told, for he had never seen the inside of it.

As galling as it was to see his decline in status, Wulfric and the warriors were not the only ones. Donato had also seen his power fettered, even though he was leader of the council. He had taken to calling himself 'mayor', a southern title. Wulfric found it satisfying that his own scheme had curtailed his rapidly growing influence. The Ambassador was deferential to Donato in public, but everyone knew who was making the decisions behind the scene. He might use the title of ambassador, but in reality he was a governor.

They had been gone for several hours, more than long enough for the ambassador to consider the loss of his latest cargo of silver, and Wulfric was keen to see if he would be provoked to reaction. With Roal delivered to the kirk where Aethelman would prepare him for his funeral, there was little more for Wulfric and the others to do but lounge on the porch of his house as they did every day.

Wulfric watched the Ambassador's house for want of anything better to do. The others were in no mood for banter, so they sat there in silence. When the Ambassador eventually appeared outside, plump and prosperous looking in a cloak of expensive furs, Wulfric paid attention. He walked purposefully toward the Great Hall, accompanied by two soldiers, and went in without knocking or waiting to be admitted—as was usually required of those not on the council. As was required of Wulfric.

His demeanour was what was of most interest to Wulfric. The Ambassador's face was dark with anger, and Wulfric prayed that this was the insult that finally pushed him to action after three long years of waiting. The blood vengeance Leondorf owed them might not be so far off. Wulfric watched in silence from the porch, knowing that Belgar would come to tell him as soon as the discussions were finished and the orders were given.

❆

Belgar strode from the Great Hall directly toward them. 'Get up off your lazy arses!'

Wulfric and the others all did as they were told. He might be old, and growing increasingly frail, but Belgar was the only member of the council they had any respect for. None of the other men had faced battle; none of them were worthy of it.

'Ambassador Urschel is displeased with losing his silver and wants to teach the Rasbruckers to mind their own business. You'll guide his soldiers north to the village in the morning.'

Wulfric felt his heart race. His father. Adalhaid's parents. The village. There were so many scores to settle, he felt he was being pulled in five different directions at once. He had waited three long years for this moment. Nonetheless, he wasn't going to roll over like a cowed dog whenever the Ambassador snapped his fingers.

'Never been there,' Wulfric said. 'Not sure if I know the way.'

Belgar cast him a filthy look. 'Don't play the ignorant Northlander with me. We want this as much as they do. Cutting off your nose to spite your face gets us nowhere. If you don't lead them, I will, and you can stay here and sulk.'

Stenn and Farlof sniggered, and Wulfric shot them as filthy a look as Belgar had given him.

'I'll take them,' he said. 'But because I want to, not because the fat Ambassador tells me to.'

'Good enough for me,' Belgar said. 'Be ready to go at first light.'

CHAPTER FORTY-ONE

ONE OF THE craftsmen who had come north from Ruripathia was a smith. Wulfric ensured his first engagement on arriving was to make him new armour and weapons. His helm bore the features of a snarling belek, reminiscent of the long dead Beleks Bane's, but far more terrifying. When a Rasbrucker saw it, Wulfric wanted their bowels to turn to water. It would mean death for them, and he wanted them to recognise it. The helm was the finest he had ever seen, and he grudgingly acknowledged the southerners' value in some things. Whenever he passed the forge wearing it, the smith paused to look at what he regarded as his best work.

If the helm was the smith's best work, the rest of Wulfric's battle accoutrements were not far behind. His armour fitted perfectly, and his sabre—a long, single edged blade with a slightly curved edge—was tailored to his preference. It was perfectly balanced, and felt like an extension of his arm. Other than a hero's blade made from the steel only found in the High Places, he was confident there was no finer weapon to be had. It had yet to shed the blood of his enemies, and he felt giddy at the thought that this would soon be remedied.

Almost the entire garrison was being sent. Seeing them gathered on the square was an impressive sight. While they lacked the individual character of a Northlander horde, there was something about their uniformity that was intimidating. Stenn and Farlof had left before first light to scout ahead, while Wulfric would guide the main body of men to Rasbruck.

They were preparing to depart when three more men arrived, dressed for a fight. Rodulf and two men Wulfric had not seen before. They had the hardened look of warriors about them, and made Wulfric think twice before giving Rodulf the greeting he usually would.

'What are you doing here?' Wulfric said.

'We're coming along,' Rodulf said. 'The council want a representative present.'

Wulfric didn't like the idea, but knew that arguing against it would get him nowhere. 'I hope your two friends will be able to look after you. The rest of us don't have time to babysit.' Rodulf smiled at him, and seemed in no way irritated, which was disappointing.

'Captain? Are you and your men ready?'

'We are.'

'Let's be at it then,' Wulfric said, as he gave the order to set off with a wave of his hand.

❈

Ritschl sat on a bench in his kirk and stared at the Stone with an emotion akin to hatred. A lone candle flame spluttered in the draughty nave, but he was oblivious to the gloom and cold. His mind was a maelstrom of disappointment, fear, and longing.

In three years of trying, he had not been able to bend the Stone to his will. He had wasted half his life desiring it, seeking it out. It had called to him, like music on the wind, but now it turned its back on him.

'Why?' he screamed. 'Why won't you listen to me?'

His exhortations were a nightly occurrence, and he knew the villagers passing by the small kirk tittered to themselves, thinking that their old priest was going mad. He didn't care. Perhaps he was.

❈

'Wait,' a young woman in the audience said.

Conradin's face darkened at the interruption, and the Maisterspaeker thought he might be moved to acts of violence if the interruption was allowed to continue for too long.

'Why wouldn't it work for him?' the woman said.

'I've given it much thought over the years,' the Maisterspaeker said, 'and I've come to believe that it *did* work for him. You see, the Stone was said to grant its possessor their greatest desires. For years, Ritschl had desired the Stone. So much had been taken from him in his life, and here was something that had been taken, but that he could take back. It granted him this desire, and once it was achieved Ritschl was spent. There was nothing else he wanted so desperately, and willing it to simply work was not enough.'

'Didn't Aethelman possess it, though?' the young woman said.

Conradin's face darkened further.

'I don't think Aethelman every truly possessed it. In his heart and soul, he didn't want it, and the Stone, in whatever mysterious way it worked, knew this.' The Maisterspaeker cast a glance at Conradin, whose impatience was near breaking point. 'Now, if you're happy with my explanation, I shall continue, before the good sergeant-at-arms bursts a blood vessel.'

❄

They arrived on the fringes of Rasbruck early the next day, having made good time. Wulfric had conspicuously avoided Rodulf, although it was not difficult as he stayed with his two companions and did not mix. Wulfric was curious why he had gone along. It was more than reporting back to the council. He wondered what advantage they hoped to get by being there.

Rasbruck looked remarkably similar to how Leondorf had before the southerners arrived, something that surprised Wulfric. It was more like home than Leondorf now was. It was obvious that they weren't expected; the gates were open and no challenge was made. At first, no one even paid attention to their arrival. Eventually someone stopped and stared at them, and was joined by others. Wulfric had never attacked a village before, and realised he had no idea what to do next. Should he charge in cutting down everyone he passed? He had thought there would be warriors waiting for them, but there were just ordinary people going about their days.

'At them, lads!' the captain shouted.

The Ruripathian soldiers charged past Wulfric, who was still staring at the village and its people. A woman screamed, and the villagers scattered as the Ruripathian horsemen spread into the village. Wulfric tried to find the hate inside of him, but couldn't. They were women, children, and elderly. No different to those at home. No different to the people the Rasbruckers had slaughtered, but Wulfric could not bring himself to do the same. Killing ordinary people was not a thing to pride oneself in. It was not what a warrior did.

Wulfric pressed farther into the village searching for a true foe to fight. He spotted a group of armed men who had finally reacted to the attack. Wulfric snapped down the belek-face visor on his helm and spurred Greyfell forward. The Ruripathians were cutting an indiscriminate swathe into the village, moving as a single unit. Wulfric charged past them and drew his sabre, roaring like a man possessed.

Wulfric, Stenn, and Farlof, the last of the old warriors of Leondorf, crashed into the armed Rasbruckers, slashing left and right, impatient to settle the blood debt they were owed.

Wulfric cleaved a man from shoulder to breastbone, then felt a tug on his leg. Before he could react, he was falling sideways, the world rushing past the eye holes in his visor. He hit the ground with a crunch of metal. His head swam as he rolled onto his belly and got up onto his hands and knees before a kick sent him sprawling across the ground.

He had lost his grip on his sabre as he fell. He scrabbled around in the dirt for it, and spotted the man who kicked him. Wulfric stifled a laugh. Rage had gotten the better of sense—the man was wearing soft leather boots, and hadn't taken time to consider the effects of kicking a man wearing plate armour. He was hobbling toward Wulfric, his face twisted with pain.

Wulfric found his sabre and scrambled to his feet. The man took a wild, unbalanced swing at Wulfric which he easily dodged. He came back with a wild swing of his own, which the lame man was unable to avoid. Wulfric pulled his blade free of the man's body and looked around to find Greyfell. He saw the horse kick a man and launch him twenty paces through the air.

The soldiers had pressed everyone back toward Rasbruck's village square, containing the villagers in one place. It was a fast and brutal encounter. Wulfric's blood was up and he craved more battle, but Jorundyr's gift had not yet taken him in its embrace. He looked around for more warriors. There were a score of bodies on the road into the village, but the resistance had ended. He had spent so long dreaming of burning Rasbruck to the ground, of putting her warriors to the sword by the dozen, that he felt deflated.

He called Greyfell, mounted, and rode over to the Ruripathian captain.

'What are you going to do with them?' Wulfric said, nodding to the frightened villagers now surrounded on the square.

'Nothing. No sense in putting a settlement to sword. Dead people can't trade. They'll know why we did this, and if they've sense they'll know not to misbehave again.' He turned to the sergeant. 'Have some of the men round up whoever else you can find and bring them here. I want as many of them as possible to hear this. Don't take any risks.'

The sergeant responded without a word. Stenn and Farlof joined Wulfric, waiting for their instructions, but Wulfric said nothing. Looting was the traditional next step, but all Wulfric was interested in was the blood of Rasbrucker warriors and it seemed there was no more of that to be had.

Two kills did not feel like enough to settle the debt Leondorf was owed, but between him, Farlof and Stenn, they had killed a half dozen warriors. It would have to do. He found it hard to believe this was the place that had wrought so much hurt on his home. As much as he hated them, he couldn't bring himself to harm the people gathered before him.

The soldiers managed to find a few dozen more villagers and added them to the group on the square. They looked at Wulfric and the others with the same hate in their eyes that he had felt for them. Now he felt oddly guilty.

'By order of his excellency Ambassador Urschel, representative of the Markgraf of Elzmark, I inform you all that this attack is in response to assaults made on the Markgraf's property. In order to make good the losses incurred, and the expense of this expedition, I am instructed to take one person in every ten for sale in the slave markets in Elzburg. The Markgraf has chosen to be merciful on this occasion, but do not mistake that for weakness. Attack his property again, and this village will be razed to the ground, and all its inhabitants put to the sword.'

It was not what Wulfric had expected.

'Pull out the ones that look like they'll fetch the highest price,' the captain said to his sergeant. 'Secure them and then have a look around for the silver. After that, the men can have their fun.'

There was nothing left there that Wulfric wanted. 'We're returning to Leondorf,' he said to the captain.

'I'll need your help with the—'

'We're returning to the village,' Wulfric said again. He glared at the captain, making it abundantly clear that the matter was not open for discussion.

The captain held his glare for a moment, then nodded his head. 'Fine. Tell the Ambassador we won't be far behind you.'

Wulfric didn't react. As with every other instruction he had been given by a Ruripathian since they arrived in Leondorf, he planned to ignore this one. He nodded to Stenn and Farlof before turning Greyfell toward Leondorf and urging him forward. As they fell in behind him, an old woman looked up at Wulfric and caught his eye.

'What are we supposed to do now? You killed my son.'

Wulfric looked at her and shrugged his shoulders.

❉

Rodulf and his two men chased the herdsman down and encircled him.

'Your herds? Where are they?'

The man was shaking, but his mouth remained shut.

'Tell me, and I'll forget I ever saw you,' Rodulf said. He lowered the point of his spear and pressed it against the man's forehead. The man whimpered and Rodulf pressed a little harder. 'Someone will tell me, and your death will be for nothing.' He applied a little more pressure on the spear.

'The east pastures.'

'Thank you,' Rodulf said. He nodded to the others and they galloped away. It wasn't an act of mercy, he simply couldn't be bothered to kill the man. He needed to chase the herd toward Leondorf before the looters found them. His father had sent herdsmen to gather them up and drive them south where they could be sold without having to share the proceeds. He needed to be quick about it. The Ruripathians wouldn't ask too many questions, but Wulfric and the others might try to cause trouble.

❉

Rodulf knew his father would be delighted when he found out how many cattle would be heading south, assuming his herdsmen managed to gather them all. It put him in an especially good mood as he rode back to Rasbruck to see what type of destruction had been wrought on their traditional enemy. He had never burned a village to the ground before, and realised the opportunity might not come again.

As he was riding back he spotted a man fleeing the village. At first he thought it was the herdsman who had revealed the location of the herds, and he considered riding over to kill him; it was his first battle and he had not killed anybody. Now that his task was completed he was at liberty to enjoy himself. He quickly realised it was not that man, however. Not that it mattered; a kill was a kill. Rodulf levelled his spear and urged his horse on to a gallop.

The man was aware of Rodulf's approach, and he made to quicken his pace, but it was futile. He moved slowly and awkwardly. He had no chance of outrunning a horseman. Rodulf had run him through before realising his grey robes were those of a priest. It was of little concern to him.

Rodulf was about to ride on, but his curiosity got the better of him. He dismounted and walked over to the body while his two minders, expensive southern mercenaries called bannerets, waited a discreet distance away. It was unlikely the priest had anything of value, but he clutched a felt pouch as though his life had depended on it. Rodulf bent down and prised the dead fingers from the bag. He tipped its contents into his hand and felt a pang of disappointment when an oddly shaped lump of metal ore fell out.

He drew back to throw it away but stopped. It seemed to tingle in his hand. Out of the corner of his eye he noticed that it was covered in engravings. He took a closer look. He couldn't read what the engraved runes said, but he could recognise that considerable care had gone into inscribing them. They meant nothing to him. It was probably a religious object of some sort, something of little value. He made to throw it away again, but stopped once more. It felt so good in his hand, as though it had been shaped to fit his palm perfectly. He took another look, smiled, and dropped it into his purse.

CHAPTER FORTY-TWO

DONATO WAS WAITING for Rodulf to return, impatient to find out how many head of cattle he had managed to drive south. He spotted Wulfric and his two cronies ride back into the village with a sense of disappointment. Part of him had hoped that Wulfric might be killed in the fight. It was difficult not to feel deflated seeing the arrogant whoreson trot into the village, rolling lazily with the horse's movement. His efforts to marginalise Wulfric and the other warriors had gone well, but it did little to quell the hatred Donato felt for him.

Looking at him, it was hard to believe that only a few years before he had been a fat little wimp. He was wrapped in that belek cloak he always wore, draped across wide shoulders that had shed every pinch of the childhood blubber. He obviously fancied himself as looking like one of the heroes of old, built like a prize bull, with braids in his long dirty blond hair and thick beard. They had probably been arrogant whoresons as well, but at least they were already dead and Donato didn't have to look at them every day. Donato imagined gouging one of Wulfric's eyes out, but it made him feel unwell. Destroying men with coin was his talent, not violence.

❧

Victory required celebration, and as hollow as it felt to Wulfric, a victory was what they had. The new inn was the only place for that. It had replaced the ramshackle old tavern that was burned down in the attack. The tavern keeper had died with his tavern, and the new inn was run by one of the arrivals from the south. It did a brisk trade, hosting the merchants who came north in increasing numbers and the prospectors in from the hills in the east, eager to spend their silver.

There had never been much use for money in Leondorf before the Ruripathians arrived. The only time anyone brought it out was to buy things from southern traders when they visited. Everything a warrior needed was provided, the service they gave in return was protection and a regular supply of fresh game from the forest. Now the Great Hall deigned to toss them a few coins when they did what they were told. The ambassador had handed Wulfric a purse of coins when he returned with news of their success in Rasbruck. It was emasculating to take it, but they needed money to survive in the new Leondorf. The smith only took coin for repairs, the innkeeper only coin for ale.

Wulfric, Stenn, and Farlof had taken a table at the inn as their own. They spent as much time there as they did on Wulfric's porch. They usually kept to themselves, but Wulfric knew they were viewed as something of a curiosity by the southerners. None of them knew how their forebears had behaved when they gathered, or in the aftermath of a victory. At times Wulfric felt as though they were boys playing at being men. There was no one to guide them in how to comport themselves. It felt awkward as they forced the behaviour they imagined the old warriors had adopted. Perhaps they would create their own traditions that the next group of young men to complete their pilgrimage would follow. If anyone else ever went on pilgrimage. Already Wulfric had seen the surviving boys of the village watching the soldiers with admiration, rather than him and the others as they lazed on his porch like old, unwanted hunting dogs.

The other great change that came with the new inn was the selection of drinks. Mead and ale were all they had before, but now southern wines and strong spirits, once a rarity, were always available. Wulfric wasn't overly partial to any of them, but some, the new councilmen in particular, took to the wine with enthusiasm. Some of the bottles cost more than an entire hogshead of ale—something the drinkers were always eager to point out. It was nice enough when he tried it, but for the price? It amazed Wulfric how quickly they embraced southern ways. There was so little left of what went before. It reinforced his desire to go on Jorundyr's Path. He would miss his mother when he went, but he was able to leave her with enough southern silver to make sure she would always be comfortable, and she could see what life in Leondorf was doing to him. She was as eager for him to go as he was. There was nothing there for him. Not anymore.

A group of soldiers came into the inn not long after Wulfric and the others. The attack on Rasbruck was the first success they had since coming north—a welcome change from escorting wagons between the village and the mines, always waiting for the next ambush. Wulfric had no interest in mixing with them. They might have to fight together, but that didn't mean they had to socialise together. The soldiers gathered at the bar, loud and jubilant, while Wulfric and the others sat quietly at their table in the corner. None of them saw it as the victory they had wanted.

'Hey, Northlanders, have a drink with us.' The call came from the bar, the sergeant that was with them at Rasbruck. His words were slightly slurred, a surprise considering how short a time they had been there. Wulfric wondered what they were drinking, or if they were simply lightweights.

'Fine where we are, thanks,' Wulfric said. He didn't want to drink with them. They weren't the worst of men, so he didn't feel the need to be rude. Had the call come from one of the councilmen, who often tried to ingratiate themselves with the warriors—a leftover hangup from days that Wulfric was gradually coming to accept would never return—his response would have been very different.

'What? We're good enough to fight with, but not to drink with?'

It wasn't the reaction Wulfric was hoping for. 'No offence meant, Sergeant. Just having a quiet drink with my friends.'

'Ah, come now. We had a victory today, come and celebrate with us. First bit of excitement we've had in this muddy rathole.'

Anger flashed behind Wulfric's eyes, and the sergeant spotted the change in his face.

'No offence meant, just miss home is all. Round of drinks for the lads,' the sergeant said, turning back to the innkeeper.

'This isn't a rathole, and we're not lads. You'd do well to remember that,' Wulfric said.

'Like I said, no offence meant,' the sergeant said.

'Just because it wasn't meant don't mean it wasn't caused,' Wulfric said. He could feel Stenn and Farlof tense up.

The sergeant turned to face them and his men gathered behind him. All the other sounds in the inn had long since ceased.

'Maybe *you'd* do well to remember that we came up here to protect this place, something you don't seem to be able to manage on your own. Respect goes both ways, friend,' the sergeant said.

'Might be time you all fuck off back home then, and leave us to fend for ourselves. Won't have to worry about respect in the big city, I'm sure.'

'After today's effort, I'd have thought you lads need all the help you can get.'

'What in hells is that supposed to mean?' Wulfric roared, standing as he did.

'Means that you and your mates there would'a taken a hiding today without us.'

'Like fuck we would,' Wulfric said, his skin starting to tingle. 'You lot spent most of your time killing women and old men. Seems you lads are a bit shy of steel.'

The sergeant walked forward. 'If you were any use, we wouldn't be here at all. You talk big and strut about the place like you're gods. You saw the treatment we gave the Rasbruckers today. If you don't watch your mouth maybe you'll get some of the same. Big lad like you'd fetch a good price in the slave markets.'

The sergeant was a big man. All the Ruripathians were, which had come as a surprise to Wulfric. He had always thought them to be small, slight, and effete. Rotted by lives of comfort like the merchants who had come north in the past. He had a face that looked like he had seen plenty of fighting over the years—a few scars, some chipped teeth, and a nose that had been broken at least once. Wulfric stepped forward and squared up to the sergeant, but he didn't back away or even flinch.

Their eyes were more or less level, and Wulfric's nostrils were filled with the sweet smell of ale from the sergeant's breath.

'Some of the same?' Wulfric said. He could feel his heart race with rage, and his hands started to shake.

The sergeant nodded. Wulfric wanted to gut him there and then, but angry as he was the voice of reason still managed to find its way through. His dagger remained in its sheath. He shoved the sergeant back and stepped forward to fill the space. 'Well, let's see it then.'

The sergeant took a swing at Wulfric, which he easily dodged. He slapped the sergeant's arm as it went past, sending him sprawling across the taproom floor. His soldiers didn't need any invitation and charged forward, as did Stenn and Farlof.

Wulfric felt blood pulse through his temples. He punched one of the approaching soldiers, catching him perfectly on the side of his chin. The soldier flew sideways, crashed into a table and sent it and the chairs surrounding scattering around the room. It seemed like it was in slow motion. Everyone else in the inn not involved in the brawl charged for the door. Someone smashed a chair across Wulfric's back. It shattered on his shoulders, but he could barely feel it.

Stenn and Farlof had the other soldiers under control, but Wulfric wanted to get the sergeant and knock the teeth from his big mouth. He was standing a few paces away holding a splintered chair leg. He raised it to take a swing at Wulfric. Wulfric roared at him. He dropped his shoulder and charged the sergeant, slamming into his chest, driving him across the taproom floor and smashing him into the bar.

The sergeant grunted as the wind was knocked from his chest. Wulfric grabbed him by the scruff of the neck and pulled him back from the bar. His mind was a swirl of rage as he looked down on the sergeant. Wulfric punched him in the face hard, again and again, until he felt his body go limp. Wulfric dropped him to the ground and turned. He spotted another soldier, grabbed him by the shoulders and headbutted him. He kept smashing his forehead into the soldier's face until he too dropped to the ground. He could feel the blood coursing through his veins, and his skin was tingling like an army of ants was marching across his body.

Stenn had a soldier in a headlock and Farlof was running one out the door. One soldier remained. He looked like he would rather be anywhere but there. He took a half step backward when he saw Wulfric coming for him. His eyes flicked to the door, but Farlof was blocking his escape. He tried to vault the bar, but Wulfric caught him mid-leap and flung him to the ground. Wulfric snarled as he grabbed the soldier and slammed him against the floor. The soldier whimpered as Wulfric started to beat down on him with fists and elbows.

'Wulfric!'

Wulfric continued to rain down blows.

'Wulfric!

Wulfric heard a voice call his name, but it seemed far away. The sound was familiar, but he could not recognise it at first. Between the blows his body was raining down, his detached mind searched for an answer. It was Farlof's voice. He stopped and looked around.

'He's had enough, Wulfric. You don't need to kill him.'

Wulfric nodded and looked back at the soldier. His face was a bloody pulp, but he was still breathing. He stood and looked at the previous soldier, lying senseless on the ground, his face also covered in blood. The sergeant was motionless on the ground, a puddle of blood and teeth on the floorboards beneath his mouth.

Wulfric had no memory of fighting either of them. He felt exhausted. 'We should probably leave,' he said.

CHAPTER FORTY-THREE

'I've HAD TO send to Elzburg for a physician to come up to tend to their wounds,' Ambassador Urschel said. 'The injuries were more severe than we sustained in the attack on Rasbruck. None of them will be capable of duties for weeks, and Sergeant Wordan is unlikely to be ever able to resume his, according to your healer…'

'Aethelman,' Donato said, in what he hoped would be a helpful fashion.

'Yes, Aethelman. He said the injuries were more like those seen after a battle than a taproom brawl. This warrior, Wulfric. He's an animal and I want him dealt with. We came here in good faith to help protect this village from outside aggression, and this is how we are repaid?'

No, thought Donato. You're repaid in bags of silver and horses worth a king's ransom. He rubbed his temples. There was nothing he would have liked more than to have Wulfric strung up by his balls, but this wasn't the time nor the right circumstance. When he turned on Wulfric, he wanted it to be certain, and final. Caging him up would only make him more dangerous. Donato had created a delicate balance to achieve his higher aspirations, and handling this matter harshly could upset that. Was it just his imagination, or was he getting far more headaches these days?

'There's not a great deal I can do,' Donato said. 'Despite all the changes that I've, that we've, ushered in over the past couple of years, he is First Warrior and that still carries quite a bit of weight with the villagers.' Donato had never directly opposed Ambassador Urschel before, and he would have preferred to maintain that record. There was too much to gain by playing by their rules. Nonetheless, sometimes things were not so simple.

'I couldn't give a fuck what he is,' Ambassador Urschel said, 'or how much weight he carries. I want this dealt with. Harshly.'

Donato had never heard Urschel swear before, and it worried him. He needed to demonstrate to the southerners that he could see their will carried out without any hitches. He had to, if he was to get what he wanted.

'The villagers have taken to your presence with far more enthusiasm than I could have ever hoped for. I'm reluctant to threaten that state of affairs.' It was weak, but the best he could come up with.

Ambassador Urschel furrowed his brow, so Donato continued quickly.

'Fights amongst the warrior class were common in the old days. Granted they didn't tend to result in beatings quite so... severe. The thing is, the people don't see anything unusual in this. Warriors are violent men, and they expect violent men to behave that way from time to time. Particularly after a victory like we won against Rasbruck.'

The Ambassador's face remained unmoved, and Donato could tell that he wasn't getting anywhere. 'Not to put too fine a point on it, if the people see their warriors being punished because your soldiers lost a fight against them, their opinion of you will change. Quickly and dramatically. That could cause us both a great many problems, and I fear that it could even interrupt the flow of silver south.'

The Ambassador's eye twitched, and Donato knew that he had finally hit on the right nerve.

'It could cause that much of a fuss?'

Donato nodded. 'If the villagers think the soldiers got beaten up and then ran home telling tales...'

'I see,' the Ambassador said.

Donato was confident that the Ambassador had gained much through his association with Leondorf, both financially and in favour for sending so much wealth back to his master, the Markgraf. He didn't want to upset things any more than Donato.

'I suppose we can leave it for the time being, but that doesn't mean I have forgotten about it,' the Ambassador said. 'When things are on firmer ground, we can revisit the matter.'

'I look forward to it.'

Donato leaned back in his chair at the head of the table and watched the Ambassador leave the Great Hall to head back to his luxurious abode across the square. It was useful that Wulfric had made an enemy of the Ambassador. Another step toward finally repaying Wulfric the price of an eye.

❋

Wulfric knew there was going to be trouble after the fight. The only question that remained was how much. He didn't like the idea of running away from anything, but it seemed like as good a time as any to go on his long-thought-about adventure.

Wulfric planned to keep his departure quiet until the very last moment. The only thing that had held him back was the thought of abandoning the village. It didn't take much consideration to dismiss that. He served no real role in protecting it any more, nor in providing leadership. Not many would even notice he was gone, and most of them would be glad of it. Everything was packed, and all that remained was to say goodbye to the few people he would miss. He had no idea where he was going, but there was a very large world to explore, and most of it lay to the south.

As he walked toward the kirk to say goodbye to Aethelman, he spotted the regular Elzburg carriage arrive and stop outside the inn. It ran back and forth between Leondorf and the city once a week. When the door opened, a young woman stepped out carrying a small valise. She had dark red hair that cascaded over her shoulders. She wore a long blue dress topped with a white blouse and dark blue bodice patterned with black thread. He couldn't see her face, but her figure alone was enough to catch his notice. One thing Leondorf was short on was attractive young women, not counting the prostitutes who had followed the soldiers north.

She looked too well dressed. A southern officer's sweetheart, perhaps? Considering her clothes, it occurred to Wulfric that she might be the Ambassador's daughter. If that was the case, Wulfric was tempted to introduce himself. One last insult aimed at the Ambassador before he left. It had been so long, he gave thought to all of these possibilities before he realised it was Adalhaid.

Wulfric didn't need to see her face. Tall, slender, with a cascade of red hair, he could tell just by the way she stood. His heart raced and he didn't know what to do next. The only thing he knew for certain was that his plan to leave was finished. He felt light headed and couldn't catch his breath. He needed to get away from the square. He wasn't ready for her to see him. He wasn't ready to talk to her.

She looked just as he remembered her, but better in every way. She had grown into a beautiful woman with grace and poise. The sound of her laughter still rang in his ears from those years before, and the thought of her filled him with both joy and despair. He didn't know what to say to her. He hadn't expected her to ever come back. What would she be like now? Another three years in the city must have changed her—she had spent the better part of the last decade there. What would she think of him now, having changed so much while he had stayed the same? Might she be married?

Before he knew what he was doing, he was on Greyfell galloping out into the pastures. He didn't stop until both he and the horse were gasping for air. He slipped down from the saddle and allowed Greyfell to graze on the thick grass. He sat and watched the clouds scudding across the sky, drifting effortlessly toward the mountains in the east. He felt the calm all around him, but none of it found its way in.

After so long, why had she come back at all? He looked down at his bruised and grazed knuckles, and realised that she wouldn't be far wrong in viewing him as an ignorant savage. He couldn't bear to think of her seeing him as that, but perhaps it was true. Their marriage promise was still in place, but that didn't mean it couldn't be broken. Was that why she had come back? To free herself of him? It was foolish for him to have thought that she wouldn't have met someone in the city. She was beautiful and intelligent, and like it or not, Wulfric knew how sophisticated the southerners could be. They had so much more to offer. After all of that luxury, what could there be in the Northlands to interest her now? He felt as though his head was going to burst.

He wandered back toward the village, Greyfell following behind, until he reached the tree, their tree, where he sat and continued to stare at nothing in particular.

❄

'Wulfric? I wondered if I'd find you here. Some things never change.'

He stood abruptly, startled by the unexpected voice. He had been there a while, and the sun was low in the sky. It blinded him when he turned, but through squinting eyes, he saw Adalhaid. He tried to say something, but no words would come. His mouth opened and closed but still he could make no sound. Adalhaid laughed.

'I'm pleased to see you too. You've gotten… bigger. Much bigger.'

'You have too,' Wulfric said, finally finding his tongue, then biting it when he realised it was not exactly a compliment for a woman, and was certainly not the thing he had imagined saying when he first saw her again.

'I've been looking forward to seeing you again for so long. Ever since I knew I would be coming back home.'

'It's been a long time. I didn't expect you would ever come back,' Wulfric said. 'When did you decide to?' It sounded cold, and wasn't how he meant it to come out.

'I always planned to, it just took longer to do everything I wanted to do.'

He raised an eyebrow.

'University. It takes at least two years to get a diploma. Once I got in, I had to find a way to pay for it all. I worked as a tutor to earn enough, and that took up a lot of my time, so it took me nearly three years to finish it. I really loved the work though. It's why I decided to come back and start a school here.'

'You didn't write to me…'

'Would you have been able to read the letters if I had?'

He blushed, knowing that the honest answer was no, but thought the comment was unfair. He shrugged. 'You could still have sent them.'

'I'm sorry,' she said. 'I just didn't think I'd be away for so long. At first I thought only a year, then it was two, then three. The longer it went, the harder it got to write. I know it's not a good excuse.' She paused for a moment. 'I thought you'd have moved on.'

'Will you miss the city?' he said, changing the subject and hoping to make the conversation more comfortable to bear.

She cocked her head. 'Not happy to have me back?'

She was teasing. He smiled. For a moment he felt the years that separated them melt away. 'No, that's not it. I just thought, after living in a city, Leondorf might seem… boring.'

'Leondorf has changed. It feels strange. There are so many faces I expected to see. It's silly really. Almost like I'd forgotten what happened.' She smiled thinly. 'It's good to see the village doing well again.'

'So. A school?' Wulfric was grasping for anything to talk about. 'What made you think of setting one up here?'

'A couple of things. If Leondorf's children are to compete in the world that's been opened to them, reading, writing, and arithmetic will be great assets. There are lots of schools in the south, but none here. That's not the main reason though.'

'What's that?' Wulfric said.

'Someone told me to learn things in the south that would help the village...'

Wulfric smiled. She remembered. It gave him hope. There was a moment of silence. He felt awkward around her, and hated it. He had wanted to see her for such a long time—but now that she was right in front of him, all he wanted was to get away from her.

'Well,' she said. 'I have to go and unpack. I just wanted to come and find you first and say hello. I'll see you later?'

Wulfric nodded, feeling torn between wanting her to leave him alone and wanting to take her up in his arms, for everything to be back the way it was before she left. He watched her go, remembering the day he had watched her ride south with her uncle. The largest matter between them had remained unmentioned—their betrothal. He felt like a coward for not bringing it up. He could face death in battle, but couldn't face a woman with his feelings.

※

Wulfric lay awake for hours that night, going over every moment of their short conversation in his head. He forgave himself his clumsiness. He had been all set to leave the village and was on his way to say his goodbyes. Her arrival had turned his world upside down, something that seemed to happen every time he thought he knew the direction his life was going in.

To his surprise, she called early the next morning and suggested they take a walk, asking that he show her around and point out all the changes to the village. When she left, it had been little more than ash and hastily built shacks. He made small talk by pointing out all the new buildings, as though they were not obvious enough, being so different from the

Northlander ones, but gradually they settled into their old rhythm. It was late in the morning when they found themselves back at the tree. Wulfric too was starting to feel as though no time had passed; that moment could be mistaken for any one of hundreds. She stood in silence for a moment, drinking in the scenery.

'I missed this view. There's nothing in the city that can compare to this,' she said.

She was silent again for a moment, and Wulfric didn't want to spoil it by saying something foolish.

'You never married,' she said, breaking the silence. 'I'd convinced myself that you would. I'm sure any of the girls of the village would be only too happy to be your wife.'

There had been plenty of opportunity. As she had said, he was an eligible husband for any of the young women of the village, and several people had encouraged the idea. Both Stenn and Farlof had married within weeks of coming of age. His mother grew impatient with him, and constantly tried to convince him to agree to this match or that, but he always refused, never with any clear reason behind it other than a seemingly general malaise.

Eventually words came to him. 'None of them were you.'

She blushed and looked away.

'You were waiting for me to come back?' she said, her voice hesitant and uncertain this time, unlike her usual self-assured tone. With the question asked so bluntly, the answer was clear.

'Yes.'

CHAPTER FORTY-FOUR

ONATO'S HAND TREMBLED as he took the parchment scroll the Ambassador slid toward him.

'The Most Noble and Puissant Markgraf has sent the necessary patents to her Royal Highness, The Princess of Ruripathia, to have them signed and sealed. Copies will be made and sent to you, as will the charter annexing Leondorf and its surrounding lands into the Principality of Ruripathia, and more specifically, as a barony within the Elzmark. All that remains is for you, as... headman of the village, to sign this deed.'

'"Mayor" is the title I believe the people have taken to using,' Donato said.

Ambassador Urschel nodded. The fruition of several years of hard work, grovelling, and negotiating was about to be realised, but they always had to make it known who was really in charge, as though that was not already obvious. He read through the document as carefully as he could considering his heart was racing. He frowned.

'There's no mention here of the other part of our agreement. There's no mention of me personally.'

'Once the pledge of fealty has been signed by you, and the patents sealed by the Princess, the Markgraf will have the authority to appoint a new baron. Until then, it's beyond his power. Anything that stated otherwise wouldn't be worth the paper it's written on.' The Ambassador smiled.

Donato drummed his fingers on the table. He had seen enough of the world to know when he was being lied to, but on this occasion he wasn't sure. Did the Ambassador plan to have the new barony of Leondorf for himself? Donato didn't think so. The man had shown no love for the place, and spoke often of how much he looked forward to going home once the annexation process was complete.

'Were a foreigner to be appointed Lord of Leondorf, I think he would find a very hostile reception.'

The Ambassador laughed. 'Worry not. I'm not trying to take advantage of you. Both the Markgraf and I appreciate the help you've been. You've done right by us, and we'll do right by you. You have my word that as soon as the charters and patents are signed, you will be appointed lord of this barony. In any event, we'd be hard pressed to find anyone competent in the south who would be willing to come up here on a permanent basis. The territory is very valuable to the Markgraf. You've demonstrated your ability to do what the Markgraf needs done here. Of course, you will be required to go to Elzburg to swear your oath to the Markgraf before everything will be official.'

'That won't be a problem.'

'Before we conclude our talks, there is another matter.'

Donato felt his smile fade and had to concentrate to maintain it. Too close for it to come to naught now. Whatever it was, he knew he would have to do it. 'Another matter?'

'Yes. Something particularly close to the Markgraf's heart.'

The Ambassador reached for a plate of dried fruits and cheeses on the table in front of them. They were all exotic items, the fruit came from Shandahar, far, far to the south while the cheese came from Venter, on the other side of the Middle Sea. Luxuries like these could not be found for at least a hundred miles around them, and they would never have found their way to that remote part of the world had it not been for Donato's enterprising ways. They would have credited the table of the Markgraf himself, and carried the price to prove it, yet Urschel treated them as though they had been hand picked from the nearest cow turd. He toyed with a small, shrivelled purple fruit before dropping it back on the plate in disdain. Donato wondered if it would always be thus, when he had sworn his oaths to the Markgraf.

'It's a... delicate matter that the Markgraf would like to have dealt with in as discreet a way as possible.'

Donato nodded in as earnest and sincere a way as he could muster.

Delicate matters that needed discreet attention could, in his experience, be very advantageous to him.

'There's a girl.'

Always a vice. Money, women, booze or drugs. What rotten lives these southerners lived. And to think the high and mighty warriors of Leondorf thought him to be a degenerate. If only they knew. He nodded again. It was ugly, but if that is what it took, then he would accommodate it.

'She was tutor to the Markgraf's two children. An excellent teacher and a fine young woman by all accounts. She chose to leave Elzburg suddenly, and his Lordship's son and daughter are inconsolable. He would very much like the young lady to return to his court.'

A tutor. His children. Of course. Donato suppressed a smirk. They had dressed it up to the point where it was almost believably respectable. He was happy to play along, if that was how the Ambassador wished to put things. It would likely cost him some money, but so be it.

'I'm delighted to be of assistance to the Markgraf in any way that I can, but I'm afraid I can't see how, in this situation.'

'Let me explain. The girl. She comes from this village originally, and I am given to believe has returned here in the past few days. The Markgraf is extremely eager for her to return to Elzburg. I can't emphasise that enough.'

'If she's here, as you say, then I might be able to influence her choice. As always, the Markgraf's pleasure is my own.'

'Her name is Adalhaid.'

Donato's head pounded with a sudden headache as though it had been hit with a hammer. It took all of his will to hold the obsequious smile on his face.

❧

Donato waited for the Ambassador to leave before allowing his mask to slide. He felt like his head was going to split asunder. He was so close to being a nobleman, of ensuring the future prosperity of his family. He had seen to it that the warrior class would never again strut around the village as though they owned it. Before he died, Leondorf would be a prosperous city with all the luxuries of the south. One day his descendants would rival the Markgraf for wealth and power. Now all that was in jeopardy because of some slut.

'Adalhaid' was the only name in the village that would pose a problem. He knew she was back. She and Wulfric had been glued to one another in the week since her return. The village was abuzz with talk of their impending wedding. Wulfric was nothing now; surely being the Markgraf's kept woman was a far better prospect. He sneered at the Ambassador calling her a tutor. Did he really think Donato was so naive? He wondered what Wulfric would think if he knew his flame-haired beauty had been the Markgraf's bit on the side. The sneer on his face faded when he realised Wulfric would gut him at the first mention of it.

He couldn't begin to imagine what the reaction would be when he suggested she return to Elzburg to resume whatever it was she was doing there before. What Wulfric had done to the soldiers in the inn would be a pale comparison to his reaction to an attempt to separate the two again. Was it too much to hope that they wouldn't find one another so agreeable after all the time apart?

He massaged his temples. Why could things never go smoothly for him? There always had to be some catch, something that made his life more difficult than it needed to be. He had nearly made his son a warrior, then his eye was taken. He had nearly made himself a nobleman… No. He would not lose this. He had put too much of himself into it. He rarely encountered a problem that could not be solved in one way or another, and he was sure this one was no different. It was only a question of how far he was willing to go for his solution. He couldn't care less if the girl went south willingly or not, but she would go and he would be made Baron. He was confident that he could manage her; a solution would come to him soon enough, as it always did.

Wulfric was a different matter. He had gone from being an arrogant pain in his neck to a truly dangerous young man. He had already got a taste for killing and he seemed to revel in violence, as his conduct in the inn had shown. If Donato tried to force Adalhaid back to Elzburg, people would die, and he would most likely be one of them.

❀

It seemed an odd, but perhaps fortuitous coincidence to Donato when his guard led Adalhaid into the council chamber only minutes after the Ambassador had departed. She was among the last few people he would expect to have call on him. Would it be too premature to start exploring her thoughts on returning south?

'Good morning,' he said, adopting as welcoming an air as he could. 'What can I do for you today?'

'I want to discuss setting up a school in the village,' Adalhaid said, not waiting to be invited to sit.

'But we already have a school. Aethelman takes classes still. As I recall you were one of his students.'

'The school in the kirk was fine for the way things were, but it's not enough anymore.'

Donato started to raise his hands dismissively, but Adalhaid cut him off.

'If people from the village can't read, write, and do arithmetic, we're asking to be taken advantage of by the southerners. If they can, they will thrive. That's good for the village. It's good for everyone. You included.'

It was a difficult argument to counter and, caught off-guard, Donato couldn't think of a reply. He didn't want her putting down roots, or starting work on a project that might incline her to stay, but he needed to be subtle in his opposition.

'If you are decided on the idea,' he said, 'I'm not going to stand in the way.'

'I'll need money to set it up,' Adalhaid said. 'Seeing as it will be such a benefit for the village, I was hoping you might advance that money from village funds.'

He wanted to smile at this first opportunity to make things difficult for her. 'That might be a problem.'

Adalhaid raised an eyebrow. 'I was under the impression there was quite a bit of wealth passing through here. Silver, I believe. It's quite the topic of conversation in Elzburg. Is Leondorf not benefitting from that at all?'

'It is, of course. We've been spending considerable sums rebuilding the village and we have to pay for the soldiers. There really isn't much left over.'

'It won't take very much. All I need is a room, and perhaps credit with some of the craftsmen in the village.'

'Things don't work like that here anymore. Coin is king I'm afraid, and without it, you'll have a very hard time getting anything done.'

'Where there's a will, there's a way, Mayor.'

Donato smiled sympathetically. 'Unfortunately, for the time being at least, I'm afraid that's not the case. Perhaps if you come back to see me at harvest time, there might be some spare coin to help you set up.'

She smiled and stood. 'Thank you for your time,' she said, before leaving.

Donato watched her go. Her years in the south had served her well. Polite, courtly, and possessed of a sharp mind. The school was a fool's errand, however. What use was schooling for mine labourers and whores?

❊

Rodulf had no idea what the stone was, or what it did, but for some reason it dominated his thoughts. He kept it with him at all times, and felt distress whenever he allowed himself to be separated from it. When alone he would study it, but its mysteries never became any clearer.

There was a knock at the door, and his father's servant appeared. The man was nervous. The last time he had disturbed Rodulf, he had been beaten him for his impudence. Rodulf wasn't in the mood for teaching manners, however. He was feeling good. It was one of those days when he believed things were going to go his way.

'Your father would like to see you,' the man said.

'I'll be along directly,' Rodulf said, his eyes still locked on that strange little piece of metal. He dropped it into his pocket and followed his father's man to the Great Hall. Donato sat at the head of the Great Table, massaging his temples. The servant exited silently, leaving Rodulf with his father.

'You look vexed, Father,' he said.

'There's been a development,' Donato said. 'A problem.'

'What now?' Rodulf said. He tried to hide the hint of exasperation in his voice. His father was a master of trading and squeezing every last copper of profit from a deal, but sometimes he seemed to lack the drive to knock obstacles from his path. Was he getting too old?

'The Ambassador wants Adalhaid to return south.'

'That's not going to happen,' Rodulf said. 'She and that whoreson Wulfric are to be married.'

'I know,' Donato said.

Rodulf smiled. At long last, he had his excuse. 'Not going to happen so long as Wulfric lives, that is,' Rodulf said.

CHAPTER FORTY-FIVE

A S BELGAR HAD aged, each old wound—even those long healed and almost as long forgotten—came back to remind him of the recklessness of his youth. On a cold, damp day, he could barely move. He had fought many battles, but couldn't remember even one that had placed as much strain on him as those he had been fighting in the Great Hall since the Ruripathians arrived. At times it felt as though he was talking to himself. If he had any sense he would just shut his mouth, but once, in a past so far away he could barely remember it, he had been the First Warrior. That mantle had passed to another when he became too slow to deserve it, but the responsibility and the sense of duty never left. He could never sit by without raising his voice if he felt the wrong choices were being made for the village, no matter how much easier it would make his life. The frustration was eating away at him though, chewing through his soul such that he feared when his turn to join Jorundyr's Host came, there would be nothing of it left.

As he had when he was First Warrior, Belgar went out and walked through Leondorf every evening to speak to the villagers and gauge their sentiment on various things. There were so many strange faces now. Whenever he asked for their thoughts on the Ruripathians, it made him want to scream like a madman. None seemed to see what they were losing, and what the future held. They only saw the luxury that the southerners brought with them, and the food, and safety.

It was some consolation that a few had made proud mention of the way Wulfric was able to beat the tar out of the soldiers in the inn. It made him smile to think of it, and he rued the fact that he had not been there to witness it. All down to his refusal to go to the inn because of its new ownership. He could remember a time when he would have been disappointed not to be involved. How quickly the years passed.

The walking helped ease his painful joints and it tired him enough to sleep, the fatigue freeing him from the frustrations of his day. It was getting late as he passed by the Great Hall, skirting by its rear on his way home from the stockade where the horses being brought in for sale were kept. It was sad to see them go, but it was sadder still to remember what Leondorf had been like after the attacks by Rasbruck. Sometimes the lesser evil had to be accepted.

His eyes fell on the spot where, as a child, he had pressed his ear to the wall to hear what was going on inside. He wondered if it still worked, what with all the new construction. His curiosity got the better of him, and his joints creaked in protest as he bent down to press his ear to the wall. He could hear voices. It surprised him to feel the youthful thrill of eavesdropping. He was perfectly entitled to walk inside to hear what was being said, but he was enjoying himself too much. Especially as there should not have been any business being conducted within at that hour.

'I've been giving some thought to the request you made at our last meeting,' a voice from within said.

It was Donato's. Belgar would recognise it anywhere, muffled though it was by the wall. Oily, smarmy; thoroughly unlikeable.

'I'm delighted to hear it. I'm very eager to send word to the Markgraf that the girl is returning to his court. I trust the situation is well in hand?' It was the Ambassador's. He was the only southerner allowed into the Great Hall.

There was a momentary silence, which even from outside, Belgar could tell was an uncomfortable one. He imagined Donato squirming in his chair as he always did when pressed on something he would rather avoid discussing.

'In a manner of speaking, yes. There is a problem however.'

'Problem? Of what nature? It's hardly the most complicated of requests. Certainly not one I would have thought beyond the ability of a man of your aspirations.'

'She's involved with one of the warriors. I believe it to be why she came back in the first place. There was a marriage promise made before she left the village for Elzburg after the disaster.'

'To whom? Pay him off if you must. I'm sure I don't need to remind you what the Markgraf thinks of those who can't carry out his instructions.'

'You're familiar with him, as it happens. That's why I thought you might be interested in discussing some options for dealing with the matter, and perhaps assisting.'

'Really? Who is it?'

'Wulfric. The warrior who bea— assaulted your soldiers.'

Belgar pressed his ear harder against the wall until it hurt. What in hells could they be up to?

'That is interesting, but as much as I'd like to see him swinging from a gallows by his neck, I do tend to prioritise things in order of importance. Girl going back to Elzburg being head of that list. Everything else is by the way.'

'He'll follow her to the ends of the earth and kill anyone that tries to stand in his way,' Donato said. 'There's no way she's going to go back to Elzburg as long as he's around, and anyone who tries to force her will end up dead. He won't bat an eyelid at money, land or titles. In the time she was gone, he didn't so much as look at another woman. Their marriage is the talk of the village.'

'So, the solution would seem to involve his death or disappearance,' the Ambassador said.

'If you want to take her back to Elzburg, he'll have to be killed,' Donato said. His voice wavered.

Belgar imagined him nodding furiously, lickspittle that he was. He could feel rage swirling in his gut. He would have to let Wulfric know as soon as he could.

'Do I detect an ulterior motive here?' There was silence for a moment before the Ambassador spoke again. 'It matters not. I know what he did to my men at the inn, and it is not my intention to allow that to go unanswered. I have no issue with killing him if it makes things easier on us both. I assume you've thought through how we will go about it?'

'We have,' Donato said.

We? Wulfric killed? Belgar pressed his ear harder against the wall, but could not hear a third person.

'Of course you have,' the Ambassador said. 'I presume it will involve my soldiers?'

'It does.' A third voice. Belgar racked his brain to recognise it. Rodulf. That one-eyed viper was always going to be involved in something like this.

'Well, let's hear it then.'

There was the sound of a chair scraping on the floor.

'Preparations are already underway for their marriage,' Rodulf said. 'I'm told it's planned for two days hence. A marriage means a feast, and a feast needs meat. That means the warriors are going to go out hunting for it.'

'And you propose to send my men after them? To kill Wulfric? In the forest? I don't think your son is playing with a full deck of cards, Mayor. Wulfric's a savage. My lads have been brawling in bars since they were weaned off the tit, and he took them apart like they didn't know a punch from a kiss. If he can do that to them in their own environment, what do you think he'll do to them in his?'

Belgar couldn't help but smile. They might not be showing Wulfric respect, but at least they feared him.

'I've thought of that,' Rodulf said. 'We split them up to get the hunting done faster. Send some of your men out with them. Say it's their punishment for the fight, and we want them to have put their differences behind them by the time they get back. Best interests of the village and all. They'll respond to it when it's put like that. They may be ignorant savages, but they'd cut off their arm for the village if it was asked of them. We send one of your soldiers with each of them. Any more than that and they might get suspicious. We can say the soldiers want to learn from them. Play to the arrogant bastards' vanity.'

'So, you've separated him from his cronies, and put one of my men with him. I still don't see how that improves our chances,' the Ambassador said. 'From what I've been told, Wulfric was responsible for most of the damage done at the inn all by himself. And that was several men.'

'He might be able to fight,' Rodulf said, 'but an arrow kills every man just the same. The man that goes with Wulfric leaves a trail for some bowmen to follow. They wait until Wulfric and your soldier are camped for the night, and fill him with arrows while he sleeps.'

There was a long pause. Belgar wanted to rush straight over to Wulfric's house and tell him what he had heard, but he needed to know everything. He couldn't go just yet.

'So, he's dead. What then? I don't give a damn about him, or settling whatever personal vendetta you seem to have with him. It's the girl I'm interested in. How do you get her to go back to Elzburg? I'd really rather not have to drag her back kicking and screaming, although I will if that's what is needed.'

'She has no family here,' Rodulf said. 'The only family she has left is in Elzburg. With nothing to keep her here, she won't need much convincing. I dare say she'll go of her own accord.'

Silence inside. Belgar felt his blood boil. He wanted to go into the Hall and kill the three of them himself.

'Fine,' the Ambassador said. 'I want it done soon, which seems to suit the timetable anyway. My tenure here is up, thank the gods, and I'm heading back to the city. I want it dealt with before then. We can bring her back with us. If it all works out, this will reflect very well on you, and confirm the confidence the Markgraf has shown in you thus far. Fuck it up, and when he annexes Leondorf into the Elzmark he'll ennoble a pig in preference to you. Am I clear?'

'Perfectly,' Donato said. 'It will work, I assure you. Rodulf and I have thought this all out very carefully.'

There was the scraping of chair legs on wood and the sound of footsteps. Belgar moved his head from the wall and rubbed his ear. He couldn't believe what he was hearing. He hated Donato and Rodulf; they were a pair of greasy, cowardly, coin-counting rats, but even Belgar could never have imagined them conspiring to murder someone from the village. That was a new low to sink to. And the talk of annexing and ennobling? What was that about? That could wait though, he had to warn Wulfric.

'Bit late for a stroll, Grandfather.'

Belgar froze in the spot; it was the accent of a southerner. He turned slowly to have his fears confirmed. One of the Ambassador's men stood watching him, spear in hand. His warrior's instinct told him what was coming, but his old and worn body could not get him out of the way in time.

❁

Donato, Rodulf, and Ambassador Urschel were sitting at the table in the Great Hall when Belgar came back to his senses, as was the soldier who had knocked him on the head. He was sitting before them, tied to a chair.

'How much did you hear, old man?' the Ambassador said.

'What? Don't hear too well. Speak up.'

The Ambassador laughed. 'Yes, very good. Very clever. Now tell me, how much did you hear?'

'Fuck yourself,' Belgar said.

Donato rubbed his face. 'This is a damned mess.'

'It's not a problem,' Rodulf said. 'One death. Two deaths. Makes no difference.'

'I agree,' the Ambassador said. 'Kill them both. Keep things clean.'

'People don't just go around murdering each other in a village like Leondorf,' Donato said. 'It's not the city, you know.'

'Really?' the Ambassador said. 'I'm glad you pointed that out. I'd not have noticed otherwise. I still don't see a problem.'

'Why do you think we've hatched such an elaborate plan for Wulfric?' Donato said. 'We can't have anything look suspicious. If they find out I'm killing off warriors, the villagers will turn against me faster than you can click your fingers, and when they're done gutting me your door will be the next one they turn up at.'

'Perhaps your son has more of a stomach for difficult decisions than you do,' Urschel said.

'We can make it look like an accident,' Rodulf said.

Donato raised his eyebrows and smiled.

'You're a fucking whoreson snake,' Belgar said. 'You don't have the guts to kill a man.' He spat at Donato, but the spittle fell short.

Donato laughed.

'Your father didn't either,' Belgar said. 'Even after he found me lying with your mother. You've the same yellow streak he did.'

This time the Ambassador was the one that laughed.

Belgar smiled. 'Poor woman needed some pleasure in her life, living with a limp prick like him. I'd have said that he wasn't up to whelping a turd like you and that you might be mine if it weren't for the fact that I only started putting a smile on her face after you crawled out into the world. I'd have said you didn't have it in you either, if that one-eyed piece of rat shit over there wasn't so obviously your boy.'

Even the soldier was laughing by this stage. Donato's face was bright red and screwed up in fury. Rodulf's was not far behind. Donato stood, walked over and slapped Belgar across the face.

Belgar swallowed a mouthful of blood and what felt like a tooth, rather than show Donato that it had caused any injury. 'Your mother hit harder than you, too.'

'Take a look at the horses tonight, did you, Belgar?' Donato said.

Belgar said nothing.

'Of course you did. You do it every night when they're brought into town. The habits of a worn out old man who's lived longer than he should.' Donato turned to the soldier. 'Take him out to the horse pen and throw him in. Make sure the job's done before that though. No blades, mind. It has to look like he fell in and got trampled to death.'

The soldier nodded and pulled Belgar roughly from the chair.

Donato turned to the Ambassador. 'That won't be a hard one to swallow. Everyone knows the sentimental old bastard likes to look at the horses. It's not too much of a stretch of the imagination that he fell in. Still think I don't have a stomach for this type of thing?'

'Fine,' the Ambassador said. 'Anyway you want it, so long as it's done.'

Donato nodded and turned back to Belgar. 'Well, off to Jorundyr's Host with you. I'm sure you're looking forward to it.'

Belgar spat at him again, but this time his aim was true.

CHAPTER FORTY-SIX

ONATO WOKE EARLY, and was agitated all morning as
he waited for Belgar's body to be discovered. Perhaps the
Ambassador was right. Maybe he didn't have the stomach for
that kind of thing. Finally, the alarm was raised. One of the stable hands
spotted something in the stockade that shouldn't have been there, when
bringing the morning feed out for the horses. Donato went there as soon as
the news was brought to him, playing the concerned mayor. The body was
bruised and battered almost beyond recognition. Either the soldiers were
very thorough, or the horses had finished what they started. It took longer
than he expected for them to identify it as Belgar.

The other warriors arrived, and Donato felt incredibly pleased as
Wulfric and his two cronies reverently lifted Belgar's broken old body from
the churned up mud and carried it back toward his house. It surprised him
how remarkably easy it was to kill a man, particularly when someone else
was doing the killing. He might have to make it a more regular feature
of his governance, although the power of life and death was one of the
prerogatives of a feudal lord. Feudal lord. Baron Leondorf. Lord Leondorf.
Some days it felt like the sun was shining on him no matter where he went.
Perhaps he did have the stomach for it after all.

He fought not to smile as the warriors walked past, trying to wear an
expression of suitable solemnity. He watched Wulfric as he went. He would
be following Belgar to Jorundyr's Host in only a day or two, and then the
road to nobility would be unobstructed. He knew killing Wulfric would be
more difficult a task than a broken-down old man, and that he was placing
a great deal of faith in the southern soldiers. Still, Rodulf's plan was sound.

There would be plenty of them, and how difficult was it to fire quarrels into a sleeping man from point-blank range? He wondered if he should arrange some poison for the tips, just to be sure.

There was movement from the broken bundle the warriors carried. Donato's gut reacted before his brain did. It twisted and he thought he would throw up. He heard a groan come from the broken body. He wanted to believe that he was imagining it. Suddenly the sun felt very far away indeed. What kind of idiot was the soldier, that he couldn't even beat an old man to death? Although alive, Belgar seemed to be unconscious. Perhaps he would die without ever waking. Was that too much to hope for?

❀

A black cloud descended over the marriage preparations when news of Belgar's injuries spread through the village. He was the last of his generation. The last of a way of life that might never be seen again in Leondorf. Aethelman said it was unlikely he would wake; that he would probably drift off in his sleep, and take his place in Jorundyr's Host.

Belgar had done well to last as long as he had. Wulfric had to be grateful for having had the benefit of his wisdom for so long. Belgar's demise made him feel as miserable as his father's death. It was difficult to put a brave face on things, but there was a wedding to prepare, and a future to plan for.

❀

A boy, no more than nine or ten summers ran up to Wulfric. 'There's hundreds of them!'

'Hundreds of what?' Wulfric said.

The boy was excitable at the best of times, but today he looked fit to burst. Every time a herd of deer or a particularly large boar or belek sighting came in, Wulfric's door was the boy's first port of call. He was perhaps the only one in the village who still adulated the warriors. The news was, however, of interest to Wulfric. With his wedding only a couple of days away, the proximity of a large herd of deer was auspicious. They would be able to hunt plenty of meat and ensure that everyone in the village went home after the wedding celebration with a full belly and a smiling face.

'Are there any harts?' Wulfric said.

The boy shrugged his shoulders.

'Well, I suppose I should go and take a look.'

The boy's face lit up in delight at the realisation that his news was to be acted upon. He followed Wulfric as he walked through the village calling out for Stenn and Farlof to prepare their things and join him for a hunt.

'What's all the commotion about?' Donato said, as he walked out of the Great Hall.

'A herd of deer have been spotted not far away. We're going hunting.'

'Hardly a surprise,' Donato said. 'All you lot seem to do is hunt and eat the village to near starvation.'

'Remind me where all the meat comes from,' Wulfric said.

Donato sniffed. 'I need to talk to you before you go.'

'About what?'

'About you beating three hells out of Ruripathian soldiers, and how you're going to fix the damage you've done to the village's safety,' Donato said.

'It can wait until I get back.'

Donato walked over to him quickly, so quickly Wulfric thought he might actually hit him. He stuck out his chin and glared at Donato, but he stopped short and spoke in an aggravated whisper.

'What if they decide they don't want to fight for us any more?'

'Rasbruck's beaten. They won't bother us again,' Wulfric said. 'Maybe the soldiers should go home, if they're afraid of it happening again.'

'You just don't get it, do you? Without the Ruripathians, every other village in the Northlands is stronger than us. Have you forgotten how quick they were to raid our herds when they saw the chance? Remember how that worked out?'

Wulfric wanted to say something smart, and offensive if possible, but he realised that Donato was right. He, Stenn and Farlof might be able to handle several men each, but there were threats in the Northlands that would be too much for them. Wulfric hadn't given a thought to how his actions could put the entire village at risk. He couldn't decide what angered him more, the fact that he had been so stupid or that Donato was right.

'What do I need to do?'

'I'm sorry, I didn't hear that?' Donato said.

Wulfric felt a flash of anger, but swallowed it. 'I said, what do I need to do?'

'The new captain of the Ruripathian garrison loves to hunt. He's a special type of nobleman from down south, ones that have earned their title through martial prowess. They're called 'bannerets', so you should get along well with him if you give him a chance. Take him out on this hunt with you. I want you best friends with him by the time you get back. I know what you think of me, and everyone knows what you think of the Ruripathians, but we still need them and will until we can put at least forty warriors out on the field.'

It would be ten years at least before that happened. Wulfric groaned inwardly, but didn't let Donato see his displeasure. 'It's a marriage feast hunt. I'm supposed to do it only with my chosen cupbearers.'

'This time, I'm sure the gods will turn a blind eye. The greater good of the village dictates it. I've already checked with Aethelman. He says there won't be a problem, that there's nothing in the writings that requires it to only be your cupbearers.'

Wulfric thought for a moment, and wondered if he should check with Aethelman himself. It didn't seem like a big issue though, and as Donato had said the reasons were good. He hated it when the bastard was right. 'Fine. I'll take him.'

'Excellent,' Donato said, a broad smile forming on his narrow face. 'Try and see to it that he bags something impressive. It will help grease the wheels.'

Wulfric scowled at him. 'Tell the captain to be ready to go at dawn.'

The Ruripathian captain was waiting outside Wulfric's house well before dawn the next morning, his horse and hunting gear all ready to go. Wulfric had expected someone similar to the previous captain. This man was different though. Tall, broad, and blond, he had a fur cloak thrown over clothes that looked appropriate for hunting.

'You new here?' Wulfric said.

'Arrived three days ago. Banneret-Captain Endres at your service.' He clicked his heels together and gave a curt nod of his head.

Wulfric gave him a suspicious look and walked forward to take a look at his horse and equipment. He might have agreed to take the captain with him, but he wasn't going to nursemaid a man who would wet his britches at the first sniff of a belek.

'You'll find everything is in order,' Endres said.

Wulfric ignored him and continued to check, looking for anything he could find fault with. He was disappointed.

'It looks all right,' Wulfric said. Maybe there was something to this military training Donato had talked about. He squinted in the pre-dawn half light, and took a closer look at Banneret-Captain Endres.

'That cloak,' Wulfric said. 'Is that—'

'Belek. Yes. I see you have one too.'

'You hunt belek in the south?'

'Yes. But only for sport. I understand that they're hunted by necessity here.'

'Yes, from time to time they can come close to the village. Not often, though.'

'They don't tend to come anywhere near towns or cities in the south. You have to go up into the forests and mountains to find them.'

'Can't say I'd ever go looking for one,' Wulfric said.

Captain Endres laughed.

Perhaps it wouldn't be such a chore after all. Their gear checked, they departed.

They rode hard for three hours in the direction that the herd was reported as being in. It took another hour to find tracks that belonged to deer, but there were not many. Certainly not so many as had been reported. That wasn't unusual. People exaggerated and he had been confident that the boy had talked up the size and quality of a herd he had only been told about. There was only so much meat that they could carry anyway. Three or four would be more than enough.

The trail, modest though it was, led them into the forest south of the village. There was a decent-sized river with steep sides not far ahead, and Wulfric was hopeful that they would be able to trap the herd against it. It would be a job for the next day though, it was getting dark and carrying on was to risk a foolish injury.

❧

It was still dark when Wulfric woke. He looked at the fire for his first point of reference. It glowed benignly, so he had been asleep for a couple of hours, not much more. Something must have woken him. He concentrated on his ears, listening for anything out of the ordinary, anything that might have caused him to wake. There was nothing. Usually he slept well, even when out in the forest.

His heart was beating quickly. At first he thought it was simply a bad dream. Aethelman had told him it wasn't unusual for men to become abnormally tense in the days leading up to their wedding. He thought the idea ridiculous at first, but as the day grew closer, he had to admit Aethelman was right. He had the additional worry now of returning without any meat. That would certainly make for a poor start to the marriage. So far they hadn't even seen a deer.

He continued to listen, lying there with only the faint crackling of the low fire breaking the silence. He knew it was more than marriage nerves, though. Even though he couldn't see any danger, his hands were shaking uncontrollably. Something was not as it should be. It was too quiet. Even with a fire to ward off wild animals, there were many small creatures that would not be daunted, filling the forest with sound. There was no sound beyond their little circle of firelight. He recalled the first time he had gone hunting, of how his father had reacted to the same circumstances. A silent forest means danger. As quietly as he could, he reached out from under his cloak and drew his sabre from its scabbard. He kept his breathing as shallow as possible as he listened.

A twig snapped and a footfall crunched on the soil. He jumped up into a crouch and backed away from the fire, moving out of its light and into the cover of the undergrowth. He threw a pebble at Endres, but it bounced off his blanket without him stirring.

Wulfric crouched on the balls of his feet, scanning the darkness for anything. His eyes were gritty and he was still fighting off the confusion of interrupted sleep. A crossbow bolt whistled out of the darkness and struck the tree beside him with a loud thud. He dived into a bush head first, and then peered out. There was no sign of the assailants. He wondered if he should call out to Endres, who still appeared to be asleep. That would give away his position though, and as amiable as the man was, Wulfric had no desire to be on the receiving end of a crossbow bolt for his benefit. If he was as skilled a warrior as Donato had made him out to be, he would be well able to look after himself.

Two crossbow bolts tore through the bush Wulfric was hiding in, each passing close enough for him to feel them go by. Two bolts being fired so close to one another meant there was more than one attacker, but he still had only a vague idea of where they were. He couldn't fight men he couldn't see. Endres hadn't moved from his bedroll, which Wulfric took as meaning he was already dead. A shame, but better his bad luck than Wulfric's.

There was no use in tarrying there. They had all the advantages. He turned and ran, hoping that he could lose his attackers in the dark confusion of the forest. He made a terrible racket as he went, but there was nothing for it; he could barely see where he was going. As he began to think he had gotten away he felt a hard punch in the back. It knocked him forward. He dropped his sword and stumbled a couple of paces, then fell to the ground. He reached behind him and felt the thick stubby shaft of a bolt sticking from his back. He could hear men coming after him, crashing through the forest, shouting to one another. He scrambled to his feet and continued to run.

He felt two more punches in his back. They felt numb rather than painful after the shock of the initial impact faded. He managed to keep to his feet, and forced himself forward as fast as he could, but it was getting difficult to breathe. He swiped branches out of his way as his run became more of a stumble. Why were these men after him? Surely reavers would have kept their distance? How was he going to make it back home in time for the wedding?

The noise behind him was getting closer. A bolt thudded into a tree beside him, and Wulfric's pace dropped to a slow walk. He felt incredibly tired. His chest felt tight. It was so difficult to breathe. The world seemed distant as he continued to stumble through the darkness.

He didn't even notice the precipice of the steep riverbank. He was falling before he knew what was happening. He didn't realise he was so close to the river. It was the last thought that went through his head before he plunged into the icy-cold water.

CHAPTER FORTY-SEVEN

'IT'S DONE THEN?' Donato said.

Banneret-Captain Endres nodded. He felt as if he was in an interview, with both the Northlander mayor and Ambassador Urschel sitting opposite him. The Ambassador had a smile firmly fixed to his face.

'I assume you brought back... proof?' Donato said.

'I was told you didn't want evidence of anything but the lie,' Endres said. 'We dumped the body in the river.' The trail had led to the river's edge. There was nowhere for him to go but down, and there was no way he survived the water with a couple of arrows in his back.

'But he's definitely dead?' Donato said. 'You can assure me of that.'

Endres nodded again. He wasn't nearly as confident as he was making out, but if the crossbow bolts hadn't killed Wulfric, the fall and the freezing water would have. He didn't like calling a job done without seeing the body going cold, but he was sure. Still, he wanted his money, so he had killed a pig and contrived the campsite to look like a lot more blood had been shed there than actually was. They left Wulfric's weapons lying around and a few scraps of cloth, including a piece of belek fur from his own cloak. He was loathe to tear it off, but the damage was small and unnoticeable, while the payment he was due to get was neither.

'They'll probably want to send out a search party for the body,' Donato said. 'I assume they'll find a campsite that looks like someone died there?'

'Someone did,' Endres said. 'Wild animals don't tend to leave meat lying around long at this time of year. Plenty of wolves, bears. Maybe even a belek. No one will be surprised to find nothing but some blood on the ground. His swords are still lying there. No self-respecting warrior would leave them behind if he was able to carry them.'

'His friends will probably want to speak with you,' Donato said. 'What do you plan on saying?'

'They're welcome, but they'll have to make it fast. I plan on returning to the city with Ambassador Urschel. I'll tell them we were attacked by a belek. I understand he had a knack for attracting them. Everyone's luck runs out sooner or later. Being a cowardly southerner, I ran.'

Donato pursed his lips in approval. 'That should work. They'd expect him to have stood his ground and fought. Bloody fool.'

'A brave man,' Endres said. 'You'd have to have seen a belek to understand. It's a pity he died the way he did. Not a good death.'

'You didn't seem to have any problem facilitating it,' Donato said.

'We all have to eat,' Endres said. 'Speaking of which. My money?'

Donato took a leather satchel and pushed it across the table. Endres opened it and peered inside. It was heavy, and stacked high with small, rough ingots of silver. He smiled.

'All things considered, I think it would be best if you were to forget about ever visiting Leondorf again.'

'I'm sure I'll be able to restrain the urge,' Endres said. 'A pleasure doing business with you.'

❋

'There can be no doubt,' Donato said. 'Banneret-Captain Endres said the attack came without any warning. It was quick and brutal, and he barely escaped with his life.'

'He did escape with it though,' Adalhaid said. 'Why couldn't Wulfric have? Did he actually see Wulfric killed?'

Donato shifted in his seat. 'No, but I sent Stenn and Farlof back to see if they could find his bod— him. I had hoped that perhaps he was just injured, or hiding.'

'But he wasn't.'

Donato shook his head. 'His weapons, some scraps of bloody clothing, a piece of his cloak…' Whatever about the rest, the scrap of belek cloak was weighty evidence. 'I don't think there can be any doubt. I'm sorry. He's a huge loss to the village.'

Adalhaid nodded, but kept her composure. 'What do you think happened?'

'Endres said it all happened so quickly it was something of a blur. He's certain it was a belek in the middle of the night. Wulfric stayed to face it. Endres ran. Not the most courageous thing to do, but...' Donato could read the look on Adalhaid's face. It was an even mix of despair and disbelief.

'His body. They found nothing?' she said. Her voice was faltering, each word uttered while she tried to restrain tears.

'I'd hoped to avoid this. There's no easy way to put this, and I know it will be difficult for you to hear, but I feel you deserve the truth. Belek don't tend to leave much of their prey.' He tried to put it as gently as possible. He wanted her to feel he was on her side, that his only concern was for her. 'I've spoken with Aethelman. He assures me this won't interfere with Wulfric's ascension to Jorundyr's Host in any way. He has already done more than enough for us to be confident that he will be welcomed by his fallen brothers. Facing down a belek is a very courageous thing to do. You should be very proud of him.'

Adalhaid began to sob gently. It appeared the lie had been swallowed. He wondered how long he should wait before broaching the next issue. He would rather have left it for a few weeks—a few days at least—to allow the grief to fade a little, and to gradually plant the thought of returning south in her head in the hope that it took root and felt like her own idea. Sadly, Ambassador Urschel wouldn't agree to that. He had said the end of the week, so the end of the week it would be. The sooner the business was dealt with, the sooner Donato could start turning his thoughts to where he would build his castle.

'I can send word to your uncle, if you'd like. At times like these it's best to be with family.'

She nodded distantly.

Donato smiled. All he had to do was get her on the carriage back to Elzburg. With that done, he had fulfilled his part of the bargain, and she became someone else's problem. Perhaps it would be easier than he hoped.

❊

Wulfric woke with a gasp and a hacking cough that spluttered water over his face. He was on a pebbly bank at the side of a river, soaked through, freezing cold and numb. He only wore a few scraps of clothing. He sat up and roared in pain. His back felt as though it had fused solid. With each effort at moving, he could feel his skin and muscle tug at the projectiles in his back.

As luck would have it, his belek cloak had caught on a tree not far from where he lay. He struggled to his feet and retrieved it, the objects in his back making themselves known with every movement. The cloak was soaking, but would dry quickly, and keep him warm once it did. If the wounds didn't kill him, the cold would. As he lay there, he realised that the cloak had already saved him. It had absorbed most of the impacts, and none had penetrated far enough to cause fatal damage.

He pulled the cloak over him and gently reached around to his back to probe the wounds. They were crossbow bolts; thick and stubby. The bolts wobbled gently and painfully when he touched them. Not deep enough to be stuck fast. He wondered what damage pulling them out would do. A hunter's arrow would be barbed, and make an ungodly mess if he tried pulling on them. The southerners were the only ones to use crossbows, which meant it was probably reavers. Still not quite a match for a belek cloak, it seemed. He wasn't going to get home with them still sticking in his back, and if he was going to die, it wouldn't be from being too timid to try and survive.

Getting a firm grip required him to stretch and contort to the point of agony. The first bolt popped free with a sickening sound that reminded him of jointing a killed animal. The second came out with little effort, raising his hopes for the third. It felt more firmly embedded, and it was nigh on impossible to get a firm grip on it. He jerked suddenly, getting his hand to the bolt and pulling it free in the same movement. Pain seared through him like a hot lance and he roared again—not the cleverest thing to do if he was still being pursued. It was time to get moving.

He tossed the bolts into the water and watched two of them bob tip down as they were washed downstream. The third floated on the surface, tossed about by the churning water. It meant that the tip of it was probably still inside him. There were plenty of things more likely to kill him than that, but he would have to get Aethelman to take it out when he got home. He checked the wounds on his back again. His flesh was still cold to the touch but there was only a small amount of bleeding, nothing to cause him concern.

He knew that if he didn't get warm quickly, he would likely fall asleep and not wake up again. He struggled up the bank, into the undergrowth and started to work his way back up river. He wasn't sure how far he had gone, or how long he had been asleep on the riverbank, but he knew of a crossing point up river of where they had camped. With luck, he could be home by the next day.

As he walked, he thought about what had happened. He felt sorry for Endres. It seemed likely that it was his death that had woken Wulfric, so in a way he owed the Banneret-Captain his life. It was no way for a warrior to die, to be robbed of the opportunity to be killed in battle with a sword in your hand. He stopped—and cursed his naivety.

It was probably Endres who had fired the shots. It was why Donato had been so insistent Wulfric take him along. Was it his punishment for the fight in the inn? He must have left a trail for others to follow, then waited until he was asleep. He cursed again. It made sense, but it seemed too elaborate a scheme if it was simply the southerners getting their revenge for the fight. It could as easily have been bandits. With all the silver passing through the country, banditry was growing. It was one of the more unwelcome things that came north with the southerners. They had reavers aplenty too. Wulfric knew that could easily explain what had happened. Nonetheless, he couldn't help but feel that Donato had a hand in it.

CHAPTER FORTY-EIGHT

WULFRIC'S HOPES OF getting home the next day were misplaced. It was six days later when he stumbled back into Leondorf half starved. The wounds on his back moved between numbness and searing pain; he was not sure which he preferred. The time he spent in the river was something of a saving grace, though; it had cleaned out the wounds in his back meaning they had not turned bad. He was exhausted, hungry, and weak beyond belief when he walked into the village. All he could think of was collapsing into Adalhaid's arms. If he could make it that far, everything would be fine.

The last time he'd walked into the village in dire straits, he had been recognised instantly. With so many newcomers to Leondorf, the first few people he encountered looked at him with the distaste they reserved for the wild men who lived in the wilderness and came to the village to trade furs and gems for things they needed.

He was caked in mud and his hair and beard were matted. They were so dirty his usual dark blond colouring was farther darkened to brown. Eventually someone managed to see through the dirt as he stumbled along the street toward his house and helped him the rest of the way. When he arrived, his mother stifled any reaction to his appearance and brought him straight to his bed, where sleep took him as soon as he put his head down.

❁

Donato found himself spending an increasing amount of time standing atop the steps outside the Great Hall. He liked to look out over the village—his domain—and watch the villagers—his subjects—go about their business. He allowed his mind to wander to the changes he would make when he was unfettered by the Ambassador's control. A filthy, scruffy wretch was limping across the village square. Donato sneered with disgust. There were a great many beggars in the cities he had visited in the south, but he wouldn't have them in his village. He was about to get one of the soldiers to drag the vagabond from the village and beat him bloody as a lesson not to come back, when he realised there was something familiar about the man.

He stepped back inside the Great Hall before anyone could see his reaction. It was Wulfric. The realisation hit him like a bucket of icy water. He slammed the door behind him and pressed up against it. He was shaking. *Fuck Endres,* he thought. And fuck Urschel and his useless soldiers. How difficult could it be to kill a man in his sleep with a crossbow? Donato reckoned that even he could manage it, even though he had never fired one. They had played him for a fool, and left him with a stinking mess to clean up.

Donato was torn between fury and terror. How much did Wulfric know? If Wulfric thought he and Rodulf had arranged for his death, there was only one way things would go. A half dozen soldiers hadn't been able to deal with him in an inn—they hadn't even been able to kill him while he was asleep. Donato took a deep breath and thought. There was no way Wulfric could know that he had anything to do with it. He might not even know what had happened. He looked in terrible condition. Retribution for the bar fight was the most obvious reason for it all. He could put the blame for everything on that. Without proof, Wulfric would be nothing more than a murderer if he killed him. Urschel, Endres, and the other soldiers involved had already gone south so evidence would be hard to come by. So long as he played it cleverly, Wulfric would never be able to tie him to it. He could suspect all he wanted, but without proof he had nothing. It was simple. The soldiers wanted revenge for the fight at the inn, and no one could say any different.

That was only one problem solved, however. As soon as Wulfric found out that Adalhaid had gone back to Elzburg, he would chase after her, bring her back and kill anyone who stood in his way. The Markgraf would be angry, and Donato would lose his barony. Donato might have liked to think that was someone else's problem now, but until his letters patent had been delivered, and he had sworn his oaths of fealty to the Markgraf, he couldn't allow anything to interfere. He had no doubt the Ambassador would lay blame for this firmly on his head if the Markgraf was angered. Wulfric could not be allowed to go after her.

※

Wulfric was lying on his belly when he woke. Someone was poking and prodding at the wounds on his back. Wulfric strained his neck to see who it was.

'Lie still now, lad,' Aethelman said. There were a few more pokes and prods before he spoke again. 'All clean,' he said. 'There was some cloth in the wounds, but they weren't so deep. And this.' He held out a small piece of metal so that Wulfric could see it. The tip of the crossbow bolt.

'You're putting together quite a collection of scars,' Aethelman said. 'Your father would be proud. You can turn over now.'

Wulfric smiled and rolled onto his back. 'How long did I sleep?'

'Two days,' Aethelman said. 'And you were gone a week before that. By the look of it, that belek cloak saved your life. There're a few holes in it that will need mending, but I suppose you have a spare to replace it with. Do you know who attacked you?'

'No,' Wulfric said. 'I didn't even see them.'

'That's what the Ruripathian captain said too.'

'Endres survived?' Wulfric said, turning over to look Aethelman directly in the eye. It added weight to his suspicions.

'Yes, he managed to get away. Said he ran when the belek attacked. First time I've heard of a belek attacking with a crossbow, but I have heard of stranger things.'

Wulfric laughed, but stifled it quickly. 'It wasn't a belek. I can't help but think it was Captain Endres.'

'When I saw the wounds on your back, I suspected as much myself. You didn't earn yourself any friends that night in the inn.'

'I suppose it's too much to hope that he's still in the village?'

Aethelman shook his head. 'He left a couple of days after he got back. Stenn and Farlof went to see if they could find any trace of you, but there was so much blood and torn cloth at the campsite that they reckoned there was no way you could have survived.'

'Can you get Adalhaid for me? I need to tell her I'm sorry for missing the wedding. I wasn't trying to avoid it.'

'Just rest. Don't worry about that. The week in the wilderness did more harm to you than the bolts. You need rest and good food.

He was so very tired, it sounded like a good suggestion, one that his body was already acting on. His eyelids grew heavy.

❉

Another night's sleep made a huge difference. Wulfric woke the next morning feeling dramatically better. His mother brought him a bowl of broth as he sat in his father's chair, looking out the small window that let him watch the comings and goings in the village. Once he had eaten he planned to go out and find Adalhaid. He needed to apologise for missing their wedding, but he was desperate to see her.

'I need to tell you something,' his mother said.

Wulfric paused with his spoon in mid air. He could hear droplets of the broth splashing back into the bowl. Conversations that began like that were never good.

'It's about Adalhaid.' She swallowed hard.

Wulfric began to feel light headed.

'Adalhaid decided to go back to Elzburg to stay with her aunt and uncle after we got word that you had been killed. When Stenn and Farlof confirmed that there was no sign of you having survived, she said she needed to get away from the things that reminded her of you.'

'That's understandable,' Wulfric said. He was disappointed, but also relieved. It explained why she hadn't come to see him. He was still a few days from being ready for a long ride south, but he would be glad of the exercise. 'Has anyone let her know that I'm all right?'

His mother let out a staccato sob, suggesting that she had been holding it back as long as she could.

'I'm sorry, Wulfric. She's dead.'

He dropped the bowl and the spoon, but barely noticed the hot broth spilling over his trousers. He felt as though he could not breathe, like the room was spinning around him.

'How? What happened?'

'The carriage she was travelling in was attacked. Brigands they think, but they can't say for sure who it was. They said she killed herself rather than be taken by them alive.' She sobbed hard. 'I'm so sorry, Wulfric, but she's gone.'

'When?'

'She left a couple of days after we heard that you had been killed. We got word of what happened to her last night.'

'Her body,' he said, his voice barely more than a whisper.

'They brought it to Elzburg. To her family…'

His mother was still speaking, but he couldn't hear anything else she was saying.

CHAPTER FORTY-NINE

WULFRIC FELT AS though he was suffocating. He stumbled outside and started to walk. He was in a daze, completely unable to order his thoughts.

'My condolences.'

Wulfric stopped and looked around to see who spoke. He had been oblivious to everything, and hadn't noticed anyone around him. It was Rodulf. Wulfric had to add surprise to his confused thoughts. 'Thank you.' He didn't know how else to respond.

'She'll be missed,' Rodulf said. 'By the garrison most of all. From what I'm told, she rushed to attend to their… needs, every time your back was turned.'

Fury cleared the fog of confusion from Wulfric's head. Rodulf really did not seem to learn his lessons. He stepped forward and grabbed Rodulf by the scruff of the neck. He pressed forward, tipped Rodulf back on his heels and drew his fist back to begin his retribution. He looked into Rodulf's face, and was surprised to see there was no fear there.

'Sure this is a good idea?' Rodulf said. 'You don't hold quite the sway you once did.' He smiled.

Wulfric hit him hard. 'Do you think it will be difficult to get about with no eyes?' He hit Rodulf a second time. Wulfric felt his teeth chatter with rage. He pulled his dagger from his belt.

'Hey! What's going on there!'

Wulfric saw Stenn and Farlof running toward him. He had the edge of his dagger pressed against Rodulf's cheek. A bead of blood appeared at its edge. Rodulf squirmed in his grip.

'Wulfric, don't be a fool!' Stenn said. 'Let him go!'

Stenn and Farlof crashed into him, knocking them all to the ground, and the dagger from Wulfric's hand. Wulfric's head felt muggy as he struggled to his feet. He looked up to Rodulf standing over him.

'You need to learn your place. Times have changed. We don't even need your kind anymore. You'd be more use yoked up to a plough. You'd do well to remember that.'

'Let him go,' Farlof said. 'He's more trouble than he's worth.'

Wulfric knew he was right, but as he watched Rodulf walk away, he had a bitter taste in his mouth.

❀

Aethelman was allowing himself one final excuse. He would remain in Leondorf to tend to Belgar, and see him depart the world of men to begin his journey to Jorundyr's Hall. It was the least he could do for his oldest friend. Then he would devote what remained of his life to ensuring no other young priest had to live with a burden like Aethelman had. He would seek out whatever knowledge of the Stones remained. He would learn how to destroy them. He would make sure this knowledge was made part of every priest's training.

There might be no more of the Stones left in the world, but a nagging sickness in his gut told him that his was still out there somewhere, waiting to fall into hands that would misuse it. Perhaps it already had. He could not leave it to hope that it had been destroyed in the fire. If he had enough life left in him once he had learned how to destroy them and passed this knowledge on with the strict instruction that it never be forgotten again, he would search out his Stone and complete his duty.

❀

'Just because you're the mayor's son, doesn't mean I have to bow and scrape to you,' the tanner said. 'You have to pay for your new boots, just like everyone else.'

Rodulf glowered at the defiance, and considered striking the tanner, but there were people watching and it would get back to his father. He had been expressly prohibited from doing anything to cause an upset after taunting

Wulfric. 'We're so close,' he had said. Him, perhaps. There was still a very long way to go before Rodulf could call himself baron.

He had to satisfy himself in the knowledge that Adalhaid lived, and that the ignorant savage would never find out. As he dwelled on it, he realised it was indeed a very satisfying thought. There was a poetry to it. Nevertheless, it did little to solve his boot problem.

'I know you're new here,' Rodulf said, 'and might not have realised how things work. You'd be making a mistake not to gift me these very fine boots.'

The tanner's eyes blazed with indignation, but Rodulf held his stare. He realised his hand was on the strange stone he took from the priest. He couldn't even remember putting it in his pocket. Odd, he thought. It felt so good to hold it, though. The boots were the finest calf leather, and the latest in southern fashion. He wanted them desperately, but the meagre allowance his father passed on to him, a poor reflection on the value of the work he did, had been spent on his last visit south. It occurred to him that it might be time for his father to step aside, to make room for fresh blood. His father was all about the money. He didn't have the stomach to get his hands dirty enough to reap the greatest rewards. Not like Rodulf.

He returned his attention to the tanner, and the boots. He wanted the tanner to give in to him, as much as he wanted the boots. More, perhaps. The blaze left the tanner's eyes and he swallowed hard. His face went pale. He held out the boots.

'Take them,' he said. 'Take them and go.'

Wulfric answered the door with one hand on the pommel of his sword. After his outburst in the square with Rodulf, and the Ruripathian soldiers trying to kill him, he had no idea who might be calling at his door, nor if they were friend or foe. The only thing he knew was that it was not Adalhaid. It was Belgar's granddaughter.

'Grandfather has woken up. He asked for you.'

Wulfric had been meaning to call on Belgar since feeling well enough to go outside, but events had determined otherwise. She remained on his doorstep, a hopeful look on her face. It took Wulfric a moment to gather her meaning, but he was nervous going outside. Leondorf was a dangerous place for him now.

'Let me get my cloak,' he said.

He followed her down to Belgar's house. There were several people gathered in his front room, and an air of solemnity prevailed. Aethelman was there. It seemed that Belgar was not expected to last long.

'I realise I've been saying it for days,' Aethelman said, 'but I'm certain of it now. He doesn't have long left.'

Wulfric nodded and went into Belgar's room. It hurt Wulfric to see how frail Belgar was. The past couple of years had taxed him greatly, draining what vigour he had left. In a way he was glad his father had died in battle. He was glad that he would never have to see him like this, wizened and drained, a shadow of the hero he had been.

Belgar spotted Wulfric. His once-bright eyes were cloudy, but he fixed them on Wulfric with an intensity Wulfric would not have thought the old man capable of.

'You're alive, boy,' he rasped.

It felt like such a ridiculous thing to say, Wulfric had to stop himself from laughing.

'I am, First Warrior. Barely, but alive.'

Belgar smiled. 'I thought I'd be too late. Donato and Rodulf. They're going to try and kill you.'

Wulfric furrowed his brow. 'What do you mean?'

'Donato's made a deal with the Ambassador. They want to send Adalhaid south. I don't know why, but it's important to them. Donato said you'd have to be killed for that to happen, and the Ambassador agreed. They're going to try to kill you, boy.' Belgar leaned forward, grabbed Wulfric by the wrist and pulled him closer. 'You have to be ready for when they try. Don't let those bastards kill you.'

Wulfric felt his blood boil. 'Don't worry,' he said. 'I'll be ready for him.'

'Good. That's good,' Belgar said. He let out a gentle sigh and slumped back to the bed, his journey to Jorundyr's Host finally started.

❊

Wulfric walked out of the old man's house, past his mother who had just arrived to say her farewells, and Belgar's granddaughter without saying a word. His hand was gripping the hilt of his sabre tightly. He headed straight for the Great Hall. Belgar's words were all the confirmation that Wulfric needed.

Showing the building no respect, he shouldered the door open and walked in. Donato was there alone, sitting at the Great Table going through papers.

'What are you doing here?' he said. 'You know you're not allowed in here.' He stood to emphasise his indignation.

'What happened to Adalhaid?' Wulfric said.

Donato took a deep breath and adopted a more conciliatory posture. 'I understand that you're grieving. Everyone in the village is. She was much loved and it's a terrible loss.' His eyes flicked to Wulfric's sword, and he took a step back. 'Now, you aren't supposed to be here. If you don't leave now, I'll have to call the guards.'

'Call them,' Wulfric said. He walked forward and pulled out a chair, the one his father used to sit in. He ran his finger along the dark, carved wood of the back. 'Belgar is dead.'

'Another tragedy, but it was his time,' Donato said.

'Perhaps. He told me something before he passed. He told me you arranged to have Adalhaid sent to Elzburg. That you were going to have me killed.'

'The ramblings of a delirious old man. You know what happened as well as I do.'

'I might have thought that too, if someone hadn't tried to kill me a few days past,' Wulfric said.

'Everyone knows the forests are full of bandits these days. You were unlucky is all.'

'Rubbish!' Wulfric said, taking a step closer. He placed a small metal object on the table.

'What's that?' Donato said.

'That,' Wulfric said, 'is the tip of the crossbow bolt Aethelman took out of my shoulder.'

'I'm relieved to know that you are healing well,' Donato said, his voice wavering.

'Do you know anything about weapons?'

Donato shook his head.

'Of course you don't. You're just a fucking coward.' Wulfric fixed his gaze on Donato, baiting him, but there was no reaction. 'This tip is interesting.'

'Really?'

'Yes. It's made from hardened steel.'

Donato shrugged.

'Bandits don't use crossbow bolts like this. Robbing from ordinary folk doesn't need an expensive tip that can punch through armour.'

'Who does?' Donato said, his voice sounding like he didn't want to know the answer.

'Soldiers. Soldiers from Elzburg.'

'We all knew that something like this might happen after the thrashing you gave those fellows in the inn. They're proud men. You didn't think they'd just forget about it, did you?'

'You seemed very eager for me to take Captain Endres hunting.'

'I did that in good faith,' Donato said. 'For the very reasons I gave you. I had no idea—'

'Shut your lying mouth,' Wulfric said.

'I've always known you are a fool, but even I cannot believe you would make accusations based on the delirious ramblings of a dying old man. I'm going to call the guards.'

'I'd trust his word over yours every time.'

Donato said nothing.

'Why did you send Adalhaid south?'

'The Ambassador wanted her to return south. I didn't ask why. I didn't care. The southerners have kept us alive, and we have to do everything we can to keep them happy. She went of her own choosing. When we got word you were dead, there was no reason for her to—'

'Enough,' Wulfric said. He could feel blood pulsing through his temples. The thought of her deciding to take her own life rather than be dishonoured threatened to tear him apart. His skin tingled and his hands shook with rage. It took all of his self control to finish saying what he wanted to say. 'The why doesn't matter. What matters is you sent her south, and she died because of it. What matters is you tried to have me killed. She was my promised. Her soul won't rest until she's avenged. Her blood debt is mine, and I will see it paid.'

'Guards! Guards!' Donato shouted. He scrambled backwards, but reached the wall and had nowhere left to go. A barony was no use to him if he was dead 'You don't understand. You're making a mis—'

Wulfric's sabre went through Donato's neck in a flash. So fast that Donato didn't realise it had happened. His mouth continued to move, but no sound came out. He lifted his hands to his throat and fell to the floor, blood flooding from between his fingers.

Wulfric heard the door open behind him.

'You there! Stop!'

Wulfric turned to face the soldiers. Had they helped try to kill him? He charged at them. They both levelled their spears, but they weren't fast enough. Wulfric struck the head from the first, and kicked the other out the door. The man fell back onto the steps. Wulfric stabbed him through the chest, twisting the blade as fury coursed through his veins.

Wulfric took a deep breath and looked around. He had just killed Donato and two soldiers. It had all happened so quickly, it felt like a dream. He looked left and right for Rodulf, but he was nowhere to be seen. The alarm had been raised, so there was no time to search for him. Wulfric knew he needed to get to safety so he could think, make sense of everything that had happened. He ran at a man riding through the square and pulled him from his horse. Leaping into the saddle, he turned it south and spurred it on.

The Ambassador had wanted Adalhaid to go south too. The whole plan was of his creation. For Adalhaid's blood debt to be settled, he would have to die. Then it would be Rodulf's turn…

EPILOGUE

While HE HAD been impatient at first, the Maisterspaeker found that he was hoping he would have enough time to finish the story before his rendezvous. Though to think in terms of finishing it was an untruth. The story didn't have an ending. Not yet, at least. He wondered how they would take it when he got that far. He would have to come up with something off the cuff to keep them happy. It could be altered later, when he had it all. If there was a later.

Nonetheless, there was a light blue glow coming in through the inn's windows, and he was too old to be drinking and talking until dawn, not with the task that lay ahead. He drained the last of his mug and stood.

'Until this evening,' he said. 'The dawn is here, and I fear I have kept you from your beds for too long. Five bells and we shall continue.'

He stood and watched them file out of the inn, their weariness finally showing. He cast his mind to the end of his tale, and wondered what it would be. A fitting end to a heroic life, or merely another chapter in it?

About the Author

Sign up for Duncan's mailing list and get a free copy of his novella, *The Frontier Lord*. Visit his website to get your copy:

duncanmhamilton.com

Duncan is a writer of fantasy fiction novels and short stories that are set in a world influenced by Renaissance Europe. He has Master's Degrees in History, and Law, and practised as a barrister before writing full time. He is particularly interested in the Medieval and Renaissance periods, from which he draws inspiration for his stories. He doesn't live anywhere particularly exotic, and when not writing he enjoys cycling, skiing, and windsurfing.

His debut novel, 'The Tattered Banner (Society of the Sword Volume 1)' was placed 8th on Buzzfeed's 12 Greatest Fantasy Books Of The Year, 2013.

Made in the USA
Lexington, KY
09 November 2017